The Burl of Meglinor

The Token Bearers — Book Five

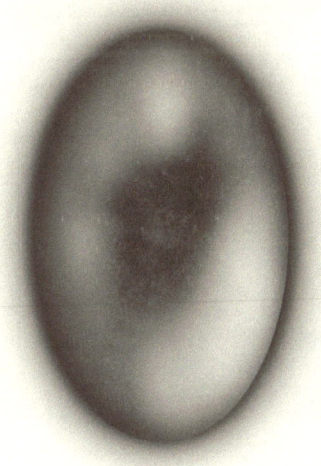

THE BURL OF MEGLINOR

DERIN ATTWOOD

The Burl of Meglinor

A Wordly Press Publication
Ashhurst, New Zealand
Phone 64 6 326 8066

First published by Wordly Press in 2017

Set in 12/18/24 Adobe Garamond Pro
This text uses English (UK) spelling.

ISBN 978-0-9941108-9-3

A catalogue record for this book is available from
the National Library of New Zealand.

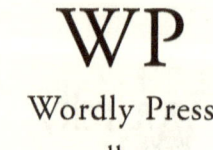

Wordly Press
www.wordlypress.com

Dedication

To my new brothers,
Cliff and Quentin,
two of the best gifts I have ever received.

ACKNOWLEDGEMENTS

Special thanks go to Llyvonne Barber of Wordly Press, for creating my amazing covers, and coming up with something remarkably similar my dream. She also copes with all the technical stuff that terrifies me.

My writing friends around the world keep me sane, laughing, and grounded. From the PenUltimate writing group, I would particularly like to thank all those wonderful friends who critique my work, keep me honest, and on my toes.

Again, I am grateful to Della Hart, who, although no longer living close enough to pop in for a daily chat and coffee, but still encourages me to create stories I never knew I had in me.

Suzanne Main, Lee Murray, and Emma Pullar, who although incredible writers tied up in their own amazing writings, always have time to encourage me, and give advice when I ask for it.

To my fans, who constantly pester me to bring out the next book, but are lovingly supportive when I don't meet their deadlines (which would have me launching a new book every six weeks).

Lastly, my wonderful family, which has expanded massively in a way I never dreamed possible. To Kirsten, Cliff, and Quentin for introducing me to new and amazing worlds. Most of all, to my son Garreth, for his encouragement, and my dearest husband, Ron, for his constant support.

CHARACTERS ON THIS ADVENTURE

Name		Relationship
From the Green Valley		
Amethyst	F	Found in the desert, adopted by Kirym.
Arbreu	M	Token brother to Kirym, Teema and Bokum.
Armos	M	Veld's second. Papa to Peet and Young Harby.
Bokum	M	Joined to Zeprah, Papa to Sarel and Trayum.
Findlow	M	Kirym's uncle, Lyndym's papa.
Harby	M	Known as Old Harby. Armos' papa.
Harby	M	Known as Young Harby. Armos' youngest son.
Kirym	F	Loul and Veld's daughter, aligned to Teema, Arbreu and Bokum.
Loul	F	Headwoman, Kirym's mama.
Lyndym	F	Findlow's daughter.
Mekrar	F	Kirym's sister, twin to Mekroe.
Mekroe	M	Kirym's brother, twin to Mekrar.
Peet	M	Armos' eldest son.
Raff	M	Leader of the People of the Hills. Aligned with The Green Valley.

Name		Relationship
From the Green Valley		
Tarl	M	Kirym's older brother. Joined to Zhins. Papa to twins, Tanwyn (F) and Shanyth (M).
Tarjin	M	Son of Danth and Jinda. Mekroe's best friend.
Teema	M	Aligned to Kirym, Arbreu and Bokum.
Veld	M	Voice and Warlord, Kirym, Mekrar and Mekroe's papa.
Walf	M	Hunter. Raff's family.
Zelriff	F	Oldest woman in the family.
From the Desert		
Garanniis	M	Leader of the Valythian families.
Morkeen	F	Garanniis' granddaugther.
Palunniis	M	Morkeen's cousin.
Tiannii	F	Palunniis' cousin.
Zyanda	F	Morkeen's sister (deceased).
From Faltryn's Tower		
Elm	M	Boatman.
Blacknight	M	Guard.
Crag	M	Hunter.
Oak	M	Guard. Wind Runner's great grandson.

Name		Relationship
From Faltryn's Tower		
Starshine	F	Wind Runner's great granddaughter.
Storm	M	Wind Runner's grandson.
Splinter	M	Guard.
Twig	M	Guard.
Willow	F	Elm's daughter. Healer (deceased).
Wind Runner	F	Headwoman at Faltryn's Tower.
Arbryn's Family		
Arbryn	M	Family head. Known as Bryn.
Dashlan	M	Eldest son.
Enliah	F	Eldest daughter.
Jeresaya	F	Bryn's wife.
Larqeba	M	Youngest son.
Quinita	F	Youngest daughter.
Rargo	M	Orphan, adopted by the family.
From The Rock		
Ashistar	M	Guard.
Baketer	M	Guard.
Borboncha	M	Guard.
Frentha	M	Gynbere's taster. Cares for grandson's Chonarth and Rintath.
Churnyg	M	Tree dwarf—Oak Family.
Gynbere	M	Leader—Yew Family.

Name		Relationship
From The Rock		
Gynletha	F	Healer.
Imolay	M	Leader—Ash Family.
Jetara	F	Shormel's maman, Oak Family.
Kwarnar	M	Ancester of above. Maker of the original qwanchel.
Lorythma	F	Leader—Willow Branch. Healer.
Maletta	F	Wise woman.
Mrilan	M	Old man.
Rookham	M	Guard.
Rosisha	F	Varitza's maman.
Sirasha	M	Leader—Beech Family. Chief Scribe—Keeper of the Histories.
Shormel	M	Son of Jetara. Larqeba's friend.
Shurlyn	F	Old woman.
Slaslow	M	Head guard.
Trethia	F	Orphan, but a mystery. Adopted by Kirym.
Tartharn	M	Leader—Chestnut Branch. Carver.
Thipin	M	One of triplets (deceased).
Vellysh	M	One of triplets, sent to pick up Ibith.
Zeffun	M	One of triplets.

Name		Relationship
From the Winterisle		
Faltryn	M	Black.
Iryndal	F	Blue.
Ubree	M	Green.
Othyn	F	Yellow.
Egrym	M	Orange/Bronze.
Arymda	F	Pink/Red.
Borasyn	M	Purple.

1

Teema Speaks

It's war!

WAR!

The word echoed around the table.

We stared aghast at the sheet of parchment Kirym held up. There was a palpable fear in many faces around me; I knew the colour had drained from mine. The only one who seemed unaffected by the news was Kirym.

She shrugged. "Gynbcre and Slaslow have already attacked, so it's no different from before. Now we know Slaslow plans to kill us no matter what is agreed."

"You think Slaslow wrote this?" asked Tarl.

She nodded. "It's the same writing as on a scroll Ashistar found in the guard's tunnel after the rock wall breached."

"Where's the scroll?" asked Tarl.

"Unless he gave it to Papa, Ashistar must still have it."

"Veld didn't mention it," said Armos.

"So," I said, "maybe Ashistar wrote it, and he didn't want

it passed around and recognised."

"I saw it," interrupted Churnyg. "It wasn't his writing. Anyway, he has no connection to the Red Stone diggings. That's Slaslow's claim."

"Perhaps a nice ploy to put us off," I murmured.

"If Slaslow plans to kill us all," interrupted Sundas, "why did he and Gynbere call off the attack yesterday. Especially when they had the advantage?"

Tarl frowned. "They overplayed their hand. They assumed we'd be too shocked to react. Had they continued the attack, we'd have beaten them. I'm inclined to agree with Kirym. They want something. But what?"

I stared at the map. "It must be the weapons. I know he refused to take the sword when Kirym offered it, but what if he thought he could hold it once Faltryn was dead?"

"Speculation, Teema," interrupted Kirym. "We now have several distinct advantages. We know where they are. We know we travel faster than they can, and they don't realise that. We also know it'll probably come to another battle of some sort. But right now, I'm hungry. It's early, but I'm sure the cooks will feed us if we beg."

"Eat? That's it?" I sounded as shocked as many of the others looked.

Oak laughed. "Kirym's right. The ovens are open and we have four days to plan." He picked Trethia up, swung her onto his back and walked towards the cooking area. Every third step he took was a hop, and I could hear Trethia giggling as they went.

After a few moments, almost everyone else followed them.

2

Kirym Speaks

We sat near the dragons to eat. Findlow, Arbreu, Starshine and Mekrar added their platters to those brought over by Oak and Trethia.

"So, what do we do to fill in the time?" Tarl asked.

"Organise your men into groups and start training them to fight together. Choose group leaders who can take instructions directly from you. They should be able to think for themselves around a fluid plan. It's just an extension of the games Papa taught us."

"Except we could die," Bokum added darkly.

"You could die out hunting, man," laughed Twig. "For goodness sake, you could have died walking to Faltryn's tower. I didn't think you'd make it, even after we rescued you from Danth. You'll get through this too." They laughed, and the tension lifted.

"So what's the plan, Kirym?" Teema asked.

"Tarl is war-lord. Ask him. He'll talk to Mama, Armos

and the other leaders who are here. Then he will make the decisions."

"But you'll help."

"Only if I am asked. I have other things to focus on."

News of the threat of war spread quickly around the amphitheatre. However, with Mama's seemingly calm composure, and support from the headmen and guild leaders, everyone accepted the restrictions and agreed to give their ideas to Tarl.

The four-day agreement and the limits to the hunting area were explained. No one wished to be shot, so everyone agreed to stick to them. Tarl suggested we all remain within the confines of the walls, unless part of a group foraging for food, or checking the squilute. The boys were specifically forbidden to leave, and the guards were charged to ensure no one left the amphitheatre without good reason.

Tarl then talked to the guild leaders and family heads, explained in detail what had happened at dawn when Vellysh Urfit gave us Gynbere's instructions.

The tree dwarves accepted the delay much better than others. Those from Faltryn's Fortress and to a lesser extent from The Green Valley were unhappy.

"Why not just go now," asked Blacknight. "This'll give them time to secure another fortress. They could kill our people before we even get there."

There were a few nods, grunts and murmurs of agreement, and although the earlier panic had disappeared, many looked concerned.

"It's unlikely," I said. "If Papa was dead, his tokens would tell us and we'd have found their bodies. One thing Gynbere does know; if any of the hostages dies, we will hunt him down. But why would he destroy his only bargaining power before he gets what he wants?"

"Kirym's right," said Tarl. "Had he wanted an area to settle in, he could have asked. If he'd wanted to live in isolation, we'd have been happy with his decision. To take hostages means he must want something he's not entitled to have."

"The dragons?" asked Bokum.

"He killed Faltryn," said Mama, "so I wouldn't think so. What do you think, Kirym?"

"At best, we can only guess. We'll find out soon enough. In the meantime, we need to consolidate and look at our choices. Then we decide how to pre-empt Gynbere and Slaslow."

"Can we?" Tarl asked.

"Certainly. Think about what Gynbere asked for first."

"His pavilion and men," said Blacknight.

"He wanted the ibith," I said.

"But that was just said in passing, wasn't it?" he asked.

"No, she's right," said Armos. "It was the first thing requested, and he mentioned it several times."

"And I plan to find out why," I said.

The cushions and draperies had been taken off the box and stacked to one side. Sundas had removed the chair. A brief glance convinced me there was nothing special about it. It was plain; the carvings on the arms were new, rough and over-gilded to compensate. Of the six uprights at the back of the chair, two had been recently placed in the middle of the four originals, and tied into place with twisted linen. All six were additionally topped with finials. A profusion of tassels and feathers hung from them. Despite all of that, it was basically a plain chair, made of a variety of woods and it had none of the richness nor comfort I'd seen with Gynbere's previous ibiths.

"It's overdone and garish," said Findlow. "It could've been found in any dwelling as a 'sit and take your boots off' chair. It reeks of 'make do'. The box though, is different. It's not been well made or cared for. The carving is rough, and it's no work of art. I'm sure it has something inside, but, there's no obvious way to open it."

"Where's Churnyg?" I asked.

"He'll be here soon," said Findlow. "He's looking for a carver who may know more about it than he does."

I ran my hand over the top, feeling the minor defects of the wood.

"The box is made of chestnut." Churnyg's voice came from behind me. "My grandsire said the panels belonged to the Willow family carvers. A payment for something, I gather. They'd never have given it to Gynbere. Harthma Chestnut knows something of its history. I've sent for him."

Harthma, when he joined us, proved to be an older man. He had the mass of thick curly hair, the Chestnut family were known for. I remembered seeing him helping in the healer's area, assisting those carrying wood and water.

"Lady Kirym." He inclined his head in my direction, but his attention was on the wood. "Yes, family history says the panels were presented to the Willow by one of my ancestors. They were not carved then, and no one from the Willow family would carve anything this badly."

"What makes you think these were the panels?" I asked.

"Many season cycles after we entered The Rock, the Willow wood-store was ransacked. Not everything was taken, but these slabs were known. They're quite distinctive," said Harthma. "This blemish was noted by the Beech historians." He pointed to a dark tree shape in the bottom right corner. "It's memorable because we are all trees, and a tree within a tree, well it's special. Now, the wood in this blemish is rotten, however, with so little access to any new source, all wood was beyond value for our families."

I nodded. "Who ransacked the rooms, and why?"

"The men were masked, but the pieces taken ended up in Gynbere's private rooms; I have no doubt he sent them, whoever they were. When someone a complaint was made, Gynbere claimed we must have been thinking of some other pieces. He said he had always owned what he held. We challenged that, and showed the written history. He said our written history was false."

"Is the chair anything other than a chair?"

"He recently called it a cathebla. My understanding of the word is that it's an ornate form created from one piece, plain, elegant and beautiful. This isn't! Gynbere has only used it on the box since we left The Rock. It was then he began to insist on being bowed to, called M'Lord and Most Esteemed Leader."

Harthma snorted. "The chair sat in his private hall for a long time. It has a minor value, because it's made up of four different woods. Recently he claimed it to be made of six woods, lovingly built by the different families to acknowledge their great affection for him. A lie. Despite that, his perception of its value was that he'd offer it to visitors he needed to acknowledge, but had no need to impress. Normally when he left his inner quarters, he used one of his ibiths. He had eight of them. Using this thing surprises me, it's as makeshift as it looks. It's not like Gynbere to accept a lesser form of anything, so there is a mystery of some sort here. Now as to the box, possibly," he paused, "probably it's worked by one of my family. We specialise in these faces. We did occasionally carve for the Yew family leaders, although they never asked for anything like this. Generally, we made small things, and mainly out of stone. There was plenty of that available."

"You don't know who made the box?" asked Churnyg. "As I understand it, your carvers have no trouble extolling their talents to everyone who'd listen and a few who had no wish to."

I glanced at Harthma to see if he was about to take offence at Churnyg's comments, but he seemed unfazed by them. "Well a workman should be proud to claim his work, and we are, but this?" he flicked the box with his fingers, "well who'd claim it? I'd say there was a lot of coercion on Gynbere's part to get anyone in my family to work on stolen wood. Just looking at it tells me that whoever did it was determined to work fast and take every shortcut they could get away with. Work done for Gynbere was never talked of, even within the hollow. A word said in the wrong place could cost a life."

"Can you open it?" I asked.

He nodded. "To open those my sire made, one simply followed a progression. They were intricate. This will be nowhere near as subtle. Assuming it is an imitation of the masters, we just need to think of a logical sequence."

I stared at the top. It was a face, not a nice face; very arrogant. The eyes were too close together; different sizes and slightly out of line. The nose was unkindly beaked and the mouth small and mean. "So, it has eyes, a nose and a mouth."

"Then that's the most obvious place to start." Harthma pushed the eyes firmly in with his thumbs. Nothing happened. He pulled the nose down until it touched the bottom lip. There was a hollow click. "Hmmm." He fiddled with the mouth; the bottom lip moved down, another click, and the nose flicked back into place. He pressed the eyes again, and this time they sank into the wood. He again pulled the nose. Nothing, so he twisted it. Something inside the box clunked and the nose flicked back, although it was now slightly crooked.

Harthma laughed. "That's it. So very basic. This would not be acceptable in our workshops, not even from an apprentice. However, I would be inclined to give it a nod, but only because of the subtle insult. If it was intentional," he shrugged, "whoever did it, seems to have been thumbing his nose at Gynbere. It's quite clever. I doubt Gynbere realised it, or the maker would have disappeared, and this would have been destroyed."

He grasped the edge of the top. It rose a hand-width and stopped. He knelt and slipped his fingers into the gap, moving them along the length of the box. Another click, and the front fell forwards.

Nestled inside was another box. The front showed a carved face, but the quality and finish was hugely different to the first.

Harthma and Findlow each grabbed the top and ends of the outer box and yanked them apart. The back fell away.

"Now this is a box," said Harthma.

It was glorious. All around me were exclamations of wonder.

The box appeared to be made of one solid block of wood, no lines to indicate a lid.

"Get it off this ghastly platform, and let's have a good look at it," said Findlow.

"The wood came from Churnyg's family," said Harthma, running his hand over the surface. "This is the quality the Chestnut family was known for, and these are two of the best I've ever seen. The face on the top was imaged on my ancestors. The front face comes from Churnyg's family."

Churnyg snorted. "So I was told. They must have wanted something, the men in my family never looked that good. However, I agree, only one o' yours could have done such quality work."

"Oak from Churnyg, carving from the Ash family. Well I'm pleased to return it to you both," I said.

"You're being a little hasty, Lady Kirym. We appreciate your generous offer, but the box was made for and gifted, with others, to your family. I'm not sure how it came to be back in Gynbere's keeping. If all I suspect is true, and the box may be of great value to you."

"What do you mean?"

"Gynbere, the second one I think, or was it the third?" He scratched his head and then shook it. "Well, he began to brag privately about owning a special box although no one dared talk about it openly. I suspect this was it. It remained in the family, known, but not talked about. The last two generations saw less need to keep it a secret. They were quite proud of owning it. For Gynbere to bring it with him, implies there is something about it he values far beyond the wood. I can't believe it's the box itself. He didn't have the aesthetic appreciation of its beauty. No, Lady Kirym, this is a real puzzle box, and by all accounts, one of the finest ever made. Our Gynbere had it open. A family whisper is that my aunt's life was threatened to force my grandsire and great-grandsire to open it. It probably remained open since then, and was shut to bring. To open it again, I imagine he would have to destroy it, unless he could again coerce a member of my family." Harthma frowned. "There's an intricate mechanism to open it. Gynbere couldn't do it, he doesn't have the knowledge, and no one would teach him."

"Presumably he has something hidden inside it. And whatever it is, he's reluctant to touch it." I said.

"How do you know that?" asked Teema.

"He wouldn't have gone to such trouble to bring the box with him. He would have gathered the contents up and brought them with him some easier way."

Harthma nodded. "Possibly. There was a whisper that

it holds something of great value. Now, there will be set steps to open it as with the copy, but this one, well, it'll be extremely complicated. It will be in a logical order, although I think it must take at least two people to open it. I'm sorry I can't help more."

"Your grandsire is not with us?" asked Findlow.

"No one holds Gynbere's secrets without paying a huge price. Both my grandsire and great-grandsire are dead. My great-grandsire was brutally beaten, although he was still alive when found. News spreads quickly in the hollows, and Gynbere sent his own physician, who took over the care. They refused to allow the Willow healers or our own to assist or even watch over him. He died, and we were not allowed to see the body. Gynbere claimed he was a close friend and gave him a great burial. It was rumoured he was poisoned, but with no proof, there was nothing to be done. My grandsire took it as a warning. He was careful, but even so, he was buried under a rock fall not long afterwards."

This box was made of oak. The top and front of the box were carved, each with a face and the grain of the wood was used to enhance them. The sides were made up of oblongs and squares, these only visible because the grain of the wood was set in different directions. They were so subtly done, one had to study carefully to realise. The uncarved parts of the box were flawless. It had been designed to sit against a wall, but even the back was polished to a high gloss. Inset into the edges was a geometric shape made of a beautiful deep purple wood.

"What sort of wood is that?" asked Sundas, rubbing his finger over it.

"We call it dragonheart," said Harthma. "It's said it was a

very special gift from The Green Valley. Only a few pieces came to us, and what we had was beyond value. Even the small scraps were carved, and shared out to the families. They disappeared; I suspect they were left in our nests when Gynbere took our freedom."

Findlow leaned forward and caressed the dragonheart. "I've never seen the wood, but I've heard stories. An old man described it to me, I think he called it heartwood. His great-grandpapa held a piece. He too talked of it being a special gift, but didn't say from where."

"You'll need help to open it, Harthma, and I can't think of anyone better to assist you than Findlow."

Findlow beamed. "It would be my pleasure to work with you," he said.

The two men turned away, instantly in a deep discussion about their chore.

Almost everyone was awake now. Many of the men still crowded around Tarl, although the crowd was dispersing.

Bryn approached me. "Arbreu told me you were present for our early visitor. Tarl has been discussing it with the men."

"What was their response?"

"Surprisingly good. The leaders accepted it and their approval meant the rest were generally fine. There were a few who wanted to ignore the warning, but the remaining leaders and the families of those kidnapped backed Tarl. As there has already been a casualty, they were convinced."

I raised my eyebrow; a silent question.

"One of the hunters was returning with game. He'd left before Urfit arrived, and had no idea what had been agreed. He staggered back with an arrow through his leg. He's all right, but it convinced everyone else they mean business."

"How badly hurt is he?"

"He'll be ready to fight in four days. Still a bit stiff I imagine, but it won't hold him back, he's furious. He feels he was shot without provocation, especially when his bow was over his shoulder, and he was loaded with game, and walking towards the northeast entrance."

Tarl still sat at the table in deep discussion with Armos, Old Harby and Teema. The other leaders came and went as they could and were needed. The men who would soon relieve the guards were clustered around the cooking area; others sat around a large fire discussing the news.

After asking Larqeba to take food over to Findlow and Harthma, I collected three platters of various foods, a basket of flasks containing broth and another of assorted juices, and took them over to the table.

"I do wish we could pre-empt them," said Tarl. "They'll know our every move. I've asked everyone to take a breath and think about it, then come to me with suggestions."

"The four days is good for us, Tarl. We can make plans, and it gives everyone time to prepare, and rest. With everyone involved, there should be some brilliant ideas we would never have thought of if we were marching out now," Armos said.

"Not much to think about though. We go there, collect our people and leave," said Teema. "That's the deal Urfit made."

"No, he didn't if you think about it, Teema." I said. "Gynbere took hostages. He didn't have to. He could have left the amphitheatre at any stage, and he had no need to come here in the first place. No, he wants something we have. Urfit said we could leave here in four days. When we get to Gynbere, the bargaining will begin."

"You're right," said Armos. "Ach, I should have thought."

Tarl patted his shoulder. "We're all tired and you're worried about your family. I should have called this meeting much later in the morning. Go, eat and get some rest everyone. We've got plenty of time."

"Be aware. Urfit may turn up here at any stage to change the rules," I said.

Tarl went pale. "Would he?"

"I doubt it, but everything is a possibility. Let's be prepared in case the worst happens. Think about what Gynbere *really* wants. Right now, he wants time, four or five days."

"How do you figure that?" asked Splinter.

"Their journey will take three days; faster than their usual rate of travel because he will push his people. He assumes we'll take four days but we know we can do it faster. So, we still can catch them unawares. If we can stop any warning getting to him, we can knock them off balance. A plus for us, if not the upper hand."

Blacknight nodded. "She's right, Tarl. We could do the trip in a day."

Tarl shook his head. "We could, but what would we prove? We'd be too tired to cope with what we find when we get there. We'd lose our advantage. Don't worry, we'll put together a plan. What do you think, Kirym?"

I shrugged. "Listen to your strategists. Sort the men into groups to practise fighting together and passing on messages without being obvious. After you've listened to everyone, and thought about what they say, make a loose plan."

He nodded, but didn't look convinced. "Oh, something you can do for me, Kirym," he said. "Have a look at the pavilion Gynbere left. Bryn poked his head in there, but otherwise, we've left it alone."

I wandered over to see Bryn, who chatted to Splinter, while they ate. At a suitable interval, I asked if he'd seen anything of note in Gynbere's last hideout.

"I didn't go in. There's a bit of stuff in there, but it meant nothing to me, so I just left a guard and told Tarl. Armos suggested asking you. Oh, he's had miffau leaves in there. I wonder why he'd put up with that."

I nodded. "I'll look, but Churnyg and Baketer may understand more than we could. Let's get them as well."

The pavilion, although not as fancy as the first one they erected, was not plain. It flowed out from a centre peak. The material was dark greyish-green, strips of dull yellow and red joined the different sections. A simple grey flag flapped from the top peak.

"The Yew family chose silver as their colour," said Churnyg, "but it's a hard colour to make, and generally it looked grey. Now they use green most of the time."

"Everyone else associated green with the Oak family though, so they tried to go darker, and highlighted with other colours to show their dominance," said Baketer.

The guard moved aside. Baketer and Bryn opened the door flaps. The astringent smell of miffau leaves hit us like a wall.

It was dark inside, but Bryn opened the sides of a hooded lamp he had brought with him. "I thought we'd need this."

"Good, and leave the flaps open, at least while we're in there," I said. "The smell explains why Gynbere sat in the door way most of the time."

The outer material was felted; held erect by a sectioned lattice framework. The bottom of the lattice sections was held open with wooden hooks. That held them rigid; they were tied at the top, to keep them together. One of the back lattices lay on the ground, still closed. There was no sign of the ground hooks for the section.

"Was the panel put up at all, or did something make it collapse?" asked Bryn.

"Well, we need to get Armos, Findlow and Dashlan to look at this and see if they can use the lattice idea in their building work," I said.

Most of the floor was covered with miffau dyed patchwork made in the same way as the ibith cover. I made a mental note to get Shurlyn to have the patchwork pulled apart and the miffau washed out. Then we should be able to find the original owners of the hangings.

Although it was all luxurious, the furnishings on one side were clearly of a finer quality than the other. There was a draped cushioned seat with additional rugs. Small tables held beakers and platters, still loaded with food. Sitting behind Gynbere's seat was a set of ornate drawers and cupboards. Nine small drawers sat on top of seven cupboards, one central, with three down each side. Three drawers and two cupboards were slightly open. Almost every surface had half burned candles on them.

"Well he made sure he was comfortable, didn't he," said Bryn. "Plenty of food and drink."

Baketer picked up a beaker. A heavy sweet fragrance wafted through the pavilion. "Klallig. Gynbere's favourite drink. I wonder why he didn't finish it. It's not like him, well not where this stuff is concerned."

"Hmm," said Churnyg, taking the beaker. "Well, I for one wouldn't drink the remainder." He paused. "The boy who was found after they left. Where was he lying?"

"He was behind the pavilion," said Baketer.

Churnyg nodded. "Baketer, could you check exactly where his body was?" Baketer left, and we continued to study the items remaining in the ibith.

The southern side was more sparsely furnished. Five low stools were grouped together. Two platters sat in front of them, one holding four empty beakers, the other, a few crumbs. A fifth beaker lay on its side against the tent edge.

"The boy's body lay where the lattice is missing," said Baketer, as he returned Pushed through maybe. But there is no seat for him, so perhaps he wasn't—"

"Oh, he'd be here," interrupted Churnyg. "He'd be either on his knees or on his belly."

Bryn nodded. "So, the boy, five others and Gynbere," said Bryn.

"Probably Slaslow, Rargo, Black-Cloak, and the two Urfits," said Baketer. He looked at his feet, embarrassed at his boldness. "Well it goes with what I saw, anyway," he mumbled.

Churnyg nodded. "I think you're right, lad. Gynbere liked everyone to sit below him, and while there wasn't a platform for him to lounge on, this would satisfy."

"Anything we've missed, Kirym?" asked Bryn.

"Gynbere makes sure of his comforts, regardless. He ate a good meal, probably in preparation for the run. He took his poisons with him, and that implies that he intended to leave here, whether he attained his goal or not."

"Poisons? Why do you think he had poison here?" asked Churnyg. "He kept them in the ibith we destroyed back at the Oak grove."

"I never really thought he'd have all of his poisons in one place. I'd say the chest there held a supply—why else would it be here? An empty chest here, and hastily emptied at that, there is residue in the drawers we should get it checked. The wood could be impregnated with what was in it, so we need to take great care. Lorythma may know how to clean it or destroy it safely."

"Well, I only hope we manage to get what he has taken with him and destroy them too," said Bryn.

I took food to Sundas, who was sitting with Trethia, and the three of us settled down to listen to the music being practised nearby.

Lyndym brought Trethia's overdress, shawl and boots to me. "Teema said you were here. I was worried, you didn't come back last night."

"I slept under the stars. I was pleased to be able to make the most of a mild night. The weather has been so mild."

"This has been the mildest winter we've had since we arrived," said Lyndym. "More like a long autumn. It would have been horrid for everyone had it been as hard as our second winter here."

Despite our inability to do anything towards rescuing the hostages, everyone was pleased to rest for the day. The usual day to day chores took over, although the cooks began preparations for the coming journey, making extra travelling food and loading the wagons they planned to take with them.

The healers likewise renewed stores, brewing the more difficult remedies as quickly as they could, collecting and drying the plants they needed.

Mekrar took care of Trethia while I spent time on the wall during the morning. The afternoon was spent socialising, I helped fold washing, and with a little of the rougher mending, not being up to anything finer in my present frame of mind. Eventually, because I was making a mess of that too, I helped card squilute fibre ready for spinning.

Since we had arrived here in the amphitheatre, a number of looms had been set up and the shelters over them were a hive of activity.

Oak had a small loom set up beside the one Rainbow, his Mama, was using. Hers was large, and she was working on a long length of material for everyday use. Everyone remarked on her speed, although she made light of it, claiming the pattern was easy. The everyday material was often more important than the ceremonial, because it was needed, and used more often.

Oak had shorn Midnight for me while on the journey from Faltryn. My spinning and weaving wasn't up to working with the fine fibres, and I agreed to leave them with him to make something. I watched him work alongside Rainbow, and it was obvious he too had talent. He had spun the fine fibres, and plied them himself, rather than hand them over to the spinners. The pattern he used was subtle. It looked flat initially, but when the light caught it, parts stood out—shinier than the background. Whatever he planned to make it into, would be amazing.

As evening approached, I went to sit with the man who had thrown the sword. Trethia came with me, and Oak joined us when he finished his weaving for the day.

"Do you think he'll wake up?" he asked.

"Jorlenta tells me his sleep is not as deep, and that's a good sign."

"But?"

I smiled. "Lots can go wrong. We can only do our best and hope. Others are improving, Hent Beech woke this afternoon, and that's to be celebrated. It was unexpected, but shows the worst scenarios have hope."

"And with this man, what do you really think?"

"That he needs to tell his story, and we need to listen to it."

Oak nodded.

As we walked back from the healers, Larqeba and Shormel ran up, their eyes shining with excitement.

"Findlow and Harthma are about to open the box. They want you there to watch them," panted Larqeba.

Teema came up behind them. "You boys should be asleep," he said. He picked Trethia up. "So should you little one. Loul was asking for you. She wants to look at your leg, and throw you in a bath."

"Oh, can we watch, Kirym? Pleeeese," begged Larqeba.

I smiled my agreement. "But, as soon as the box is open, you must sleep, else you'll miss all the exciting things that are planned for tomorrow. Trethia, you can watch too, but then you must go to Mama. Teema, can you make sure they all do as they're told?"

Night had fallen, but the area around the box and the two men was well lit. Eight lamps in all, and a good-sized fire. Already they had an audience. Word had spread very quickly.

Findlow glanced up as I approached. His eyes shone, he was obviously enjoying himself. "Harthma's ancestor was a true artist," he said. "I thought the secret drawer in the chest found on *Dragon Quest* to be special, but compared with this, it was child's play."

Sundas chuckled. "You must be right, Findlow. As I remember, a child found them after you and the other men had thoroughly searched the chest."

Findlow laughed. "Aye, well it made me more willing to search for the unusual, but this box is beyond even my wildest dreams. I'd never have even thought of some of the tricks the artist has routinely used." He drew me in close. "Watch now, Kirym. Harthma was right, it's a natural progression. There are thirty-seven movements, plus others that happen automatically if it's done right."

He moved the whole section with the eyes on the top of the box to the left and held it there while Harthma pressed a diamond shape on the right side. Then Findlow slid one of the left side strips up. The eye section slipped back into place. Harthma pushed the eyes on the front section in.

It took time, and long before they had finished, most watchers had disappeared.

On and on it went, each movement being carefully checked on a written list. Two moves were done with Findlow's ear to the chest.

"This way I can hear the faint click that tells me I have gone far enough," he said. "If I go too far, it negates the whole exercise and we begin again."

Finally, the two men straightened up, smiling broadly.

"Lady Kirym. Would you please close the eyes on the top?"

I did; there was a soft click, and the lid lifted a little. Findlow held it up with one hand.

"Now twist the nose on the top," said Findlow.

Again, there was a click and the lid rose further.

"And open the eyes on the front panel."

This time the lid opened fully. Delicately carved wooden chains at each side allowed it to lean back, without straining the hinges.

The interior of the box was beautifully finished, with strips of dragonheart interspersing the golden oak. The walls were satiny smooth, but the bottom was lined with a thick, rich blue material.

Sitting atop four oak columns was a large oblong dragonheart tray, covered with a curved latticed grill. Nestled inside was a feather quill and a box. A small scroll sat on top of the box.

Two large linen bags balanced on either side of the lattice. Harthma hauled out one bag; Findlow the second, and they placed them on the table.

Findlow went back to the box, and studied the tray. "The

tray thing comes out," he said. "Help me lift it, Harthma. It's too unwieldy for me to handle by myself."

Together they lifted it out and sat it on a nearby table. I studied it as Harthma opened one of the bags and inspected the contents.

I looked up when he gasped. He held a scroll, one of many, and was staring at the notations carved around the top.

"Oh, my goodness." He'd gone quite pale. "These belong to Sirasha Beech. I'd best go get him."

While he was gone, Findlow and I studied the grill that sat over the tray. It was amazing. From what I could tell, the lattice was made of one piece of wood, the joins, if there were any, were seamless.

"You know, I'd almost swear this was a tree root," said Findlow. "But it would be impossible, wouldn't it?"

"I've seen a lot of impossible things here, so perhaps you're right."

"I can't be, it's impossible."

Harthma returned with Sirasha, four sons and two grandsons. Their attention went first to the tray and grill. Harthma and Findlow carefully lifted the lattice off, and carried the box to a clear section on the table. It was big, and heavy.

Sirasha studied it briefly. "For you, I think, Lady Kirym."

The top was dark blue, with a raised silver pattern. It was divided into nine sections, the middle three being double the height of the top and bottom. Similarly, the centre sections were twice the width of the sides. Each section had a picture or scene in it.

In the very centre was a large white stone, circled by six coloured shapes. They reminded me of tokens.

The section to the left of the centre showed nine poles. Three looked like stellon, three were made up of people and animals, and three had holes and lines on them. They were reminiscent of the stones that made up the three circles we had discovered at the beginning of spring.

The picture to the right of the centre was a large ball, covered with swirls of purple, pink and silver. The way it was coloured gave the impression of mist. I wondered what it was.

The four corner sections showed different types of dwellings, one made of wood and stone, similar to those built in The Green Valley. The second showed a wide ledge with caves in the cliff behind it. The bottom left corner showed a tall block with a tented top and arches in the two visible walls, and the fourth showed a massive tree with holes in the trunk, and what looked like large bird's nests hanging from the branches.

The centre top showed boats, copies of those we travelled to this land in, except one had a dragon's head as the prow.

Teema's intake of breath told me he too remembered seeing a similar head on our own Dragon Quest, thought of as a simple trick of light at the time. Now I wondered what it meant, and what happened to the head.

"Is it Dragon Quest?" Teema murmured.

I shrugged. "Perhaps this is the third boat, the one that disappeared, or maybe another we aren't aware of."

The bottom middle section showed a lake, or possibly a pool with a waterfall to one side. Behind the lake was a cave, beside the cave, a dragon.

It wasn't a box. Words curved around the circle of stones told me what this was.

Ledger Sixteen

Life of the Token Bearers

Jeresaya came to collect Larqeba and Shormel, who were strenuous and vocal in their objections to going with her. "Do you want me to take Trethia as well?" she asked.

"Yes please. Mama wants to check her leg and bathe her. Tell Mama she hasn't eaten yet."

Having kissed Trethia on the cheek and handed her to Jeresaya, I pulled the book close and opened the cover. The interior sheets were fine parchment, each covered with writing and pictures. Where there was no writing, the parchment was transparent, and yet words from one side did not show through to the other.

I wondered how they did it, it was a splendid effect.

In the corners and down the centre where the pages joined, were pictures to coincide with words written.

I carefully turned the pages, taking great care—they appeared so fine.

This book was continued from a previous one, there were references back to earlier incidents. I wondered what had happened to the other books.

On the fifth page was a picture of the seven dragons. The next page told of them arriving in the land and talking to the guardians who, I presumed, had written the book. Either the guardians were giants, or the dragons had grown a lot since the image was drawn.

Several pages spoke of something called The Burl of Meglinor. The writer described its amazing size and colour, the ceremonies over the time of accepting it, and the honour they felt at being given such an amazing gift. I wished they had pictured it. It was something big, but even after reading all they had written, I had no idea what it was.

The word *REF* with a number appeared occasionally. I took these to be references to other subsidiary books, and wondered if they expanded on the story.

Ledger sixteen covered several generations. Many pages described trips made with the dragons. Sections of maps were sketched in. Some I recognised from Borasyn's pictures; some from my own travels.

One section near the centre of the book told of a trip to the forests of Leniarm. It described a great hunt for a wild creature that was attacking the people who lived there. The picture of the animal showed massive spiralled horns on a chunky shortened head with sharp fang-like teeth. Its body was long, sinuous and snake-like, with thick stumpy legs and long claws. The men pictured next to it were tiny by comparison.

This creature was bigger than Faltryn, but although it was the same artist, I wondered if the size comparison was right. However, with all other pictures of men, dwellings and trees, the scale was perfect.

Some pages further on, I learned of a feast where the people gathered for a great summit to sort out the minor problems of people living near each other. Most of the people were brought to the summit by the dragons. They carried large packages, much as Egrym had when we went to collect Garanniis' people.

There were maps scattered throughout the book, generally aligned to journeys taken. Most of the book however, was about season to season living and the interaction with the dragons. At one point, there was a picture of the caves in the canyon followed by a comment from the writer.

Headman Arjin:

After a hard winter, the spring has been quiet. Little has been needed from me, other than to decide a direction for hunting, when we would plant the crops, and on what day we would go to the cave to see if Aidrall and Ysteral's child would be given a token.

We still mourn for my son, Aidrall. His sudden death mystifies me, and with no answers, my family feel unsettled. Many have wished aloud that Aidrall's child had been a son who could lead us in the future.

The dragons joined us in the canyon for the ceremony, not something they did often. Aidrall's token was returned on the evening of our arrival at the caves.

In the morning Miarta named the child Kirym, a name we have not heard before. The cave chose to give her two tokens, both darker than those we are used to.

Ancient Brinleatha spoke for the first time in seventy springs. She declared the two tokens foretold strange events in the future, and that this child would have a place important in our family. Brinleatha had me write the following: "She is a serene child, but she sees the world with eyes of an aged sage. When she speaks, you must listen and act. Her words will have great weight."

Here a drawing of seven faces, the first a baby, then the same face, but each time older until she was about thirteen.

I turned over more pages, now near the end of the writing, although there were a lot more between Arjin's record of the naming and the end. I quickly read the last four pages. They told an interesting story.

Acting headman, Varl:

I have been caring for the family while Arjin—our headman and my papa—is away visiting those tribes distant from us. The trip will last until autumn unless they decide to winter over in the summer-lands. Their plan is to introduce the dragons to the people of Valythia. It will take some special care, Valythians are so tiny in stature, and yet from all we can gather, huge in spirit. If Arjin can make this happen, it will mean we can come together as a whole nation. Then we can have what we have always planned—a gathering of all the tribes under the care of The Green Valley. Of course, it will not be easy, but Arjin will take what time he needs. If any of his arguments do not work out, then we will see them sooner than planned. We hope however, this will be the final move that brings total peace to the land, and integrates the dragons into our whole community.

All here is settled, and the early spring warmth and soft rains promise a bounteous harvest.

~ ~ ~ ~ ~

The men who had travelled with the dragons returned far more prematurely than any of us expected. Although the trip they took was expected to last until the end of autumn, they walked into the settlement before spring was half gone. This, in itself, is different; the dragons always delivered them back to the settlement and joined us as we celebrated their return.

The men do not appear to be themselves, having no memory of the dragons at all and none of the events over the last four season cycles.

Kirym, having now seen her thirteenth spring suggested Arjin read through this book, and the 'articles of friendship' we hold with the dragons.

He did, and became very angry. He wants now, to take the book and approach Faltryn beneath the great oak where we pledged homes to Churnyg of the Tree People, when they first requested our protection and land to live on. It was in the same place where we accepted the friendship of the dragons, and brought them into our family.

27

Arjin will request Faltryn's help to find out what has happened. He will enlist the dragon's assistance to rectify everything.

Kirym suggested I encourage Arjin to go, when he awakens from his sleep, for no other reason than he is headman, and needs to know what has occurred.

Brinleatha just stared at me, and she says so much without uttering a word. Everyone is terrified of her, except for the child, Kirym. My late brother's daughter is fond of the old lady, and they seem to understand each other. The world as I know it becomes more inexplicable by the day.

Beyond that, the pages were empty.

Lyndym brought Trethia and sat her on a stool beside me. She was in a sleeping robe, smelled sweet, and her hair glowed in the candle-light.

"I'm sorry, Kirym," said Lyndym. "I put her to sleep with Sarel and Nysia, but she wouldn't settle. Every time I looked up, she was on her way out the door. It was beginning to disturb the other two. Where should I take her?"

"Oh, leave her with me. I'll settle her."

Lyndym nodded with relief and handed her to me. "I must get back. Who knows what mischief they'll be getting up to? I asked Dashlan to watch them while I brought her over, but I think it might have been less disruptive leaving them alone."

"I hope not. If he has created a fuss, make him stay until you're absolutely sure they've all settled again. Keep him there until at least midnight. It'll teach him a good lesson."

She left, laughing.

I wrapped my cloak around Trethia. "Have you eaten?" I asked, as I pushed the nearest platter towards her. She nodded, but took my flask and drank. I smiled to myself, suddenly understanding why Mama always checked I had eaten.

I glanced down at the book, thinking of all I'd learned. The maps had been useful, as had the pictures of the settlement, the layout they'd used—not unlike ours—and the different types of dwelling around the Green Valley, all known to me, and now confirmed here. The portion of the book written in was well under half, they obviously planned to use it for many more seasons. I wondered why they had stopped recording their history. I closed the books and studied the cover.

The spine too was decorated. A token, a tree and a dragon. As I turned it to the light, I felt a pattern on the back cover, and turned it over.

It had an image of three bolts, held together at the centre. Three bolts, three different heads, one wide and heavy, the second narrower and serrated, the third slim and pointed. The heads and shaft of each were covered with silver scrollwork.

Trethia leaned over and ran her finger down the centre shaft. "Those are your bolts, Kirym."

"How did you know about them?" I asked quietly.

"I watched you pick them up."

I stared at her, shocked that she had been in that part of The Rock.

"Why didn't you come to me then?"

She glanced up; her eyes wide. "It wasn't time."

Sirasha leaned over and studied the picture. "They're a true work of art. I've never seen the like. My ancestors said those from The Green Valley were the cleverest artisans in the land."

"Why would they be pictured here?" asked Teema.

Trethia reached over and lifted the back cover of the book.

I was surprised at how thick it was. It felt very different to the front cover, which was quite firm. The outer side of the back was the same, but the inner section felt spongy.

I realised the back cover was, in fact, the base of a box. The sides of it had been cleverly painted to look as if it was made up of many pages, and was seamless when closed. The final page of the book section, a piece of fine creamy parchment, was glued to cover it. There were faded letters along the top.

I brought the lamp closer and read, the words, *Maps of the Land.*

"Open it," said Trethia. She lay on her tummy on the table with her chin on her hands, staring intently at the book.

Oak ruffled her hair. "Such enthusiasm. Shall I get a knife?"

"I have mine here," I answered, "but I'm wondering if there's someone else who is more entitled to open it."

Sirasha, sitting further down the table studying scrolls, looked up. "Go ahead, Kirym. Harthma and Findlow feel as I do. It belongs to you and The Green Valley. We've already seen sections of the maps as you turned the pages, and it's probably just an overview of them all. You understand maps far better than we do."

"I was thinking more of Mama. She is headwoman."

"I told her about the book when we first found it, Kirym," said Findlow. "She felt you would have more understanding of it. She expects you to tell her of anything important, but go ahead."

I tried to slip the knife under the edge, but it was truly stuck.

"You may have to cut it. It's fixed tight with tree gum."

Trethia's words registered, and I looked up to see Harthma and Sirasha's shocked expressions, which must have echoed mine. "How do you know?"

"Because I stuck it down," she said.

"Why?"

"So, it couldn't fall out by accident. If it was opened, it would mean someone had chosen to open it."

"Who would have looked?"

"Gynbere."

"But surely, they would have been seen when the box was first opened," said Oak.

She shook her head. "They knew they didn't have the right to touch it. Anyway, they feared it."

"They?"

"The Gynberes. Right back to the first.

"Then why do you think I should look in it?" I said.

"Because it belongs to you."

I thought over what she said, now more mystified than ever. "You were in Gynbere's rooms?"

She nodded.

"She's lying!" Girk stepped out of the shadows. He carried a bow and arrows, and had obviously just come off guard duty. "With all the guards, no one could enter those rooms. Anyway, what little tree gum there was within The Rock was highly prized. There is no way she'd get it."

"And yet it is stuck with gum just as she said. What other explanation could there be?" I asked.

"She must've heard someone talk about it. She's a sneaky little troll. Always turning up where she isn't wanted."

"Who else would know about the book?" I asked.

"Gynbere, Slaslow, possibly the triplets," said Sirasha. "One or two of Gynbere's more influential personal guards. There's no way she'd hear anything from them. None of them would speak of Gynbere in front of anyone else."

Oak pursed his lips, frowning. "You're right. How would she get close enough to them to hear? If they'd found her listening, they would've killed her. From all I've heard and seen, she was belittled by pretty much everyone within The Rock. The guards were particularly nasty towards her."

Girk snorted. "It's because she was a liar and a thief."

"What did she steal?" I asked.

"Food mainly," interrupted Sirasha. "I heard she picked up a rug that had fallen on the ground. A couple of times she picked up toys left lying in a corner, a doll, similar things to that."

"Things most dwarflings would have been given as a matter of course," said Oak.

"She's not a dwarfling," snapped Girk.

"She is a child," I said. "She should have been protected; cared for by everyone."

"Kirym, I agree with you," said Sirasha, his face red, although it could have been the reflection from the fire. "However, the situation within Gynbere's realm was difficult. Those who helped her were threatened, their own dwarflings punished. People look after their own first. No one knew where she came from, and she was so different."

"And yet many of your people have continued to treat her badly since they were freed. Someone attacked her with a knife or sword yesterday." I said.

"It doesn't matter, Kirym," said Trethia. "Just open the box."

Sirasha sat on beside Trethia. "Child. Trethia. I am truly sorry for what happened. Possibly we could have stopped it had we stuck together and shown a united front. I'm embarrassed to admit we always allowed internal arguments to take over. I should have stopped them and insisted we make things right. I will endeavour to change things from now on. You will have protection in the future, from me personally, and from my family for the rest of time." He stood and walked away into the darkness.

I waited a few moments. "Invite him back please, Findlow. He needs to see what's in here."

Sirasha returned and again sat opposite me. His eyes glistened, and he looked shamefaced. Trethia leaned over and patted his hand.

"There's a liquid that may loosen the gum," said Findlow, breaking the silence. "If we're careful, it won't affect anything else." He brought over his work kit, and set to work. Shortly after, he stepped back. "See how that is."

I carefully slipped the tip of my knife under the corner of the parchment and began to ease it back on three sides. As the gum softened, it became easier to separate the two edges.

Inside was a large piece of fine velum, folded and then rolled to fit into the box. I opened it out and laid it on the table. It was covered in a jumble of letters, symbols and pictures, all laid out on a diamond grid around a central picture of a dragon. Some of the pictures were coloured, faint lustrous colours that glowed in the lamp light. The letters and symbols were joined diagonally with thin lines. Tiny curlicues, some blue, some yellow, were on many of the lines.

"It's a qwanchel." Sirasha sounded surprised.

"What's a qwanchel?" asked Oak.

"Usually they pass on a memory of someone special, or perhaps a momentous occasion. We make them for many reasons. I carry one made for me by my sons, and grandsons." He pulled a skin pouch from his jerkin, and laid out a large square of parchment. "I value it for many reasons. The givers, the time it was given and the message it holds. A qwanchel contains four elements. In mine, there's a beech tree, a scroll, a quill and a bladder of ink." He pointed to drawings as he named them. "These are items of great value and meaning to me. The surrounding words describe me, and the things I value. Qwanchel are often passed down from generation to generation. They frequently give part of the history of a family." He glanced at the Velum. "This artist however, didn't seem to have even the basic knowledge of the needs of a qwanchel. The word means four things, initially the artist, the brush or quill, the ink and the parchment. But it's generally more than that. When I create one, the brush I use for instance contains four elements, perhaps the handle made of three different materials, and hair, linen or flax fibres for the head, although there could be variations. Add the parchment made up of four layers and it's divided into four sections. Qwanchel are drawn on parchment, but this is velum and therefore very wrong. I think it's just a piece of art as opposed to a message or memory. As you see, there is only one element here, the dragon in the centre and variants of it elsewhere. I suspect the artist couldn't read because there are no words, just letters, although they're beautifully drawn. The colours are not quite true, not the pure bright tones we use, although the lustre is compelling. I will try to replicate it at some time in the future, but not for qwanchel. These things are tied by tradition. This piece however, is of minor value."

I gently touched the letters. "In itself, it's a beautiful piece of art, but it looks so complicated there must be a reason for it," I said.

I pulled the lamp closer and stared, trying to see a pattern.

Trethia's finger traced a line, and I suddenly realised she had followed the letters of one word, and then another.

It took only the two words, difficult because each word was written backwards, as well as there being twists and turns within the words, and I realised the turns were indicated by the curlicues. It was effectively a message in a maze. The first word she showed me was dragon, and further along the line, homage. I followed the hints and finally read the first sentence.

My homage to the dragon is the beginning.

Once I figured out the sequence of letters, words and sentences, I explained it to Sirasha.

His eldest grandson was called to help. "His eyes are better than mine, and perhaps his mind more open. I discounted it because it was different, and I shouldn't have," Sirasha said.

Once they were settled with it, I turned my attention to the scroll.

Sirasha had shown me the differences between those written by his family as part of their historic archives, and those by others, all indicated by the marks on the scroll rod ends, and sometimes by comments at the beginning or end of the scroll.

This one was written in the same pattern as those even now written by the tree people, but it was larger, and the scroll rods were carved differently and gilded. However, in this case, the scroll rods gave no indication of the author. It was open, that is, half rolled onto each cylinder.

I sat another lamp on the table and trimmed it for reading. After perusing the writings for two sections, I returned to the beginning of the scroll and began to read from there. Left and right, up and down, each letter contained in a grid, the story was captivating. The language was a little different to ours, but there was enough similarity for its content to be clear.

3

Teema Speaks

Kirym was immersed in the items from the carved chest, until after midnight. When she finally looked up, she was frowning and distant, obviously still lost in what she had read.

She rerolled the scroll and called Findlow over. Harthma, dozing, his head on his arms at the other end of the table, started awake when he heard her.

"You too, Harthma," she said. "First, can you put the bigger box back together?"

"Oh yes," said Harthma, "but why?"

"We may need to return it to Gynbere and it'll be a better bargaining tool if it appears intact." She handed them the book and the scroll. "Take these and hide them in a place where neither Gynbere nor anyone else will find them. No one should read them at this stage. However, they may be needed in a hurry, so keep them close. I need you to close the smaller box and hide that as well. As it didn't ever belong to Gynbere, it will not be returned to him. However, if most people think it's back in the bigger box, there will be less speculation."

"Gynbere will never get his hands on it ever again, Lady Kirym."

After replacing the tray and lattice, the two men closed the box and walked off, their heads close together as they discussed where to hide the book and scroll.

Sirasha, his sons and grandson were still making notes at the far end of the table.

"We're almost finished. I'm sure I will soon have a wonderful story to tell you, Lady Kirym."

"You should rest," I said. "You'll have time in the morning to finish reading."

Sirasha nodded, collected the scrolls together and blew out the lamp he had been using.

Kirym glanced at the sky. "I need to sleep, Teema. Can you have someone waken me as the sun rises, please? It'll be a busy day."

I nodded, although I would have loved to allow her to sleep until midday.

Trethia had long since closed her eyes. She lay on the table wrapped in one of Oak's cloaks. I wondered when he had exchanged his for Kirym's, and wrapped hers around her shoulders. It was cold and I was annoyed I hadn't thought of it.

Together Kirym and Trethia curled up on a rug near the northern wall.

"It's too cold out here. You should go into a dwelling."

"They'd feel compelled to move people to make room for me. I don't want to disturb anyone; it's not fair." She quickly fell asleep.

Workers wandered around the open area. I felt a few eyes on me as I walked away from Kirym, and realised I wanted her to be guarded overnight.

I grabbed Bryn as he passed. "Who's in charge of the guards tonight?"

"Churnyg. Why? Are you worried about something?"

"I dunno. I just feel someone should watch over Kirym while she sleeps. I'm probably being stupid."

"No, no, if you have a feeling, you need to go with it. The dragons aren't here to watch over everything, so yes, perhaps we do need to take more care of Kirym. Is it her or the wee girl?"

"I don't know."

"I'll see to it. I think you need to rest too. You get some sleep and I'll organise something. There are a few good men around, and a group of them will watch her overnight."

Bryn woke me as the grey dawn streaked the eastern horizon.

"Here lad," he said as he handed me a flask of hot juice. "Come on, drink up, there's a bit o' time before you need to waken Kirym. Ah, here, eat something too."

Dashlan sat a platter of bread stuffed with meat beside me, after taking a hefty slice for himself. "I love Ma's cooking, but this stuff is divine. I hope she learns how to make it for us. Why're we getting up so early, Pa? We don't go off to war today; we could all sleep in."

"If we slept because nothing was planned, we'd never plan anything," said Bryn. "Teema wanted an early start, so we're obliging him by bringing a meal over."

"And I need to be awake because Kirym asked me to make sure she didn't sleep past dawn," I said.

"So why didn't you just ask Pa to sort Kirym out, and then you and I could've slept."

I laughed. "Doesn't work that way, Dash. Kirym asked me. Bryn offered to help, but it's still my job. I'll tell you this for what it's worth. She has plans for today. You'd be silly to sleep through them."

Dashlan looked crestfallen. "Ach, I have to move the squilute to the river meadow this morning. I'll miss it all."

"I'm sure she'll give everyone time to finish their tasks. It won't happen before," I glanced at the horizon, "well much before midday. She'll do her usual rounds of the sick, the prisoners, the children, and our visitors. Then she'll talk to the dragons. You'll hear whatever she has learned. I'm sure everyone will. Even those on the wall."

I glanced at the sun. "How high can I let the sun rise before it's no longer dawn?"

"Ah well, it depends how angry the person you're dealing with will be," said Bryn. "Go and have a wash first. I'm sure Kirym will wait that long. I'll go and relieve the guard there."

"I'll get Kirym something to eat," Dashlan volunteered, and he raced off towards the cooking area.

"He's planning on a third meal for himself, I'm sure of it," laughed Bryn. "Can't think where the lad puts it all."

Blacknight was just walking away from Bryn as I approached. Kirym still slept, and I regretted having to disturb her. Before I had the chance to, her eyes opened. She smiled sleepily, sat up and carefully wrapped her cloak around Trethia, who slept on. "Has anything happened overnight?"

"It's been the quietest night since we arrived here," said Bryn. "Dashlan is going to allow us to share his third meal o' the morning," he said, as a filled platter was put down in front of us, a large wedge of it already missing.

"Growing lad needs his food, Pa," laughed Dashlan.

"What are you planning today, Kirym?" I asked. "Will you tell us what you learned last night?"

She took a bite of her loaf. "Possibly. There are other things I must attend to first. Now, how is Starshine?"

I looked at her blankly.

She laughed. "The first and most important thing. Has there been an agreement for her and Mekroe to join?"

"Oh, I know. Well, I think," Dashlan said. "They were in a long meeting with Loul, Tarl and a pile o' the Guild men during the evening. When it broke up, Starshine spent the night with her people and Mekroe went back with the other single men. He didn't say anything, but he looked happy."

"Good, it seems they will be joined today."

"The best time will be late morning," said Loul. "Larqeba tells me you will have a tale to tell. Just me, or everyone?" She hunkered down beside Kirym, kissed her on the head, and handed each of us a flask.

"Everyone, I think, Mama. And I need to tell the dragons why Faltryn did what he did."

Loul looked surprised. "You've figured it out?"

Kirym nodded. "With help, and I hope I have enough to rectify the damage done. But I want to tell you a bit of it first, Mama."

"Will it waken them?" I asked.

"I don't know."

"What? Wake them? I thought they were dead," said Dashlan.

Trethia stretched, rolled over and winced as her back touched the ground. Kirym immediately took her hand and in the flurry of sitting her up and giving her food, left Dashlan's question unanswered.

Platters of food were prepared and taken to the healers and their patients, the prisoners and the men coming off guard duty. Quickly the open area became a bustling, but organised chaos, and Loul was inundated with people, reluctant to approach a 'war-lord', but wanting information and advice.

"Was it too soon to take the rugs away from the prisoners?"

"Should the animals be taken to a nearby field to eat, or given food from stores?"

"If they went to the fields, would they be in danger from Gynbere and his guards?" "Would Gynbere take exception to the hunters going out?"

She dealt with most by simply sending them to ask Tarl to make the decisions as the 'Voice for the Headwoman', or pass on those already made.

Starshine approached Kirym just before mid-morning, the mixture of joy at Loul and the guild leader's agreement for her joining, and worry for those kidnapped. "I still wonder if we should wait until everyone is rescued, Kirym. I don't want Wind Runner to feel she's missed out."

"It needs to happen as planned, Starshine. Wind Runner wouldn't ask you to wait. We do have the time now, and it'll be good to take everyone's mind off what may happen in the future. Mama and Tarl have to make the decisions on how to approach Gynbere. Together you and Mekroe can assist them far better together than separately."

"Will there be a battle?" she asked.

"I hope not. We'll try everything else we can before it comes to that. Go and get your flowers and get dressed. We need a celebration."

Kirym's smile was very reassuring, and I wondered how she could be so calm.

The joining ceremony from Faltryn was quite different to ours, but aspects of our ceremony were included. It could not happen in quite the way we wished because of the situation with Gynbere unresolved. However, we were determined to give them as much of their celebration time as we could, and hope everything would be back to normal and have a special celebration when the hostages were back with us.

Two temporary dwellings had been erected at the back of the crowd for Mekroe and Starshine to use for their preparations, and a walkway created between them and the family heads who were taking the ceremony.

Slate, of the carer's guild, Loul, Findlow, and Mole stood together to officiate. I wondered why Findlow was there, and then realised he had taken the position Old Harby normally took. I would have expected Armos to take over, but realised he was still mourning Peet's death.

Oak and Tarl represented the two families.

Mekroe walked to his position in front of the officials. He wore clothes given him while visiting the Fortress of Faltryn. Arbreu was with him as support. It shocked me, he hadn't told me he would do that.

Arbreu's clothes were traditional formal clothes from The Green Valley. It was rare for anyone to wear them, generally they were worn only when a new headman was sworn in, or when someone very important was joining. I wondered if it meant Arbreu was now rejecting any claim Bryn, Jeresaya and their family had on him, and acknowledging his adoption into the green Valley. I had long thought he should; his loyalty should be to Kirym.

I was hurt Arbreu hadn't told me what was happening, but when I tried to connect with his token, Mekrar got in the way. I wasn't used to her being there. It was wrong, Kirym should be the most important person to him, as she was to me.

Background music had been arranged, and the variety of instruments from the four families blended well together.

Vandara and Sarel, came out of Starshine's dwelling first. They scattered flower petals around them as they walked.

I glanced over at Morkeen, expecting her usual scowl of disapproval at the waste. However, she leaned forward as Sarel passed, and picked up a petal to show Amethyst.

Then Starshine appeared. She wore a festival dress from The Green Valley, a gift, I imagined, from Loul.

Mekrar walked beside her. She wore a new dress in a style I'd never seen before. It took me a while to realise it was made up of aspects from clothes worn by those from Faltryn and The Valley.

They both looked exotic in their different clothes.

It was strange not having the ceremony in the cave, and with no cave, there were no tokens. Earlier in the day Loul had spoken to those from The Green Valley. Everyone had accepted the absence of the cave and tokens; new circumstances with new families.

Slate spoke about the responsibilities of marriage, and the delight he, and was sure everyone else, felt on this happy occasion. Findlow talked of how the marriage would strengthen the bonds between the separate families and tribes.

I was pleased though, that he included many aspects of our ceremonies, and especially pleased when he put our usual wish to all the families.

"Mekroe has requested a joining and he has chosen Starshine. Is everyone happy with his choice?"

His friends responded with cheers and catcalls.

"No objection here," called Splinter. "That scar gets him far too much attention from all the pretty girls."

This was greeted with a roar of laughter.

A similar request by Loul for Starshine was treated with

far less noise, but a lot of happy nodding and I was pleased to hear Loul, Findlow, Slate and Mole end the ceremony saying: "They are joined."

Instead of the final comments we'd been told Mole would impart, Findlow stepped forward again.

"Arbreu has requested a joining, and chosen Mekrar. Is everyone happy with his choice?"

After a moment of shocked silence, everyone cheered. Loul repeated her request for Mekrar, with the same enthusiastic reaction.

I realised I was the only one not cheering, but again I was hurt I'd not been told. I didn't think they'd told Kirym either, and I felt for her. But when I looked over at her, she was clapping and smiling broadly.

She glanced at me. I was surprised at the concern in her eyes. But then Mole had finished his comments, and everyone stood and pushed forward to congratulate the two couples.

I was walking away when Kirym caught up with me.

"What's wrong, Teema? We knew they would join."

"They shouldn't have elbowed in on Mekroe and Starshine's ceremony. It was wrong."

"Mekroe and Starshine wanted it. They wouldn't join unless the ceremony encompassed them all."

"Arbreu didn't tell me." I sounded petulant, but I didn't care.

Kirym pulled me down to sit in the shelter of a wagon. "Teema, with all that has happened, they've scarce had time to breathe. Did you not wonder why Arbreu was dressed so formally? Why he was so excited and busy over the last evening? Why he didn't do his usual guard duty, although he would have. Tarl had to order him not to."

My face went red. I hadn't even thought of Arbreu lately. "Mekrar should have had you stand by her. You didn't get the chance to support Halse."

"I'm sure Mekrar would have liked it to be different. Arbreu would have liked you to stand by him, and Tarjin would have liked to support Mekroe. But these are difficult times, so everyone needed to adjust."

"So, I'm being selfish."

"No, not at all. But everyone has been so busy. None of us have had time to note everything that has happened. You've been tied up with protecting me, and don't look at me like that," she said, noting my look of outrage. "I was very aware of it, and although I thought it unnecessary, I appreciate your care of me. I knew objecting would do no good. However, you need time for you as well. Now let's go and talk to the two happy couples."

I let her guide me over. The crowds had thinned a little, and Arbreu turned to me with such a big smile, I instantly forgave him for not telling me his news in words of one syllable.

With the formalities and congratulations over, the two couples collected their traditional sweet loaves from the food pits and approached everyone there, giving them a taste and accepting more good wishes. Eating it signified approval of their joining.

"What about those who aren't here?" asked Starshine. "Can they object to the joining?"

Kirym shook her head. "Normally the whole family is with us when someone joins, but I talked to Mama and Tarl this morning and we decided to have more acceptance loaves when everyone is back together, and we again celebrate you joining. Objections need good reasons behind them, and I don't think anyone could have any. Those not with us will support your decisions."

"Shame we can't have a huge celebration now," said Mekroe, as he offered me a piece of sweet loaf. "My friends feel they've been robbed."

"They'll get over it," Kirym said. "But something is planned, so pass around your bread, and tell everyone it begins at midday."

She hugged them all, and reminded them to include the prisoners and those in the healers area.

4

Kirym Speaks

Having collected the scroll, I glanced at the sun. It was nearing the meridian. I explained to Teema and Bryn where I wanted people to sit for the next part of the day, and although they were not part of the watch, they arranged for a few of the men to guide everyone to seats near the stump, where they could hear. People could listen if they liked, and by the look of the crowd, everyone had decided to. I ensured the six dragons could hear, and be included.

Those who were prisoners had been given the opportunity to join us there, having given their word they would not attempt an escape, nor harm anyone else. Most agreed, although a few held out and stayed resolutely in their cage.

As the sun reached its highest point, I threaded my way through the crowd and climbed onto the great stump. I sat cross-legged and Trethia snuggled in beside me, almost hidden in my cloak, needed because of the cold breeze.

While waiting for everyone to settle, I began again to read

the scroll, starting from the beginning. Teema leaned over my shoulder, reading along with me.

The scroll had been written by Gynbere, an ancestor of the present dwarf with the same name. He began by stating his pride at being able to read and write, and his annoyance at not being presented with a special award, given to the best of his group at the beginning of each spring. He realised the award would influence family position in the future, and despite being provided by Churnyg Oak, held great prestige. He felt it should have been given to him.

Then he wrote:

> *I am angry! Furious in fact. Forced by my sire to bend my knee to the cursed Churnyg Oak, I have left my family tree and I intend to NOT return. Ever!*
>
> *Now I sit in another cursed Oak, the only tree of substance here, and the only one in the area I can adequately hide in. I have pissed on it, kicked it and broken a branch, but I swear this. One day I will destroy this tree. Destroy it in such a way, everyone will know I am bigger and better and stronger than IT, and the people who take their name from it.*
>
> *Aghhhh! Why do they grow so well, live so long? Four times longer than my beautiful Yew. Cursed? I curse him! Them! Those! These trees! Those people! The Oak family! Him in particular. Churnyg Oak!*
>
> *And so, I ran from my home, my sire's oaths ringing in my ears. He said I was NOTHING! I'll show him!*
>
> *For now, I sit hidden, and I cannot even leave, for a dragon has come to lie below the tree, and just when I thought he would leave, the fool who leads The Guardians has arrived to talk to him. Another man I hate. We foolishly consider them our overlords. Just because they are the owners of the land and our trees, which we stupidly begged from them,*

instead of taking them by force. We should have killed those of The Green Valley if they challenged our ownership.

Another oath! I will somehow subjugate them! Grind them under my heel, and have them bow to me. They will beg me to rule them, and I will consider it, after I perhaps show my power by killing the few who annoy me most!

Something is not right though. Normally, they are as thick as thieves, but the dragon is distinctly nervous of the human.

Arjin demands a truth—reminding the dragon of past promises.

The dragon agrees to talk, and what a story I heard. So much I learned, and I can use it to rule my people. I know so much now about the dragon, Faltryn, he can refuse me nothing. I will have everything I want. The world is now mine for the taking, and I will take all of it. I will demand it be laid out for me to use as I see fit.

This dragon is devious, almost as devious as I. He promised to tell the man all, and he did. But he put him to sleep first.

If only I had this information earlier, I could have ruled the trees. No! More than the trees. With this information, I could rule the land, the universe, and I will. Eventually. Still, it will be enough initially to give me rule over the people of the trees. That first, and then I will demand everything else.

This is what I heard.

"Oh my," said Teema. "Will you tell everyone this? Gynbere will be ruined when his people know it."

"I'll tell Faltryn's story, and I'll pass on some of the rest, but not Gynbere's reasons stated here. This dwarf died long ago, and the present ruler has enough to answer for. He should not have to account for the actions of an ancestor. It needn't be more complicated than it is."

The last of the crowd slipped into their seats, and the healers helped those who were able, to come closer. The music that had been quietly playing in the background came to a halt. From the stump where I sat, my voice carried across the amphitheatre, ensuring everyone could hear. Oak brought me a drink, and I began the story.

"When the dragons came to the land, they talked first to the guardians, those who cared for the people and the land. An agreement was written up. The dragons would assist the guardians in the work they did, and their payment was to have a place of their own, somewhere they could live in peace and comfort. Those they called the guardians suggested a formal meeting every fifth spring, to make decisions for the time ahead. Although that was set in the calendar, the dragons were eager to begin being useful in the land, and to their new neighbours.

"Beyond those plans, the dragons were offered the freedom of the land, but it was requested they be circumspect in approaching the other inhabitants until the guardians could make the proper introductions. Almost always, the dragons met the guardians at their spring festival, and celebrated with them, although the place changed to encompass the various tribes as they met them. Trips the dragons and their riders made together could be short, less a season, but also, if need be, last several season cycles.

"When not helping the guardians, the dragons ranged widely, sometimes together, but more often one or two would go off to explore. In this way, they learned about the people of the land and the ways they lived." I paused as the murmur of comments fluctuated around me.

"This, however," I said, "is Faltryn's story, and so we will talk of him. Faltryn loved watching the inhabitants of the land. He was delighted when able to meet them, and he went out of his way to help them where he could, taking messages from one family settlement to another, carrying loads, helping to bring in and prepare building material, or entertaining the families as he was able. He was intrigued by the different people and their diverse customs. He was delighted at how welcoming they were, once they met him, his brothers and sisters. Initial meetings were at the great circle, but he soon learned where all the different settlements were.

"He flew over the dwellings in The Green Valley as they were built and enlarged. He scrutinised the people as they grew food, hunted, lived, and celebrated together. He found them to be a welcoming people, as diverse in their ideas as the buildings they created.

"He watched the people of Nythia build hollows and nests in the massive trees along the Wyist River. Over the seasons, they built a multi-level bridge, added walkways between the hollows, and festooned the trees with flags and banners. They grew masses of exotic flowers to encourage the insects and birds of the land to join them, and to help decorate their homes and the trees."

The dwarves murmured excitedly as they heard about their past.

"We were called Nythians," said Mrillan. "Churnyg always said so. How many other things has Gynbere lied about?"

Others sighed wistfully as the story of their past gave them new insights into the lives their people used to live.

"The trees," I continued, "gifted to them by the guardians, prospered with care and company, and grew to massive heights.

"Faltryn studied the people as they collected food, and prepared it for use. He watched their celebrations, the huge fires, the feasts, dancing and singing. Although he had been introduced to them, he was aware the Nythians were wary of him because of his great size, so he still wasn't able to have as much contact with them as he would like.

"When he visited the cliffs by the river, he saw the small dwellings built in the huge caves and at the back of the wide ledges become a great fortress as the people learned the art of cutting blocks from the rock to build massive ramparts. The more substantial dwellings protected them from the icy winters. He watched as they too celebrated, together and with those who had become the dragon riders. He was delighted when, with the other dragons, he was invited to join their celebrations.

"All these things were an obvious progression of family life within the land. In watching the growth of the settlements, he understood the essence of the different communities.

"The one group of people he did not understand were those who lived in the desert. The great walled city of Valythia was an enigma. The walls were higher even than those being built by the cave people, and thicker beyond anything he had ever seen. The whole city of Valythia was covered with tented canopies. These protected the people from the blistering heat of the desert sun. Even the gardens were shielded whenever the people tended them, although they were uncovered on other occasions, for plants need to see the sun. The shelters also stopped Faltryn from seeing the day to day life of the people who lived under them.

"Each of the four walls surrounding the city held a massive vaulted gate. When they were opened, the thickness of the walls formed a long dark tunnel, so even then he couldn't see the people. He could only imagine what they looked like, based on the height of those gates and the massive size of the city. He was inquisitive and his inability to realise his curiosity rankled."

Now it was Garanniis and his people who sighed as their city, thought of by many as being simply a myth, was confirmed as being real.

"Seasons passed," I continued, "and in his spare time Faltryn flew over the city hoping the canopies would somehow be drawn aside. When he was finally there with the dragon riders and his siblings, the suggestion of him entering the city and meeting the people didn't come up. He found himself requesting time away from the riders to rest and get over the long flight. This was the time of death for them and Faltryn would watch over his siblings until they were reborn."

"That's what you meant?" said Dashlan, amid a wave of comment. "How does something get reborn?"

I smiled. "It's the way of the dragons, Dashlan, and hopefully we will all see it happening sometime soon.

"On this occasion, the other six dragons died almost as soon as the riders had left them. Faltryn eagerly watched from the top of the dune as the riders made their final approach to the city on foot. They pulled a thick rope that hung at the huge gate. Deep inside the walls, a great sound rang out, rich and intriguing, but interspersed with lighter trills. To Faltryn they sounded as if the voices of many waters joined the echo of the wind in the hills and the thundering of the waves against a cliff. Faltryn shivered at the sound.

"The gate to the walled city slowly opened and Faltryn stared into the deep, dark tunnel that led through the wall. The riders disappeared into the gloom, the gates closed, and again he saw nothing of the people, nor their city.

"He was frustrated and angry. He sat in the dunes above the desert plain and hoped the city gates would open and the people would stream out and invite him in.

"It was not to be.

"Through the rest of the day, he watched the city, ignoring his siblings as they lay dead behind him. The only movement was an occasional vulture drifting high above them, and the lizards that basked in the sun and darted across the hot rocks.

"He was aware of his riders, now richly dressed, feasting inside the city and being entertained by their hosts. He knew when they were finally taken from the banqueting chamber and shown to a place put aside for them. He knew when, exhausted from a day and night of entertainment, they fell into a deep sleep."

"Faltryn could see what his riders were doing, so why couldn't he see us, the people of Valythia?" asked Palunniis.

"Dragons need a reference before they can do that. They can't know what they have never seen."

Palunniis nodded.

"As the riders slept, Faltryn had an idea. His plan depended on the riders not seeing him, for they would recognise him instantly. They had to remain ignorant of what he was about to do. If they found out, and it was resolved satisfactorily, there would be no problem. If something went wrong and his plan failed, he could deny involvement, although if need be, he resolved to tell the riders about the death of the other dragons. He would explain he had sat over their bodies, caring for them as he had always done.

"First, he ensured the riders would remain asleep throughout the rest of the day and night. Then he created a protective dome over the other dragons. It ensured no one would disturb them.

"Taking a roundabout route, he flew to the western side of the city, but landed out in the desert, far beyond the sight of those behind the walls. He could not disguise his size or colour, but he laid his wings flat on his back to hide them and altered his way of walking to mimic the lizards he had watched through the day.

"He approached the western gate of the city, the late afternoon sun hiding his advance until he was almost at the walls. He was aware he'd been seen, by the uproar within them, but when he got to the tall gates, they remained closed to him.

"He began to climb the wall, digging his sharp claws into the bricks to get to the top. He intended only to push aside the canopied roof, lift it back and peer in. He reasoned that when the people of the city realised he meant no harm, they would be as welcoming of him as they were of his riders.

"As he clung to the top of the great wall, part of it crumbled away. More of the wall fell as he grabbed a new hold and he looked down into a large open area. He suddenly realised the walls were hollow, appearing thick only because the inhabitants had made their homes within them.

"However, his impressions of the people did not align with the rooms he now looked into. They were large, but not in the way he had thought they would be.

"With the height of the gates and walls, he had imagined an extremely tall elegant race. They would have to bend double to fit into these rooms. He was mystified. More of the wall fell away, exposing another room, and suddenly taken by a frenzy of discovery, he pulled at the bricks to expose yet another and another. Each of them, although big by many standards, certainly had nothing in height to accommodate people who needed such gates.

"Searching for more clues, he slit the canopied roof and hauled it back to expose the city. Below him was an enormous square. Smaller buildings dotted the area, masses of trees and hedges lined paths and parks. In the centre, a large tower reached up to hold up the canopies that shaded the open square.

"He hunted for answers that made sense to him; pulled down section after section of the walls in a frenzy of destruction. Windows looked over the city and they provided an excellent anchor for his claws. He clambered over the debris and worked his way deep into the centre of the city, searching as he went. Once beyond the walls, he found many smaller buildings, most of them roofed. *Perhaps they hold an explanation of the people,* he thought, *or maybe they hold something of great value.*

"When those too had been crushed to dust giving him no answers, he searched through the prolific parks and gardens, ripping out plants and uprooting trees. *Maybe in the desert heat, they live underground, and the dwellings in the walls are just for their visitors.*

"In the centre of the gardens, he came to the tower. This was the one building that could house those he imagined lived here. The lower part of the structure was buried deep in the ground. Unlike the other buildings, there were no windows here to look over the city, and no door for the people to enter. Steps spiralled up the sides of the building, and he grabbed them to pull himself towards the top. However, they pulled away from the walls, and to stop himself from falling, he dug his claws into the bricks that made up the wall. They gave less resistance than he thought they would, and he slashed a long gash in the side. A great wave of water washed over him.

"Faltryn had discovered the water storage for the city. There was no repairing the building, and he could only watch as the water carried away the dust and debris from the demolition. A fountain of water erupted from the ground where the tower had been, but even as he watched, it suddenly disappeared back into the sand, creating a whirlpool, that for a short time, pulled water, bricks, and sand, back into the ground. It quickly died, and the wet sand settled.

"Throughout his destructive foray into the city, Faltryn had found himself under attack, *ants and gnats* he had called them, as he swiped them away. Yet they returned again and again, and when they were not attempting to drive him away from the city, they tried to gain access to the one remaining piece of the wall still standing.

"*They're trying to get to the dragon riders,* he realised.

"He knew if the riders were woken they would recognise him, and he would have to answer for all he had done.

"At that moment, he came to his senses. He was appalled at the damage he had created, and ashamed of his actions. Instantly he realised what the city was, and understood what the gnats and ants who had harassed him were. They were the inhabitants of this great city.

"He wanted time to think; needed it desperately.

"He drove the tiny people out into the desert to a sheltered place behind a dune, and bade them sleep.

"He brought his riders from their rooms, and up onto a high dune. As they climbed, he crushed the remaining buildings to dust and created a huge storm to blow the debris into the desert. As it swirled around the dunes, he collected his riders, and removed from them the memories of the desert citadel.

"Although the men had travelled to the desert on the backs of seven dragons, he had no trouble transporting all of them. He was the biggest and strongest of them, and the dragons rarely ever flew fully laden.

"He then returned them to a place near their home, and gave them the desire to walk the remaining distance.

"The riders continued to be mesmerised. They were unaware of the destruction of the city, because Faltryn had taken from them the whole memory of the trip. As he flew them back to their land, he removed their desire to fly with him, his brothers and sisters, and indeed, their memories of the dragons.

"He then returned to the desert, wondering what to do about the people he had just made homeless. He hoped they would go out into the desert and build a new home there, rebuild their great walled city, and he resolved to help them in any way he could.

"To his surprise the people were not where he left them. They had wandered away into the desert as soon as the wind had died. His removal of memories about the location of the city from the dragon riders had rebounded on them. He watched over them for a while, and realised they were quickly adapting to desert living.

"However, it was when he approached the sleeping dragons that the import of his actions finally hit home. He could not sing to them as he usually did, because it would tell them what he had done while they were dead. He didn't want the embarrassment of having to face everyone with them knowing how appallingly he had behaved.

"He sat beside his brothers and sisters for a long time, wondering if they would ever waken without the knowledge they needed to grow. When eventually they did, they had not grown at all. They were as they had been when they died. Their questions brought new lies, and Faltryn realised he would have to maintain those lies forever. No one would grow, because he could never die.

"He managed to quickly mesmerise his siblings, and convince them of a trip back to the green lands with the riders. The subterfuge was tiring, and towards the end of the trip, he removed the figments of their imagination, and told them the riders had decided to carry on without them and not travel with them again.

"He led the dragons back to Winterisle, the land given them by The Guardians, and insisted they remain confined there while he ostensibly went to talk to the riders.

"In reality," I said, "he came here. He wanted time to think about what had happened, and make sure he had covered every eventuality. He wanted to memorise the story he had created.

"His plan fell to pieces almost immediately, for soon after he arrived, Arjin, the leader of the dragon riders, came to talk to him. Although he had lost his memory of the journey, his family hadn't, and they did more than ride the dragons. They mapped the land, and noted what was happening when they travelled. They also wrote of their journeys and adventures in huge books.

"Once Arjin read of the ongoing travels they'd been doing, and of the promises made, he knew he needed answers and he came to this place to demand them.

"Faced with the ultimatum, and unable under old law to refuse to tell, Faltryn bade the man to sit and rest.

"Faltryn knew the promises to Arjin and his ancestors were binding, but as he settled under the tree facing the man, the dragon pulled one more trick. He caused him to fall into a deep sleep. Then he told his tale.

"Unbeknown to them both, Faltryn's story did have an audience. High in the tree sat a dwarf, one of the Nythians. He listened to all Faltryn said and, scroll in hand, wrote down what he heard.

"Faltryn finished his story satisfied he had covered all contingencies. Then the one he hadn't predicted climbed out of the tree and challenged him.

"For a moment, Faltryn panicked, but the dwarf assured him he had no intention of passing the story on, and particularly not to the guardians."

"That was Gynbere?" Bryn asked.

"Well, an ancestor of the present Gynbere, and I'm assuming it was many generations ago," I said.

"Call him Gynbere," Sirasha said. "Since he took over as ruler, all firstborn and rulers of that family carry the name. My family is the same. My sire, grandsire and his before him many times over, carried the name Sirasha. It's the same with most of the families, although the Chestnut family use two alternate names, Tartharn and Shallern. Of course, most of the rulers have family names, although with each generation there are one or two who don't."

I nodded and continued. "Gynbere proposed a deal to suit them both. With his scroll in his hand, he knew Faltryn couldn't mesmerise him to forget all he had heard. The price of his silence was power. He wanted to rule the six tree families. He demanded the ability to control them and promised he would ensure they wouldn't ask awkward questions. He advised Faltryn remove the memories his people had of the other people of the land, and suggested the dragon allow him to implant a story in their minds to keep them compliant. While he didn't tell Faltryn what he planned to tell his people, Gynbere assured him it would not include references to anyone else in the land, nor the dragons.

"Faltryn agreed to the suggestions, although he had little choice if he was to keep his secrets.

"Gynbere advised him to leave the sleeping man where he was. He assured Faltryn he would be cared for. 'I will waken him when you have gone and I'll convince him the meeting he wanted was with me,' he said.

"Faltryn agreed and left.

"However, Gynbere didn't waken the man. Instead, he robbed him of his weapons and the book he brought with him, and walked away, leaving Arjin asleep on the ground.

"When he reached the trees, he found the people in a dreamy state and he was able to plant his story, delighted Faltryn had kept his part in the bargain."

"You told Iryndal that everyone was deceived," interrupted Teema. "But surely Faltryn and Gynbere weren't."

I shook my head. "Gynbere convinced Faltryn that he was eager to care for his people. Faltryn, for his part, wanted to believe Gynbere would be a benevolent leader. However, the dragon was aware of the corruption of power, and understood that those who demanded what wasn't theirs by right, were more prone to abuse their supremacy. He was annoyed he had been blackmailed into agreeing to Gynbere's demands.

"So, when Faltryn took the history of the tree people away, he planted a layer of memories, some true, some false, in one of the families. These would be triggered if certain things happened. He assumed it would create discussion and rebalance the power. So yes, they were both deceived.

"Gynbere's initial plan fell to pieces quite fast when his sire found the scroll and read of his plans. He privately challenged his son. The argument was brought to a quick conclusion when young Gynbere made good use of the sword, and killed his sire. He used it as a threat to control the rest of his family.

"He set harsh restrictions on his people, but there were murmurs of revolt. To keep control, he convinced a number of personal friends to become his bodyguards. These men were bullies by nature. Gynbere's offer came with promises of vast wealth. They readily agreed to support him. He allowed his bodyguard to carry weapons, but to ensure there could be no revolt, he had all other weapons collected together and hidden. Gynbere's bodyguard were encouraged to spy on each other and report back to him.

"Then a hunter brought news. A large group of The Guardians were in the area, seemingly aiming straight towards the tree communities.

"Gynbere raced to intercept them.

"Varl, son of Arjin, led the group. When Arjin had failed to arrive at an agreed meeting point, Varl went to find him. He found Arjin wandering near the amphitheatre, more confused than ever and now without his weapons. The book Arjin had taken with him to refresh his memory was also missing.

"Varl approached those who lived in the trees, to ask for their help in searching for the items. Before he could get near to the hollows he, fortuitously he thought, met a group of men led by Gynbere Yew.

"Varl's story was met with sympathy, but a reluctance to assist.

"Varl reminded Gynbere of agreements made when the tree people came to The Green Valley. They were obligated to help their benefactors in any way when requested.

"Gynbere didn't want Varl and his men approaching his people, for it would render his plan to nothing. While frantically thinking of how to cope with this problem, he assured Varl that his people were as loyal as they had ever been, and that although he and his people had seen nothing, he would send out his hunters and guards to search for the book and weapons. 'If they find them, I will personally return them to you,' he said.

""Now Gynbere wanted Varl and his men out of the area, and he didn't want them to return for any reason. He explained that a sickness had hit some of his people. Past experience showed that this particular sickness was extremely contagious and could decimate other families, although the dwarves seemed to have a natural immunity. He expressed concern for friends and neighbours, but urged Varl to keep his people away for at least four seasons.

"By the time the illness passed, he was sure everything would be back in its place. 'Possibly Arjin, while his mind was confused has dropped these items as he wandered,' Gynbere said. He again swore a deep friendship to Varl's family, and invited them to visit once the contagion had died. The two parties separated.

"Gynbere ensured Varl left the area, and then he returned to his people, and set about solidifying his leadership. It was not smooth going, and a number of people died. Then when the stories of the Oak family as dragon riders began to circulate, Gynbere assumed Faltryn had planned from the beginning to cheat him.

"To offset these stories, Gynbere added another false story, that of the destruction of the desert city, the opal and the baby, whose skull he conveniently presented.

"He used the guilt his people would feel over the death of an innocent baby, and he played on it over the seasons that followed. He piled more and more guilt on the family of the man he personally hated, and who he suspected, was spreading the stories. The skull was set up as a constant reminder to everyone, and the memory of such an act divided the people."

"Where did Gynbere get the skull from?" Oak asked. "It seems to have been a bit of a mystery from the beginning."

"Well I will get to that. Please be patient," I said. "but accept that the story of the opal and baby was totally false. There was no opal, your ancestors did not destroy a city, nor did they kill a baby."

There was an audible sigh of relief, a few people wiped tears of relief away.

Churnyg stood and bowed in my direction. A generous salute.

"Now Gynbere was fearful that Faltryn was actively monitoring him, and would return to exact revenge," I continued, " He also worried that Arjin would regain some memory, and tell The Guardians. What if they came looking for him? He wondered if using the sword or lying to the Guardians could have made things worse. He felt the need to get away.

"The tree people had long used the tunnels and caves in the rock. They had been given the use of them by the guardians with permission to mine them for gold, silver and precious stones. A portion of these were paid as a tax to the guardians, for they owned the land, but the remainder were kept by the Nythians and used to buy items they were unable to or unwilling to grow or make.

"To ensure he could retain control, he told his people they had lost the right to live in the trees. The loss of their home in the trees was punishment demanded for the destruction of the desert cave. The only other place they could go, was into The Rock. There were complaints, and again, there were deaths."

"That's terrible," gasped Starshine. "How could he do that?"

"Oh, he could do it, if he had any similarity to his descendants," snarled Sirasha. "I just wonder why we let him get away with it."

"The lies worked because you are, for the most part, a gentle and kindly people," I said. "Gynbere worked on his ability to make you feel guilt for a horrid crime. Many of the Yew people feel the same, but remember, they and their families were personally threatened, and they saw the result of crossing Gynbere. He got away with it for a long time. Bullies are hard to get rid of once they attain their desired position. They attract other tyrants to support them and encourage their thinking.

"Eventually though, the generation who had moved into The Rock died. Their children and grandchildren began to question why they should also be punished, especially as many of them hadn't been born when the alleged crime was committed.

"The Gynbere who ruled at the time, became aggressive. He wasn't prepared to give up his position. He hoped Faltryn had died, but even had he not, Gynbere was sure the dragon must have forgotten about them. This Gynbere ruled on a divide-and-conquer basis, richly rewarding those who supported him and trying to destroy those who didn't.

However, he also started to train an army, and ordered that they be the only ones to hold and use weapons."

"Where did the large dragon we saw in Gynbere's hall come from?" asked Arbreu.

"I have the answer to that, Kirym," Sirasha interrupted. "The history we held was old, but not as old as the dragon. I knew for instance that sometime after we entered The Rock, the Yew family invited us to a feast to celebrate a new beginning. Nothing came of the things spoken of, but when we returned to our hollows, a fire had gutted our archives.

"Suddenly our history, so carefully written, stored, and remembered over hundreds of seasons was gone. All we found was a pile of ash. We suspected that Gynbere had caused the fire to be set, but we had no proof, and making those sorts of accusations had proven to be dangerous in the past.

"Strangely, the memories we had of the contents of the scrolls, also disappeared. For some reason, we failed to reinstate them. That was unusual, because each of my family was obliged to read through the archives every tenth winter. Most of us could recite our history with no prompts. Something happened along with the destruction of the scrolls, to ensure the information vanished and never returned.

"Last night, however, Kirym found and returned those scrolls to us. The ash had been placed to make us think they'd been destroyed. Gynbere had taken them and retained them over the seasons. My sons and I read through them to find the memories we had lost. Despite that, there was still a gap in our knowledge. The dragon wasn't mentioned in any of those scrolls, and nor was its creator. Now this was information we did not know, and it would have continued that way had Lady Kirym not discovered a qwanchel." Sirasha waited until the buzz of speculation died down, and then explained what a qwanchel was, to those who didn't know.

"This qwanchel held an interesting history, and it filled a few holes in our knowledge. In fact, I now believe it was the first qwanchel ever made, and those following were mere shadows of the original." He turned to me. "May I describe what was written, Lady Kirym?"

I nodded.

"This is what we learned," said Sirasha. "Our Gynbere is the eleventh to use the name since the loss of our trees. It was he who first imprisoned us in the rock. When Vinric, his sire, found out what his plans were, they argued. Vinric objected to the subjugation of those he looked on as friends.

"Young Gynbere explained his dream, but Vinric labelled him a fool, and told him that leadership had to be earned. He stated he would tell his friends, and have things return to what they'd been.

"Gynbere was furious. He had organised this and he was determined he would be ruler. Above all he wanted his own sire and older brothers to bend their knee to him, acknowledge his greatness, and allow him what he saw as his due.

"The result of the argument, was the deaths of Vinric, an older brother, a sister, and her husband. This was a warning to the rest of the Yew family. Their new leader was ruthless in his drive to conquer and rule. The deaths also warned the other families to take great care. Never-the-less, more deaths followed, but eventually Gynbere became supreme leader.

"Many moons after the second Gynbere became leader, he planned a huge celebration. His family and supporters were told in advance. Explorers had found a large natural cave deep in The Rock. The only entrance was high in the wall, and very narrow. He had workmen dig a wide tunnel of an impressive size to become the new entrance. Others, using the original narrow tunnel, began to decorate the walls to show Gynbere's imagined exploits, his wealth and magnificence. Galleries were created and festooned with carved garlands. Finally, the work in the cave was finished. He wanted every part of the hall and its approach to impress his allies and daunt his enemies.

"The workmen left the cave, and Gynbere planned that no one would enter before he did, when the final piece of the wall was breached at the grand opening. The hole was closed off, and a date was set by a family sage.

"The day came for the grand opening. Gynbere ordered everyone to be there to see his greatness.

"The wall was finally breached, and the people assembled for the opening. Gynbere entered the cave, followed by his guard. Everyone surged in behind them. For maximum impact, the cave was darkened. The galleries lit up one by one amid the ooohs and ahhhs of the crowds, as the various galleries and carvings were revealed. As the top gallery was illuminated, the dragon suddenly swooped into sight.

"Gynbere was shocked, and although he rallied and claimed he had planned it, he was visibly shaken. He told everyone it was placed there to watch over those who, because of their greed, had killed an innocent baby and annihilated the desert city. 'The dragon will warn me if the Oak dynasty and their friends plot again to continue their murderous schemes,' he said. 'For they still plot and plan to destroy you all, anyone who stands in their way as they grab power and riches.' It was another tacit warning to those who supported the Oak.

"The people did not respond as he had expected. There was an uproar. While none of them wished to be spied on, many knew those of the Oak family and respected their hard work in caring for families who needed help for one reason or another. While Gynbere offered much in assistance, it didn't filter down to those with little or no influence. These people turned to the Oak family, and although they believed the original story, they were also sensible enough to judge those they knew, by their actions."

Around the amphitheatre, there was a swell of comments, and a lot of nodding.

"If this is true," came a voice from in the crowd, "we owe Churnyg and his people an apology and more."

"We do, and I have already approached them as leader of my family," Sirasha said.

"The hall appeared to be unused except for the hanging dragon, Sirasha. Not as I would have expected. And yet lights shone occasionally." Arbreu said. "Why?"

Mekrar handed Sirasha a flask of water. He smiled appreciatively, drank and continued his story. "The lights shone intermittently to see if the dragon ever left. However, the hall was never used as Gynbere planned. He initially decided to close it off, but many people felt it would be an insult to the dragon, to pretend it wasn't there, and there would be nothing to stop it from moving to another hall. Gynbere began to believe Faltryn had placed the dragon there to watch him. While initially tempted to destroy it, he became convinced that Faltryn would take offence and expose him. He tried again and again to find out how it got there. He questioned everyone, but no one had knowledge of the dragon. Those who discovered the cave said the dragon wasn't there when they first found it, and they pointed out that it was far too big to get in that way. Gynbere was reminded by his family that he'd set guards everywhere, and had been the first to enter the cave.

"So, the hall became a shortcut between three areas in the rock, but Gynbere never ever entered it again. Before long he had renovated anew in the only other area big enough to impress in the way he wanted. Unfortunately, the new hall sat beside Churnyg Oak's back door.

"Annoyed at having to be so close to the Oak seat, Gynbere

tried to drive them out. These attempts were met with heated resistance, much of it from the other families who saw this as a precedence. What would stop Gynbere from doing the same thing to them, should the whim take him?

"The qwanchel told you all of this?" said Bryn?

Sirasha nodded. "Now the artist behind it was Kwarnar, Gynbere's youngest brother. He was a potter and had discovered the recipe for making white pottery. He made the skull which sat on a shelf in his tree hollow. Gynbere remembered seeing it in the past, and it's possible his memory of it triggered the story of the desert cave. He visited Kwarnar, and took it. He assumed it to be a real skull.

"Kwarnar was incensed when Gynbere used the skull to enslave his people. He knew about the deal Gynbere had made with the dragon, but unlike his older brothers he continued to object to what Gynbere was doing. Being the youngest, he was restrained by threats to his maman, sisters, his wife and children. Knowing of Gynbere's ruthlessness, he decided to keep quiet. He kept to himself, and concentrated on his work as an artist and sculptor.

"Kwarnar, made likenesses in wood, but he also worked with fine clay. He was very talented. He was left to do what he wanted in his workshop, provided he occasionally came up with a novelty piece for his brother. Fearing for his family Kwarnar made a point of never allowing Gynbere to see any of the white clay, nor objects made from it. He passed the art onto his sons; he didn't want them to be lost, and he made sure his sons and grandsons understood the importance of the secret they held.

"The dragon was made of many thousands of shards, each of them locked into the pieces around it. He had gained access to the cave through the original awkward entrance, and he and his sons erected the dragon together. He hoped it would keep his brother on his toes. Whether Gynbere realised who had made it is unknown, probably not, in view of his reaction."

Sirasha sighed deeply. "Ah, what a document. It was inspiring, and I'm sure that reading it again will allow me to learn many new things from the past. It fits right into the one blank area we had in our written history. Of course, coming down to today, our Gynbere decided the skull and the dragon were more of a liability than an asset. The argument for punishment was getting thinner and thinner, and even those who supported him were beginning to question his actions. To stop any revolt, he changed the stories, forbidding many and creating new ones." Sirasha slowly sat down amid a growing murmur of speculation.

"Kirym," said Oak. "Borasyn said the skull wasn't real. He said you told him that. How did you know?"

"It's the wrong shape to be what Gynbere claimed it to be." I was silenced by the buzz of questions, and waited until they had died before continuing. "Compared to a real skull of a similar size, you'd notice the similarities and the differences. A baby's skull is flatter comparatively, and wider from front to back. The top of the skull is different too. A child's skull is not just a small version of the adult, but that's what Kwarnar sculpted. I wonder if he did that on purpose. Probably not, he never intended it to be the skull of a baby. However, no one realised that until Salcan saw it.

"The original sculptor, Kwarnar, passed his talent on to his children, and the skill continues to this day. Salcan too had a talent in making likenesses of the things he saw around him. The present Kwarnar liked Salcan and invited him into their work hollow. Salcan watched carefully and discovered the recipe for white clay. Salcan had only to glance at the skull, to know it was a fake. He heard the story around it and realised the whole reason for being in The Rock was false. He hated unfairness, especially to the dwarflings."

"Salcan? You're talking about the giant who stayed with us in The Rock?" asked Lorythma.

I nodded.

"How would he see what we had missed over hundreds of seasons?" asked Lorythma.

"Salcan knew bones. He had always been fascinated by them, and he'd studied those he found back in Raff's hills. When he came here, he dug a cave into a hill, and found human bones. He cared for them, but he also learned the differences in the ages of bones and ways of death. He was also an artist, and studied detail. Above all, as you know, he loved children, dwarflings, anything small. He knew something was wrong, and he challenged Kwarnar who told him at least part of the story.

"The two men had a mutual desire. They wanted to stop Gynbere, but the threats against Kwarnar's family were still there.

"Salcan thought if the skull disappeared, Gynbere would lose enough prestige and the people could oust him and leave The Rock to again live in the trees. Too late he realised it would make no difference to Gynbere."

"Salcan was right," said Jetara. "Gynbere simply added another accusation against Churnyg Oak. He tried to use it as another way of getting rid of him."

"What about the weapons? Where did they come into it, Sirasha?" Arbreu asked.

Sirasha shook his head. "I don't know. Do you, Lady Kirym?"

"Yes, I do. It's an interesting part of the story from the scroll the first Gynbere began, and was added to by his successors," I said. "The original Gynbere had the sword and shield displayed in his private rooms, but his successor soon had second thoughts about them, and his suspicions were passed down to his son. When the white dragon was found flying in the hall, Gynbere had a disturbing nightmare. He dreamed that Faltryn was searching for the weapons and planned to kill whoever had possession of them. The dream must have seemed very real, because Gynbere had the weapons placed in the back of a cupboard, and hoped they would simply be forgotten. However, a family sage issued a decree, saying that Gynbere must personally return them to the rightful owner or their ancestor. This was an hereditary obligation, and if unfulfilled would ruin him and following rulers of the Yew family. He also told Gynbere that touching the weapons would be a death sentence.

"Feigning sickness to explain an absence, Gynbere travelled to meet The Guardians. He planned to tell them he'd found the weapons dropped in a thicket. He'd accept their thanks, and hope it would put them in his debt.

The settlement was deserted. He was shocked. Initially he thought that Faltryn had put a curse on the weapons, and by making it impossible for him to return them, was condemning him to death. The theft became a weight he could never be rid of. But understanding that neither Varl, Arjin or any of their family could now challenge him for his ownership of the weapons. He convinced himself that The Guardians feared him. Feeling more and more immune to retaliation from them, he broke into the store houses in the settlement, and took everything the Guardians had locked away. These included their bows and bolts, the box they kept their current ledger in, and the special container they had kept the weapons in before he stole them. He smuggled everything back into the rock and stored them, thinking to train his army to use the weapons.

"His arrogance did not last long. Soon after his return to The Rock, his nightmares returned. He now believed that any attempt to use the stolen items, would rebound on him and his soldiers. In a fit of pique, he had the ancestry of the sage researched. When in the deep archives he found a tenuous, and perhaps false, connection to the Oak family, he declared the sage and the Oak dynasty were in league with the dragon. However, despite his outward bravado, Gynbere balked at ordering the death while the sage stared at him.

"Gynbere was in a quandary. He couldn't return the items, and he feared the dragon more than ever. Before he could think of a way to solve the problems, he died and the responsibility passed to his son, who was even more stubborn than those before him. He resolved that if he couldn't use the weapons, no one would. Now he looked at the possibility someone would expose the whole conspiracy and remove the stolen power he had inherited. He kept the weapons concealed, and hoped that passing time would dull everyone's memory of them, but to be sure of his safety, he trained personal guards, and a spy system to rout out any insurrection within the community. When the two men he used to place the weapons in the box died, he dreamed the dragon told him that touching them was a death sentence to all except the rightful owner. His fears continued, and he passed them on to his children." So, the problem passed down from one Gynbere to the next, until the present Gynbere took the throne.

"How did Gynbere and his family know all of this, when we knew nothing?" asked Shurlyn.

"The first Gynbere took a leaf from the Beech dynasty and had his family listen to a version of the original scroll on a regular basis. He instilled in his sons the need to keep the subterfuge up. He said they'd all be killed if ever anyone found out. However, he also passed on his fears and worries. That reading habit died quite quickly, but the story came down through word of mouth.

"The present Gynbere resolved to do what none of his ancestors could—he would destroy the entire Oak family. It was not as easy as he had hoped, and the talk of the dragon riders and the mysterious weapons continued, getting bigger and bigger with each telling of the story.

"The weapons still sat in the box in his rooms. He had a guard open the box and look at them, and then ordered one of his sons to look. Neither of them died, although he had the guard killed. However, he felt it safe to look on them himself. He didn't die, so he decided he'd be the one to carry them and use them. Almost immediately he began to have the nightmares that plagued his ancestors, and he dared not touch them. When the weapons disappeared from the box, he thought Faltryn had entered his rooms and taken them; somehow had free access to The Rock and could do as he liked. In an act of bravado, he burned the box. He told a few people that it was sacrificial, that he was the chosen holder, and was waiting for the perfect moment to declare himself.

The truth was, he was terrified. He was more sure than ever that the dragon was behind the upsurge in stories about vengeance on those who instigated the persecution of Oak family."

"But, if it was so," said Oak, "Faltryn could have taken his vengeance on Gynbere; killed him at his leisure. He didn't."

"Gynbere wasn't able to think clearly. The fears and nightmares had built up over many seasons. He concluded the dragon was playing with him. Each unusual circumstance or death around him, he blamed on Faltryn, until he would neither move nor eat without protection. Gynbere then had the rumour passed around that he had destroyed the weapons and their malevolent influence when he burned them and the box. It didn't stop his own nightmares and his paranoia continued."

"What did Faltryn think he was doing when he took our

memories, and yet gave my family false recollections?" asked Churnyg.

"Faltryn knew the false memories would be a thorn in Gynbere's side," I said. "He fed back into your hearts and minds enough of your own history to inspire you. He hoped this would keep you all arguing the facts for many hundreds of seasons, until no one knew the truth from the lies. He wanted it to create a balance within the community, and return it to what it was. He didn't know about the tunnels in the rock, and had no idea what Gynbere's actual plans were. He also thought The Guardians would eventually sort it out, as they would have before the dragons arrived."

"Does that mean the stories of the power Mellith, Oakenrock, Tamweir and Zandahem have are false?" asked Findlow.

I shrugged "I don't know. Nothing is written of them; well nothing that's been found yet."

"There is a power there," said Sirasha. "From the dawn of time, my family believed the weapons were made so only one person could carry and use them in their lifetime. However, there was the added ability for that person to have an assistant. Partly it was because of human frailty. The memory has stayed with my family, along with the knowledge that ownership did not belong to us."

"And the present holder is Kirym?" asked Larqeba.

"She has been carrying them," said Sirasha.

"However, things are changing," I said, "so maybe not. Faltryn's death may have affected that. I don't know."

Well, I for one, wouldn't pick any of them up," said Sirasha.

5

Kirym Speaks

Everyone dispersed over the open area, discussing what they had heard from the scrolls. I sat for a while with the dragons, joined, one by one, by a few close friends. "I wonder if there is anything else I can do for them," I asked.

Mekrar shrugged. "Do you think they heard the story?"

"I've no idea, but I'm hoping so. Maybe Faltryn needed to be alive. Possibly he had to tell them, and just maybe it wasn't enough of the story to make a difference."

"Kirym," Teema interrupted, "Tarl has said nothing about his tactics for the coming battle. I know we'll go after the hostages, but he hasn't told me how he plans to do it. He hasn't changed the guards schedule on the wall; it's as if nothing has happened. Everyone is uncertain."

I took a deep breath, pushed aside my worries. "Have you asked him?"

"Well no..."

"Would you have asked Papa?" I interrupted.

"No, but he'd have told us,"

"He would have eventually, Teema. Tarl needs to follow the same progression Papa does. He'll think about the possibilities first, and let everyone else offer ideas. He'll talk to Mama and then tell you. We have plenty of time, and rushing into a set plan could spell disaster. There are a lot of unknowns he needs to think about. So allow him at least the same time you'd allow Papa."

Arbreu squeezed Teema's shoulder. "She is right. He's asking questions, studying the map and making notes."

"Notes won't win a battle."

"Oh Teema, do you think Papa doesn't do the same? His notes tend to be in his head now, but he still does it. Mama kept quite a few from when he first became The Voice. Grandpapa did the same thing, as did quite a few others. Look, I'll see what I can find out, but we know the agreement Tarl made, and this is only day two."

I made my way over to Tarl.

He smiled warmly when he saw me. "You tell a good story, Kirym. You took their minds off their worries, kept them entertained while I try to organise this mess."

"What have you decided?"

Tarl sketched out a loose battle plan, showing how he planned to use his men. "I don't want to approach him in the evening. We'd be at a disadvantage."

"I saw you talking to the men. Have they offered any good suggestions?"

He frowned. "The ideas all clash. And what if I don't want to use their ideas? Papa never—"

"Papa listened to everyone," I interrupted. "These men are leaders. Their people are with Papa, and you'll honour them by listening. You don't have to accept what they say, but you should pay attention. If you show interest, you may hear something important, and you'll be surprised at how many of them will think parts of your final plan come from their suggestions."

"What if they don't agree with my decisions?"

"Let your supporters handle that, but some of their ideas will coincide with yours. Acknowledge them, even if you thought of it first. Think how Papa handles contentious situations. He listens first. Then he makes suggestions, and finally he sets out his plan. You are Papa's son, and this is The Green Valley. That's a powerful strength."

Tarl nodded, but he still looked strained. "What if my supporters don't agree with me?"

"They'll talk to you privately," I said. "Keep your plans fluid. We don't know what we'll meet, nor what Gynbere will demand, and that may mean a quick change of plans. Get to know your men. Train them, and trust them."

Tarl rubbed his hand across his eyes, a gesture reminiscent of papa. "What if I miss something?"

"If your plans aren't set in stone, you'll be able to re-adjust them whatever comes at you."

"When Teema chased Gynbere, he couldn't get close enough to see what was happening. He was continually stopped by lines of arrows. What if they do the same thing when we leave here?"

"Was Teema stopped in the same place each time?" I asked.

He shook his head. "No, the line moved with Gynbere."

"Have any of your men been shot since Urfit left?"

"Only Shingle. He got an arrow in his thigh. He went to check a couple of snares he'd set up before dawn on the day Urfit arrived. Urfit's men got him as he returned. It was a bit unfair, he obviously couldn't have known about the agreement."

"Teema was stopped because Gynbere wanted time. But he wants us to find him."

"I think you're wrong, girl," said Lelth, who had approached with several other men. "Gynbere wants a fight. We need to attack first. It's the only way to get our leaders back."

"No, Lelth," Sirasha Beech said. "Think about it. Kirym found the note about war by accident, but that means we're forewarned. Urfit came to negotiate for time. Gynbere doesn't want us to turn up before he's prepared. Otherwise why would he go to the trouble of annoying us to the extent he has? Would you enter The Rock again?"

Lelth frowned.

"None of us would, Lelth. Gynbere will feel he has the upper hand at the tor," Sirasha said. "We'll find him quickly enough, and because we travel faster than he'll anticipate, we'll still catch him unawares."

"And if he's not there? What then?" asked Girk.

"We'll know if he's taken a different direction, and we can track him," said Tarl. "There are too many of them to move with no trail, and if he did return to The Rock, we'd catch him long before he got there."

"Maybe only part of The Rock fell down. An area could be intact enough for him to use. It's stood since the birth of time. Why would it collapse now?" Bryn asked.

"Gynbere removed a lot of rock from the interior," I said. "More than the structure could cope with. His men created big halls and wide tunnels. The extra rock was dumped over the eastern wall. When part of the outer wall fell, there was nothing to support the halls. The rock collapsed under its own weight. When Borasyn flew me over the rock, I saw what Gynbere had taken out. A lot of rock was dumped there."

Sirasha Beech nodded. "He did, and his sire before him, and before them also. We all knew they were doing it. Tailings have been dumped over that wall by most of the Gynberes. There were warnings against it. Anyway, how would Gynbere know if an area was left intact? He told us all it was a prison built by our enemies. When we learned of the collapse, he claimed he had destroyed it, so our enemies couldn't force us back into slavery in it. No, he wants something, and I don't think it has anything to do with The Rock."

Tarl nodded thoughtfully. "It still begs the question, if we travel fast and get there earlier than he expects, will Gynbere kill our people?"

"If Gynberes kill anyone, he'll have less to negotiate with. We have to be prepared for any eventuality," I said. "Their first lookout is by the stream. If we take those guards with us, they'll tell Gynbere we obeyed his rules."

"Why should they tell?" asked Lelth.

"Why shouldn't they?" Bryn asked. "Are those men known to be dishonest?"

"How do we prepare for the unknown?" interrupted Girk.

"We have time to train. We'll learn to fight together," Bryn said.

"We don't need training for that," snarled Lelth.

"Not killing," said Armos. "Any fool can kill. We learn to defend ourselves and each other. Work as a team. We also want to save all the people Gynbere is holding against their will."

"And I'll happily listen to every suggestion," said Tarl. "We have plenty of time to plan."

Sirasha nodded. "What if Gynbere has already killed everyone?"

"Veld is alive," said Loul. "His token tells me that, and he's not distressed. He would be if anyone had been killed."

"I think Kirym's right," said Bryn. "Without the hostages, he has no power to get what he wants. Here, he wanted the weapons, but then he didn't take them. One of the hunters overheard Gynbere ask Slaslow if Faltryn's death would mean he could claim the weapons. Slaslow said, 'Maybe, but what about the other things?' So, what else does Gynbere want?"

"He didn't take the weapons, even though he killed Faltryn. Why not, Kirym?" asked Armos.

"Faltryn wasn't dead when Gynbere left, and the old man who threw the sword appeared to be. Gynbere had no proof the prophecy had changed."

Tarl nodded. "So Gynbere had two plans."

"More likely Slaslow," I said, "with help from the Urfits, no doubt. Anyway, without the hostages, they'd have nothing of value."

"They could change the rules again, though." Tarl shook his head. "What's to stop Urfit from returning and telling us something different?"

"If they make any changes, it would negate the original agreement. We'd be free to follow them immediately," I said.

"Lelth nodded. "Assuming you're right, why don't we just leave now?"

"Because I gave my word," said Tarl.

"And Gynbere is ruthless," I said. "If he thought we'd would recapture the hostages before he's ready, he would kill them. But he'd have to do it in front of his people, and I suspect there would be little appetite for murder in cold blood. Especially when many of them are elderly, one is a young girl, and a few are revered. And there are things we don't know. We have information about what happened to begin Gynbere's rule, but he has knowledge of the land long gone from our memories. Because of his definite path, I'm sure he knows the land very well."

Lelth snorted. "What if his position is impregnable? If we lose the battle, any chance of getting our leaders back will be gone."

"Gynbere wants to negotiate," I said.

"So why didn't he take the sword with him?"

"Because he's scared the curse is still there." I said. "If picking up the sword could be a death sentence; he won't risk it."

Tarl sighed and sat down. "Oh, I wish Churnyg would just take it back and go and sort out the problem."

"What gives you the idea it belongs to Churnyg, Tarl?"

"Arbreu saw pictures in a room in The Rock. He told Papa about them. You must have seen them."

"Yes, but a painting doesn't prove something is true. It showed them as dragon riders, but the memory and the painting come from the falsehoods Gynbere gave them. It was drawn when Gynbere's persecution appeared to be having its desired effect. The treasures weren't part of the picture, although we found them in the same room. If the weapons belonged to Churnyg, he would have claimed them when we first found them. The treasures and the dragons go together. Churnyg's people have their feet very firmly in the trees, I'd be surprised if any of them ever sat on a dragon before Churnyg did recently. The dragon riders came from The Green Valley."

"But—but, us? We can't do that."

"Do what? Ride a dragon? You've already done it, Tarl. It wasn't difficult. The guardians were our ancestors, and that's why we must sort this out. We're the protectors of the land and the people. We've always done it anyway, even in The Land Between the Gorges."

Tarl stared at me. "Really? Does Papa know?"

"Mama knows, so he might. If not, he soon will. In the meantime, do what is needed here to prepare. Bury the dead this afternoon, and sort out the needs of the journey"

"Kirym's right, Tarl," said Bryn. "Other than guarding here to ensure there is no lightening attack back on us, don't think about moving out until we're ready. I know it isn't normal practise with a declaration of war, but this is different. We gain much more by waiting."

"They'll have a better battle position if we wait," said Tarl.

"Gynbere doesn't want to fight," I reiterated. "He's scared that if he kills any of us, we won't give him what he wants. His problem is he's not sure what he wants."

"Why not?"

I laughed. "Because, Tarl, he doesn't know what we know or may know. He'll never be sure. That's always been his problem; he's always been beset by indecision."

"I know how he feels," muttered Tarl.

"You're doing all right, lad," laughed Armos. "Every leader wonders, but you, along with the best, take advice. Gynbere doesn't, because he thinks it's a sign of weakness."

The burial ceremony during the afternoon was moving. Every family had connections with those who died. We each handled death and burials differently, and the mixture of rites melded well.

I felt deeply for Armos who was far too contained. Both his papa and remaining son were hostages, and I knew he was imagining two more bodies in the ground with Peet. I thought had it not been for Lantiah, he would not have attended the ceremony. She gathered his grandchildren around him, and they did what grandchildren are supposed to do in the circumstances, made him accept that life continued, and he was needed.

Despite his youth, Peet's son Parlansho talked about his Papa. He was quite a serious boy, and he spoke of looking after his mama and sister, and asked for Armos' help and guidance. With Peet's daughter in his arms, Parlansho standing tall beside him and young Harby's children clustered around, it was what Armos needed.

The evening was quiet, and most people stayed with their families, following what customs they had when someone died. Mama and Tarl visited all of them, offering what support and help they could.

After spending time with Armos and his family, I decided to sleep early, having not spent an entire night asleep since I left the gorge having helped find the Desert people.

As I walked towards the food area to collect a large flask of water for the dwelling, Garanniis approached me and asked me to join him at their fire for a time.

Bryn and Jeresaya were there, chatting to Paluniis. I sat and accepted a platter of vegetables, bread and fruit, pleased because I hadn't eaten since midday.

Morkeen joined us, something she had stopped doing after I returned Amethyst to her family. She still held the wee girl close, her love for Amethyst was obvious, but I felt a familiar ache, wishing she was in my arms, even for a few moments.

Initially the talk was about the events of the last few days, answering queries about the wellbeing of the families who had lost people in the battle.

Slowly the conversation drifted to a halt. I had the impression they had something planned, but for the life of me, I couldn't figure out what.

Morkeen was visibly upset. She cleared her throat a few times.

We waited.

"Ummm," she cleared her throat again.

Paluniis took her hand and squeezed it.

"When we left the sands," she said quietly, "I had only just learned that Zyanda was pregnant. It was so unfair that I'd miss her journey, because the bridge had been destroyed. She died..."

I took her hand. "I understand how hard it was for—"

Morkeen held up her hand, stopping me. "Zyanda died five days after we left the riverbank." She placed Amethyst in my lap. "She is yours. Amethyst couldn't belong to us. We really don't know where she came from." She buried her head in Garanniis' shoulder, sobbing softly.

Amethyst cooed and gurgled. I'd so missed her. It was wonderful holding her again. She grasped my finger in her hand, and pulled it into her mouth.

"There were three or four groups that we knew of," said Garanniis. "Paluniis' family found the remains of two separate heaps of possessions as they travelled north. No people though, and little indication of who the owners had been. The remnants of a third group were already sheltering in the thorns when they got there."

"We can go back and search again."

"No, Kirym," said Garanniis. "When Ubree took you to Bryn's lodge, I asked Iryndal if there could be other families somewhere in the sands. She said there were none." He hesitated, looking distinctly embarrassed. "I hadn't passed the news on to Morkeen before you returned and gave Amethyst to us."

"We've been in a quandary over the situation. While we knew, we felt for Morkeen and..." Paluniis paused, and shook his head.

"I shouldn't have taken her, Kirym. I knew Zyanda could never have given birth to her," said Morkeen. She covered her face with her hands.

My pleasure at holding Amethyst was marred by the grief in front of me.

"Morkeen." I waited until she looked up. "Amethyst is a child from both worlds. She must learn about her heritage, and she needs you to teach her that."

I looked down and stroked Amethyst's token. "This token proves she is part of me and mine. As her mama is dead, we can share her."

Morkeen's sobs grew louder. "I was so horrid to—"

"You were distraught at losing your sister, and so many other people. Amethyst will help pull our families together, and she'll learn far more from all of us, than any of us could have passed on alone," I said.

Garanniis grasped my hand. "You are very generous."

"I know all of the families here have invited you to live with them, including Mama and Papa. If you're with us, or nearby, it'll make it easier for her to be with all of us, to integrate into both families."

Morkeen stared at me in stunned silence.

"We don't deserve this, Kirym," said Paluniis.

"But, perhaps Amethyst does," said Jeresaya. She took Morkeen in her arms and hugged her. "Really though, you all do. There are so many broken families here, but perhaps together we'll become whole."

Garanniis cleared his throat. "Bryn, you and Jeresaya are here because I hoped perhaps you would be happy to move to a dwelling beside us or even in with us. With more people, the spaces won't seem so empty. The dwellings Veld gave us are huge, and we rattle around in them."

Bryn smiled and stood. "I'll get the boys to bring over the essential things for tonight and tomorrow we'll sort out the details."

Jeresaya beamed. "Oh it'll be so nice to be surrounded with people again."

"Will you stay also, Kirym?" asked Garanniis. "Well for tonight anyway. I know you have a large family, but I—well

I thought maybe…" He shrugged.

I hesitated. This was awkward. "I also have Trethia to think of."

"We want all of you here," said Morkeen. "Trethia is Amethyst's sister, as much as you're her mama."

"Let me talk to her."

Amethyst had fallen asleep. I kissed her and handed her to Morkeen.

Trethia crawled out of the shadows near the dwelling entrance as I approached. I was amazed at how well she managed to hide, although the ability was what had kept her alive until now.

I sat against the wall, and put my arm around her.

She snuggled close to me.

"You should be inside asleep, honey."

"You weren't there."

"No, but Lyndym was, and she cares for you to."

I told her about Amethyst, and the invitation to sleep in a different dwelling. "It won't be as crowded. You already know Larqeba; he'll be there with his family also."

She stared at me, frowning. "You gave Amethyst away?"

"I introduced her to her mama's family. She needs to know her history. It's lovely that Morkeen is now ready to acknowledge Amethyst's claim to us, to you and me."

She became very stiff as I explained. "Are you going to give me away, too?"

"Oh, my darling," I pulled her onto my lap, held her tight, and kissed the top of her head. "You are mine! You will always be mine. It's quite different with Amethyst, and remember, Amethyst came back to us. You know at some stage; you might choose to go on an adventure. That won't change us, and Amethyst will always be part of you and me. She is your sister, and my daughter."

Trethia relaxed, put her arms around my neck and hugged me. "I'll never ever go away."

"Most people do, you know. They grow up and join or marry. Sometimes they'll choose to live with a different family or travel with another group to see the lands around us, maybe for a short time, sometimes longer."

I pulled my cloak around her. "I left my mama at the end of last winter, and went on a long journey. If I hadn't gone, I'd never have found Amethyst. Everyone here has had to travel, but if I had stayed home, I wouldn't have found you or the dragons. But she's still my mama."

She nodded.

"You'll never be forced to leave, but you don't lose your family when you make new friends. And nothing will ever change my love for you. Now, will we go and spend some time with Amethyst and her other family?"

She thought for a while. "What if they don't really want me?"

"Morkeen said specifically you should come. You're Amethyst's sister, and Morkeen will love you as much as she does Amethyst. Jeresaya already loves you, and I know you'll like Garanniis. I think they'll all be very pleased to have you there."

"What about your clothes?"

"Let's choose what we need for tonight, and then tomorrow we can collect the rest, or we could leave some of it, in case we want to come back."

Oak approached carrying a large flask. "Thought you'd need this here."

"We're going to stay with Amethyst," said Trethia.

"Well, I'd best get a flask for there, too. Would you like me to help carry your rugs over?"

We arrived to find the dwelling buzzing with talk and movement, as everyone settled in. I fed Amethyst when she woke, changed her clothes and then happily settled down next to Trethia, with Amethyst in a hanging basket nearby.

Again, I was not destined to sleep the night through.

The moon had only moved two hand-spans above the horizon when Jeresaya woke me.

"Lantiah needs you in the healing area."

I carefully tucked the rugs back around Trethia, checked that Amethyst was settled and slipped through the door, wrapping my cloak around me as I went.

Dashlan waited outside for me. "The dwarf who threw the sword at Faltryn is awake. His healers thought you'd prefer to talk to him before anyone else did."

"Has he said anything?" I asked.

"No. Evidently he just stares at the stars."

Lantiah met me before I reached the healing area.

"We weren't sure we should even call you yet. His eyes are open, but he appears to see nothing. He hasn't responded to anything." She sighed. "He seems very unhappy. His name may be Frentha, although no one seems too sure. No one has asked after him. I'm not sure what he was able to hear while asleep, but some of the younger healers are not as understanding as they should be. They blame him for their predicament."

"Ensure Lorythma knows. He'll talk to them. In the meantime, let's see what we can do to help your patient."

A shelter had been erected to protect the patients and healers from the weather. The outer walls were removed when the weather was fair, allowing easy movement in and out, but as the night was cool, most of them had been replaced.

The old man lay on a pallet, covered by an old rug. He had been given a spot against the western wall, isolated from the other patients. Jorlenta sat with him.

Both she and Lantiah looked tired, understandable under the circumstances.

"Neither of you should be here," I said quietly. "Armos and Harnita need you both, and you need them. There are others who can help here."

"They're both asleep. I couldn't settle, and the other healers are busy," Lantiah said. "I'm better if I keep myself occupied."

"No excuses. Go and rest. Care for each other. I sent them both off and sat down beside Frentha. It was as if I wasn't there. The only movement he made was when he blinked.

"You're not going to die you know," I said. "What did Gynbere hold over you?"

There was a long silence. Then he quietly began to cry. I held his hand and waited.

"My grandsons were all I had left."

"Gynbere took them?"

"He said I could choose, their lives or mine. He knew I'd do anything for them. Gynbere told me he'd give them their freedom. He didn't or they'd be here. They haven't been seen, have they?"

I shook my head.

"He'll have killed them. The sooner I join them the better."

"How old are your grandsons?"

"Chonarth had seen twelve winters, Rintath, eight."

"There were no boys that age among the dead. Gynbere may still have them with him, and in that case, they'll be alive. He'd not carry dead bodies."

"Gynbere made Chonarth drink something, 'to encourage

me to get it right', he said. "Told us he'd give him the antidote and leave both boys here to explain. He laughed when he said that. I didn't trust him, but I—"

"Didn't have a choice," I concluded for him. "No one else from The Rock knows you. Why not?"

He shrugged. "We were kept away from the public eye. Gynbere holds something from our history. My grandsire said no one would work alongside us, and his great-grandsire took the only job offered."

"And that was?"

"Gynbere's official taster. He has always feared someone would poison his food or wine. We were kept isolated and guarded. At any feast, I was heavily cloaked. It's been the same for many generations."

"What happened to your children, the boy's parents?"

"Food tasters die. Sometimes food is poisoned just to see that the taster does taste, or maybe to see how a poison will affect the imbiber, or even to accuse someone who Gynbere or Slaslow wanted dead."

I was struck by a sudden thought. "Your grandson. A pale thin boy?"

He looked deflated. "His body is here, isn't it?"

"If it's him, he is here, and he's alive. You say he was given a potion?"

He nodded. "Can I see him?" He struggled to sit up, but with no energy or strength, sank back.

I looked around to see who could help me. The guards were delivering full water flasks. Vimble, who was in charge was talking to one of the healers.

"Vimble," I called. He came over and I asked him to find Churnyg for me. "And send someone to help me here now."

Vimble raced away, and moments later, Twig was at my side.

"Can you assist Frentha? He wishes to sit with his grandson."

Chonarth did not look good. His eyes had sunk into his head, and his skin had lost even more colour.

Frentha's pallet was carried over. He looked more animated, but had little energy. He showed little reaction until he saw Chonarth. With tears in his eyes, he took my hand.

"Oh thank you. I can be with him until he dies."

"Now we know he has been poisoned, we can search for an antidote," I said.

Frentha looked beaten. "No. He will die. No one recovers from Gynbere's poisons."

"I did!"

He looked at me, surprised. "Well—"

His comment was drowned out by the thud of boots that heralded Vimble and Churnyg's arrival.

I explained what Gynbere had done to Chonarth.

Churnyg shook his head. "He has about ten potions he likes using. All have different effects. Most of his victims died in agony. He probably thought he was being kind by allowing Chonarth a long painless death."

"Other than those that cause pain, what comes to mind?" I asked.

"Gynbere had a bowl of small red seeds beside him, when he told me what he'd done," said Frentha. "Do you know what they were?"

"I know them," said Lorythma. He had arrived silently, and was standing quietly at the end of the pallet. "They slowly depress breathing, until it stops. I warned Gynbere not to play with them, the poison can even enter through the skin. If that's what the boy has been given, then I can think of nothing to help him. Death is taking its time, so I suspect the boy has had a very minor dose, but that means nothing, because the result is always the same."

"Get everyone together who may have an idea. The healers, the wise men and women," I said. "In the meantime, can you treat the symptoms?"

People were quickly summoned; most were still wearing night robes. Lorythma explained the situation, and they settled down around Chonarth and Frentha. There was an immediate flurry of suggestions, and a few arguments began.

I was pleased to see Mama and Seba with them. Mama brought her large remedy kit, and pulling her huge shawl around her, she and Seba began searching through the lower layers to see if there was anything that could be a possible antidote, or assist in any other way.

I squeezed Frentha's hand. "You will both be well cared for. These are the best healers we have. Eat and drink. You'll need your strength when Chonarth wakens. I'll see you in the morning." I slipped out of the crowd. I would be in the way if I stayed, and I had nothing more to add.

I climbed gratefully back under my rugs, and snuggled into Trethia, delighted my leaving hadn't woken her. I was almost instantly asleep.

I woke sometime later. It was still dark, and I was thirsty. The large flask was empty, and because Jeresaya was comforting a fractious toddler, I went out to get a refill. The night was three parts gone. The air had a damp icy feel about it, cold enough for me to soon wish I had worn my cloak and boots. Moon dark was tomorrow, and I wondered if it would rain although the sky was dark and full of stars.

I was hauling the large flask back to the dwelling when Oak ran up. "I'm glad you're awake. I was just coming to find you. Something's happening to Faltryn's body. I don't think it will be there for long. You said to let you know if there were any changes. Do you want to be there?"

"Yes, I do. Hold on, I'll just take the flask back."

"I'll take it," he said. "I'll get your cloak, too." He handed me his lamp.

I smiled my thanks, and ran towards the dark area where Faltryn's body lay. He was difficult to see in the shadow of the wall. I held the lamp high as I walked the length of his body. Up close he seemed more silvery than black.

I arrived back at his head at the same time as Oak. He carried a thick rug, a pair of highly decorated boots Storm had given me, and the delicate black cloak Oak had made for me when we were still in the fortress city of Faltryn.

"It seemed a good time for you to wear these," he said, as he wrapped the cloak around my shoulders.

I was again surprised at how warm the cloak was. It was light, soft, and appeared to be too delicate for anything cooler than a summer evening. I thought back to the first time I felt the silky warmth, and was thankful for the darkness that hid my reddening cheeks as I remembered the kiss that went with the gift. My first romantic kiss.

Oak stared again at Faltryn's body. "Is this colouring the effect of the worms, or does it happen to them when they're killed?" he asked.

"I don't know, but could you check the other dragons, please?"

He ran off and I sat on the rug to tie my boots. He was back before I had finished, and brought another hooded lamp with him.

"The others haven't changed. There's not even a glimmer of silver on them."

As he sat beside me, a section of Faltryn's body suddenly sank into the ground.

"That's what I meant," he said. "It happens in fits and

starts. It's almost as if the ground is swallowing him."

He was right. Already Faltryn's back feet and the middle part of his tail had disappeared. There were also constant smaller movements downwards, although it was the larger movements that had the biggest effect. Again, the body lurched downward, and this time his tail disappeared. Moments later, the end of Faltryn's nose vanished. Watching his head pulled away from his neck to leave a great cavernous hole was decidedly disturbing. Immediately his nose sank up to his unseeing eyes, allowing us to see into his now seemingly empty body.

"I'm not sure what I expected," I said, "but not that."

Faltryn's nose sank further, and I had the impression of shadows moving inside his skin-covered ribcage. I remembered the worms that had fallen on him and forced their way into his body on the night he died.

"I've come to say goodbye to Faltryn," Trethia said, as she snuggled beside me. I cuddled her close and ensured my cloak wrapped around her as well. When I turned my attention back to the dragon, two big eyes stared out from inside the cavernous hole.

Almost immediately, they disappeared.

Oak gasped. "What was that?"

I moved the lamp and narrowed the beam to shine directly into the hole, as the head sank further into the ground and disappeared. I still couldn't see much because of the shadows, but deep inside, something moved, and I saw an occasional glow as one or both eyes reflected the light.

I leaned forward. "Hello. Who are you?"

Again, the face appeared, although in the dark cave-like body, it was hard to see details. Whatever was in there made good use of the shadows.

"I wish it would come into the light so I could see it."

"Do you think it's one of the worms?" asked Oak.

"It's too big. They didn't have eyes, and anyway, what happened to the rest of them?" I asked.

"Well it might have eaten them all," he said.

"Well," I said with a half-laugh. "A large carnivorous worm is something we don't yet have."

"Do you think it is…"

"No, I don't," I interrupted. "But until I know, I have no idea what to do, and well—." I shrugged. "I do wish I could see it."

"I'm going to get a couple of guards and some weapons—just in case."

I grabbed his arm. "The dragons have never hurt us. Why would they begin now?"

"Because this may not actually be a dragon, and Faltryn caused a lot of damage to Churnyg's people," he said.

"If you think about it, Gynbere caused a lot of damage to his people. Faltryn just didn't stop…" I paused.

Trethia had suddenly leaned forward, staring intently into the darkness. I realised that whenever Faltryn's name was mentioned, the little face inside the cavernous body came momentarily into the light.

"Faltryn?"

Again, the face appeared, and then retreated. The eyes were most prominent, big and dark in pale skin. It had a small dark nose.

The dragon's body gave another lurch, and began to settle faster.

"If it doesn't come out soon, will the ground swallow it too?" Trethia asked anxiously.

Oak frowned. "Perhaps that would be for the best. We don't know what danger it brings."

"No, that mustn't happen," I said. "Whatever it is, it should live, and we have to help it."

Trethia took a deep breath as what was left of the body sank lower. Now the belly and half the legs had disappeared.

"Faltryn, come here," I called softly. "Come on, come to me." I held my hand out, trying to entice him.

There was a slight rumble, a flash of white and we were enveloped in thick cloud. When it cleared, the body was gone.

"Amazing! It's as if it wasn't even there," Oak said. "Nothing left, not even a mark on the ground. Perhaps it's for the best."

I smiled. "Only the corpse is gone."

Trethia giggled as she felt what had slipped under my cloak in the mist, wound around behind me and squeezed between us to climb onto my lap.

A small white face peeped out at me.

Oak stared, his mouth open. "What in Faltryn's name is that?"

"Well, I'd say it's probably Faltryn. Isn't he gorgeous?" I said with a big grin.

"It can't be," he gasped. "It's white. Faltryn is, well was black."

"Grown Faltryn was black. This is Faltryn, reborn."

"You mean the story Borasyn told you and Teema about them all coming back was true?"

I nodded. "Why would he lie about it?"

"It just sounded a bit far-fetched, and when the others arrived, well it wasn't mentioned. I thought it was just a good story. But what do we do with him now?"

"I've no idea."

"Baby squilute are offered water soon after birth. More often than not, they drink. So perhaps some water." Oak disappeared towards the cooking area. Trethia and I tickled Faltryn's chin and tummy until he returned with a deep platter of water.

The small dragon lapped it up, and yawned.

I picked him up as his eyes closed. "They both need to sleep, but what do I do? I can't take him into my old sleeping shelter. But I don't want Garanniis and Morkeen to feel awkward about me leaving after being there such a short time."

Oak laughed. "At the beginning of summer, you had only you to think of. Now you have a baby, a child and a dragon. I'll go and talk to Garanniis. We'll work something out." He picked up Trethia, who also yawned and snuggled into his shoulder.

He was back a short time later. "Garanniis and Paluniis are setting up a corner for the four of you. Garanniis was a bit worried about Faltryn's size, but once Trethia got over her giggles and explained, it was fine. They're a good community for you all to be in to be in."

True to Oak's word, there was a lovely little corner ready by the time we got there. The set I slept on had been far too long for me. They had moved the sleeping pad towards the bottom, leaving an area for Faltryn. There was a thick rug for him, and Paluniis had upended an unused set against the top section. to give Faltryn a modicum of privacy.

"There, you're all together," said Garanniis, as he showed us.

Faltryn sniffed around his area, moved his rug around a bit and curled up happily.

Cuddled up to Amethyst and Trethia, I must have fallen asleep almost immediately. When I next opened my eyes, it was daylight.

Oak and Teema sat nearby. I had the distinct impression they were guarding us, both had weapons on the seats beside them. Amethyst lay on a rug nearby, trying to put her toes in her mouth.

I sat up and stretched. Faltryn had crawled in next to Trethia and they both still slept. I tucked the rug around them and wandered over to wash the remains of the night away and change into clean clothes.

Platters of food had been recently brought in from the cooking area, and although everyone else had already eaten and left the dwelling, there was plenty left for me. The wonderful smells made me realise how hungry I was.

Teema picked up a platter of hot food and sat it on a table between the three of us. "Amethyst has been fed and Morkeen will come back soon to see if you need any help. I have a message for you from Loul. The boy Chonarth is awake. Still sleepy, but getting better. Frentha has slept, and would like to see you sometime."

It was great news.

"I was about to come off the wall," Teema continued, "and I thought I saw Faltryn's body move. Then the mist swirled around it, and when it cleared, he was gone. I thought that was the end of him. By the time I finished my report, you were back here and asleep. I asked Oak if you were upset about Faltryn's body, and he told me what happened." He shook his head. "He's so small. It's hard to imagine he came out of that huge monster."

"He wasn't a monster," I said. "Just frightened. If he'd wanted to, he could have destroyed everyone who knew about him. He didn't, and in a way, he ensured we would continue to do what we've always done."

"What was that?" asked Oak.

"Look after the people and the land. Now we have a dragon to care for as well."

"What about the others?"

"I don't know. I know they've never all been dead at the same time. Normally when they're reborn, the older dragons awaken first. But everything has changed, so we'll have to wait and see."

"Could it be that they don't—well, now can't come back?" Teema asked.

"It's possible, but we won't know until—" I shrugged, "well, until we know."

"It could take a long time, Kirym. Seasons or even season cycles. We can't just wait for them. What about Veld and the others?"

"The rescue of the hostages will go ahead as planned. I'll ask for a few guards to help me protect the dragons, while the rest go with Tarl."

"But you'll be needed with Tarl," said Teema.

"Mama and Tarl will make that decision, not me. I'll do what I'm told."

They nodded. I pushed the platter away, suddenly not hungry. "Did anyone see anything of Faltryn's rebirth?"

Teema shook his head. "A couple of guards commented on the mist. There was a bit of talk about the corpse disappearing. A few of the boys asked Tarl if they could play there."

"And he said?"

"He told them it was still a dragon area. There are a couple of guards there to keep everyone away."

"I see no reason they shouldn't play there, if the ground is safe," I said.

Teema nodded. "I'll get Bryn to check it out. He knows what to look for. Do you want to have a ceremony there to—I dunno, what do you do to a place where a dragon deceased?"

"As the dragon in question is very much alive, maybe I'll ask him first."

There was a flurry under the rug and a small black nose peeped out and sniffed at Trethia's face. She stirred, pushed his nose away and turned over. With the rug still over his head, he looked sweet and funny. I tickled him under his chin. He came out further, and I saw what I missed in the darkness. A blue lump on his forehead.

"If there was any doubt about it being Faltryn, it's gone." Teema and Oak nodded.

Trethia's eye's opened. She smiled at us. Faltryn spun around and his head came up beside hers. They touched noses. "I'm hungry," she declared.

"We all need to eat. Then we have some work to do," Oak said. He brought over a platter of water and Faltryn drank as we ate.

"When will he start talking?" asked Teema. "If he could tell us what to expect next, it'd make it easier."

"He's a baby, so it may take some time." I was distracted by Faltryn shaking his head vigorously. "It'll happen soon?" I asked him.

He shook his head.

"A season? Two?"

Again, he shook his head.

"Four? Six? Oh, dear. Longer?"

He nodded.

"A lot longer?" I paused. "So, you can't sing to the other dragons."

He sank onto his belly and put his head on his front feet.

"We've told them all we know. Will that be enough?" I asked.

While he didn't shrug, he may as well have.

"Do we tell them you are alive?"

He continued to look miserable.

"What's the problem?" asked Oak.

"As I understand it, the oldest doesn't die until the others have been reborn. Faltryn was killed. That and his rebirth has changed things. If they heard Faltryn's message as he was dying, and the story I told after, how will they react when they awaken? It scares him."

6

Kirym Speaks

Most of the children had been taught to allow a new-born to be at peace, but this was a dragon, and they were all eager to get close and touch. It took some convincing, and eventually Tarl stepped in and ordered them to give him space to learn to be a dragon, and asked Oak to watch and see no one unwanted, came too close. Even then, a group of girls watched Faltryn's every move, oohing and aahing as he walked, ran and fell on his nose. They increased their distance when I took him over to Borasyn's pictures.

"Why show him these, Kirym?" Oak asked.

"Two reasons. I don't know what he can recall, and this might trigger some memories. If he doesn't remember, then he'll begin to learn something of the past and the land around us."

"But surely he's far too young for that to mean anything."

"Dragons are different. They're born with memories that

need to be activated. This is the best I can do, but just maybe, it requires a dragon to teach him, or possibly the memories should be sung to him." I was distracted by Faltryn's reaction to the pictures. He rushed past the drawing of the massive tree with his head averted after the first glance. When he saw Borasyn's depiction of Valythia, he backed away looking scared.

"He recognises them." I picked him up. "It's all right, little one. The past is over. The desert people now live here, and we look after them. They're safe and happy. You didn't destroy the tree, others did that, but Borasyn gave us a special gift. He made the tree beautiful. Come and look at it."

I showed him the stump, and sat him on the top. He studied the patterns on the polished surface.

When he had finished the inspection, I took him over to the sleeping dragons. He sat in front of Iryndal for a short time, and then walked over and nudged her. When there was no response, he tried again.

Oak frowned. "What's wrong with him?"

"This is the only time in their history when the youngest has been here alone. There was something Borasyn said when he first talked of the dragons being reborn. When he was the oldest, he taught the youngest, Arymda at the time. I think that's how they grow."

"But the other dragons are dead. They can't do that."

"So, I have to."

"Can you?"

"I can try." I picked the wee dragon up. "Faltryn, your family has a connection to the land and to us. You have a token connection, just as I do." I showed him each large token as I placed it on the surface of the stump.

He studied each one for a short time, and moved them it onto a mark on the stump. When he had all except the rainbow token on a mark, he inspected the pocket, and shook it.

"He's looking for the yellow," I said. "Oak, can you please find Larqeba, and ask him to join us."

When they returned, Larqeba readily placed his yellow stone on the stump.

Faltryn inspected it, and pushed it onto the space he had left for it. Then he backed away as if inspecting the line, but in doing so, casually shoved the rainbow token off the stump and into a clump of grass.

"Why did he do that?" asked Larqeba.

"I don't know," I said. "Just watch."

Faltryn then sat in front of the blue token and stared at it.

"He knows there's a connection here. Perhaps it's time I formally introduced Faltryn to his siblings." I picked him and the blue token up and sat in front of Iryndal.

Faltryn followed the token.

I rubbed Iryndal's forehead bump, amazed that her skin didn't have the cold solid feeling of a dead human. However, she felt very different when she was alive.

Faltryn put his head on my knee and stared up at me.

I rubbed his forehead also. His little blue bump pulsed as I touched it. "Faltryn, this is Iryndal. She is the oldest dragon in your family. She is very wise and gentle. Her ability is sight; she can see many things, past and present. She is very compassionate, and she can pass the pictures of her understanding on to others. Hers is the gift of knowledge."

Faltryn stared at her in awe. It was as if he was seeing her for the first time.

Trethia stroked Iryndal's token bump. Then she touched it with her forehead.

Faltryn tried to copy her, but was too small to reach. I lifted him up so he could connect his forehead to hers.

"Will that bring her back to life?" asked Oak.

"I don't know. We'll have to wait and see." I clicked the blue token to my tokens, and then to Iryndal and Faltryn.

We sat there quietly for a time, and then I placed the token back on the tree stump, and picked up the green token. It led us to Ubree.

And so Faltryn learned about his family, Ubree the brave, who possessed the gift of healing, clever Othyn, Egrym the dreamer, gentle Arymda, who had the ability to be invisible, and Borasyn the artist.

With each of his sisters and brothers, Faltryn listened to what I knew of them, touched his token bump to theirs and to the large tokens.

"They have a better chance to wake up now," said Trethia. "They needed to know him too. Now they just need the final request."

"What request?" I asked.

She shrugged.

"How does Trethia—where did that come from?" asked Oak.

"Her knowledge is a mystery, but she's been right about many things. Maybe this too. I just wish I knew what the request is."

Faltryn climbed onto my boot, and I picked him up and sat him on the stump. He looked at the patterns and tokens again, pushed the tokens together and over to where I was sitting. While he was doing that, I picked up the rainbow token.

Faltryn saw it and darted away. I grabbed his tail before he was out of reach, and suddenly he was airborne.

I scrambled to my feet and ran a short distance with him, raising and lowering his tail slightly to get him used to the feeling and to learn what happened, when he eventually flew alone.

Faltryn suddenly realised he was above the ground, and

twisted around to see what was going on. In doing that, his wings closed and he nosedived towards the ground.

I grabbed him under his tummy. I was still holding the token, and when it touched his skin, he dived away from it. I dropped the token, grabbed him as he fell and put him on his feet, keeping hold of his tail. He strained to get away, and finally twisted around to look at me.

I picked up the token. "It won't go away," I said quietly. "The other tokens are important to your brothers and sisters, so does this one has significance to you?"

He sighed, sank on to his tummy and put his head on his front feet.

"If it connects to you, does that pass your history to the other dragons?"

He shook his head.

"Why are you frightened of it?"

He couldn't answer, and I wondered if he knew.

"The unknown is more frightening for not being faced. Ignoring it won't make it disappear. That connection could be important to your brothers and sisters. It might not be, but you don't know. Touch it or not, it's up to you. "Just ask for it when you want it." I wrapped the tokens up and packed them away." I handed Larqeba his yellow stone, and thanked him.

"Why does it do what the other tokens do?" he asked. "Would all coloured stones do that?"

"I don't know, but I doubt it. There's a history to that stone. Something to do with the dragons or the tokens."

"Does Gynbere know about it?" asked Teema.

"Ask Churnyg or Ashistar. They may have some idea, but the significance could be lost in time."

"I wonder how much Ashistar really knows," said Teema, as he sat beside me. "Did you know he disappeared before Gynbere attacked?"

"I knew he'd gone," I said, "but I didn't know the moment he left."

"I know you've always supported him, Kirym, but it's possible he's really working for Gynbere." Teema said. "If he knew Gynbere was going to attack, he may have left early to make sure he wouldn't be compromised. He knows so much about us."

I smiled. "Many things are possible, but with Ashistar, no! He has an agenda to follow, and he does it his own way. He is loyal to me, and therefore to Mama and Tarl."

"Teema thinks Ashistar totally supports Gynbere, and I I'm told Churnyg isn't sure of his loyalty," said Oak.

I glanced up at Teema, who went red, but tried to stare me down.

"But—but Ashistar's hate for Churnyg could sway his judgement."

"Teema, where did you get the idea he hated Churnyg? Had Churnyg claimed him as his son while in The Rock, Ashistar would probably have been killed, and he knows that." I paused. "I'm sure you've both heard a lot of stories. Don't listen to them. Churnyg's doubts, if he has them, may have been fed by the guilt of his response to Ashistar over the seasons. But since he claimed Ashistar as his own, he has never said anything against his son. Ashistar deserves our support until there is plain proof against him."

"Some people say there is the proof. There've been fights over it." Larqeba rubbed his jaw.

"Oh dear. Don't fight over it, Larqeba. Just walk away, please" I said. "Ashistar being absent at times is not evidence of anything. Remember, he was rejected by everyone for a long time. He's used to spending time alone. He has his loyalties, and he serves them as he sees fit. Please don't fight over it, any of you, but if someone makes accusations, demand proof, and make them talk to Mama."

People had paused to watch the wee dragon play as they wandered about their chores. At times, there was quite an audience, but they did keep their distance.

Tarl and Armos came and sat with us. "He's a bonny wee thing, isn't he? How soon can he help us?" Armos asked, as he watched Faltryn chasing and being chased by Trethia.

"He's a baby, Armos. What would you have him do?" snapped Oak.

Armos winced at his icy tone. "Can he do anything the other dragons could do?"

"He has to learn those things." I said. "I'm teaching him as much as I can, but we don't expect this much from any other new-born. Please don't expect more than you would another."

"Aye, he can't even fly, can he" Armos said.

"Nor walk," Teema said, as Faltryn tripped over his tail. "He's a liability we could do without."

"When we left the settlement last spring, we knew nothing of the dragons. So why have you become so dependent on them, that you require answers from one who's too young to have them? We do what we would normally do in the circumstances."

"You're right, Kirym," said Tarl, "and I have to realise I can't plan the unplannable."

The day passed quietly, but plans were made to eat together in the evening, and perhaps listen to music afterwards. For some it was a farewell celebration for those who had died.

7

Arbreu

Mekrar, Arbreu, Starshine and Mekroe had been allowed a few days with no specific duties. Now with the journey looming so close, they took more interest in the details and arrangements. In the afternoon, they joined everyone else to hear what plans had been made when the deadline finally expired. Once the noise had died, Tarl stood and cleared his throat.

"These plans are fairly final. Everyone should know now who they stand alongside, and what they do when we reach Gynbere. However, we need to leave men here to guard those unable to join us. So, the guards who are about to go on the wall will be reduced by half and do all the guard work from the morning of the day we leave. Those in charge of the healers and cooks will similarly choose a small group to care for those who are staying. Everyone else capable of using a bow, spear, sword or knife will be prepared to travel by mid-afternoon so we can leave as soon as I order it."

"I'm in charge of those about to go on the wall," said Bryn. "I'll choose the people to stay here and let them know during the evening. Any who need to stay for family or other reasons can talk to me, and relieve one of those men. I'll sort out their shifts and who will be in charge. I'll have a list for you in the morning, Tarl."

Tarl frowned, and then nodded as a wave of comments swept the area.

"Starshine has given permission for us to use what wagons we need. The cooks, and healers get first choice and then others will be loaded with necessities. Kirym will give you what advice she can, and will liaise with everyone after we've gone. Let me know your decisions when they're made. We will travel as far as we can tomorrow, and the final part of the journey on the following morning. I want the sun behind me when I approach Gynbere."

"He doesn't rise until late," said Arbreu. "What's the point in getting there early, if we then have to wait around?"

"I don't intend to wait. We'll march in, take the hostages and leave. If he wants it different, he'll wake up fast. Now I don't expect it to be quite like that, but that's the simplified version. Now get the necessary preparations done." Tarl stared at the maps.

Teema leaned over the table. "Um, we need Kirym with us, Tarl! She has the weapons. She understands Gynbere and—"

"No," interrupted Tarl. "Churnyg can advise us."

"Armos, talk to him" said Teema. "He's wrong."

"He's not!" Kirym said. "Churnyg understands Gynbere, and Tarl also has Baketer to help—"

"What use could Baketer be?" interrupted Teema. "He's a fool. So useless, Slaslow didn't even consider him worth taking when they left The Rock."

"The lowest of the low, I heard," said Tarjin.

Kirym swung around, her eyes blazing. "Baketer has knowledge so important, Slaslow felt he had to be destroyed at all cost. Those looking up, often see far more than those looking down. He has already given us invaluable information. Why would he turn on those who are loyal to him, and return to those who would kill him on sight? His value is that Slaslow considers him to be a threat."

"You may be right, Kirym, but he can't even tell us why Slaslow wants him dead. It's possible he doesn't, and this is just a story to con you." Teema turned his back on Kirym before she had a chance to comment. "You shouldn't take him, Tarl."

Arbreu glanced at Kirym. She was furious, but there was something else. It took Arbreu a while to realise it was grief.

Kirym's information on the map was the best they could get. No one else could add any changes, none of the hunters had gone in that direction; the herds had avoided the marshland, so the hunters did also. While Arbreu wondered how dangerous the marsh was, he was more interested in the sketch Kirym had done of the land Gynbere had chosen to make his stand.

"A smaller hill in the centre of a big hole," said Crag, Wind Runner's map maker. "Why would he choose to make his stand there? Is he being so badly advised?"

"No!" Kirym was emphatic. "He knows this land. He's there for a specific reason. That was his original goal when he left the rock. Coming here was an afterthought."

"We'll have the advantage of space, Tarl," said Blacknight. "Kirym says he's probably put his people in the hole. If she's right, he'd have to leave them if he decides to run, but his escape path is very limited."

"That means he won't have any defence; there's nowhere for his archers." Twig said. "Maybe he's setting a trap and plans to bring them in behind us."

"He won't do that for two reasons," said Kirym. "First he won't trust anyone to lead them in case they decide to cross him, and second, they're too good not to use. I suspect he'll mix them in with his people."

"So you think he has no intention to fight us?" Blacknight asked.

"I didn't say that," she said. "His archers are good. They can place their arrows where they want them, even if they can't see their goal. And they'll have plenty of time to practice. As they're surrounded by women and children, we can't shoot back."

There was a stunned silence.

"Yes, that's precisely how he would do it," said Churnyg.

"But what about those words written on the back of the map?" Arbreu asked.

"It depends who has control. If it's Slaslow, they may order an attack even if we give them what they want," Kirym said.

"What we need," said Churnyg, "is good shields."

"Which we don't have," said Armos. "Do we have time to make them?"

Tarl frowned. "We don't have the facilities to make enough, but the armourers are already doing what they can.

"How can we defend ourselves?" asked Girk.

"Hopefully it will all pass very peacefully," said Tarl. "If anyone is ordered to fire at us, we aim our weapons at Gynbere and Slaslow. They're the vital people in this."

Lelth snorted. "He'll have so many people in front of him, we'd have trouble getting him. He'll probably have time to escape around the tor, and that implies the marsh isn't as extensive as we think."

Tarl acknowledged the comment. "We have to handle it as we see it. In the meantime, check with whoever's in charge of you on guard duty to ensure you are each as prepared as you can be, and can work together with your group. Then spend time with your family. It seems we will have a quiet celebration tonight. Enjoy it."

The celebration began with music before the sun set, and everyone who could be there, was. People initially sat with their families, but the families were large intermixed groups now and it was sometimes hard to tell where one finished and another started. Smaller groups were brought into the bigger, and soon everyone was mingling.

Arbreu joined Kirym's family, happy that Bryn, Jeresaya and his siblings were there too, and with Mekroe and Starshine now being joined, many of those from the Fortress felt they too belonged.

Initially it was a quieter gathering than usual. There was an air of sorrow at the beginning of the meal, but soon a few people began to dance and the beat of the music increased. We ate at dusk. The night was dark; we didn't expect to see the new moon for three nights. However, the stars were vivid against the inky blackness around them. With hunger satisfied, everyone settled back and the music began again, interspersed with chatter and laughter.

It was very dark around the walls, and although the fires lit the centre of the amphitheatre well, they were smaller than usual.

Parlansho had just asked Armos to sing his favourite song when there was a sharp challenge from the guards, followed by the warning whistle, that meant an intruder had breached the outer wall.

Arbreu glanced around, as many of the others did, but Kirym was instantly on her feet, holding her bow and grabbing a handful of bolts from the quiver by her feet.

Arbreu hadn't noticed her weapons prior to that. She was one of the few who had a weapon with her, the others being those about to go on guard duty.

8

Kirym Speaks

I ran towards the north-western entrance, but stopped as the next signal sounded. I waited, my bolt still nocked, but not drawn.

Dashlan was at my shoulder. "I'm still not sure of the calls, Kirym. The first part was danger, but what did the last bit mean?"

"That they've contained the situation, but we're all to stay alert—for now."

"Oh right. It was that inflection at the end I didn't know."

I glanced back to check that Trethia had remained beside Morkeen and Amethyst. Garanniis and Paluniis stood over them, Garanniis holding a knife, Paluniis his spear.

Faltryn was at my heel. I was surprised at how quickly he had followed me.

Everyone was quiet, the men poised and alert, ready to get to where they were needed if called on.

Mama, Tarl and Starshine were joined by Bryn, Bokum and Armos, and slowly the group around them grew. Everyone in the amphitheatre was alert and ready to act at a moment's notice.

It was dark near the entrances. From where I stood, I couldn't see what held the guard's attention. Soon though, I heard thumps, bumps and an occasional curse. The dim shape of a scuffle came closer, and then two guards hauled a cloaked figure over to Tarl and threw him on the ground. Two more hauled a large sack up and dumped it beside him.

A third signal resounded across the circle.

"Ah," murmured Dashlan. "That means all clear. The warble at the end, that's calling in a few more men, isn't it?"

I nodded. "The next guards will begin their duty now, and there will be a cross-over for the rest of the night."

As some of the men melted away to follow the order, and Findlow, their leader, joined them.

The cloaked figure on the ground rolled over, his face still hidden in the folds of the hood. Two guards grabbed him under his arms and dragged him to his feet.

"He'd almost made it in, Tarl," said Gorjh, the head guard for the shift, "and would've, had his sack not scraped along the side of a wagon and alerted us. Otherwise he'd be in here doing his worst." He leaned forward and pulled back the hood.

"Baketer!" snarled Teema. "I knew it! This is proof."

Baketer looked terrified.

"Proof of what?" Mama asked.

"That he's in league with Gynbere. He was there when Tarl told everyone to stay in the amphitheatre. He must have gone out to talk to Slaslow or one of his men."

"I'll hold judgement until I have a little more information,

Teema" said Mama, "Kirym, perhaps you'd join us here. I believe you know Baketer. Everyone else step back or return to their celebration while we sort this out."

While the circle around Mama moved back a step, no one left. They wanted to see what would happen. In fairness, although there were a few murmurs, no one showed overt antagonism, leaving it to Mama and Tarl to decide.

Teema stepped in front of me, trying to block my view, and stood over Baketer. "Well then! Who were you seeing out there?"

Baketer shrank away from him.

Tarl pulled Teema away. "That's not helping, Teema. We'll learn nothing if you scare the man to death. We do this fairly. He can explain himself, and then we'll make some decisions. I will not have him bullied." He helped Baketer to his feet. "Kirym!" he called. "Here, please."

Teema scowled as I stepped past him.

"Baketer looks tired. He needs a seat and a drink." I led him over to a nearby bench, and sat opposite him.

He took the offered flask and half drained it. "I did nothing wrong, Kirym. Nothing!"

I nodded. "I know. So just tell me what you were doing."

"Well Tarl said we didn't have enough and I realised it made no sense having them out there, and the simplest thing was for me to bring them in." He spoke in a rush, obviously still scared. "It wasn't just about stopping Slaslow from using them."

Everyone looked as confused as I felt.

Baketer looked up at me, hesitated and realised it had been a bit garbled.

"They're in the sack. I was bringing them in." He jumped up and dragged the sack further into the firelight.

Dashlan gave him a hand and together they tipped the contents onto the ground. A number of metal, wood and skin oblongs fell out with a clatter. Dashlan picked one up, turned it round and grasped two straps on the back.

"Pa, remember that statue back in the settlement? The old man. He was holding one of these, wasn't he? It's a shield. Different from those Slaslow's guards hold, but—"

"I think you're right." Bryn took it from him and settled it on his arm. "Yes, I'm sure you are."

"Baketer, where did they come from? Why were you bringing them in?" I asked.

"Tarl said we needed more shields, and I thought these—."

"Where did you get them?" interrupted Tarl.

"They were outside under some branches."

"Tarl, that implies Gynbere intends to come back and attack," said Mekroe.

"Getting us out of the amphitheatre is just a ploy," snapped Teema. "Once we're gone, Gynbere returns and all of his armour's here waiting for him. He marches back in and has even more to bargain with. Our families, the dragons and he'll have any resources we leave. Tarl, this is proof."

There was a rising wave of comments. But Baketer was shaking his head.

"Quiet!" bellowed Sundas. "Kirym, what do we do?"

"Listen to Baketer's whole story before we jump to conclusions and start panicking. Now from the beginning, Baketer. Who put the shields under the branches?"

"I did. Slaslow had them stored in some big chests ready to take with him."

"And no one objected to you taking them?" said Mrilan dryly.

"Why would they? Guards do what they're ordered to do. No one explains why we should do it. Slaslow and his assistants consider everyone below them too stupid to understand anything. Men have been killed for asking a question. Four men were told to guard the chests. They wouldn't have known what was in them, and they wouldn't want to know. For one of them to report what I was doing, he'd have to leave his post. That's never good. His superior wouldn't have known what he was guarding or why. To go higher, well why would you call attention to yourself when you didn't need to? And just because they didn't know what was going on, wouldn't absolve them from guilt nor punishment. No one would get involved."

"Baketer's right," said Churnyg. "That's exactly how it would have happened. What he did was extremely brave. Slaslow would've killed him had he known. We should thank him for what he's done."

"How many shields there, Bryn?" asked Armos.

"Twelve. That's a heavy load, Baketer. You should've asked for help. We can quickly train a group to protect Tarl, should anyone shoot at him."

"There are more," interrupted Baketer. "I put a couple of loads in one of the wagons earlier."

Tarl stared at him. "How many trips did you make before you were caught?"

"Four."

Tarl started to laugh. "I think we need to retrain our guards. How many of Gynbere's men can have done that over the last few days?"

"None."

"Why do you say that, honey?" Oak picked Trethia up so Tarl could see her easily.

"The others were noisy all the time. He wasn't, because if he made a noise, they hit him or made him do the horrid jobs."

Tarl nodded. "Well that's a relief. So, we probably have about fifty. They'll be a great help."

Baketer shook his head. "There's over eighty there. I

had a bigger sack, but it split. There are more to bring in though."

"You've done well, Baketer. Let's leave them until morning." Tarl raised his voice: "Mek, can you get this brave man a platter of food?" He turned back to Baketer. "We'll give you a hand to collect the rest tomorrow?"

"I can do it. I should have it finished by midday."

"How far away are they?" I asked.

"In the trees. Just by the rock fall by the stream."

"But that's quite close," said Tarl. "How many loads do you reckon?"

Baketer shrugged. "Twenty, thirty or so. There's some armour there, too. And some loose stuff, and then there are some sacks I've not opened."

"Wait on," interrupted Teema. "This is wrong. Gynbere's porters aren't stupid. They would know the difference between empty and full. The weight of the chests alone would warn them something was wrong."

"Oh, they weighed the same as before. I filled them with branches, rocks and tree-cones."

Armos laughed and slapped Baketer on the shoulder. "Impressive! You've really helped us. It'll make the confrontation with Gynbere a lot safer. How many men do you need to bring the shields here?"

"Depends how quickly you want them."

Tarl smiled. "Very quickly. Will ten men be enough?"

"Twenty would be better."

"Bokum, can you organise that for tomorrow? It seems we are getting more help than we realised."

"Um," Baketer seemed ill at ease. "I found out where some o' the watchers are too."

"Did you not listen to anything Tarl said after Urfit gave his ultimatum?" Teema was incandescent with rage. "If you've even been seen, Gynbere will have an excuse to break the agreement."

"I stayed inside the lines Lord Tarl drew. I just looked for their camps."

Tarl pulled a map out of his tunic. "Let's at least note the information you have, and then worry about if you were seen."

He spread the map out and Baketer pointed to seven spots on the trail going east, and three more going north.

Tarl frowned. "I know you had the best of intentions, but you must have strayed past the lines I set, Baketer. I do wish you hadn't."

"I didn't cross the lines, Lord Tarl. I promise. I went at night. They all have big fires. Easy to see, even from a distance." He pointed to a spot on the map. "I went no further than there. I was in the trees and they were on the ground. They don't ever look up, and anyway, it was dark, and they blind themselves in the firelight,"

"When did you do this?" I asked.

"Last night and the night before."

"But you did guard duty through the day, and you helped with the squilute," said Dashlan. "When did you sleep?"

He shrugged. "When I needed to."

"Tarl, we owe Baketer a great deal of thanks," I said. "This information will be invaluable when you travel."

Tarl nodded. "We'll talk about it tomorrow. Now, we are celebrating, and Baketer, you will join us and enjoy yourself." He leaned close to him. "If you have anything else in mind, please talk to me first. I'd hate to be planning something only to find you'd already done it. They'll begin to think you are Warlord." He looked up, knowing I'd heard. "Tell him, Kirym. He's too valuable to lose. Now, let's celebrate."

Baketer beamed, feeling for perhaps the first time in his life, he was valued.

9

Kirym Speaks

Baketer's interruption hammered home how close tomorrow's separation was and the memory hung over everyone. The moon moved less than a hand-span while we celebrated, and then the fires were damped down for the night.

I lay beside Trethia and slept, knowing I'd be awake for Amethyst through the night. She slept longer than I'd expected, waking just before midnight. I fed her and changed her wraps, and slept again, only to be woken soon after by Faltryn snuffling in my ear.

"Is he all right?" whispered Paluniis, the wake person for the dwelling for that part of the night. "Maybe the other dragons are waking."

Faltryn stopped and shook his head frantically. Then he nosed through my possessions, and dragged out the bag of tokens.

"The rainbow token is calling him. He's ready for it," said Trethia, sleepily reaching for her boots.

Faltryn didn't look enthusiastic, but he nodded.

I dressed warmly and wrapped Trethia in a thick cloak. Carrying Faltryn, we walked towards the other dragons.

As usual at night, there was very little light within the amphitheatre. The healing shelter had been walled to keep everyone protected from the cooler damp air of midwinter. The cooking fires had been damped down. Food, being prepared for morning and the trip, was either under the ashes, or in large chests surrounded by dried corn husks and fush grass to keep them cooking overnight. The wagons were all in darkness.

The sky was amazing. With no moon, the stars seemed to have multiplied. The two rivers of stars that snaked across the sky seemed particularly crowded, the glow from them made it seem almost as light as daytime. To the north, the Dragon Star sat by itself in a small pool of darkness, and with no light around it, it seemed even bigger than I remembered. I pointed it out to Trethia. "It's my favourite star."

"Mine too," she said softly. "When I came here, it was the first star I saw. I always feel better when I see it."

The six dragons lay as they had since they had died, but the top of the stump shone, the swirls where Faltryn had laid the tokens starkly obvious in the starlight.

I sat Faltryn on the ground; he walked over to Iryndal so I placed the pocket beside him. He pushed his nose into the pocket opening.

"Can I help?" I asked. He nodded. I took out each of the tokens and unwrapped them.

Oak raced over to us. "You should have called me, Kirym. How can I protect you when you wander off alone?" He placed a platter holding a warm bun filled with fruit and nuts, the remains of his meal, beside Trethia. "Eat up sweetness. I'll get more if you're still hungry."

I refrained from asking what I needed protection from. I

had the horrid feeling he would have a list of possibilities I could find little to argue against.

Faltryn watched Trethia bite into a bun, and dragged the platter towards Iryndal.

"Does he want a meal for them?" said Oak. "I didn't think the dragons ate. Does he not know that?"

"Yes, he does know. I think it's the platter he wants."

Faltryn dragged the platter over to the tokens, and pushed the tokens onto it.

My fingers itched to help him, but I felt he needed to do this alone. When all except one were on the platter and arranged to his liking, he lay with his head on his front feet and stared at the one he'd left on the grass, the rainbow token.

The pattern he had made with the stones was a tight spiral, following the pattern on the platter, which was one Findlow had made soon after we arrived in The Green Valley. The wood had been an offcut from Papa's dwelling. Findlow had been intrigued by the pattern on it, which swirled first one way, and then spiralled out in three places to spin in the opposite direction. We hadn't found any wood with similar patterns before, and he had kept the platter simple and let the pattern take over. It was his favourite.

Faltryn had only used part of the platter, he kept the centre clear. There was an empty space where the yellow token would have sat and space beside the purple. There were two logical places Faltryn could put the rainbow token—in the middle, or at the outer edge.

When he pushed it on to the platter, it was not into either place I had thought obvious. He positioned it right at the far edge, opposite the other tokens.

He pulled the platter carefully over to a place beside Iryndal, and sat opposite it.

The night seemed to get darker, although when I glanced

up, the sky was as brilliant and as memorable as when I first came outside.

When I looked back at the tokens, the blue began to glow, just a little at first, but it built up and finally light seemed to explode out of the stone, connecting with Iryndal's forehead, the rainbow stone and my three tokens. We stayed connected, and the green token and Ubree joined us. Despite there not being a yellow token here, the shadow of one formed between and green and orange, and it mirrored the others, connecting with Othyn, the rainbow token and mine. Then the orange token and Egrym, Arymda and the red stone, and Borasyn with his purple all joined them.

The connections stayed static, and I had the impression of searching, not for the yellow token, but something more, and then a scene formed—a dark tunnel deep and I was travelling down it.

Despite the dark, I was aware of massive coloured shapes, mainly circular approaching from the sides and either rushing past or twisting around us and racing away.

I began to slow down. Now I could see the tunnel walls. They gave me the impression of being fluid, flowing in the opposite direction to that I was taking. We stopped opposite an arch. I was reminded of the rocks that arched over the entrance to the inlet that led us to The Green Valley, although this one was not made of rock, nor anything else I could identify.

Set in the middle of the arch was a double gate, shut and locked. It was dark beyond the gate, but there were shadows moving to and fro. Something, or someone who accompanied me, grabbed the ornate bars of the gates and rattled them. They didn't open. The shaking became desperate and then violent, until one of the gates cracked, a hinge broke, and the gate twisted and sagged to the ground. I caught the glimpse of a face at the gate, and then it backed away.

Slowly the scene darkened and disappeared. When the light returned, the gate shimmered as if this were a dream that was fading as night finished. I went through the arch, but what had been with me in the tunnel remained there. Once through, the light disappeared and I felt I was drawn through the darkness at speed, but slowed when I joined a group of shadow figures travelling towards a far distant glow.

The glow grew larger, and then a dark robed and hooded figure loomed up in front of us. The shadows halted, and the figure appeared to grow. It raised its heads and opened its eyes, deep red against the black of the hood.

For a long moment, the shadows watched, and then they sped up as the figure spread its arms in welcome. Its mouths, red like its eyes, opened. "Haaaaa!" The long drawn out exhalation sounded as if two jagged rocks had been dragged across each other, and the shadows ahead shrivelled and disappeared in smoke.

The figure laughed—the sound sent shivers down my back. It lifted its left arm pointed at a tree on the right of the path. Flames erupted from its fingers and the tree almost exploded from the ground, enveloped in fire. The figure pointed again and again, and trees on both sides of the path caught alight. Then it swept its arms forwards and pointed at the path. Flames erupted from its fingers and consumed many of the shadows.

"I! Rule! Now!" The figure screamed it out, and the words echoed around me. The figure turned and floated away, flames flowing from its fingers, engulfing the land to each side and beyond.

As suddenly as it appeared, it disappeared, and I was left on the path, flames soaring up around me. Eventually as the sky lightened, they died, leaving the land black and dead. I felt immeasurably sad.

I heard a sound nearby, and swung around, fearing the figure had returned. Nothing on the path, but I could still hear the noise, more a whimper than a whisper.

A small movement in the blackened ashes at the side of the path caught my eye. Two tiny shadows were pushing up through the burned undergrowth.

As soft as the message was, I understood it.

The land is no longer whole. They disappeared. We need help. Everything must return to how it was.

The light faded and disappeared and I was again in an all-encompassing darkness. It seemed to get smaller and smaller until it was but a dot, and the scene in front of me—the amphitheatre—was as it had been before.

I felt that eons had passed since I had seen it last. My tokens were still connected to the large tokens and the dragons. That surprised me. Trethia was snuggled beside me, Faltryn sat opposite, staring up at me, and looking troubled.

"That told them what happened?"

Faltryn looked unsure, and then nodded.

"And that's what you're scared of?"

He looked terrified as he nodded again.

Each of the seven tokens sent up a bright rope-like ray. The rainbow token absorbed the light around us, while the colours of the other six stones stood out brightly. The rainbow of six colours twisted together, and swooped over us to curl around the black. Slowly the colour drained out of them all, leaving a spiral column of black cords. Then the column melded into one cord, white light appeared from the dragons and as the cord drained, it slowly filled with colours again. The colours separated, arched up and swooped down to replace the white. The bright multi-coloured cord reached gently towards Faltryn, and touched his token bump.

Then all I could see was the spiral of tokens, glowing on the platter. For a long moment, I was held enthralled by the colours, and the lights slowly faded. The rainbow token now sat between the purple and the blue.

Faltryn crawled onto my lap. I stroked his head, thinking of what I had seen.

"It was very brave of you to tell them. The tokens accepted you. That acceptance had to come from their owners."

"They know what happened now, Kirym, but they won't react until they waken." Trethia began wrapping the tokens and stowing them in my pocket.

"How did she know that?" asked Teema.

I looked up, surprised he was there. "I didn't hear you arrive."

"I couldn't sleep. I'm glad, I'd have hated to miss that. I'm surprised that the whole camp isn't here watching."

I glanced around. "Perhaps they weren't supposed to see it." I slipped the pocket over my arm, and picked Faltryn up.

Oak took Trethia's hand. "Come on, we need to sleep."

10

Kirym Speaks

Morning brought more surprises. Amethyst woke soon after dawn, and after I had cared for her, I ate with the others in the dwelling.

We emerged as the sun bathed the grass, to see piles of equipment in front of the table. Baketer was in the process of emptying another sack of armour out and sorting it, with help from Larqeba and Shormel.

As we approached, Twig staggered over, deposited a sack beside the others, and sank to the ground.

"I don't know how he does it. He carries twice what I can, and he seems unaffected by it. He had a pile of them sacked up, and others on hauling frames before I even woke, and while I hauled this sack in, he made two trips." He gratefully accepted a flask and drank deeply.

"How much more is there?" asked Teema.

"This is just about half."

"You're not supposed to do it all alone, Baketer," laughed

Oak, as Baketer jogged in with yet another huge sack over his shoulder. "I thought the idea was to have a group of us doing it."

Twig stood, still red in the face. "I thought we weren't supposed to start until later, but he just turned up and got going."

"I don't mind," said Baketer. "Everyone needs to be with their families. I don't have one."

"Yes, you do," said Oak. "You're part of Kirym's, part of mine. Now come on, we're all here. Many hands," and a group of men who just arrived, all trooped toward the north entrance.

By the time the morning chores were done, there was a mountain of armour waiting to be sorted. The women and children waded in and soon there were many smaller piles as helmets sat together, leg and arm covers, shields in two sizes and body armour in four different piles, according to size. And Baketer still hauled in bulging bags and frames.

"It's an impressive pile, and even more so when you realise that Baketer hauled more than half of it in by himself," said Arbreu.

Drinks were handed around while Tarl talked to the armorers about distribution and training.

Hiffit, the chief armor was ecstatic. He quickly sorted the men and handed out the correct sizes, and explained the use of the various parts to those who had never used them. Most interesting were the large shields. They slotted together to form a solid wall, and were large enough for a man to stoop behind for safety.

"They are now your responsibility," Hiffit said. "Care for them and they'll last many life times. Oil them to protect them against rain. Cover them when they're not in use. Practise with them, and learn to use them in cooperation with the man next to you. Your whole squad should be able to act as one person."

Tarl then explained the schedule for the rest of the day, mainly practicing with the new armour. "But be prepared to leave as soon as the sun sits on the horizon. I intend we travel at least to where the eastern path intersects the north."

"What about the watchers?" asked Bryn.

"We know where they are now, thanks to Baketer, and we'll handle the first fairly quickly. Baketer says there are six of them by the stream. Any four of you could take them, but I intend there be no deaths, and we also need to be sure none escape to warn Gynbere. So, ten men will approach them, with another six in reserve to make certain there are no problems."

"Why so many?" asked Mekrar.

"They may see us approach. However, they've stayed on the ground, so most of the men will travel in the trees."

"Does that mean," interrupted Paluniis, "you're only using those from The Rock?"

Tarl smiled. "Oh no. Others have been training with them. Dashlan, Blacknight, your Giimjji, and Tarjin will join them, and they'll be led by Churnyg. Raff will lead the reserve." Tarl allowed the comments to swell and then die.

"Tomorrow," he continued, "we'll finish the journey and then rest ready to travel the final distance at sun-up. A warning! We will have a cold camp on both nights. We can't chance anyone knowing where we are, so no fires. There will be a heavy guard presence around the camp to ensure none chance upon us by accident. Food has been and is being precooked, so you will have a hot meal tonight. After that, it'll depend on the outcome of our confrontation with Gynbere."

"Borboncha will get information to you Tarl, if he can."

"Baketer has proven himself, Kirym, but I'm not sure

where Borboncha's loyalties sit. He's an unknown," said Tarl, eyeing the men around him.

"Comments made by Borboncha saved your life, and mine. He later put himself at risk to tell us what was happening in Gynbere's camp."

"The reality is, he accidently dropped some things which you were lucky to recognise, Kirym," said Teema, "and the message he sent you, arrived too late for you to do anything about it. Anyway, it doesn't matter one way or the other. He disappeared without a word, and so has Ashistar. In fact, since we've been here, the only time either man has been seen, was when wearing armour. Only Gynbere's guards wear armour, and even they take them off occasionally. It proves they've been collecting information for Gynbere or Slaslow."

"It proves nothing, Teema. Ashistar told me he was going. He doesn't know what we plan to do, so he can't pass anything on."

"He could have a collaborator here," snapped Teema, "and if a hint of our actions is passed on, we'll be at a disadvantage."

Tarl massaged his temple. "Right now, we're doing the obvious, Teema, except for the speed of our journey. I haven't told everyone everything because many decisions will be made as needed."

Teema leaned over the table. "Perhaps they are the reason we need Kirym with us, Tarl. She reminds the likes of—"

"No, Teema," I snapped. "No one needs to be reminded. Anyway, we didn't always understand what Papa intended when he made his decisions. Tarl is war leader. Don't assume he's wrong. Let him lead. He'll tell you what you need to know, when you need to know it."

"The weapons—"

"Teema," Tarl interrupted. "If we place no importance on

the weapons, Gynbere may begin to doubt himself and his previous beliefs. That may resolve the whole situation."

"But if you're wrong!" snapped Teema. "It'll take three or four days to get a message here and for Kirym to get there."

"He must then allow more time. He didn't demand we bring Kirym. She could make the trip faster, but even if it did take that long, a lot can happen in those days," said Tarl.

"Yes. The hostages could be killed." Teema was now white with anger. "What if Gynbere plans an attack on the amphitheatre once we've gone? He could capture Kirym, the weapons and Faltryn, and then we'd have no bargaining power at all."

"Teema," I interrupted. "The amphitheatre is well defended. That won't change."

"With half a guard unit!" Teema glared at Tarl. "They have to sleep, eat. That means long shifts, and too few watching."

"There are as many people on the wall as there has ever been," said Tarl, patiently.

"Really?" sneered Teema. "Women and children. We need proper guards."

"The women are as good as the men, and most spend some time up there anyway. They're only staying here because of their children," said Armos. "As for the children, they're learning."

"I'll stay and help you, Kirym. Then if Tarl needs you…"

"No Teema!" interrupted Tarl. "I need you with me. You can contact Kirym if I need her. That'll be far more useful. Arbreu, and Bokum also. If we need to attack, I want to be able to split my fighters in three groups, and your ability to communicate with each other is vital. Starshine. While your people are yours to command, would you be happy to leave Oak here to guard Kirym?"

"Will Twig accept orders from Tarl now Storm is no longer with us?" Walf asked.

"He won't need to," Starshine said icily. "He'll take them from me."

Walf reddened under her glare. "But you won't have Oak—"

"Oak is not indispensable. None of my fighters are. Mekroe will stand beside me, but make no mistake. Until Windrunner returns, I lead my people."

"Jeresaya will join you, Starshine. She can care for my fighters, and can make decisions for them."

Tarl smiled an acknowledgement to both Bryn and Jeresaya. "I know I will have good advisors," he said.

I was pleased he refrained from mentioning the irony of Dashlan being Bryn's 'fighters'.

"It seems any number of able-bodied people will stay and go." Armos turned to me. "Try to teach that little dragon a few things. He may yet be the only weapon we have that Gynbere doesn't know about."

"Look at this," called Paluniis, holding up his shield. "I oiled it as Hiffit said. The brown stuff was a coating. It all came off and this was underneath it."

On the front of the shield, a yellow token was engraved into the surface.

The men clamoured to get cloths and oil, and soon they had all been cleaned of the mud-coloured coating.

"Tarl," called Oak. "If you look carefully, well they're slightly different sizes—the shields, that is. I think the token image-colours and sizes match. Perhaps we need to organise them to colour. It'll look stunning, and this may be the answer to the occasional problem we've had clipping them together smoothly. They may clip to their similar colour easier."

"Hiffit, that's your job," said Tarl. He picked up a wad of parchment and strode over to talk to the cooks.

I sat in the sun playing with Amethyst, Trethia and Faltryn, watching the men practising with their new armour.

"I brought you something to eat," said Tarl, sitting beside me, and placing a platter in front of me.

"You're getting as bad as Papa, or did Mama put you up to it."

He laughed. "She did say, but then she's the same with all of her children, me too." He paused. "I wanted to ask. Can you think of any way I can organise it so Bryn comes along with me?"

"No!"

"But, he's too good to leave here."

I nodded. "But think who would have to stay if you took him."

Tarl sighed deeply. "Oh! Yes. Armos."

"Armos is Papa's assistant. If something happened to you, he would step in. Anyway, with his papa and son being held by Gynbere, it would be unkind to leave him behind. The other head guards would do it, but there would be a lot of resentment. None of them could successfully take over Bryn's group. Men work better with those who trained them. So, you'd be asking for men who are preparing to go, to change their plans. Whoever you leave here has valuable attributes. They're all talented in their own way. That's why they have the positions they have."

He sighed. "I should have thought before I made the decision."

I shook my head. "I really think Bryn is the best choice. By the way, Tarl. Make Larqeba and Shormel senior under-guards. Have them report directly to Bryn. Otherwise they'll follow you."

He laughed. "I hadn't thought of them, but you're right. Anyone else?"

I nodded. "Put Tarjin with Findlow. He needs more training, and he's feeling a little isolated now Mekroe is joined."

"Why not Armos? He's always taken an interest in Tarjin, and it may be good for them both."

I smiled. "That's true, but Armos has other things on his mind at the moment and anyway, Tarjin isn't interested in Armos' daughter."

Tarl's eyes opened wide in surprise. "Lyndym? Oh, right then. Reciprocated?"

"I think so, although it's early days. There's a favour you can ask Starshine. She has a man, Shale. He's hard of hearing, but he reads lips. Some messages are passed on quietly, and Shale may be able to read them. Stand him just behind you."

"That's a talent we should encourage. I must mention it to Mama," said Tarl.

"Good idea. One other thing, Tarl. Those robes we found in The Rock. Give one to each of the people travelling within your group. Have the men walk with the hoods up, especially when you approach Gynbere. But not you or the other leaders. You must be identifiable. Oh, not the dwarves either, but give them our warmest cloaks so they're not disadvantaged."

"Why shouldn't they have the robes too? They'll feel we don't trust them?"

"You'd have trouble getting them to wear elven robes. The thing is, the robes won't hide who the dwarves are, and that may kill the illusion. The whole idea is to have a mysterious group of elven soldiers. You want to play on Gynbere and Slaslow's fears."

"What if Gynbere accuses us of theft. That would cause

problems I don't need."

"He can scarcely accuse you of stealing something he stole from our ancestors," I paused. "I doubt he'll link those you wear with those he left in The Rock. He knows the rock has fallen, and if he thinks of them at all, he'll assume they are still safe where he left them. He only used them the once, and even that terrified him."

"But he knew they were stolen from the settlement?"

"The facts were written, but most of his and his sire's information came to them by word of mouth. Partly, they learned the same story tales their underlings were taught. That's the elven story. So, whether he thinks there were more robes at the settlement, or assumes the elves support us, he will be shaken. And especially if a large section of the army approaches him wearing them. His ancestors have used the threat of the elves over the seasons. I think this Gynbere believes the stories."

Tarl nodded. "I always wanted a robe like papa's. It was special. Yes, they'll be useful. What if Gynbere does claim them?"

"Something locked in a Green Valley storehouse is scarcely abandoned. Demand payment for hundreds of seasons of use," I said. "At best, he'll claim they were found somewhere, but challenge that, and ask him which one fits him. I guarantee he never ever wore one."

"Why would he think they were elven robes if they came from The Green Valley?"

"You remember the underground area between the four big trees?"

Tarl nodded.

"If I was storing these, the bows and bolts, that's where I'd put them. Armos said it would have taken considerable force to enter that area. The doors were still intact, locked. Old Harby found the key to them under a rock at the edge of the old fireplace."

"But you can't prove Gynbere did it, Kirym."

"Who else would have? By his own admission, they were the only people in the land. Gynbere doesn't know we don't have it all spelled out in our history. His fear of the Elves is so great, his guilt will eat away at him. He won't think straight. Anyway, he has used the Elves to threaten his people for many generations, and they'll believe."

"Hmmm, yes. I always wondered if those trees are part of the settlement." Tarl frowned, as he thought about it. "But you're probably right. You always said the original buildings had been ransacked. Papa and Old Harby agreed with you. What about the armour? Almost every piece has some indication of tokens stamped or engraved in it."

"Oh, definitely ours. The third Gynbere raided the settlement when he realised we'd left. Do you remember Armos remarking on the number of storehouses we repaired when we first arrived?"

"I remember him saying it, but I never quite figured why he called them storehouses."

"Dwellings have windows and doors. The storehouses don't. Also, remember the building over by South-Hill? It had that huge underground area, too. We found seeds and very shrivelled root vegetables there. It was probably mainly used for food storage, but it was big enough to hold more, and Mekroe did find a spear and some arrows in there. It was a good place for food though, and that's why Papa was so careful in beginning the reconstruction above it. He wants it built up properly for our use. It was going to be the project for next summer. Now, I guess it'll wait until everyone has somewhere to live."

Our archers were given a choice of elf bows and bolts or their own bows and arrows, and while many stayed with the weapons they knew, some were happy to change. Tarl put them into a single group to fight together.

"My elven group," he called them.

The robes were accepted with an amount of indifference, but once the first men had put them on and realised their value, they all clamoured for them.

I had not realised how many hundreds of robes there were. Everyone was given one, and there were many more to spare.

The healers, support people and remaining guards were very grateful to have them, especially as the thicker cloaks the guards usually used were going with Tarl. Some adjustments were needed for the children who were on the wall, but the seamstresses soon had everything ready.

Throughout the day, the guards came and went from the wall, and everything worked smoothly. I spent time up there from early-afternoon until Tarl was ready to leave. Three boys and two girls joined me on the section Oak and I cared for. They were learning good skills, and all showed great potential.

Faltryn slept through most of the afternoon, and then he and Trethia stayed beside Morkeen until I returned. Oak and Trethia helped fill the water flasks in each of the dwellings while I spent time with Amethyst.

As soon as the sun sat properly on the horizon, the first sixteen men left. The initial ten led by Findlow raced up the trees opposite the eastern entrance. They were all adept at moving from one tree to another. They waited a short time for Raff to get his group into position near the stream, and then they were gone.

Little time passed before they herded six terrified men into the amphitheatre.

"Are you sure you got them all?" asked Tarl.

Raff nodded. "There were six mugs, platters and cloaks. Food for them for another seven days. It adds up." He pointed to one dwarf who had the markings of the Chestnut family. "That's Corlain, their leader."

Corlain took a deep breath. "So, kill us and get it over with. Gynbere knows you're coming."

"Where would you get the idea we want to kill you?" asked Tarl, looking as shocked as he sounded. "You have a choice. Stay here, eat and rest, or come with us. After all the arguments have been sorted, you can join us, or return to Gynbere. You'll be fed and cared for, no matter what you decide. All we'd like you to do is assure Gynbere we stuck to the agreement, and remained here until the sun sat on the horizon today; that we followed the path he set, which, if you accompany us, you'll see."

The men conferred together while Jeresaya and Harnita brought over platters of stew, flat bread and a flask for each of them.

They each took food and ate quickly, then Corlain turned to Tarl. "We'll all go with you, and we'll tell Gynbere what happened here. Rest assured, we will tell him honestly."

Raff had packed their possessions into packs, and now handed them back. "Right, let's go, men."

"Go? Now? Ya—ya can't," spluttered Corlain. "It's almost night. Ya won't see the trail."

"It's a clear night; there are stars and the track is clear. We'll make it."

Calls went out, everyone shifted into their groups, and the army moved out.

While they looked formidable, I knew many of Gynbere's fighters had been trained to kill men. Whether they would, was unknown, but it was a concerning thought.

The amphitheatre appeared empty once the army left. The children who would normally have raced around playing, took their new responsibilities as guards very seriously. Children who had seen seven full winters did shifts at various strategic places, and learned the rudiments of watching. They were eager to learn and did surprisingly well. Many had spent time on the wall with their parents over the seasons, but now, they had the responsibility.

The guards left with Bryn, were divided into seven groups. That way, he could put as many guards on the wall as usual. The men and women did two shifts to the children's one, and only the older boys and girls were used at night. It worked as smoothly as it ever had, and better than Bryn had hoped.

When the tramp of boots had faded, I helped to clean up the eating area, and stacked the remaining robes, cloaks and armour in one of the wagons. I spent some time taking water to those on the wall, and visited the patients in the healing area. During the day another man had died, but the rest were doing well.

Frentha still sat by Chonarth, as he had since he woke to find his grandson poisoned, but alive. He had scarcely slept. Chonarth had not yet woken, and I talked to the healers, before going to sit beside them.

"The healers think Chonarth will waken tomorrow. I know you want to be here until that happens, but you need your strength. Chonarth will need you to be alert then, so I'd like you to allow the healers to move you onto the set here beside him. That way you will be here, but you can also sleep. A healer will sit with him, and rouse you if anything happens, or seems likely to."

Frentha looked resigned.

"You're wondering if it will happen at all, aren't you."

He nodded guiltily. "There've been moments when I thought he would and didn't. Other times I think it'll never happen and I count his breaths, expecting each to be his last. He's the only reason I'm here and not with Churnyg and," he paused, "What's the leader's name?"

"Tarl."

"I wanted to go to search for Rintath. But the healers keep telling me I'm needed here."

I nodded. "And they're right. Tarl has tasked all his men to watch out for Rintath. If they find he has been poisoned, the healers know what to look for and what has worked for Chonarth. His recovery would be faster."

"Only if Gynbere uses the same poison."

"True, but poisoning Rintath would only work if you are there to be hurt and used. Gynbere may have allowed him to join the others. Either way, he'll be cared for when he's found. Had you gone with the army, they'd be carrying you back right now."

I watched while he was helped to lay down. His eyes closed almost immediately.

"Yes, I'm aware he needs a lot more care, Kirym," said Harnita, as she sat between them. "I'm not as good as Lantiah, but she has explained what I need to do. Jetara and I will share the watch until the boy is awake, and probably beyond. I've talked to Lorythma, and he will keep an eye on them too and help if need be."

Trethia and Faltryn played together through the evening, although not as boisterously as usual. Eventually they crawled onto the rug beside Amethyst.

I stroked Faltryn's forehead. He seemed no warmer or cooler than usual, but he looked tired. Concerned, I picked him up. He snuggled into my neck and sighed.

"I think he needs to be with the other dragons," I said.

Morkeen picked up Amethyst and she, Trethia and Oak followed.

I took Faltryn first to Iryndal, and helped him touch his token bump to hers. He did the same to Ubree, Othyn, Egrym, and bypassing Arymda, Borasyn. He returned to Arymda, touched hers and then my three tokens separately.

"It's time?"

He nodded, reached over to Trethia and licked the tip of her nose. I put him on the ground and sat beside him. He climbed onto my lap and closed his eyes.

I stroked his head and back for a while, then took him over to Arymda and snuggled him in under her wing.

Oak and Morkeen looked mystified.

"What's going on?" asked Morkeen.

"He's dead," said Trethia, matter-of-factly. She turned and walked towards the open shelter where Bryn was writing his reports.

Oak looked shocked. "Are you all right?"

"Yes." I took a breath. "The youngest dragon is never alive alone. I'm surprised he lasted this long."

"What about Trethia? That's not a normal reaction. She was so fond of him."

"She'll be all right. She's faced death many times before."

11

Arbreu

Tarl had said it would be a swift trip, but Arbreu had no inkling it would be as fast as it was. Knowing the wagons could not keep up, Tarl assigned enough men to ensure they did not need to stop.

"The squilute are capable of travelling continually for about six days," Twig said, "although they'd then need an equal time to rest up. They'd manage the journey to the tor and back with no rest if needs be. We brought extra teams in case something goes wrong. Never known it to happen, but Tarl is allowing for every possibility."

The men travelling with the wagons were not as resilient as the squilute, but there were enough there so at least half of them could sleep in the wagons at any time as they travelled.

Walf, who oversaw the wagons, organised the usual guarding system, differing only in that their guard area moved with them.

The main party went ahead. They travelled at a fast trot, and paused to rest only when they were in sight of the next group of watchers. Then a smaller group went ahead to capture them. Baketer's information was extremely accurate.

The ibith travelled with them, Tarl hoped Gynbere would agree to accept it in exchange for the hostages. The heavy platform and the thick covering had been removed, making it light enough to be carried by four men. These men wore elven cloaks, and would do so when approaching Gynbere.

Gynbere's seven guard groups on the eastern trail were easily captured. They slept once the sun set, leaving a single guard to watch. In most cases the guard was snoozing in front of the fire, although one group had two men awake; playing with long sticks in the flames.

A few astute questions showed none of them had any idea of how to organise guards. In the days since Urfit had left them, they had sat around their fires eating roasted kellich and admiring the trees. Even when they slept, the guard was there only to feed the fire.

"Anyway," Corlain told them, "Gynbere assured us that no one'd leave the amphitheatre for at least another four or five days, because you'd all be arguing about who'd be leader."

"Did Urfit not tell him that Tarl was in charge?" asked Arbreu.

Corlain looked a little embarrassed. "They all said Tarl was too young to engender confidence and loyalty."

"All?"

"Well Gynbere, Slaslow and the Urfits. No one else was asked, and only a fool would offer a different opinion."

Tarl halted them at midnight. Guards were set to watch for the rest of the night, and waken them before dawn. They would continue their guard duty until the army marched away. This was an unusual change in the guarding system,

the watch being somewhat longer than usual. Those men
could then wait to be picked up by the wagons which were
not far behind, and rest while travelling with them, if they
were too fatigued to walk.

The first group Urfit left on the northern path was captured
soon after dawn. They were quite happy to join Tarl's army,
especially when they realised they could not warn Slaslow of
the approaching army's imminent arrival at the tor. As they
had been asleep when captured, they deemed themselves
safer to claim Tarl's protection, although Arbreu felt that
if it came to a battle and Gynbere won, the men would
maintain they had been taken by overwhelming numbers,
and kept prisoner.

The third group they met in the morning were the only
ones to put up a fight. Three of the seven men seemed
determined to try to stop the whole army by themselves,
although why they thought they could win against so many,
was never discovered. Even when it was pointed out that
their job had been to watch only, they refused to back down,
stating that Gynbere didn't expect anyone for days, and they
planned to make sure Gynbere got what he wanted.

Tarl was in no mood for time consuming nonsense. He
assigned a small group to contain them and keep them
occupied or wait them out, while the rest of the men
bypassed them. After watching the first men pass them, with
calls from some about how they'd be sure to tell Gynbere
and Slaslow how diligent but ineffective they were, they
advanced on the men assigned to capture them.

These men, led by Eagle, one of Mole's nephews, simply
retreated until one of Gynbere's men rushed them. He was
surrounded and Eagle quickly disarmed him. While he was

being tied up, another three rushed them. The fight was short, and fortunately wounds were minimal. A couple of knife scratches, two black eyes, a bruised jaw and sadly, a broken arm. All of them were cared for by the healer's wagon which approached them soon after. The prisoners were given the choice of walking with their guards, or travelling in the wagon. The two who led the fight refused to walk, and found themselves tied up and stretched out on top of a load of lumpy linchim roots. By the time the sun was two hand-spans above the horizon, they all opted to join their companions and walk.

Tarl called a halt soon after midday, when one of the advance guards returned and reported hearing noises up ahead. He had not checked further, his orders had been to allow a specialised group of trackers do that, to ensure no one was spotted.

Tarl led them off the path to rest. When the trackers returned, they confirmed that the tor was quite close, and although they could not get close, they did identify Slaslow and both Urfits.

With guards set around the camp, they spent the rest of the day and night watching, keeping quiet, and ensuring their weapons were sharpened and ready.

Dawn hadn't touched the sky when they began their approach to the tor, still unsure if Gynbere was expecting them. Although they had moved with lightning speed, they were ready to face a trap of some sort. One of the men set to watch for them may have managed to warn Gynbere.

Corlain had repeated every instruction given him by Urfit and Slaslow, who seemed to believe that whoever did lead the army they would travel slowly, being disinclined to meet with Gynbere's superior army.

Slaslow believed that even if inexperienced, untried Tarl did win out over the other rivals, he would be reluctant to make decisions. More than that, most of the men would be unwilling to follow him because of his extreme youth, and the older family members of the Valley family would continue fighting for the leadership position.

Although Corlain seemed to be genuine in his belief, Tarl privately admitted to not totally accepting it. "It's quite possible Corlain and his fellow watchers have been fed information on the assumption that one or two of them may be captured. If we believe them, it could put us at a disadvantage. So, we hope he's right, but expect him not to be."

They had slept well, or as well as they could under the circumstances. As with the previous night, there had been no fires, however, this time, there were no hot meals or drinks. It was a cold clear night that promised a frost before dawn. The guard was tripled, but everyone took a turn, so no one was awake for long through the night.

Many of the men had worn their robes as they travelled, especially in the early morning and late afternoon. The men and women doing guard duty all used them, appreciating the added warmth they offered, but also knowing they were less visible in them.

In the distance, the glow of a huge fire on the tor reflected against the sky. Again, Gynbere was making the most of the ample supply of wood available outside The Rock.

12

Arbreu

They began their final advance in the grey time before dawn, wanting to approach to the tor just as the sun tipped the horizon. It was a perfect dawn; the sky was clear. There was a heavy frost, and around the tor, rising mist intermingled with smoke from Gynbere's fires.

"That'll be good," Dashlan said quietly. "Something more to help mask our approach."

"But a mixed blessing," said Arbreu. "If they can't see us, we won't see them."

The men who still wore the robes now walked with their hoods up, as much for warmth as camouflage. The rest of the men wore their normal cloaks. These were mainly dwarves, and a few of those from the desert.

They rounded the final stand of trees, swung around an outcrop of rock and fanned out to see the whole area for the first time. The sun was only just tipping the horizon when they breasted the rise to the wide area in front of the tor.

The contours of the land assisted in hiding them as they approached. The ground around the tor, being slightly higher, was more visible as the mist settled onto the lower levels where they stood, although the tor itself was still wreathed in mist.

This area was devoid of trees. The boulders Kirym had spoken of were lower than the land they stood on. They sat near the edge of the pit slightly south and east of the army. Straddling them was a massive tree stump. The thick ropey roots snaked over the rocks. It appeared to be staunchly holding them in place. The trunk, chopped down as those opposite The Rock had been, lay further south. Wide steps in the hill created a path between the boulders and a bridge that accessed the tor.

"What a horrid waste of good solid wood," murmured Arbreu. "No leaves on it; it's been down for many seasons."

"Obviously Gynbere only sees it as firewood," said Dashlan.

The ground was different to anything Arbreu had seen. It was covered with the same thick grass as elsewhere in the area, but on the ground between them and the tor were thirteen long humps, most above knee height.

"I wonder what they are," said Arbreu. "They're not natural, and to me, their being on the ground points to Gynbere's involvement."

"Perhaps they're fallen tree trunks. Trees rarely exist alone. Anyway, what leads you to Gynbere? Possibly he just found them here," said Twig.

"The big tree didn't fall," said Arbreu. "Gynbere was adamant there were no other people in the land, therefore it must have been him. These ones, well why would they all fall at once?"

"It points to some sort o' intervention," said Twig.

As they moved forward, they could see more and more of the

tor and the areas around it. Standing next to the rocks was a solitary guard. His armour was different to that worn by the other guards. His black tunic fell to his knees. His legs were armoured, and his helmet included a facemask. Everything was black from head to toe. He carried no weapons, and seemed to pay no attention to anyone or anything.

Findlow leaned over and murmured in Tarl's ear. "I'm sure that guard saw us, but he turned away."

"He can't have seen us. He'd have warned them otherwise," muttered Twig.

"Watch carefully," said Tarl, "but keep moving. The closer we can get, the better."

Arbreu tried to take in all the details of the place Gynbere had selected to make his demands. On the surface, it seemed most ill-chosen, even though it had a slight height advantage.

The flat top of the tor was bigger than Arbreu expected from the description, and the trench around it wider. While seemingly indefensible, it was accessed only by a narrow bridge, a very limited entrance that could cause problems for both sides, later.

The top of tor, where Gynbere and his guards were, was level. A clear path, a good three strides wide, ran around the edge of the tor. Just in front of the bridge, the unused area was wider.

A misshapen object rose above the heads of the sleeping guards. "Is that the pavilion? Dashlan asked quietly. "It looks nothing like it did."

"With so many guards crowded onto the tor, there's no room to erect it properly," said Tarl.

"I'm surprised they haven't used the area around the edge, though," said Dashlan.

"I guess even the biggest idiot understands the importance of being able to send messages to other areas," said Tarl.

"As I said, I'm surprised."

"Wonderfully vigilant, aren't they," murmured Jeresaya. "Almost all of them are asleep."

"They don't expect us at all," said Tarl, wonder showing in his voice.

Arbreu glanced across the width of the tor, now visible in the strengthening light. "Over there, Tarl. To the left."

Veld and the other hostages sat in a line on a wooden platform opposite the boulders. Veld was closest. The back third of the platform was balanced on the edge of the tor, the front two thirds overhung the ditch. Three poles, butted to the wall of the cliff below, helped hold the front up. It looked very flimsy. Above the hostages was a horizontal pole, held up by two vertical posts.

The hostages were wrapped in cloaks and rugs. Above each of them a looped rope, a noose, hung from the horizontal pole. The other end of them seemed to be tied around a fat log sitting on the ground behind them.

Tarl's men could easily have leapt across to the platform, but its footing was so flimsy, it would have collapsed into the gully, taking the hostages with it.

A guard stood just behind Veld. He faced the south and appeared to be taking no notice of anything happening around him. He stood out because he was dressed in the same manner as the guard by the stump on this side of the tor and like him, was not asleep.

Three sleeping guards lay on the ground beside the log. They were nestled in a small mountain of rugs.

Arbreu glanced back at the men following him. They walked in silence as instructed. The Elven Group carried their weapons openly, but most other weapons were hidden in the folds of robes and cloaks to ensure the approach was not marred by the clank and clash of weapons. The Elves were led by Teema and marched to Tarl's immediate right.

If I didn't know who was under the robes, I'd be very intimidated, Arbreu thought.

Tarl, Armos, Churnyg, Starshine, Jeresaya, Garanniis and the dwarves were not wearing robes. Loul and Tarl had agreed with Kirym, that Gynbere and Slaslow must be aware of who led these men. Corlain walked just behind Arbreu, also in his own clothes. The other guards they'd collected on the way were back with the wagons.

The men walked solidly across the open area towards the tor. Their approach had been well timed and managed, the first cries of shock and wonder as they loomed out of the mist told Arbreu that not only was their approach unexpected, but *what* approached was a shock. *Wearing the robes was a brilliant idea,* he thought.

Cries of, 'eeeee the Elves', 'the Elves have come, and 'now the Elves are agin' us too', drifted over to them. Other comments showed the suspicions Churnyg's people had about the Elves, and their reaction to the desecration of the tree, were confirmed. Many feared the Elves had come for retribution.

Once the alarm had sounded, there was a flurry of activity across the tor with guards being roused and warnings shouted. A short time later Vellysh Urfit raced up to the bridge screaming manically.

"You were told—"

He got no further. Slaslow appeared beside him and yanked him backwards so violently, he lost his footing, and hung in Slaslow's grip for a moment before regaining the ground. Slaslow spoke in a low voice for a short time. They then had an equally quiet argument.

Arbreu could hardly hear Shale as he repeated the conversation back to Tarl.

Slaslow looked over at the prisoners. "Get them ready," he screamed at the guard.

The guard in black slowly approached Enliah and took her rugs and cloak away one by one. He carefully and methodically folded each one, and placed it in a pile before moving on to Imolay, who sat next to her.

The other three guards still slept, shielded from Slaslow's view and the noise by a pile of equipment.

"You've broken your word," yelled Slaslow. "We were specific in our instructions. You accepted them. You lied to us. We warned—"

"We followed your instructions," interrupted Tarl. "I gave my word and I kept it. Urfit left guards to watch us. You can check with them if you doubt me. We've brought them along. They'll verify it." He glanced around. "Corlain, please."

Corlain stepped up, standing just in front of Arbreu.

"Eeeee, Sorr," he called, bowing deferentially. "He be telling' the truth, Sorr. Them elves, Sorr. They's brought us here on wings, Sorr. Each step they took covered more'n I could do in a mornin', Sorr."

Arbreu made a concerted effort not to appear shocked by Corlain's message or broad accent.

Slaslow was obviously not pleased with the answer he got. "I'll speak to Lord Gynbere." He turned away.

"Slaslow!" called Tarl.

Slaslow paused and turned back.

"Make it fast, or we'll take matters into our own hands. We kept our side of the agreement."

As Slaslow disappeared into the group of soldiers gathered in front of the pavilion, Arbreu nudged Corlain. "What was that about?" he asked quietly.

Corlain chuckled. "They think we're morons because we're just lowly guards. If I sound like an idiot, Slaslow is more likely to believe me. He thinks I'm too stupid to lie. You people have treated me well, even though I left with Slaslow.

He used my family to get my co-operation. Slaslow holds my sire and my son, so I needed to step carefully. My wife however, chose to keep our daughter back in your camp. Slaslow said you'd torture and starve those who stayed behind, but I saw them when I was eating, and they looked happy and contented. I'd never seen my daughter look as healthy and happy, good food was the reason. So, I made my choices as and where I could."

Arbreu nodded. "And you told Tarl?"

Corlain's broad smile gave him the answer.

Four men in elven robes carried the ibith forward and sat it at the edge of the ditch to the right of the bridge.

There were murmurs from those on the tor. Arbreu heard comments about the strength of the Elves, and that Gynbere needed twenty men to carry the ibith.

Arbreu glanced around. With the mist rising rapidly, he could now see the whole area clearly. A large group of women and children waited on the far side of the hole. They looked cold and scared. Guards stood between them to cut them off from the approaching group or, *more likely*, Arbreu thought, *to stop them running for protection.* As he watched, a guard grabbed a girl from the arms of a woman and held her over the edge of the hole.

One of Tarl's Elves immediately shot an elf bolt over to land between the guards' feet.

"If that child isn't returned to her maman instantly, my aim will change."

The guard jumped and stared at the bolt. The woman grabbed the girl back, and he quietly slunk into a nearby group of soldiers.

Arbreu recognised Sundas' voice, but he was stunned at how it reverberated around the tor. For some reason, it seemed to come from everywhere. It was quite eerie. Weird too, because he was sure Sundas hadn't trained as part of the

Elven fighters.

As the voice died, there was a flurry of movement from the pavilion. Gynbere was hoisted onto the shoulders of his guards. He looked around, saw the elf bolts aimed at him and ducked out of sight. A short time later, he pushed his way angrily through the guards to peer across at Tarl and his men. He was obviously not prepared for, or happy about the confrontation. He wore a sleep robe with chest armour over it. The shoulder catches were loose and it had slipped down his body and needed to be held up as he walked.

"You cheated," he screamed. "And you're lying. You must have left early."

"Nee, Sorr, Sorr. On ma life, Sorr," called Corlain. "I ha' counted the days proper, and they done as they was told Sorr. They truly did, Sorr."

"You've joined them," screamed Urfit.

Corlain shook his head fervently and looked affronted. "Oh no, Sorr. I is as loyal to you, Sorr, as you is to us, Sorr, as my men will tell you. We is all in wonder, Sorr, at the abilities of them there Elves, Sorr."

Slaslow, Vellysh and Zeffun joined Gynbere and they whispered together.

Arbreu glanced at the platform holding the hostages. It was closer to the stump than he had realised. Now the mist had risen, he could see to the bottom of the pit there. Although the rocks and stump appeared to sit back from the tor, sharp boulders showed in the wall and three lay at the bottom of the ditch below the platform.

He pointed them out to Jeresaya. "They don't look as if they've been down there for long. So, what caused them to fall?"

"Who, more like," said Jeresaya. "The bridge and the platform are new. Kirym didn't mention them, so I'd say Gynbere's been here a few days at least. I wonder what else he planned to do before we got here. Our position is more defensible, and he'd have trouble escaping, but I suspect he doesn't intend to leave. I want to know why he came here to make those demands."

"Kirym said he wants something," murmured Arbreu. "He thinks he has the upper hand because he has the prisoners."

"Times up, Gynbere," called Tarl.

"Now!"

Arbreu wasn't sure who shouted, but suddenly a volley of arrows arched up from the void behind the hill.

"Cover!" called Bokum.

They had rehearsed for this. The large shields slipped from under robes and were lifted to protect the front rows. More, along with smaller shields were held up to protect heads and shoulders of those further back.

Arrows thudded into the shields, although no one was hurt.

"Do that again and I—"

"Tarl!" Gynbere stepped out from behind his guards and smiled maliciously. "Young Tarl, is it? Well, well, well. The claimant. The infant leader. The pretender." There was an audible chuckle from those near Gynbere. "So now you'll listen to me. You will give me the secrets I demand, and I will hold the power in this land."

He glanced across the assembled men and elves. "Hmmm! Didn't bring your little sister? Not a mistake your sire would have made. Still, send a child to do a man's job and there'll be slipups. Well, you'll learn the lesson because this one'll cost a life."

Arbreu could hear the men behind him muttering angrily. Many had expressed concern at Tarl's decision to leave Kirym back at the amphitheatre, and almost immediately it seemed he had made a fatal mistake.

"Which one though?" Gynbere stared over at the prisoners."

"If one of them even looks as if they'll be hurt, Gynbere," said Tarl, "one hundred arrows and bolts will instantly fly in your direction. Whether they hit you or your men at the beginning matters not, because they will be followed by one hundred more and another and another, and sooner or later one will get you because we will keep firing until one does."

As Tarl spoke, the front row of elves knelt, and they and the rows of robed, hooded men behind them raised their bows.

Gynbere went pale.

"An idle threat," shouted Slaslow. "He wouldn't put our prisoners at risk."

"Really?" Tarl shrugged. "Well despite my desire not to have their deaths on my conscience, with them all dead, I rule everyone. And let's face it, I don't even know most of them."

There was a short silence culminating in a wave of laughter and comments from the men around Tarl, although Dashlan muttered angrily.

"Part of a plan, Dash," Arbreu murmured. "It's something Gynbere would say and do. He'll see himself in the statement and have doubts. Very clever, Tarl."

"Well I only hope it doesn't backfire," said Dashlan. "I wouldn't like to see my sister hurt for all I've sometimes wished she'd disappear."

"Ignore him," shouted Slaslow, although he pulled several guards over to partially block the arrows aimed at him. "He'll never do it. He'd lose his followers."

"Really?" Sundas' voice again echoed across the area. "We're all sworn to him already. He holds the shaft of power. It's all he needs."

"What in Faltryn's name is Sundas on about?" Twig asked quietly.

Arbreu followed Gynbere's bug-eyed stare back to Tarl.

Tarl held a magnificent multi shafted staff. The five legs seemed to move, each independent of the others.

The head that sat above the legs was also strange. Arbreu could see through it, and like water it seemed to flow, and occasionally disappear.

"Where did that come from?" he gasped.

"How does he make it do that?" asked Jeresaya.

Dashlan laughed quietly. "The knots and markings on the wood give the appearance of movement. From a distance, it must look alive. More disturbing than I thought."

"But what's the thing on the top?" asked Arbreu.

"I thought it was something we held," said Jeresaya, "but ours doesn't do that."

Suddenly colours erupted out of the clear head. They seemed to hover over Tarl and for a moment, looked like a dragon.

"How in Faltryn's name did that happen?" murmured Dashlan.

"It's a fake!" screamed Rargo, pushing his way through the guards to stand beside Gynbere. "I held the shaft of power for almost a season, and I gave it to you. You hold the real power."

"You rejected that shaft, Rargo," called Jeresaya. "You held such power and considered it beneath you? That would reduce it from what it was," she paused, "or it would if you'd held the right shaft. But would a shaft of that power allow a miniscule weed like you to manipulate it? I think not."

Gynbere went pale. He pushed Rargo roughly away, and stood taking deep breaths, his eyes darting along the hooded throng in front of him.

Gynbere had almost regained his composure when Tarl

held the staff high, and again a misty dragon appeared. This time it seemed to breathe smoky fire in Gynbere's direction, and they heard a strange noise.

There was a lot of movement on the tor as the guards and soldiers vied for position as far away from Gynbere and Slaslow as possible.

"I don't think it likes you, Gynbere," called Armos.

"I wouldn't like to be in Rargo's boots," said Twig. "But, is Tarl doing that, or are the dragons back?"

Before Arbreu could answer, there was a gasp from those on the tor, mirrored by Twig and Dashlan. It was only when he glanced towards Gynbere that he realised what he and many others had missed as they watched the staff.

Standing to the left of the bridge was a small robed figure.

The shaft crackled loudly, many there jumped, and all eyes glanced towards it. When they looked back, the robed figure held the sword, shield, and knife.

Kirym pushed her hood back. She was wearing a band around her head. Arbreu had seen her using it on occasion lately. Although he knew she valued it, it seemed a bit frivolous under the circumstances.

Oak, also wearing an elven robe, stepped into place beside Arbreu as Dashlan began the cheer, although he beat everyone else by only moments. Arbreu smiled as even a few of Gynbere's men joined in, before self-consciously stopping.

Gynbere was pale. "How—where did—umm." He took a deep breath. "How did she get there?"

"You saw the dragon! Who did you think it brought?" called Dashlan.

Many of Gynbere's men nodded in agreement with his statement. Gynbere glanced fearfully at the sky. He was almost white; it was obvious he did not expect this.

"The Elves, the dragons, everyone is against this, Gynbere," shouted a soldier. "Stop before it's too late, or we'll all be condemned."

Slaslow took a deep breath. "No!" he screamed. "It's a trick! It's the same as the lies they told about travelling so fast." He swung around to Gynbere and spoke very fast, gesturing at the prisoners, the tree stump and Kirym.

"He says they still have the upper hand," murmured Shale. "He thinks they should stick to the plan."

"Arbreu, help Oak protect Kirym," muttered Tarl.

As Oak and Arbreu moved to flank Kirym, Arbreu glanced at the prisoners.

The uniformed guard was still removing and folding cloaks and rugs, now up to Wind Runner. Zeffun Urfit had kicked one of the sleeping guards awake, and was gesturing angrily. As he walked away, the guard rushed over to Enliah, dragged her hands behind her and tied them. He pulled the noose down and placed it around her neck, tightened it, and moved on to Imolay Ash.

The guard who wore black glanced up, saw what was happening, and continued removing the cloaks and rugs.

Gynbere waved Slaslow away and turned back to Kirym. "Well, as you're here, you know what I want. There's a place for them over there." He pointed at the stones. "You'll see where to put them."

"Don't be hasty, Gynbere."

Arbreu was distracted. He scanned the tor, trying to see who had called. It was a woman's voice, and he had seen none over there.

A great pile of rags sitting to Gynbere's right started to move. They shivered, shook, and wobbled. Arbreu watched, as did everyone, fascinated. The rags shuddered and slowly turned. Two beady eyes stared out from the swath of tattered scraps wrapped around a wizened old woman.

She ponderously pushed her way past the guards to a place where she could see Kirym and Gynbere.

"The prophecy, Gynbere. Remember the prophecy. Formally request your heart's desire and describe each item precisely. Unless you get it right, nothing will work."

Gynbere scowled, and took a deep breath. "First I want Mellith, Tamweir, Zandaheim and Okenrock. Put them on the platform."

"Ahhhh, details, Gynbere. Details. Be more specific," croaked the old woman.

He glared at her. "The sword you carry, the knife and the shield. You'll see where to place–" He was distracted as the old woman cackled.

"Not yet explicit enough," she called, with another screech of rusty laughter.

Kirym still hadn't moved.

"First!" yelled Gynbere, clearly losing his patience. "Mellith! The Great Sword of Power." He looked over at the old woman.

Her eyes disappeared and the pile of rags seemed to shrink down to almost nothing.

The centre of one of the flat outcrops of stone had been roughly brushed clear of leaf debris, although it was still covered with thick moss, and a curtain of moss covered the wall behind. A line down the middle of the moss stood out, with a shorter line intersecting it about a quarter of the way down. There were various indents visible and in places, smaller lines showed in the moss. Kirym traced three on the right with her finger, on the wall.

Arbreu frowned when he realised she had outlined three letters.

LIN

He stared at it. "What...?"

"Don't," she interrupted quietly, glancing over at the guard, He was close enough to hear what was said, although he appeared to be concentrating on the prisoners.

"What does it mean?" Arbreu whispered.

"I don't know, but it makes no difference until this is over," she murmured, as she drew the sword from its scabbard and laid it on centre line. More than half of the blade hung over the edge; it threatened to topple off. However, Kirym pushed the pommel under a small lump in the rock to keep it steady. The cross-guard sat well below the shorter cross-line.

"Do you have to do as he says?" Oak asked quietly.

"What price would you put on Wind Runner's life? Papa's? Zelriff's? Enliah's?"

He had no answer, and she turned back to Gynbere.

"Tamweir! The Knife of Supremacy, using Zandaheim, the link from the wise ones to connect them," called Gynbere.

Kirym lay the knife on the sword. It clicked audibly as it connected.

"And Oakenrock, The Shield of Sovereignty."

Kirym sat it at an angle above the sword, leaning it against a thick ropey root, and in doing so hid the letters she had traced in the moss.

"Now place the tokens."

"No, no, no," called the old woman, suddenly visible again. "Details, Gynbere."

"One day, crone, you'll have no more knowledge, and I'll take delight in removing your head from your shoulders and you from my life."

He sighed audibly as the old lady cackled loudly.

"A green token. Green for the trees that I, as leader of these people, own," he called.

"That's not right," called the old lady, before Kirym could move. They could see her eyes again. "It doesn't symbolise those things, Gynbere."

He cursed and paused, then sighed with frustration. "The green token. Green for the Valley and people who own the land."

The old crone screeched with laughter.

Kirym unwrapped the token she pulled from her pocket and placed it on a small dark spot of moss to the right of the cross-guard.

"A blue token. Blue for the waters of the land, the waters directed by the child of the ruling family of The Green Valley." He paused as Kirym placed the blue token on a small dip beside the green.

"And the black. Black for that accursed dragon."

There was a moment of shocked silence, followed by a swell of comment.

Arbreu felt cold, wondering what Kirym would do. "Where did he get that idea?" he asked. "What'd we do?"

Kirym delved again into her pocket. "Trust the tokens," she murmured, pulling out a third wrapped package.

As the cover fell away, there was an intake of breath from those who had seen the tokens before. No one had any inkling of a black token.

"I didn't know the rainbow token could do that," Arbreu said.

"It didn't," she said sitting it on another mark just above the other tokens.

Followed by Arbreu and Oak, she climbed the steps to stand in front of the bridge. "You have what you want, Gynbere, now release our people."

Gynbere stared at the pile of rocks. "Slaslow! What happened? You said—"

"She cheated you," snarled Slaslow. "Kill them!" He

pointed at the prisoners.

The guard in black moved from checking the rope around Enliah's neck and hands, over to Imolay Ash.

"No!" A tall man in a black cloak ran forward and confronted Slaslow. "You promised you'd free them. You said there'd be no deaths."

Slaslow tried to push him aside.

He stood firm. "She gave all you asked for. Keep your word."

Gynbere and Slaslow whispered together and then Gynbere shoved Slaslow away.

He slipped on the grass, and fell to one knee. "You'll regret that!" he snarled.

But Gynbere just stared at the ground where Slaslow had fallen. Suddenly he lunged forward.

Slaslow glanced down, and snatched up something he had dropped. He stood, pointed over to Kirym. "I told you they'd cheat. She cheated you." He punched out at Gynbere, but missed.

Gynbere immediately slashed at Slaslow with his switch.

Slaslow staggered backwards out of reach, and turned towards the prisoners. "Kill them," he yelled. He rushed past the cloaked man, who caught his arm and swung him around.

"No!" screamed Black-Cloak. "You gave your word!"

Slaslow moved in close to him, his hand on his shoulder. He spoke a few words very quietly then shoved him away, and pushed past him.

Black-Cloak staggered back, lunged at Slaslow and grabbed the back of his jacket.

Brought up short, Slaslow twisted around so they were face to face and with a roar of rage, punched downwards with his fist, hitting Black-Cloak in the belly.

Black-Cloak screamed, an almost inhuman sound, and the

ground beneath him was suddenly covered with blood. He staggered back clutching his belly as Slaslow punched him again, hitting his shoulder.

Again Black-Cloak screamed. Blood oozed from his shoulder and sparkled redly in the morning sunlight.

Arbreu couldn't work out what had happened. Slaslow appeared to hold no weapon, had never held one. What had caused those inhuman screams? Where the blood had come from?

Everyone was frozen, except the guard checking the prisoner's bonds, who was now checking Storm.

Black-Cloak slowly sagged to the ground, and everything became chaotic.

Slaslow raced towards the prisoners. "Kill them," he screamed. "Now!"

Two of the three guards standing behind the prisoner's platform kicked some rocks away from the log the nooses were tied to.

Most of the ropes pulled away from the prisoners, but not Veld's.

Because his was the only rope attached, the log swerved towards Veld's end of the platform. The rest of the prisoners were already stepping back off the platform, but Veld was pulled up as the rope tightened.

The guard, who had been bent over Wind Runner's hands, raced along the shaking platform, jumped over the log and grabbed Veld's legs.

Arbreu saw the flash of something fly towards the rope holding Veld. He was sure it came from Kirym, but he was distracted as she darted across the bridge. Not towards Veld, as he thought she would, but to the cloaked man lying on the ground.

Movement in the trench below, caught Arbreu's eye.

Two of Gynbere's guards were racing towards the bridge,

and Arbreu realised they were trying to get to ropes hanging off the long log holding the left side of bridge up. If the log was pulled away, the whole structure would fall, leaving Gynbere with the prisoners and Kirym, and giving Tarl's men no way to get across.

Arbreu heard someone shout a warning about the fragility of the bridge as he shot an arrow down to land in front of the guard. His second arrow pinned the toe of the guard's boot to the ground.

The guard stopped, but his companion barrelled into him and they both fell forward. Another two arrows in front of their noses encouraged them to begin to slither backwards.

Arbreu grabbed the arm of the man beside him. "Watch them! Don't let anyone get to those ropes. Shoot them if necessary."

"I'll watch too," shouted Dashlan, wrapping something around his arm as he grabbed his bow from his shoulder.

Arbreu pushed his way through the crowd of men waiting to cross the bridge, to check it wasn't similarly booby-trapped on the far side.

It was, and already men were racing along the trench to get to the ropes. He shot an arrow into the ground ahead of them and glanced around as they paused and looked up.

The ibith stood near the edge of the trench. Arbreu fired another arrow into the trench and grabbed the man next to him. "Help me push this in," he yelled, and put his shoulder to the box.

Three other men joined him, and the ibith toppled over the edge effectively blocking those attempting to get to the ropes.

"We'll watch they don't climb over it, sir," said one of the men.

"Above all, keep them away from those ropes, said Arbreu. He turned to look at the bridge. He realised the flimsy nature of the access was part of its defence. The men couldn't run across it and only a few could use it at once.

He glanced at the battle on the far side. There was fierce fighting in the area where Gynbere had been standing, although he was nowhere in sight.

Slaslow, Vellysh and Zeffun had also disappeared.

Arbreu winced as an arrow whizzed past his right ear.

"Steady, lad. Just start shooting," came Moon's calm advice. "Shoot strategically, a lot of Gynbere's guards aren't fighting."

Abreu took in the scene as he nocked an arrow to his bow. Many of Gynbere's men were already on their knees, their hands behind their heads or in the air. However, the battle was by no means at an end.

Those fighting on the tor were at a disadvantage. Because Gynbere had packed so many men around him, there was little room to manoeuvre. Those he placed at the front fought, but were being overwhelmed, and the pockets of battle elsewhere were fast diminishing. Several men had simply jumped or been knocked away from the battle, ending their fight in the trench below.

The crowding disadvantaged Tarl's men also, for they had only a narrow path around the edge of the tor to fight in, and in many places, could only move in single file around the perimeter. Nevertheless, they were pushing into the massed men, and many had been and were being injured on both sides.

Arbreu joined others who were using their more distant view of the fight to aid those friends who were being overwhelmed. Gynbere's fiercest fighters were slowly being removed from the battle, but it wasn't all one way.

Many of his guards had cottoned on to the same ploy, and were firing into the army opposite them. They had a slight advantage. Anyone they hit was an enemy, whereas Arbreu's companions needed to be careful not to hit their own men nor those who had already surrendered.

Some of the men on the tor were not the most accurate shots, and Arbreu was delighted to note that of the arrows hitting them, few were killing shots. Loul had been adamant they kill no one unless it was deemed necessary to save lives. "They are still my people," she had said.

Arbreu was pleased when one of the hunters pulled him behind a growing wall of large shields, now being used as they were designed, slotted together to protect them. Although his vision was more limited, the barrier reduced the injuries, while allowing them to continue their fight in relative safety.

Arbreu's worries about those he loved were relieved somewhat when Mekrar hunkered down beside him.

"Mekroe sent a message, Papa's safe, but wounded. The other prisoners are fine I think. I don't know about Kirym though. She's in the thick of the battle, and she wasn't armed."

Arbreu fired six arrows while trying to concentrate on Kirym. "I think she's al..." He suddenly felt his green token drain. He felt empty.

A ragged cheer started somewhere to the right of them.

"It's pretty much over," Splinter yelled.

Mekrar turned to Arbreu, but her smile faltered when she saw his stricken face. "Kirym?"

He couldn't concentrate, couldn't figure out what had happened. "I—I don't know."

13

Kirym Speaks

I grabbed my stone knife, the only weapon I still had, from under my hood, threw it towards the rope holding Papa. Then I raced across the bridge, aware from its movement to my footfalls, that it was too flimsy to take more than two men at a time. I frantically tried to pass the message back to Teema and Arbrcu to warn Tarl and the men who would follow me.

From the vibrations on the bridge, I knew one person was behind me, Oak, I presumed.

The black-cloaked man lay just in front of me. I fell to my knees and rolled him onto his back. The smell hit me first. His belly wounds were ragged—not survivable. The weapon had been very sharp and had at least four blades. His guts, flecked with grass and dirt, were spilling out onto the ground. He would not have the nicest death. Whatever weapon Slaslow held, it would do a lot of damage to anyone fighting him.

I pushed Black-Cloak's hood back. He wore a kellich-skin mask.

I eased the mask up onto his forehead. It was already blood smeared from his stomach wound.

Now I understood the message Borboncha had tried to give me, when he dropped a reed figure wearing a similar mask. Here was the answer to the puzzle I had agonised over. The reeds had been specifically chosen, a water variety, to indicate a boatman.

"Elm!"

His embarrassed smile quickly ended in a grimace of pain.

I fumbled for my remedy pouch, but he stilled my hand.

"It can't be healed." He grasped my arm tightly. "Listen, I don't have long. I was wrong. Very wrong. I was always so angry at everyone. It coloured everything I did and thought." He panted as he talked, trying to control the pain. "Gazania wouldn't marry me. I knew she was pregnant, although she denied it. When the baby was found in Faltryn's passage, she said it was nothing to do with her or me." He gripped my hand hard, gasping, his eyes tight shut; then relaxed as the spasm passed. "So, I punished everyone. Her initially. Willow when Gazania died and you when Willow died. I tried to make it right in the end, but dealing with Gynbere and Slaslow. They have no concept of right..." He gasped again as the pain hit him.

"Small breaths. It helps." I placed a massive pinch of powder on his tongue. It would reduce his pain slightly, but I knew the amount he needed to control the pain, would stop him from talking.

He tried to smile his appreciation, but his face contorted as the agony again took over. Then it slowly became bearable.

"How did they capture you?"

He looked surprised. "Ah, so you sent someone else to

trail me, and they didn't figure it out. You would have. They didn't capture me. I went to Gynbere. I followed the path back to the top of the stream bed. Then I did what I've watched you do. I grabbed a branch of a tree, swung to another and another, and stayed hidden in the tree until the others returned to the camp. Then I followed Gynbere. I caught up just after dark. I just walked into their camp." He shook his head. "Idiots! I was almost at the pavilion before I was noticed, and then only because Slaslow walked into me. He got such a shock—bundled me inside—in case I was seen by someone else. I'd made a deal before midnight."

I nodded. "You told them Churnyg was still alive, and you gave him the carvings Salcan gave me."

"I didn't tell Gynbere everything. He assumed the dragon saved Churnyg and told you the whole story. Evidently the dragons can do that somehow." He gripped my arm. "I didn't tell him everything. He swore he just wanted the weapons, the tokens and the land. No one would die. I wouldn't have stayed otherwise. Later Gynbere said the carvings had been stolen from him. I figured he just didn't want to give them back, but I was angry. That wasn't the agreement. He accused me of stealing them. I thought it was just a ploy to keep—" Again, a spasm of pain hit him.

I was aware of the clash of swords and grunts and screams of hurt men around us. I tried to block the sounds and concentrate on what Elm was saying. I gave him powdered poppy seed, the strongest pain relief I carried with me. Too much would kill him, although he wasn't going to survive long, and eventually it might be the kindest thing to do for him.

Blood trickled from his mouth. I wiped it away with the corner of my robe.

"There's other danger though," he continued. "Rargo. He's evil. If he's to be believed, he's killed over fifteen people, and I believe him. He attacked a young lad a few days ago, simply for walking across his path. The boy only survived because the guards intervened. He'll continue unless he's stopped. But Danth is a bigger threat."

Elm suddenly gripped my shoulder and pushed me violently away from him.

I rolled across the ground bumping into the legs of someone who was fighting nearby. I glanced back at Elm.

Another black-cloaked man was astride his chest. His raised hand held a knife. Elm was struggling to hold his arm high, and was weakening fast.

I rushed at the attacker, barrelled into him and knocked him away.

I checked Elm. The attacker had sliced through the inside of his arm. His blood was pumping out.

This was a serious wound, and could kill him more quickly than the stomach wound. As loath as I was to extend his life, he had more to tell me. And I needed that information.

"That was Rargo," he said. "I proved him in a lie. He wasn't happy."

With no knife to cut material from my skirt, I wound the ties of my pocket tightly around his arm, trying to stem the blood flow.

A shadow loomed over me, Rargo's black cloak brushed my hand. I leaned over Elm, trying to protect him. I had no weapons, and could do no more.

Someone charged into Rargo, knocking him away from us.

I heard choking sounds and glanced over. Rargo lay on the ground convulsing, a knife in his chest. His green-cloaked killer sat beside him, watching him die.

The sounds of battle had moved away to the south. *That's where Papa is,* I thought. *I hope someone has given him a weapon and some armour.*

My tokens throbbed so firmly; they gave me a headache. I pulled the token holder off so I could concentrate on Elm.

He gripped my hand. "Danth. It's important. You may be able to stop him, Kirym. He wants you dead. You and everyone else, but especially you. He's too scared of you to do it himself. He's gone to get help." He pushed his hand into his cloak, and dislodged the strings I'd tied around his arm. Blood spurted over us both.

I grabbed the pocket again, trying to tighten the ties again.

His arm was slippery with blood, and they wouldn't hold firmly.

I tried again, beginning to panic. The more blood spurted out, the harder it was to keep the ties in place.

Elm took my hands. "It's better this way, Kirym. I'll die anyway. This'll be less painful. There's one good thing I've done for Willow. Wind Runner taught me to read and write. I hated her for making me, but now I'm glad she persevered. I wrote down what happened. It'll be my salute to my daughter. I loved her so much. I just couldn't," he paused and tried to take a breath. "Try and remember me for that."

He pulled the pocket away, handed it to me, and fumbled with his cloak. The flow of blood pumped strongly for a few beats, and then lessened.

I held his hand and watched. His breath was ragged, and his chest moved less often, and then his breathing died and he was still.

I closed his eyes, and as I straightened his arms, something fell from his robe. A small scroll, the outside smeared with blood, rolled towards me. This was what was so important to him. I'd make sure it got to Wind Runner.

I rubbed as much of the blood off as I could, and slipped it into my bodice. My pocket, where I would normally have put it, was too sodden with blood to use.

The battle sounds had diminished, but there was still a lot of shouting, an occasional scream; sounds of men in pain. The smell hit the back of my throat. Sweat, fear, and blood, were foremost, but the stench of Elm's belly wound overpowered everything here. Already I could hear the buzz of flies. It would get worse as the day passed. I glanced at the sun, just after midday, I thought. I had expected it to be much later.

I picked up my remedy pouch and looked around to see who needed help. Belatedly I realised my tokens were still throbbing in my hand. I slipped them back onto my forehead.

I knew something had happened to one of my token brothers, however, I had no time to concentrate on them. The dying and injured must come first. There was such a lot of chaos here, the screams, groans, moans and sobs of the badly injured, or worse, the silence of those near death. These people were my priority.

I first checked Rargo.

He was dead.

His assailant still sat with him, and I finally saw the face of the person who had just saved my life.

"Enliah!"

She didn't move, just stared stonily at Rargo. She showed no emotion. She held the knife she had used to kill him. She had taken it from his chest and now held it pointed at her the base of her throat.

"Enliah, give me the knife."

She clutched it tightly; the point pierced her skin.

I gently pulled her hand from her throat, and began to pry her fingers off the hilt. She suddenly jerked away, twisting the knife from my grip.

The blade sliced a curve from the base of my forefinger

across and below the middle of my palm, down around my wrist and along my arm.

I gasped at the pain. Blood dripped onto Enliah's hand. She saw it, dropped the knife and started rocking backwards and forwards.

I touched her forehead—she was very cold—wrapped my robe around her, and picked up the knife.

While trying to think what to do, I cut two long strips from the hem of my dress and wrapped my throbbing hand and arm up tightly.

There were others who needed my help—people who were dying. However, I suspected Enliah was a danger to herself and I didn't want to leave her alone.

I grabbed the arm of a person walking by, pleased to see Blacknight's kind face. His arm was in a sling, his eye was bruised and his cheek was swollen and raw.

Before I could ask, he nodded. "I was one of the first to catch an arrow. I twisted, fell over and that did the rest. Only good thing about it was I got to the healers before the crowd. I came to help, but I'm not very good for much.

"Can you watch Enliah, please?" I asked.

He nodded.

I briefly explained what had happened. "She just saved my life, but there are others who—"

Blacknight nodded. "Killing a person demands a price. I'll care for her. You go and see to others."

Relieved, I checked the first man I came across. It was one of Gynbere's guards; he was already dead. The next body, Grass, I thought his name was, was unconscious. He had a large lump on his head, but was breathing easily. I rolled him onto his side, grabbed a cloak from the ground, covered him and moved on. I was now aware of the cries of those hurt, the occasional scream from the healer's area, and even the calls of those still on the tor.

Someone grabbed my arm. "Help my brother, please." These men came from The Rock.

The brother had a long cut on his upper arm, and an arrow in the flesh at the top of his shoulder. He wore no armour, and sadly, the arrow had Yew markings on it.

I sprinkled powdered calendula petals on the cut and bandaged it—more strips from my dress—a difficult chore because of the wound on my hand. I was pleased the brother could help a little.

We helped him to his feet. "There's a healing area set up on the other side of the bridge. They'll cut the shaft to get the arrow out, and treat the wound. Your wound is minor. You may have to wait until they've dealt with those whose wounds are life threatening, but they will deal with it as soon as they can."

They both nodded, thanked me and together walked towards the bridge.

Someone spun me around and hugged me tightly. "Thank goodness you're all right. I thought you'd be with Bokum by now," Mekroe said.

I suddenly realised what my throbbing token had been telling me. "Is he being cared for?"

Mek nodded. "You still should see him. Now, Kirym!"

Bokum lay on the tor, just west of the bridge. His eyes were closed, his face a massive bruise.

Gynletha knelt beside him, trying to stem the blood gushing from just below his ribs. I could do nothing to help him there, she was very experienced.

I took his hand and held it to my cheek. His eyes opened. His breath was laboured, his face contorted with pain. He took a short rasping breath and squeezed my hand tightly until the spasm eased.

"Tell Zeprah I love her. Sarel and Trayum, tell them o' the silly things I did when I was young. Help them to do the same things." He looked past me. "Teema, look after Zeprah. Make sure she's happy." He closed his eyes.

Arbreu touched his cheek. "We'll take care of her and the babies until you're well enough to take over."

Bok tried to shake his head, but stopped and grimaced. His eyes opened.

I glanced down at what Gynletha was doing. His chest was covered with blood, and more was spurting out.

"I hate stab wounds," she murmured.

Pink bubbles dribbled from Bokum's mouth. I pulled the left side of his armour away, and saw the wound she couldn't heal. An arrow head still protruded from his chest, blood oozed out around it; more pink bubbles.

"What can we do?" asked Arbreu. "Pack the wound or—"

"No," I said quietly.

Bokum squeezed my hand; I kissed it, it was the only thing I could do. His breath came in ragged puffs. "We had fun, aye, Kirym."

I nodded. "Yes. The best times."

He exhaled. His eyes closed.

"He's gone," said Gynletha. "I'm so sorry." She stood. "I have to help others."

"Yes, go," I said. "I should too."

"But, Kirym!" Arbreu grabbed my hand.

"He's dead," I said gently. "Others aren't."

He nodded bleakly.

Findlow grabbed my arm. "You all need to see Tarl."

One look told me it was too late. Two strange blades had

pierced his throat, the tips of them still visible.

I knelt beside him and felt his chest. His heart had stopped. "Oh Ubree, I do need you. I wish you were here," I murmured.

Teema helped me to my feet.

"Can you see that he's—" I paused, lost for words. I shook the blank feeling away. "Find out where to take him."

Teema nodded. He, Findlow and Arbreu lifted Tarl's body to their shoulders and walked towards the healing area, knowing the dead would be placed nearby.

I glanced around. All over the hill, clusters of people gathered around prostrate bodies. "Who else needs help?" I asked, brushing away my tears.

Mekrar put her arms around me. "It's not fair. He had so much to live for."

I clung to her briefly. "I'm needed," I said.

She took a deep breath. "Yes, I'll help too."

The next man had an arrow in his leg. I grabbed a man who was passing. "Can you get a stretcher and get this man to the healers. Then come back for others." He nodded and walked to where stretchers were being stacked near the bridge.

Mekrar was already leaning over a young man; a deep wound on his leg needed bandaging. It was easier with her help, my right hand was throbbing unbearably and almost useless, although I made myself use my thumb and forefinger.

"What about your hand," Mekrar asked.

"It's minor," I said. "Like all minor cuts, it just needs time. It's annoyingly inconvenient though."

"Kirym. Mekrar. It's Veld. You both need to come now." Oak took my arm.

Mekrar pushed him away. "We'll—there are others. We need to help them."

Oak shook his head. "They'll be cared for. Veld needs you."

"Not Papa too," she sobbed.

Then Arbreu was there, his arms around her. "Come on. He's alive, but he needs to see you."

Papa had been taken to an area on the far side of the bridge. I wondered why they had moved him.

The circle of people opened as we approached.

He lay on a stretcher, and didn't seem to be in pain. A healer cleaned a cut on his leg. Although it was deep, it seemed to be an insignificant wound to deal with when there were so many others in worse need.

I remembered the healer's face, he was from Faltryn, and I struggled to remember who he was. Calendula came to mind, but I knew that wasn't right. I was angry with myself for forgetting.

Mekrar took Papa's hand, Mekroe and Arbreu knelt one on either side of her.

I knelt at his head and felt his forehead. It was cool, *too cool*, I thought.

"He fell with the platform," said the healer. "Evidently, he landed on a guard, and that probably saved his life, but he has a lot of broken bones, and for some reason, he isn't feeling any of them. He does have a sore head though."

"How did they get him out, Comfrey?" I asked, remembering his name.

"A stretcher, I think."

"And what of the guard?"

"No one told me, so he's probably fine."

I shivered as a shadow moved over the sun.

"Kirym! Look!" Oak grabbed my arm and pointed.

I looked up reluctantly, following his finger.

Above me hovered a dragon.

"Ubree! Oh, thank goodness." I stood up as he landed carefully beside the nearest wagon. "Can you help Papa?"

He was a darker green than he had been, but he still had the scar on his shoulder and the bandages on his front foot, although not his tail, which looked longer and thicker.

He put his nose briefly on Papa's chest. "I can heal you, Veld, but once I do, you will need to lie still for the rest of today and all of tomorrow, possibly longer. I will need to work on your injury two or three times, possibly more. To do it all at once would incapacitate me for too long, and I'd be unable to help others. So, once I have started, you must not move. If you do, all I do will be undone. Do you understand?"

Papa closed his eyes once, and then opened them.

"I'll make sure he does, Sir," said Comfrey.

"When the sun has set, he can drink if he wants to and then sleep. But absolutely no food until I've seen him in the morning." Ubree sank to his belly and put his nose on Papa's forehead.

Suddenly Ubree's neck, back, front left leg and both back legs twisted grotesquely. A long cut appeared on his shoulder, deep cuts and grazes on his legs. His head sank lower, oddly misshapen. He closed his eyes and lay still.

I felt his forehead, it was as cool as Papa's had been.

"What's happened?" asked Mekroe.

"Papa had broken bones in his back or neck," I said. "That was why he couldn't talk move, or feel any pain. His arm and legs were also broken, but really, they were minor by comparison. Ubree has taken Papa's major wounds, and is now trying to heal himself. He's breathing, but he's very weak. Perhaps I asked him to heal too soon after his rebirth."

"Wouldn't he have told you it was too soon?" asked Papa.

I was so relieved to hear his voice.

"How are you feeling?"

"Strange, but I'm fine. I can feel my arms, legs and feet now. I couldn't before. They feel a bit weird, I never thought I'd welcome pain. Ask one of the other dragons to help Ubree."

"They're not here, Papa. Perhaps they have other things to do with the rebirth."

Ubree's neck slowly righted itself, and he appeared to breathe easier.

I glanced around. The injured and dead were being brought across the bridge. Work was being done to widen and strengthen it, and captured soldiers were being herded to an area to the north.

I grabbed Twig as he walked past. "Are people being brought out of the chasm?"

"Just started, Mam. Those long ladders we made are doing the job. We've put them over the far side, it's not so busy there."

"Good. Are there more ladders?"

"Yes, Mam, but they're not quite long enough. Our builders are working on it."

"Would they be long enough to reach the bridge? It's slightly lower there and the climb will be quicker."

"I should have thought of that, Mam. I'll get on to it. I'll need to get that box out first, but four men and a few ropes will make short work of that."

"And Twig, are the cooks working? We'll need to feed these people. Most won't have eaten since their meal in the amphitheatre."

Twig looked shocked. "Gynbere's already eating, quite a feast I understand. His men served him, and they have plenty for themselves." He paused and shook his head. "I'll never understand the man. I'll let the cooks know, and make sure everyone is cared for." He paused. "Mam, who do I take orders from? Most of the guild heads are reluctant to make decisions. Wind Runner is with the healers. She's all right, but I don't know, in shock I think. Starshine was wounded, but not badly. Storm hit his head. He's still groggy. Findlow is busy with the injured, Tarl is—umm," he hesitated.

"I know he's dead, Twig, and Papa won't be able to do anything for a while. Ask Armos and Mekrar to take over for now."

"What about Mekroe?"

I shook my head. "He'll be tied up helping Starshine and Wind Runner. Mekrar will know what to do."

He nodded, and looked relieved.

"Um, Twig, one other thing. Check where they've taken Tarl, and recover the weapon that killed him. Treat it carefully; keep it safe. Ask the healers to cover the wound carefully. They probably won't deal with it until tomorrow, but I want it done before Mama and Zhins see him. And be careful, the blades may have poison on them."

He nodded, and I watched him walk away.

"Ubree's all right," said Oak. "In a short time, he'll be as good as ever." He wrapped a cloak around my shoulders."

Ubree was quickly on his feet, and I asked him to look at Tarl and Bokum.

"Kirym," he said gently, "I can't bring the dead back to life. I can only work on the living. Now who needs my help most?"

I guided him over to the healing area, and he set to work. Most wounds that could be quickly healed, were left until later, while he concentrated on the most damaged.

Mekrar, Armos, Churnyg and Twig were dealing with everything efficiently. The dwarves were still being brought up. That would take until well into the night, and possibly through the morning.

I re-crossed the bridge, looking for what needed to be done. Bodies and body parts were still dotted around the tor. The smell—faeces, vomit, and drying blood—was stronger now. Already there were a lot of flies, and I knew by morning, they would swarm over whatever remained. Rain would reduce the problem a little, but with a clear sky, that seemed unlikely. Carrion birds floated overhead, the few alighting to test the chance of a meal were being chased off.

A dwarf, sitting nearby seemed lost in thought. I touched his shoulder. He glanced up, his eyes were red.

"Girk! Are you hurt?"

He shook his head. "Such a waste—all those young lives. It's—it's..."

I nodded. "Your son?"

"Near death, they said."

Tell him his son is fine, asleep, and will recover fully.

I passed on Ubree's message.

Girk looked relieved. "Our boys did well. Your brother was a good leader. I heard he'd—"

"War is never good," I said quickly. "But there's lots to do. Have you eaten? There's food over by the big fire, and then you should see your son. Can you send a worker over here? I need to organise the collection of the body remains for burial, and some water-carriers to wash away the worst of the blood and debris."

He stared at me. I didn't think he comprehended, but then he wiped his hand across his eyes. "He's all right?"

I nodded. "Yes, go see him."

"If he's fine, I'll stay and help. I'll get the water containers, and a few other men to help."

"Thank you." I watched him walk away, looking much happier. I turned back to check what else needed to be done.

A few bodies lay without attention, and I wandered over to see why they'd been left. The first body I came to was a gory mess. Lifting him could not be done without a stretcher and whatever was used would need to be cleaned or burned. With nothing nearby to cover the body, I used my cloak. Although it wasn't long enough to cover more than the worst of his injuries, it was better than nothing, and discouraged the flies.

The next man was alive and comfortable. His leg was badly broken, and would need a splint before he could be moved.

He was surprisingly cheerful. "I'm fine, Mam," he said. "Others needed the help, and I said I'd wait. One o' the lads has gone to get me a rug and a hot drink. I'm just a bit cold."

I felt his forehead. He was hotter than I liked. "Ubree will come and heal your leg."

Then Ubree was at my shoulder, and took over.

I wandered on.

The next man, a dwarf, was lying as he'd fallen. I turned him over.

It was Slaslow.

I felt the bile rise into my throat and sank to my knees.

He had a deep wound between his neck and his left shoulder. His hand was around the knife—my stone knife—that caused it.

How on earth did my knife end up in you? I wondered.

He'd been trying to pull it out—a mistake, he had bled out very quickly.

I killed him.

I was shocked.

I looked to where I'd been when I threw the knife, and I tried to figure the angle from there to the rope holding Papa, and then down to here.

I killed a man.

The angles didn't make sense, but my mind kept skittering off the problem. *I killed him! I killed him!* I couldn't push the thought away. *I. Killed. Him.*

"Come away, Kirym. You shouldn't have seen that." Teema grabbed my arm and tried to pull me away.

"Stop it, Teema," I said, shaking him off. "I should see it, because I am responsible. I killed him!" Tears streamed down my face. "But, how did it happen?" I swallowed, not wanting to be sick in front of him.

"It doesn't matter. It's a problem gone. He'd have been difficult to manage even as a prisoner." Teema offered me his flask, and I took a mouthful of water, gagged and vomited.

I glanced around, wondering what Slaslow had done with the weapon he'd used against Elm. There was nothing there, and I knew I had seen nothing, even when he attacked Elm. It was a disquieting thought.

I vomited again, mainly bile, I had nothing left in my stomach. I felt stupid; I couldn't stop the tears.

"Come on, lass. Drink this." Sundas held a flask to my lips. "Careful, it has a wee bit o' skarfarhn in it."

I could smell the raw spirit, and took a small mouthful. More skarfarhn than water, but it steadied me.

"A little more," he said. "Just a few more sips."

I took another mouthful, and felt the warmth settle in my stomach. "That's enough." I pushed the flask away. "I'm so sorry."

"Ach, it hits us all." Sundas pushed the stopper into the flask. "Do y' want to go and lie down?"

"Oh, what a ridiculous idea, Sundas. No! I do not!"

I rounded on Teema. "Slaslow was not *just* a problem to be rid of. Don't ever diminish a person in that manner again. I killed him; it's a responsibility I will live with. Forever. He was a person, and he meant something to someone."

I walked away from them, but Teema followed me.

"He called the attack, Kirym. And he struck the first blow. Because of him, Tarl and Bokum—"

"Yes, Teema, I know." I sighed. "But his was also a life, and I will regret every life lost here. Always." I turned away and continued to check the injured, dead and dying.

Teema followed me for a while, but I ignored him and eventually he stopped, and watched me walk away.

The bridge was now sturdy, and ladders were being used to bring a few of the injured from the pit, and allow workers to go up and down.

I skirted groups of people helping those on the ground, and my path took me to the edge of the tor where the platform had been. I glanced down. The platform that had held the prisoners lay in a broken heap. Men were throwing the wood up, bit by bit to others on the far side. Lying across a rock to one side was a body. This was the guard who had been on the platform with the prisoners. The shield I'd placed on the stone oblong lay against him. I wondered how it got there.

"Why isn't anyone helping that guard," I called.

No one answered, although I was sure they had heard me.

The bridge was nearby, and I ran for it. As I got there, a line of lightly-laden men arrived at the bottom, and began climbing. Now I knew they were attempting to stop me.

"Clear this ladder now."

They looked uncertain.

"NOW!"

Four men who were near the top of the ladder came on and those further down reversed and stood aside allowing me access to the bottom. I ran to the guard.

"Mam, someone else will deal with this. We're just—"

"No one will go near him because of the shield, will they?"

He looked shame-faced. "We were going to bury him where he is."

"Would you have buried my shield as well?"

"I hadn't thought, Mam."

"You should have called me straight away. I'll deal with it now."

I lifted the shield away, and rolled him onto his back. He was dressed in the same uniform as the guard beside the weapons. As far as I could see, the helmet was part of the tunic he wore. I fumbled with the straps on his chest, but was frustrated by the tightness, the number of them, and my damaged hand. With no other option, I used the knife I'd taken from Enliah, to slice through them and expose his chest.

With none of the tools I would have used in the healing area, I put my ear against his chest to listen to his heart.

"Kirym!"

I glanced up.

Teema looked shocked. "I'll get someone, um a healer to look at him. You shouldn't do this."

"Everyone else is busy, Teema. Anyway, why shouldn't I? I've worked in the healing area and I know what a man's chest looks like. Would you be happy for him to die while I turned away?"

Teema's eyes narrowed.

"He tried to kill Veld. You shouldn't be the one to save—"

"We're caring for Gynbere. Why should those he ordered under the threat of death be given less attention? Anyway, if I don't work fast, he won't be alive. Get some men and a stretcher so we can lift him to the top. It's too narrow down here for Ubree to come to him."

Teema was angry. "He's dead, Kirym. Come and have a meal and I'll organise his burial—"

"He's alive!" I really wasn't sure. His skin was cold, and the bruises that covered his chest made it difficult to see the usual changes I'd expect. I thought his chest had moved, although that may just have been his body settling. What cuts he had were not bleeding, not a good sign, but there was no way of finding out at this stage, so I decided it was best to be positive.

"He is alive," I said.

"I'll help," said Oak. "What do I do?"

"I need some men here to—"

"I'll get them," Teema said sourly.

I felt the guard's neck. There may have been a slight flutter; I really wasn't sure. He was so pale and cold, I wondered if I could keep him alive until Ubree was free.

"Is Ubree still busy?" I asked.

I'll be there as soon as I am healed, came his message.

Oak started to rise. "I'll check."

"No." I grabbed his wrist. "He knows I need him and he'll be here as soon as he can." I touched the guard's skin. "He's very cold. The healers should have warmed rugs. Could you get someone to bring one?"

"Use this in the meantime." He took off his robe and handed it to me.

"It's generous of you, Oak."

"Hmphh, you've done it more than once today. Do you want help to get his helmet off?" he asked.

I shook my head. "Leave it. It's a weird uniform, not to be put on or off in a hurry. I'm hoping it supports his neck."

"Then I'll organise the rugs, and look for someone who knows him."

"No one will claim him, Oak. Not in view of his position guarding the prisoners."

Corlain and three men arrived with a stretcher. He'd chosen men from Faltryn, and I was pleased, thinking they would be less superstitious about the shield, but the stories had obviously spread and they went out of their way to avoid it and were reluctant to touch him. Corlain helped me roll him onto the stretcher.

"Take him to the tor," I said. "It's less crowded, and there'll be more room for Ubree. The less he's moved, the better. His injuries may be worse than Papa's. He fell the same distance, but I think he hit the rocks."

I picked the shield up, wishing it was already with the other weapons, and followed them.

The men struggled to manhandle the stretcher along the narrow ditch. With only one ladder, he couldn't be carried up, but there were ropes to haul up some of the larger pieces of debris. Corlain took charge there, and he tied ropes to the handles, and climbed the ladder, steadying the stretcher as it was hauled up.

Ubree hovered overhead as the stretcher was levered onto the bridge.

"Add an extra ladder here, Corlain. It'll make it easier for everyone. A couple on the other side too."

"Yes, Lady Kirym. I'll see to it straight away."

I grasped his arm. "Thank you."

Ubree was again badly affected by absorbing the injuries.

"Oak, when the guard is healed," I said, "he needs to be treated in the same way Papa was. He can't move until Ubree says it's safe, and I imagine that will be sometime after Papa. Can you make him comfortable, ensure someone is with him all the time, to tell him not to move and see if he needs anything? Leave the helmet on until Ubree agrees to it being removed."

Oak nodded. "I'll put him with the man who stood beside the rocks. They wear the same uniform."

"I'm reluctant to use a guard who would be unable to

defend himself let alone another if there was a problem."

Teema looked shocked. "Why shouldn't that guard care for him? We're caring for his friends."

"Are we?"

Teema just stared at me.

"Teema, a uniform means nothing. They may not know each other. We care for the needs of each person. No one should have responsibility thrust on them in that way."

"We shouldn't be caring for this one at all," said Teema, sourly.

I frowned. "So, what would you do, Teema? Kill him? Explain that to Ubree after has gone to such trouble to heal him. Where's Papa?"

"He was put in one of the big wagons. Comfrey and Malaaran are caring for him," said Oak.

"Good, put this man there too."

"NO! Kirym! He tried to kill—"

"Right now, Teema, he can't even move. It makes sense having him there. Comfrey and Malaaran know how to care for Papa. This man will need the same attention. Put guards outside the wagon. I want him alive and well when we get back to the amphitheatre." I turned away.

Teema grabbed my arm and swung me around. I staggered and almost fell.

"He tried to kill Veld. Put him anywhere, but there. Placed beside Veld, he may just finish the job."

"I imagine Papa will heal faster. Both will sleep. I doubt this man will even be able to move for quite a long time."

Teema was still furious.

"Add an extra guard there if you feel it necessary, Teema, but they mustn't get in the way of the healers."

"NO!" I'll do nothing to help him! Teema turned and stamped away.

"I'll make sure he's cared for, Kirym," said Mole. "I'm

between chores. I'll ask Twig and Eagle to find reliable guards, and I'll stay until they've sorted everything."

I knelt between the guard and Ubree. "You will need to remain still for quite a long time for your body to heal and settle. Otherwise you will undo everything Ubree has done. Can you do that?"

He remained silent, but his eyelids fluttered briefly.

The other guard still stood by himself beside the rocks. I had a good look at him as I placed the shield beside the sword and knife.

"Is there anything I can get you?"

He shook his head.

"I presume there's a reason you don't wish to remove your helmet yet, and I'll accept that for now. But sooner or later, you'll have to, if only to answer some of my questions. I will not allow you to die, I intend to ask someone to stand guard here. For your protection, and to help you guard the weapons and tokens. If you have an issue with the person I choose, let me know, I don't want you to be in any danger."

He inclined his head. I glanced around the tor, wondering who I could choose.

"Paluniis!" I called.

He came over and agreed when I explained what I wanted of him.

"I'll have food brought over to you, and organise someone to relieve you later."

"Ach, don't worry too much. It'll be nice to have an excuse to lean against the rocks and rest."

I wandered back over the bridge to check on Ubree and the other guard. The light was fading, and torches were being brought over to light the work still being done. The air was already icy; smoke from the fires hung low over the hill-top. Food smells mixed with the smell of burning wood and wafted over. Normally I would be hungry, but now I just felt nauseous.

Enliah still sat on the ground, rocking backwards and forwards. Sundas chatted with Blacknight who was still watching over her.

"How is she?"

Blacknight shook his head. "She hasn't responded to anything, Mam. Dashlan came to get her, but she didn't acknowledge him. He offered to bring Jeresaya, but I suggested he wait to see if you knew of something better for her."

I nodded. "Leave her for now." I turned to Sundas. "Can you get warm rugs, food and hot drinks for Paluniis and the man he's guarding? Get them anything else you think they'll need. I doubt they'll ask for anything. Rugs for Enliah too."

Sundas ran towards the bridge.

"A good man, that," said Blacknight.

"Yes, one of the best. Are you all right for a while longer? Ubree will come and help Enliah soon."

He nodded, and I walked back to Ubree. He was beginning to stir. His back had been very distorted, *broken*, I thought, *in many places, breaks in both legs and arms*. His head had been swollen and strangely twisted also. "I'm all right, Kirym. I'll be ready soon."

"Don't rush. Perhaps you'd best rest overnight, do no more until the sun rises."

"One or two need my care soon, or the damage to them will be irreparable."

Sundas arrived with a large platter laden with food and drink—enough for half of the army, it seemed.

"Mekroe and Dashlan are bringing the rugs, Kirym," he said. He left a portion of food and a flask with Oak, and took a share over to Blacknight. Then he wandered around handing food to any who were tied up with work over here. He returned finally to me.

"What would you like?"

I shook my head. "Later perhaps."

The smell of the food made me feel nauseous, so I walked to the centre of the tor. The pavilion lay on the ground having fallen when the guards moved away from it. I had studied the pavilion Gynbere had left in the amphitheatre, and this was made in the same way. Here though, the guards had held it up. I wanted to see why and began to haul the outer material aside. A huge pile of cloaks and rugs covered the ground. The interior latticework supports had not been pegged to the ground to hold it rigid. They lay stacked on the ground inside the entrance

Most of the rugs and cloaks were dull green or grey, *belonging,* I thought, *to Gynbere's people. I wonder if the offering was voluntary.*

I pulled the nearest cloaks away. Beneath was a beautiful slab of chestnut. It ensured that even without the cloaks, no ground dampness would even get near Gynbere.

Three men walked past with a boy a little older than Larqeba.

I stopped them. "Could you try to find the owners of these cloaks, and then take the wood across and stack it. Tartharn Chestnut should know the owner. Otherwise ask Churnyg Oak."

"I know most of the owners of the cloaks," said the boy. "Many of them are still in the pit. They'll be pleased to get them back, they've been cold these last few nights."

When they returned from taking the first load across the bridge, they brought four other men to help.

"Why did Gynbere take these?" I asked.

"The pad Gynbere normally used was left in the

amphitheatre," said the older man.

You're Buish Ash, aren't you?" He nodded. "Why didn't they use the latticework walls as they did before?" I asked.

"Evidently there's rock under here, and they couldn't hammer the hooks in." Buish picked up another arm-full of cloaks and walked towards the bridge.

A steady stream of people climbed from the ditch on both sides of the bridge now. A few needed help; they were being taken straight to the healers.

Ubree hauled himself to his feet. He quickly dealt with Blacknight's arm, and then walked over to Enliah.

He watched her for a few moments. "More than anything, she needs a long sleep, and that's what I'll give her now. Then take her to Jeresaya. I'll see her again when she wakens. If she needs more healing, I will handle it then, but it would be better for her to understand and accept what she did, and the sleep will allow her to sort through the emotions and put them into some perspective." He touched his nose to her shoulder, she stopped rocking, and Blacknight gathered her in his arms and disappeared into the gathering gloom.

"What's wrong with her?" asked Oak.

"She's having trouble accepting that she killed someone she'd convinced herself she loved and thought to spend the rest of her life with," I said.

"She had a lucky escape from what I've heard of Rargo," he muttered.

"Now what about you, Kirym?" Ubree asked.

"Oh, I'm fine."

There was a long silence.

"Others still need your help, see to them," I said.

Ubree stared at me intently, and I felt tears very close to the surface. I blinked hard to keep them at bay. "I don't want sympathy, and I don't want Slaslow's death diminished or hidden in the recesses of my mind. I caused his death, and I'll own it and live with it. I know he was evil, and he damaged a lot of people. Just leave it with me for now."

He continued to stare at me, but then bowed his head in acknowledgement. "Don't let it overwhelm you. Try to see it as if the situation had happened to someone else. Think about how you've admonished Enliah. Don't allow other wounds to fester." He turned away to another man who still waited for attention.

It was fully dark now, and almost everyone who had been on the tor had crossed the bridge and were gathered around the food wagons. Of those left, four men were about to cross the bridge, and Sundas and Mole still sat with the guard.

"Move him now before the night mist settles. He must be cared for at least the same time as Veld," said Ubree. "Take care with the guards though. There are those on both sides who would happily eliminate him and the guard at the rocks. Now I have one more thing for you all to do. Go and check on those you value. See that they are all right. Then eat, and sleep."

Mekroe and Arbreu came to help Sundas and Mole take the wounded guard over to the wagon he would stay in.

Others brought more ladders to sit against the bridge, and realising it would soon be teeming with people, I took the opportunity to cross.

The main activity focused on the fires where those who were eating gathered to talk about the day. Dashlan and Sundas came towards me, Sundas again carrying a massive platter of food, and a basket of flasks over his shoulder.

"Mama said to thank you for caring for Enliah," said Dashlan. "She's settled in the wagon Wind Runner will be using. Gynletha is with her. She was reluctant to leave the healing area, so this allows her to rest. She'll keep an eye on Wind Runner, so I guess they'll both watch Enliah. Now is there anything else you want me to do, Kirym?"

"You should be with your friends around the fire."

"Nah, they're just rehashing their bravery, and it's growing with each arrow fired. Pa taught us to get the work done first. People are still coming up, and the men directing them will need to be relieved soon. I'll volunteer there if there's nothing else to do."

"I could use you. Can you help Paluniis care for the guard at the rocks, and watch over the weapons?"

"What's more important? The guard or the—"

"The guard, of course," I interrupted. "But he too is caring for the weapons, and I suspect he will be most diligent in that task."

As I smoothed my blood-stiffened dress, I suddenly remembered the scroll. I needed to hand it over to Wind Runner.

I detoured first to check on Zelriff and the men who had been held captive with Papa. They were all together, gathered around Papa so he could be included. The side canopy of the wagon had been lifted, and a second wagon sat alongside, so there was room for them all. I stood just out of the circle of light and studied each one. Even from a distance, I could hear their laughter.

Most of the men appeared fine, although Old Harby looked tired. I knew he, Papa and Young Harby would have spent much of their time watching out for the others.

Armos was between the two Harby's. For the first time in days, he looked contented. Zelriff sat on the far side of Young Harby. She held his hand, and they talked quietly. I couldn't quite make out his face. He and his grandpapa would now know how Peet had died. However, they were surrounded by those who loved them and there was nothing I needed to do for any of those there.

As I watched, all except Armos and Old Harby stood, left the wagon and wandered away.

Mole climbed up and spoke to Papa. At his signal, the far canopy was lowered, and the stretcher holding the guard was levered up. Mole helped to settle it. The guard appeared to be asleep, but I noticed Armos and Old Harby glance at him occasionally. A small hand signal from Armos told Papa there was no danger.

Guards stood around the wagon. They seemed to be enjoying themselves as much as those they guarded, although they were still alert enough to watch everyone who came close.

I was turning away when I realised there was one face missing from the group. Findlow.

I glanced around the open area. He wasn't in any of the places I expected him to be.

He's guarding Enliah.

I thanked Ubree, and walked towards the wagon she was in.

Vimble and Blacknight were at the front entrance. Findlow leaned against the back, so lost in thought, I was beside him before he was aware of me.

"Tell me," I said.

He seemed surprised to see me.

"A bit tired, I think. Perhaps I should get another guard and get some sleep."

"You have too much on your mind to sleep. Perhaps sharing it will help."

He took my hand. "Ah, I was just remembering all of the good times. Travelling with Natia, finding Sundas. Holding Lyndym for the first time. All great memories. It'll all be different now."

I suddenly had a bad feeling. What hadn't I been told?

He glanced at me, and realised I had no idea.

"A spear. Natia was in the way. It was a fluke. Quick."

"I thought she was helping the healers."

His smile was strained. "She was carrying some water past where the extra weapons were stacked, and somehow one of the stacks fell. She walked into a wall of spearheads. One of them nicked her throat. Lots of blood. Gynletha said she…" He took a deep breath. "She said there was no way Natia could survive. She died almost immediately."

Tears flooded my eyes. I wiped my face on my sleeve, realising by the stiffness of the material that even that was covered with blood.

Findlow put his arm around my shoulder, hugged me and kissed the top of my head. "It's been a hard day. Lyndym knows, and she seems all right. Loul is with her. I'm glad they both stayed in the amphitheatre."

"How did Sundas take it?"

Findlow nodded slowly. "He was practical. He was told first, and came to tell me, although I knew. He gives good advice, does Sundas. Said to think later, and remember the best of times. I guess he knows. He lost his whole family. His mama met a spear as well. Coincidences huh."

We sat quietly together for a while. Then he took a deep breath, stood up and helped me to my feet.

"He's right you know. There's a lot to do, and we need to keep busy. What were you doing before you came to find me?"

It took me a few moments to remember. "Oh, I was looking for Wind Runner."

"She's still in the healing area. I'll organise a different guard for here. Then perhaps I'll join Veld and celebrate."

Wind Runner was in the healing area under duress, far

preferring to sit with the other leaders and be part of that conversation. She looked tired though; her eyes were shut.

I stood at the edge of the light, hesitant to disturb her, but as I turned away, she called to me.

"Come and sit with me, Kirym. They won't let me leave here until I've eaten, and then they want me to go to a wagon and rest. So, I'm waiting for a ridiculously large meal. Of course, by the time it arrives and I've eaten enough to satisfy them, all the fun will be over and everyone else will be asleep." She took my hand as I sat on the edge of the set. "I've heard little of what happened. So, you can fill me in. You're one of the few I can rely on who'll not treat me as if I would drop dead at the slightest hint that something distasteful has happened."

I smiled. "I'm amazed they've been able to resist you. I'm sure you've picked up most of the details."

"I know the dragon has done great work. How you got him here, well that was clever. Now tell me what he couldn't do."

"Oh, he did everything possible. I messed up a bit. I was unable to save Tarl and Bokum. I've only just heard about Natia. And I couldn't save Elm."

Her head came up, and for the first time since I'd known her, she looked shocked. "He liked fighting as little as he liked company. What made him join you?"

She must have seen something in my face. "All right, you'd best tell me. What did he do?"

"In the end, he felt great remorse. He sent his sorrow and appreciation to you. He wrote down what he did and why. He specifically thanked you for teaching him to write." I handed her the scroll. "I'm sorry about the blood. I wiped it off as soon as I could. It's dry now. I hope it hasn't affected the legibility."

She stared at the small scroll. "Such a small amount left of a sad waste of life." She shook her head. "Such a shame," she whispered.

"He did make a difference in the end. He tried to save all of you prisoners. He made a deal with Gynbere. When he realised that Gynbere and Slaslow had no honour at all, he gave his life trying to protect you all. And he saved my life too. By doing that he died quicker, and although he wouldn't normally have survived with the injuries he received, Ubree may have been able to help him. I just couldn't keep him alive until Ubree got here."

"I'm sure you did your best for him, Kirym. I suspect he was happy for his life to end. He was one of those people who was always consumed by his regrets. I imagine this will be depressing reading." She stared at the scroll. "I'll need a lamp."

"Wait until you get back to the amphitheatre, or even The Green Valley, Wind Runner. I doubt there's anything in there that's of much importance for now. Get your family settled, and then read what he had to say."

"But his body will be recognised when they bury the dead," she said. "I've never been at a loss for words at a burial, but my mind is blank when I think about him. What do I say that won't cause anger and resentment?"

"Tell of his delight and expertise with the boats. His love of Willow. Of his sacrifice when Rargo tried to kill me."

"They'll question why he was there."

"And if you say nothing, they'll assume there was a plan they weren't told of. If anyone asks directly, tell them he died saving lives."

She nodded wistfully. "You have a great deal of wisdom, Kirym. Yes, there are some stories that don't need to be told until later."

"Or perhaps ever," I murmured.

Sundas sat a platter of food in front of Wind Runner.

"Will you allow us to have a few bites of your meal, Sundas?" I asked.

"Oh, it's all for Wind Runner."

My laughter sounded brittle. "That could feed ten hungry men. She'd explode if she ate even a quarter of it."

He sat beside Wind Runner. "Aye well, perhaps I was a little generous when I dished it. I'll join you, as long as you eat too, Kirym."

The thought of eating turned my stomach. "I'm more thirsty than hungry. I'll get a drink and I need to see that Ubree is all right."

Sundas took a breath to object, but Wind Runner placed her hand on his arm. "Yes, the dragon needs to be cared for, Kirym. Come back and talk to me later."

Ubree lay at the edge of the healing area. His eyes were closed, but I knew he was aware of everything that was happening around us.

"What decisions have been made?" I asked.

"Veld wishes to return to the amphitheatre before anyone talks about what happened here. Veld doesn't want to tell it twice, here and there. That would be too hard."

"There will be arguments against that. Can you help it happen?"

"We've already discussed it, and it will happen as he wishes. Right now, I need to rest."

"I'll organise a guard so you can sleep," I said.

"No one has any present desire to hurt me. Sit with me and talk to those who have questions to ask."

14

Kirym Speaks

I was pleased to sit, lean against Ubree's warm body and rest. I closed my eyes, not eager for anyone to approach me. I was exhausted, but knew I'd not be able to sleep.

"I know you're awake, Kirym."

I looked up. "Come and sit, Arbreu. I'm trying to avoid making decisions that can be made by others. How's Mekrar?"

"She's fine. She's with Veld, making sure he isn't overtaxed. She wanted to tell him about the joining when there are fewer people around. I think she wishes we'd waited."

"She doesn't. Papa already knew and approved. She's close to him and he reads her tokens well. But it'll do her good to be with him."

"How did you get here, Kirym? I thought Tarl told you to remain at the amphitheatre. Did I hear that wrong?"

"No, that's what Tarl wanted everyone to believe. We felt that no one should expect the weapons and tokens to solve the problems we faced. We also thought that anyone passing on messages to Gynbere or Slaslow would have nothing to pass on. I didn't think anyone would do that, but Gynbere could see I wasn't there."

"Where's Faltryn and Trethia? I haven't seen them."

"Trethia agreed to stay with Mama, otherwise I would've brought her. Faltryn died the morning after you left."

He looked mystified. "When did you leave? You—my goodness, I thought we did it fast."

"I left soon after Faltryn died. We took a shortcut. The path through the marsh. Vimble and Oak came with me. We spotted your camp when the moon was a hand-span from setting."

Arbreu looked horrified. "But we promised Urfit we'd not take shortcuts. What if they find out?"

"Tarl did what he promised and followed the path. Once he'd left the amphitheatre, well I was free to do what I liked."

"What if the marsh path was—?"

"I'd have had to take the longer path," I interrupted. "Mama and I discussed it with Tarl, and he had a few plans."

"But how did he know which plan to use?"

"He wouldn't rely on something that involved me unless he had word I was there. Vimble got a message to Churnyg just before you began your final march here."

"Why did you choose Vimble?"

I giggled. "He's quick. He shoots accurately, and he's great at climbing all sorts of things, large rocks, trees, anything really. We knew he wouldn't be missed as some of the other more obvious choices would have been."

"And no one knew."

"Mmmm, only Mama, Tarl, Armos, Churnyg, Sundas, Vimble, Oak. Oh, and me."

"So almost everyone. But not Teema, Bokum and me."

"And that was necessary. You and Teema in particular, were both so annoyed with Tarl for leaving me behind, no one thought there was any subterfuge at all. We had to keep it that way. You would both have been too complacent had you known. I did as Tarl wished. He was war-lord, and he did an excellent job."

Arbreu looked thoughtful. "I wish I could apologise to him. Both Teema and I said some nasty things. I should have trusted you both. What about that thing he held? That was just weird. Why did Rargo think it was fake?"

"You really need to talk to your parents and Dashlan about it. It belongs to your family."

"Oh, really? Ah, the head thing. I vaguely remember it, but it sat in the corner next to the fire-mantle. I always thought it was just an ornament. But it sat on a different pole, didn't it?"

I smiled and shrugged. "Perhaps the head wasn't needed so much when you were young, or maybe they used it more when you were off exploring. I can tell you this much. When Rargo stole the original staff, all he got was a tree branch. Dashlan found the replacement when he was helping to save the dwarflings. He remembered the trouble Larqeba had holding the staff when he was little. He thought the multiple legs would allow it to stand alone, with just a hand on it. He got me to help him because I already knew about the head. The dragon hadn't been seen before, it seems it appears when the sun shines through it. Prior to this, the head had only been used in dappled light or at night. The mist was a bonus."

"Wow, I can't wait to tell people about it."

"Be circumspect. It's a family secret, and Bryn should be the one to tell, if he decides to share."

He nodded. "Sometimes I feel I'm not part of them anymore. I usually don't mind, but every so often..." His voice drifted away.

"It's up to you, you know. If you involve yourself in their lives, they'll be more than happy to include you. They don't want you to feel they are pulling you back to them, or away from somewhere else you'd prefer to be. They remember making that mistake the evening you found each other."

"I don't want to take Dashlan's position. He's been the eldest for ages, and it seems unfair to take that off him. And now there's Mekrar to consider."

I took his hand. "Talk to Dashlan. You may be surprised at what he sees for the family future. He'd love to have an older brother he can share with. Arb, you're at a stage in life when you'd be moving on anyway. Joining does that. But you can be part of two families or more. Most people are. Mekrar loves your family—all of them. Be yourself and allow it to happen. Now go and see Mekrar and let Papa say what he needs to. Then go and talk to Jeresaya and Dashlan. They'd be happy to tell you about the staff. Dashlan is very proud of his ideas."

15

Kirym Speaks

"Why are you so restless, Kirym?"

"Are you delving into my head now, Ubree?" I asked.

"Hmmm!" He was amused. "I have no need to do that. Your breathing hasn't slowed as it would, had you fallen asleep. You also use that as a diagnosis tool."

I silently acknowledged his argument. "I was just thinking about how wrong this place is."

"Wrong? In what way?"

"The tor, this hill. It's not natural. Gynbere had problems erecting his pavilion."

"And that's significant?"

"Gynbere said the tor was a huge rock, but the walls aren't made of rock. As for the ditch, well although there is a lot in nature that has amazed me over the seasons, it seems to me there would be growth on the walls, and debris layering the bottom. And yet the corners between the floor and the walls of the tor are sharp and crisp."

"There are things here that mystify me as well. If I don't concentrate on the tor, I forget it's even there. Every time I see it, it's as if I'm seeing it anew. That can't be because of Faltryn, because I understand he has died. So, something or someone else is blocking or altering my memory. Whoever or whatever is doing it, is powerful."

"Could that be what woke you up?"

"I don't know. Before now, we have always been woken by an older sibling, and yet I can't identify any dragon flying the land."

"If the ditch has been created, what happened to the dirt that came from it? This hill isn't natural either."

"You could be right. So, I will think about how to deal with that presently. Now tell me about the tor itself. If not a rock, then it could be that the soil is so dry and compacted—"

"If that was the case, the grass would show stress. The grass on the tor is different from this springy stuff that's almost everywhere else. On the tor, it's similar to the grass we have around the dwellings, but over time, that grass gets taller. Here it hasn't. Something has changed here, and the tor is the place to start."

Lights suddenly lit up in the healer's area, and Ubree was gone.

We'll discuss it later, came his message.

16

Arbreu

Sundas, Paluniis, Findlow and Dashlan shared the job of watching the guard and the weapons. Arbreu joined them when he could.

The guard continued to stand, even when encouraged to sit or sleep. He neither ate nor drank, even though Sundas brought meals over.

Just after midnight on the second night there, Arbreu woke with a start, aware of a shadowy figure beside the weapons. He glanced around.

Dashlan was asleep next to him; Findlow beside Dash. The others seemed to have disappeared. He slowly got to his feet, and reached for his knife.

"You won't need that, Arbreu."

"Kirym. Whew, I couldn't see who it was. Where are the others?"

"I sent them off to wash and eat."

"What is the point of you having guards here, if you send

them all away?"

"Silly. The guard is still here, so are you, and see," she said, "now you've woken Findlow and Dashlan."

"What are you doing?"

A narrow beam from a hooded lamp shone onto the rock. "I wanted to look under the moss, but I didn't want anyone to be aware of my doing it. So, the best time is when people are asleep."

"Hmm, you have been busy," said Findlow. "But what does—oh my goodness." He stared at the rock. "This is done by an expert. I couldn't be so precise with a chisel on rock. Those lines are perfect."

He moved aside so Arbreu could see.

The line where Kirym had lain the sword, was etched deep into the centre of the rock. The shorter line crossed it at about a quarter of the way down, and another longer line was carved above it.

On the rock behind it, a scroll was engraved into the rock. It contained the words,

THE BURL OF MEGLINOR

PRESENTED

TO

THE PEOPLE OF THE GREEN VALLEY

WITH DEEP APPRECIATION

FOR YOUR ASSISTANCE

IN BRINGING PEACE

TO OUR WORLD

Underneath was a curved line that turned up at each end. Three holes sat to the right. The top one was round, the next a small slot, the third a wider slot.

"It's fine work. Well except for the holes there. I would have done them all the same size. It spoils the whole effect," said Findlow.

Dashlan nodded. "Maybe they were already in the rock

before the rest of it was done. What do you think, Kirym?"

"The Burl of Meglinor was mentioned in the qwanchel," said Kirym quietly.

"So, what is it?" asked Arbreu.

"I have no idea, but I suspect the answer is here somewhere. As soon as the burials are over, I'm coming back to find out."

They woke to a frost and heavy clouds, although the threatening rain held off. People huddled around fires, and the cooks were worked hard to provide enough warm, hearty food. The day passed in a flurry of organisation.

Scribes noted names and details and cross-checked family connections to see if anyone was missing. Of course, no one could be totally sure until they returned to the amphitheatre and studied the lists there.

The bodies were prepared for burial and placed on a wagon base ready to be transported back to the amphitheatre. Everyone was grateful for the cold winter day; the bodies would be welcomed by the ground before decomposition set in.

Ubree was kept busy with the injured, and he slowly emptied the healing area. He spent time with Veld and the guard, helping them heal faster. Even so, they were forbidden to move until at least the morning of the second day after the battle. Despite that, Veld decided they would begin their journey home before dawn on that day. A few of the other leaders objected, suggesting that an extra day or two would make little difference to most, and would give the injured time to rest after recovery.

Veld was adamant. "It's unfair on the families back at the amphitheatre to wait longer. Most don't know what has happened to their loved ones. Although those from The Green Valley can tell them the battle is over, most won't believe their loved ones survived until they see them."

Kirym seemed to be in a daze. She did what was needed, but without her normal spirit. Arbreu didn't see her eat or sleep, but assumed she must have.

She avoided people where she could.

Arbreu wasn't sure who to approach about her, everyone else was dealing with the dead of their families, and mending breaches where possible.

The only time Arbreu saw Kirym sounding anything like her usual self, was when they found a lad called Rintath.

He had been twice thwarted trying to slip past the guards. When questioned, he didn't answer and was sent back into the camp. When he was caught the third time, there were raised voices, and Arbreu took charge of the boy, taking him to Kirym because he had no other answer.

She instantly knew who he was, and gave him a message from his grandsire. Quick questioning showed that Gynbere had given him nothing even remotely poisonous. Once he knew his grandsire and brother were alive, he settled happily in the healing area where he could be fed and cared for until they all returned to the amphitheatre.

17

Teema Speaks

I dreamed.

The night was dark. There was no moon, although there also seemed to be no stars nor clouds. The usual night sounds were absent.

I followed a path through a misty marsh. Although I was surrounded by water, I stood on firm ground, and followed the man in front of me, but I remember no details of him. If he turned to see who was following him, I didn't note it, and I likewise did not check to see who was behind me. As attuned as I am to checking these details as I travel, in this dream, I didn't.

I remember seeing Kirym astride a massive dragon. I couldn't figure out which one she rode, but wondered if they were alive, or had they just joined me in this asleep-awake dream.

The dragons seemed to be everywhere, leading the line of people, lending a shoulder to push a wagon out of a boggy hole, or thwarting an attempt of a group of men to leave the line of travellers and disappear into the mist behind us or the marshes around us. Kirym was with each of them, guiding and chiding as the need arose.

At what I assumed to be midnight, although the moon hadn't risen to tell how long after sundown it was, I heard a hair-raising snarl, and turned to see a dragon, scales erect and eyes narrowed in anger. A group of men, Gynbere being one of them, were wading back towards the path, although one, held by the dragon's left rear claws was still in deep muddy water. His eyes showed fear, and he held tight to the dragon's foot. Once the others were safe, the dragon lifted the man from the marsh, and deposited him mud-covered and shaking, onto the path beside his friends. The squelch as the mud released him sounded over-loud in the dark silent night.

The dragon laughed, and I started awake as the dream of it echoed through my head.

I lay on grass, wrapped in my cloak, still bone weary, and I wondered how long the journey home would really take.

Oak nudged my shoulder and handed me a warm flask. "Drink up and we'll get going. That was the weirdest night, wasn't it? I'm assuming the dragons did it." He noted my confused expression. "Did you not realise? Last night we were brought to within a short walk of the amphitheatre. We'll be there before midmorning. My stars, what an amazing journey. I can't wait to see what else the dragons can do."

I smiled. "I thought it was a dream. It felt unreal. I've had a dragon induced sleep before—twice actually—although the second one wasn't really a sleep. They were both just as weird, and different from last night. How many dragons did you see?"

"Oh." He frowned. "You know, I'm not sure. Only ever one at a time. Kirym will know who did what, though. She's still asleep, but with everyone stirring, I guess it won't be long. I feel as if I've slept the whole night."

"Strange, I don't! Maybe I've had other things on my mind."

No one seemed particularly stunned to find themselves on the path towards the north-western entrance to the amphitheatre. I was surprised at how they just accepted it.

"Why the frown, my friend?" Oak asked.

I shook my head. "I feel a little out of step with everyone. I mean, they accept where we are. They don't question how we got here. I'd have expected to be approaching the east entrance, not this one. You're happy with it, but I'm—." I shrugged.

"I did the trip the other way, remember, so I recognised the path. My only real fear was getting stuck in the mire and having to be hauled out by a dragon."

He paused and stared intently into my face. "You should talk to Kirym or Arbreu."

"Kirym's too busy, and Arbreu's tied up with Mekrar." I thought Oak would laugh at me, but he didn't.

"Y'know, Arbreu felt much the same as you for a while, but Kirym helped him. She has time for everyone, and particularly those she loves. Arbreu may be married, but he's still your brother. He always will be."

Dashlan raced up to us. "You two are wanted up at the front. Veld wants the families of the fallen warriors to enter first."

"But I'm not—" I began, but Dashlan had already run off.

"You are related, Teema. Through Kirym," said Oak. He took my arm and firmly propelled me forwards. "She's your token sister, and that makes Tarl your brother too. Your relationship to Bokum is the same as hers. Zeprah will need your support. Other than her children, who is there for her? Come on, you've more right to be there than I have. Bingas is related because my aunt married his uncle. The more support they get, the better. Anyway, Loul has been your mama since you could walk. She'll need you too."

He ignored my bleats of protest, and soon, I was in a large group—much bigger than I'd anticipated, walking towards the entrance.

We were met by Bryn and a token group of guards, three men, Larqeba and Shormel.

Veld's formal request to enter was accepted, and he walked in as Voice and Warlord of The Green Valley. Bryn clasped his shoulder as he passed, and then we caught a glimpse of the families waiting for us.

Loul stood at the head of the group. Somehow messages had been sent, and all of those who had lost loved ones stood with her.

I realised with some regret that I didn't know many of those who died. Loul would, and I strongly suspected Kirym did too. Every family was approached by someone from the group. Veld of course went straight to Zhins and Loul, Kirym approached a dwarven family I didn't know. I wondered what she'd say to people who were strangers.

I was part of a second line, and was beginning to panic when Oak suddenly leaned in front of me and began to talk to Dashlan, who stood on my left.

"Would you mind, Teema," he said, and changed places with me to have a quieter conversation.

I was a little annoyed, it seemed the wrong time to be chatting about inane things, although my irritation lasted only moments. Then I realised what he'd done. I now stood behind Raff, who was talking quietly to Zeprah. He stepped aside, and I was face to face with her, and for the first time in her presence, I was at a loss for words.

She seemed to know and understand, because she put her arms around my neck and hugged me. "Oh, Teema. I am so very sorry."

"No, no, no," I murmured. "Your loss. I'm only sorry I didn't protect him better—" My comment suddenly seemed trite and inadequate. All I could think of was to hug her as our tears mingled. I felt small arms around my legs and looked down. Sarel's face was pressed into Zeprah's skirt.

I bent down and picked her up. "Where's Trayum?"

"Morkeen kept the little ones with her, so I could," she shrugged. "Sarel was there too. I should take her back."

"No, keep her here with you. I'll go and tell Morkeen. Then I'll come back and help." I was pleased at the excuse to not make more comments that, even to my ear, sounded tired and insincere.

Zeprah nodded blindly, and turned to the person behind me in the line.

I suddenly realised I hadn't spoken to Loul, Lyndym or Zhins. I glanced back, torn between the chore I'd volunteered for and the obligations I had to them. Sundas was talking to Zeprah and Larqeba had distracted Sarel. Everyone was supported by someone. I wondered how they could all do it so easily.

18

Kirym Speaks

The time spent talking to the families of those dead was initially difficult for many. My guilt at not having managed to save more lives was not quite so overriding now, although I knew I would feel the pain of it for the rest of my life.

Eventually I was able to approach Zhins. I wondered what to say, but she turned her back on me when she saw me move towards her. I was trying to decide what to do about it when Mama stepped in between us and hugged me.

"She will get over it, you know. She hasn't thought beyond her personal loss, not even as far as the children. Sometimes it takes a little longer."

"I wish I could have done more for Tarl, Mama. And I didn't even know about Natia. You've lost your sister as well as—"

"No more than you. Less in fact, because you lost Bokum as well. As I understand it, more would have died had you not been there." She paused. "I notice you haven't been to see the dragons."

"They're still dead. I have no need to see what I already know, Mama. I really knew it at the tor. I don't know what to do for them."

"Then perhaps as you care for yourself, Trethia and Ubree may be able to help you work out how to waken them."

The burials took place just before midday. Again, the different family traditions melded together well. The overwhelming feeling was that it could have been a whole lot worse. Over and over, Ubree was hailed as the hero, as indeed he should be.

While watching the shroud-wrapped bodies of Tarl, Natia and Bokum, being lowered into the ground, I felt as though my world had ended. Everything around me seemed black. I thought back to Halse' burial so many seasons earlier. Now Peet, Bokum, Natia and so many others gone long before their time, the deaths caused by the needless megalomania of fools. I hadn't been able to stop the killing, and I felt very bitter about it.

During the ceremonies, I realised I had a headache, and the throbbing in my hand increased. As soon as I was able, I asked Oak to care for Trethia for a short time, and found a quiet spot outside the amphitheatre to clean and re-bandage the wound.

The powders I'd sprinkled on the cut hadn't worked as well as I'd hoped, and signs of poison showed on my arm. The cut still bled; the bandages were badly soiled. I added more powders to the cut, and rebandaged it. The bandage was awkward to tie one-handed. I managed, and pulled the sleeve of my dress down over my hands, pleased for the style that allowed for this. That, and the fact that this dress was a little too big for me, meant the sleeve successfully hid the dressing. I mixed several powders in water, and drank it, knowing they would work better had they had time to steep. I prepared another dose and wrapped them in a spill of parchment ready to use when I the opportunity arose. I buried the soiled bandages and walked back into the amphitheatre.

On the way past the cooking area, I asked for a flask of hot water, and quietly added the powders. I would let it steep and sip it through the afternoon.

I then resolved to put the annoyance of the wound out of my mind and carry on with the necessary tasks. What I couldn't do with my right hand, would need to be done with my left. However, the relief I felt at having made that decision was negated by my excessive fatigue.

I was accosted by Larqeba and Shormel as I walked away from the cooking area.

"Veld asked us to get everyone over near the table," panted Larqeba, having raced over from the healing area. "He wants to hear about the things that have happened, and the things we found out while he was away."

"Although we told him most of it just after the burials," interrupted Shormel.

Larqeba looked at him as if he was a child. "He'll be wanting to tell everyone who was with him. They need to know too."

"So why does he need to have everyone else there?" demanded Shormel.

"I'm sure there will be other things to explain as well," I said. "Did you think Sirasha told everything he'd found out?"

Larqeba's eyes widened. "There's even more? Wow, can we tell people?"

"Perhaps you'd best wait until the headmen make that decision."

"We've saved you a seat near the dragons," said Larqeba grabbing my hand to pull me along.

As my arm straightened, I fell to my knees, clutching my arm to my body, and gasping at the pain.

"Are you all right?" asked Larqeba.

"Oh yes," I said, breathing deeply to gain control. "I tripped on the hem of my dress. It's a bit long."

"Mama will sew it up for you," said Shormel.

"No need, I'll change into something else later."

I gingerly got to my feet, and walked over to where Oak and Trethia were waiting with Morkeen and Amethyst.

Morkeen frowned, but then handed Amethyst to me. I carefully took her. I had more trouble holding her than usual, and didn't want to lie her on the ground. It was still a little damp.

"Did it rain recently?" I asked.

"No," said Morkeen. "There was a heavy dew last night though. Kirym, can I do anything to help—"

"No, no. I might have twisted my arm when I slipped over. It'll come right."

I took my cloak off, and lay Amethyst on it. She promptly rolled onto her tummy and started to pull herself towards me.

"Why is no one talking about the scrolls and book, Kirym." asked Teema, as he and Zeprah joined us. "Is Ubree behind that?"

I shrugged. "Ubree and Mama haven't told me their decisions."

He raised an eyebrow. "I thought they told you everything?"

"Who? Mama or Ubree?"

"Well, Ubree."

I laughed. "Ubree talks to Mama, because he's answerable to her as Headwoman of the land."

"Well it isn't normal human nature, so I think Ubree must be behind it," said Oak. "Twig mentioned that when we came to the amphitheatre, Gynbere and many of his men chose to enter last. There were no guards behind them, but they didn't try to escape. It would have been the ideal time."

"Or perhaps," I said, "they still hope to find whatever it is they're looking for."

"What happened to those two guards?" asked Mekroe, as he and Starshine joined us. "The ones all in black."

"I didn't see them through the night," said Teema. "People were complaining about them, Kirym. People on both sides. Gynbere says they caused the battle. I think he's right. They should be accountable for their actions."

"Really, Teema? I'm sure Mama will find out who did what, before arbitrarily condemning someone to death," I said.

"Well, maybe someone already has. I haven't seen them at all."

"They travelled in the wagons with Wind Runner, Mek," interrupted Oak. "They're still in there."

"What!" Teema looked shocked. "Veld travelled in that wagon. No wonder people complained. I wonder who decided to put them all together."

"I imagine Veld and Wind Runner did. Wind Runner was waspish about any complaints she heard. Even without Veld, she'd have kept them safe." Oak picked up an empty platter. "I'm getting something to nibble on. Anyone else?"

Mama and Papa were joined by Bryn, Garanniis, and Findlow at the table in the centre of the amphitheatre.

They would make up the inquiry panel, although Mama made it clear that everyone who wanted or needed to be heard, would be, including any guards on the wall.

There were four empty seats along the table, and Oak asked me about them.

"The seat next to Mama is for Wind Runner, who is supposed to be resting. Tartharn Chestnut will represent the dwarves. The two others I don't know."

The wagon Papa and Wind Runner had travelled in sat near the table. Seven guards stood around, not obviously guarding it, but certainly, to my eyes, more alert than I would have expected had they been relaxing there.

The back entrance of the wagon opened, and Wind Runner appeared on the top step. Immediately one of the guards was there to hand her down, an action she accepted with barely hidden exasperation.

Findlow walked over and shooed the guard away. He escorted her to her seat, talking quietly as he did. She leaned towards him to hear, and in doing so, took his arm.

"Oh, very clever, Findlow," breathed Oak. "I must remember that."

The noise around the open area diminished when Mama stood.

"I demand that I be allowed to speak," yelled Gynbere, as he jumped to his feet. "I was prepared to discuss peace between our people until my men were attacked and murdered. I demand satisfaction, although with your panel as one sided as it is, I'm doubting I'll be allowed to even speak."

Papa stood. "Sit down! You will be heard, but at the proper time. The panel is made up of many family heads, and is open for two more people. I will allow you to choose one of them. As you have lodged a formal complaint to the panel already, you cannot be that person."

Gynbere looked surprised, but then smirked. "I choose Vellysh Urfit."

"Why him, Kirym?" Oak asked, as Gynbere and Vellysh started a frantic whispered conversation.

"It would have been him or his brother. Both have reason to hate us," I said.

"Gynbere!" Garanniis called. "Perhaps you should choose someone else. Vellysh seems so reluctant to join us."

Vellysh jumped up and almost ran to accept his seat, leaving Gynbere's whispered instructions unfinished.

Teema was incensed. "How will that help the inquiry, Kirym? Gynbere has just told him what to do."

"The truth can't hurt and it's only an inquiry panel. They'll listen to Gynbere along with everyone else."

"His version maybe. He'll want payment of some sort. I have a bad feeling about this."

"Vellysh is only one person on the panel. They all have an opinion, and they will listen to everyone before making decisions."

"Sirasha Beech. I'd like you to join us," said Mama. "It's good to have an uneven number of people on panels such as this. Your ability to notate what is said is renown, and your memory for detail is legendary."

Sirasha stood. "Lady Loul, it would be easier for me to sit with my sons and grandsons, recording what is said and done here today. We do have a system, and it's easier if we do it as is usual for us. I would suggest my seat go to another, perhaps a member of Gynbere's family." As he cleared his throat, I glanced at Gynbere noting his smug look of satisfaction. "I would suggest you ask Kwarnar Yew. I'm sure he would accept."

"Who is he, Kirym?" Oak asked.

I smiled. "Not Gynbere's choice by a long shot, but he can hardly complain. It's his youngest brother."

Arbreu frowned, and then grinned as he remembered learning of the first Kwarnar noted in the discovery of the qwanchel. "Does this man follow his brother or take after his ancestor?"

"He chose to teach Salcan the secret of the white pottery," I said. "He was most upset that Gynbere had hounded him from The Rock, and very distressed to hear he had died. He may feel a little bitter towards Gynbere for that, but from what I know of the man, he wouldn't allow that to influence him against his brother, or anyone else. He's a very good choice."

I stopped speaking as Gynbere again jumped to his feet. "I demand again to be heard. A few days ago, there was a foul murder, and I want the culprit punished. I demand their death for this unprovoked attack on one of my treasured, people. A gentle man who worked tirelessly to bring about a peaceful resolution for my people." He stamped up to the table and as he arrived there, brought something out of his robe and stabbed it into the table.

Embedded in the wood was a slim sliver of stone.

My shard knife.

"This was handed to me on the night of the murder. It was removed from the body of my loyal companion, Slaslow, by someone who felt the killing should not be overlooked. A life should pay for this"

"So, someone loyal to Gynbere is still free," Teema said.

"Many, I imagine," I said. "But that isn't the problem here. It is my knife and it was in Slaslow's neck, I saw it myself. Gynbere wants an answer, which he deserves. Personally, I'd like to know how it happened too."

"But he wants you dead, Kirym. He's trying to have you killed! What will you do?"

"Tell the truth."

Vellysh jumped to his feet and cleared his throat. "I think this should be considered first. I believe this incident began a battle that would never have otherwise happened."

"Wait just a moment!" Oak was on his feet, his face black with anger. "You declare war on us, and complain when one of yours gets hurt! The responsibility is yours not ours."

"Slaslow was the first person to be attacked. Killed!" snarled Gynbere. "How would that be us declaring war. Our sole desire was for peaceful resolution."

"Kirym," called Findlow. "What do you know about the circumstances of Slaslow's death?"

I stood. "Nothing. I did throw the knife, but not in Slaslow's direction. I have no idea how it came to be in him. However, he wasn't the first person attacked. In fact, he was the first to attack."

"That's a lie," said Zeffun. "It's well known he carried no weapon, so he couldn't have attacked anyone."

"Slaslow was armed." Twig was on his feet. "May I speak Veld?"

Gynbere again jumped to his feet. "Veld should not be on the panel. Nor should his woman. They clearly are biased because their son died in the battle."

"If they were of a mind, Gynbere," said Wind Runner, "you would be dead. All you have done over the seasons, and even your actions in the last few days, would give them the right to sentence you to death. Loul is headwoman of The Green Valley. She could sit alone if that was her desire. It's her generosity that allows all of us to have a say." Wind Runner waved him away. "Continue, Twig."

"Before taking Slaslow to lie with the other dead. I removed his gloves." He held one up, the black leather dull with the blood that had dried on it. "Any who look can see his name and crest carved into the wrist strap, and I'm sure many will recognise them. My hand is too narrow to do the gloves justice, but they are very interesting." He slipped one on, pulling it taut and hooking the strap into place.

"What's this nonsense? What do his gloves have to do with this? We of The Rock have seen this glove and its companion many times." Gynbere waved his hand dismissively, although he may have been wary had he glanced down at Zeffun who was trying desperately to get his attention.

Twig wandered over to Gynbere, and held his arm out, his fingers about a hand-width in front of Gynbere's face. He tightened his fist.

Hooked blades suddenly stood out from his knuckles. Parts of the metal glinted in the sunlight, the rest was covered with dried blood.

Gynbere jumped back, his eyes wide.

Lantiah stood, and was acknowledged by Veld. "I was one of those assigned to check the dead. One of Wind Runner's men had wounds I had never seen before. His belly was ripped in several places. The wounds were ragged and irregular. The nearest I've ever seen before was a hunter who had been savaged by a bear. Findlow wears the animal's eye-teeth. I said nearest, because the wounds I looked at were more irregular than those. The weapon Twig holds would have created them perfectly."

All eyes turned back to Twig and Gynbere.

Gynbere took a deep breath and batted Twig's hand away. "My Chief of Security was allowed to protect me against your men. Men who secretly infiltrated the ranks of my guards and planned to kill me. Slaslow should not have been killed for protecting my life."

"Secret infiltration?" Findlow allowed his scepticism to show. "At a head and a half taller than any of you, it could scarcely have been a secret when Elm arrived in your camp. When you were here last. You kept him hidden in your pavilion, resorting to have him transported there in a basket to keep his existence secret from us. Not something you'd have done if you suspected he planned to kill you. Elm was nowhere near you when he died, so he could scarcely have been a threat to you. Now enough of this nonsense. Slaslow was ordering those whom you kidnapped, to be killed. That is an end to the matter."

"That's a lie," shouted Gynbere. "He was calling his brother."

"He has a brother called Kill Them?" Wind Runner sounded amused.

Gynbere wasn't fazed at all. "His younger brother is called Killium. You misheard his call."

Sirasha stood and cleared his throat, accepting a scroll from his son, as Papa acknowledged him. He unrolled it and studied it to find a section and cleared his throat.

"Ahem! The birth of the child named Slaslow was unusual in that the maman had the child while alone. She handed him over to the first person she met after the birth, and then walked away." He studied a section in the scroll. "Hmmm, yes. Yes, when the child was handed to the man in charge of the red-stone diggings, he set a search for the boy's maman. A woman was found dead, lying twenty paces into East Far tunnel. She was identified by the man who had been handed the baby. No one claimed her or the baby. Domina, a childless widow, was approached with a view to caring for the child. With no other close family, she agreed." He looked up. "I can guarantee there was no other child born to the boy's maman." He rolled the scroll up and handed it back to his son.

"However, the girl did kill Slaslow, it's her knife. When and how she did it matters not." said Vellysh. "It can't have been then, because she was by the bridge. She had to have killed him later in cold blood, and in view of her size, I suspect she stabbed him while he was unconscious. A cowardly act. She needs to pay for the crime and I demand—"

"Oh, I scarcely think that's been proven yet," interrupted Tartharn Chestnut. "All we know is that this knife was found in him. Veld, did you see what happened?"

"If I did, I have no memory of it. I heard someone shout

'kill them', and then everything went black until Ubree was standing over me."

"Did anyone on the east side of the ditch see what happened?" asked Garanniis. The silence lengthened. "Teema? Arbreu?"

Teema shook his head. "Once Slaslow ordered the hostages death, I watched them."

"My eyes were on Kirym," said Oak. "She never went near Slaslow until after he was dead. But other strange things happened, and perhaps we should deal with them now."

"What strange things?" asked Veld.

"When Slaslow called for your deaths, you were the only one who was strung up. A guard there grabbed your legs. What were his orders, and who gave them to him? Perhaps Gynbere can answer to that."

"I requested Slaslow set a guard there to ensure nothing untoward happened to any of you. I know nothing of the guard's actions. Slaslow organised that side of my empire," said Gynbere dismissively. "Only he could give that answer."

"So, does that mean you have no control of your empire then?" asked Kwarnar Yew.

Gynbere scowled. "Slaslow gave orders to those under him. If his men chose to ignore his orders, I can't be held responsible for that. Zeffun was his helper."

Zeffun went pale and frantically shook his head. "No, no, no! Thipin was. Thipin helped Slaslow, not me."

"Let's not rush into accusations against dead men," interrupted Loul.

"Anyway, this guard wasn't dressed as our guards are," snapped Vellysh. "He must have sneaked into our ranks. Perhaps he planned to dump the uniform and return to his own people once all sorts of heinous crimes were laid at our feet. He is responsible for the attack on you, Veld. But of course, he's been hidden so my people are blamed."

"Perhaps we should discover what happened before anyone is found guilty in absentia," said Veld. "The guard was hurt, and needed to lie still for some time. When can I talk to him, Ubree?"

"He's ready now, Veld. I've asked Paluniis to get the two men who wore that uniform," said Ubree.

The two men climbed out of the wagon Wind Runner had been using. Murmurs of anger surged around the area.

Vellysh snorted "The smaller one was seen grabbing your legs, Veld. That would obviously show his intention to break your neck or back, and thereby kill you. That is guilt. I can scarcely think he has any excuse for that."

Veld frowned. "Shall we allow him the opportunity to give his story?"

"I'm sure he has had plenty of time to concoct some falsehood," snarled Vellysh. "I think we should take his actions as we saw them, and make our decision from that. There were no other witnesses, but his guilt is obvious. We need to quickly take the sad but necessary action. He must die now!"

"I saw what happened." A clear voice rang across the grounds. Enliah stepped out of the wagon Wind Runner had used at the tor. She went red as everyone looked at her. One of the guards raced over to help her down.

"I'm sorry, I've been asleep. I only just heard what was being said." She looked nervous as she stood in front of the leaders.

"Wh—when," she took a deep breath. "Slaslow ordered our hands tied and the ropes be readied for when he shouted the order. The guard in charge of us, the man in black, allowed the nooses to be readied, but he didn't tie our hands. He gave us rugs and cloaks. But Slaslow ordered the nooses to be checked and tightened when he saw the approaching army.

The man in black came and took our cloaks, but another guard dressed in the same manner as Slaslow followed him. He tied my hands, put the noose around my neck and made sure the rope above my head had no give in it. He was in a hurry, and pulled the rope really tight. Then he went on to do the same to Imolay." She paused, and clasped her hands together tightly, obviously nervous.

"When Kirym put the weapons and tokens on the stones, the guard wearing black came and loosened the nooses. Then he checked the rope around my wrists, put a rope in my hand. He told me that if the platform began to fall or the rope pulled away, I should step back quickly to the grass. Then he made sure my cloak couldn't fall off and went on to Imolay who sat next to me, and then to Young Harby. After that, I couldn't see what was happening to the side, but I heard someone shout, 'Kill them', and felt the ropes pull away. Then the platform started to tilt."

She waited as a tide of comments faded. "The guard in black had been talking to Wind Runner, and he immediately raced towards Veld. Our ropes flew upwards, but Veld's didn't, and he was pulled off his feet." She frowned. "Then lots of things happened at once. The guard grabbed Veld's legs and tried to climb the side pole while holding him up. That made the rope loose and took the tension off Veld's neck, but he hit his head on the side pole and slumped over. That pulled the rope again. Kirym threw something towards the top pole, and at the same time, the guard who was over by the rocks grabbed something and threw it. The guard's thing hit Kirym's and knocked it to the side. Then whatever the guard threw hit Veld's rope and sliced through it. Everyone else had stepped off the platform; it was beginning to fall. Imolay pulled me back onto the grass, but Veld and the guard fell with the platform."

In the silence that followed, she went red.

"Thank you, Enliah," said Garanniis. "That gives us a lot to think about, and a few questions as well."

Vellysh snorted. "I think it shows a vivid imagination and a desire for attention."

"If it were that," said Wind Runner, "then the fuzzy details would have been filled in, I should think. It seems the guard by the platform—"

"Tried to kill Veld," interrupted Vellysh. He stood and pointed his finger at the guard. "Had he not grabbed your legs, Veld, you would have been able to step off the platform. Proof of his guilt, I think." He sat down, looking smug.

"However," said Kwarnar. "The guard cut the other ropes. He could not, in my estimation, be blamed for not reaching Veld in time. Wind Runner, what do you remember?"

"What Enliah says rings true. The guard was speaking to me, but then was gone. I was knocked against Storm, who lifted me off the ground, and then the platform had fallen. My hands were still tied, but the rope had been cut above the noose."

Kwarnar nodded. "The guard saved lives by cutting the ropes, and he nearly died. The healers said he would have, had it not been for the dragon. Veld's life would have been very different and hard to cope with, but he would have survived, solely because when they fell, the guard landed on rocks Gynbere's guards had left there, while Veld landed on the guard."

"So, it was planned between the two guards," interrupted Gynbere "The murder going wrong is no excuse. They should both accept responsibility and both be punished severely."

"You would punish those men," said Wind Runner, "when Enliah saw one cut the rope and the other attempt to—."

"You have only one person's word for it," interrupted Gynbere, "and that's not enough."

Zelriff cleared her throat. "More than enough I think.

The rope around my neck was intact when it was placed there. It wasn't just wound around my neck, it was tied, and in its original state, would have killed me. Later I had the opportunity to look at all those ropes. They'd been cut by a blade, quite close to the noose knot. That hadn't happened earlier, because I tested the rope. The cut on your noose, Veld, was way above your head. There was no way the guard who saved us could have cut it." She waved Gynbere away. "What did the guard by the rocks throw?"

"There was nothing. That shows the girl is lying," said Velysh.

"No, she isn't," I said, standing up.

Everyone was suddenly quiet; waiting.

"Mama, may I speak?" She nodded. "Enliah's account explains the one thing I couldn't understand. The guard by the stones threw the shield. That's how it came to be beside the guard in the trench, Papa."

19

Teema Speaks

The uproar continued unabated for some time, before Veld stood and demanded silence. When everyone settled, Mekroe stood to be acknowledged by Veld.

"Does this mean the weapons don't affect people who touch them?"

All eyes turned to Kirym.

Gynbere jumped to his feet again. "Yes, it does. If the guard touched the shield, then it's obviously not of the weapons those of The Green Valley claim. They should now be returned to me. I've already proven they were stolen from The Rock."

Sirasha stood. "With your permission, Lady Loul, and before any claims for possession are looked at." Loul inclined her head. "In the days of waiting until we could rescue you, I spent the time reading through some historic scrolls that were recently discovered. They explained the happenings of our history. Several those scrolls are, I believe, vital to this discussion. The writings in them shed light on who may handle the weapons, and more importantly where they came from. If I have your permission, will explain."

Loul nodded and Sirasha continued. "If we accept that the Gynbere who took us into the rock as Gynbere One, he was the first of that name, and the present leader of the Yew family as Gynbere Nine, it allows us to put this into the place of our history."

There was a murmur of acceptance from the Tree People.

"The weapons were brought into the Yew family by Gynbere One just before he took us into The Rock. They had not been part of his family possessions before then. There was a suggestion he used the sword to kill his sire, but that was only ever a rumour. Initially the weapons were hidden, and Gynbere refused to talk about them. However, after everyone was settled or as settled as they could be, he ordered them to attend a gathering to show the weapons off. They had been placed on a moulded pad made especially for them. Gynbere declared himself to be the lawful holder of them, and this ownership allowed him the right to rule all of the families."

"That aligns with some stories my grandsire heard from his ancestors," Mrilan called.

Many people nodded in agreement.

"Gynbere one," Sirasha continued, "said he would explain the full significance of the weapons the next day, and use them to find the traitors who plotted against him. He retired to his hollow for the night. The next day, everyone gathered again, but the day went by without him making an appearance. The guards allowed everyone to leave. The following day they gathered again, but Gynbere remained locked in his hollow."

"Typical of many of the gatherings called over the seasons," Laymal shouted.

Imolay frowned at his youngest son.

Sirasha cleared his throat loudly. "Eventually the whisper passed around that Gynbere had been beset by nightmares. In them he was warned against touching the weapons ever again. Death was promised if he dared to tempt fate. That was when the declaration was made of who could hold the weapons. Only the owner of the weapons now had the power to touch them without dying. The weapons were never mentioned again in that Gynbere's lifetime."

"Well if that is Kirym, how come the guard held the shield?" asked Raff.

"That will be answered soon," said Sirasha. "Before he died, Gynbere One wrote down a full accounting of how he acquired the weapons, along with his actions and plans for the future of the Yew family. Now, at the relevant time in our history, the ruler from the Yew Family known to us as Gynbere Four, decided he was the chosen one, and would hold the weapons of power. He called everyone together to see him take them up. The open box sat on the platform in the hall. As he reached for the sword, the lid snapped shut, almost taking his hand with it. He retreated in shock initially, but rallied and ordered his guards to reopen the lid. They couldn't. Gynbere ordered the lamps over the people extinguished. Moments later, he yelled that he, the rightful owner now held them, and his enemies should fear him. A deep voice interrupted him. This is what was said. 'Only the true owner can hold these weapons. Any imposter who claims them, will pay the ultimate price. The load is heavy and they who are chosen need good hearts and an ability to care for the families of the land. Because of the number of weapons, there can be one chosen helper. That helper is tied by loyalty to the holder. They would cross the true holder at their peril. This tie will last until one of them dies."

Sirasha laid the scroll down, paused and turned to Kirym.

"I have no wish to know if you are the rightful holder, or the nominated assistant. But I ask this, for it will tell me. Who is the person who threw the shield?"

Kirym nodded. "He's known as Ashistar."

There was a gasp of shock from those who knew him, although many people looked mystified.

I was appalled.

"He's a traitor," screamed Gynbere. "He turned against us, his people."

"Sit down and be quiet!" Veld was on his feet, and he was very angry. "For all of your accusations, you, Gynbere, have a lot to answer for."

"But—but," he spluttered. "You can't hold my ancestor's actions against me."

"It has nothing to do with your ancestors," Loul said quietly. "You chose to be a tyrant. Despite the peaceful aspect of the meeting here, you made the decision to attack. Lives were lost because of your actions. Ashistar took no lives. I will be proud to shake his hand. Now Kirym, before we find clothes to suit these brave men, do you know anything about the other guard, the man who, it seems, saved my life."

"This is my friend, Borboncha."

Again, I was aghast. I grabbed Kirym's arm. "How could you?" I tried to keep my voice low. "They both work for Gynbere. They've passed on all sorts of information. Of all the people you could have trusted."

I should have thought, and should have kept my mouth shut, at least until I could have got her alone. Even then, it would probably have made no difference. She was incandescent with rage.

"If it's any of your business, and it isn't, it was my choice. Ashistar and Borboncha risked their lives to save those kidnapped, and have no doubt, Teema, Slaslow would have made a point of killing them all. Would you have them dead just to prove your point? What else could Ashistar have done to convince you? Have you thought that maybe he's the holder, and I'm just his assistant?" She wrenched her arm away and stormed off.

Although we had kept our voices low, those closest in the group we were in, heard every word and understood what was going on.

I got to my feet, unable to meet anyone's eye. I knew I didn't want to go after Kirym, I had no idea what I wanted from her, or from me. Just not this.

I walked in the opposite direction towards the northern wall.

Mekrar found me a short time later.

"You took your time," I snarled.

"I'm not here to argue with you, Teema. The other holder of the weapons was always Kirym's decision. I just hate that you two are fighting."

"Well what else can I do when she keeps making stupid mistakes, despite all o' the warnings we gave her."

"What if you're wrong?"

I stared at her. "You think I am?"

"There is no proof Ashistar has done anything to show disloyalty. You haven't found proof, or you'd have told us. So, I'm wondering what's really annoying you?"

"I have a feeling about him. He'll hurt Kirym, and I can't convince her to even be careful. She should be playing with the other children, not having to defend herself against murder charges. She shouldn't have even been at the battle, shouldn't have to be dealing with people's guts spilling out, blood and vomit all over the place, and—"

"That's it, isn't it?" she interrupted. "You still think of her as a baby. Halse was younger than Kirym is now when you asked her to join with you. The only reason you didn't have the ceremony immediately was because Halse wanted two full season cycles with Raff and Soojee without the chance of being pregnant. Kirym has grown up whether you want it or not. She has more understanding of people than most of us. Have you ever known her to be wrong about someone?"

"No," I said reluctantly, "but she won't always be right, and this time I think—"

"Perhaps you think too much, and it's clouding the truth. I know you love her, but you constantly push her away. Then when she doesn't confide in you, you blame her. Grow up, Teema."

She stalked away.

I didn't know whether to scream or cry.

"You're wrong," I yelled, "and so is she!"

Everyone was staring at me, but I didn't care.

I waited until they got sick of looking, stood up and walked away. Initially my thought was to leave the amphitheatre and go off for a few days, but at the entrance I was stopped.

"No one's allowed to leave."

I tried to push past the guard, but he grabbed my arm and held on. "Veld's orders, sir. No one, for any reason."

Two other guards paused close by, not obvious in their support, but ready to step in if I decided to be a problem.

Reluctantly I turned back and found one of Wind Runner's wagons. As I climbed in, the people behind me began to clap and cheer. I wondered what was going on. I forced myself to ignore it. Anyone who was watching would see that.

I lay down on the floor, pulled my cloak around me and tried to sleep.

20

Arbreu

While waiting for Ashistar and Borboncha to change clothes, the cooks had drinks and light food available for those who wanted it. Oak, Trethia and Mekroe went to get a basket of drinks for us.

Mekrar returned from talking to Teema, her cheeks bright red, her mouth compressed into a thin line. As soon as she sat down, Arbreu began to massage her shoulders.

"He'll come right," he said. "Shall I talk to him?"

She shook her head and sighed. "You'd have more luck talking to the wall. Don't waste your breath. He won't listen to anyone."

"Bokum's death hit him hard," said Arbreu. "Tarl an—"

"It's nothing to do with them!" Mekrar snapped. "This problem began while we were at Faltryn. He's being stupid. I can do no more to help him—I *will* do no more. He drives Kirym away and sulks because she's gone. There's no reasoning with him."

"She'll miss him."

"Will she? She won't want for friends or company."

"Perhaps Loul, Veld or Old Harby."

"He won't listen." She paused. "Maybe—hmmm! I'll think about it, but the way he is at the moment, I'd avoid him if I were them."

Twig hunkered down beside Kirym. "The healers handed me the blades from Tarl's wound. They were the same, Mam. They'd broken off, but I'm sure it was a similar weapon."

"Slaslow's other glove?"

He shrugged. "It's possible, unless he had others made. I have a left glove and it's intact, although covered with blood."

"He hit Elm with his right fist, so it adds up. There could be others, tell Papa and Armos to warn the guards. And just watch and listen."

Ashistar and Borboncha appeared looking quite different in their new clothes. As they climbed out of the wagon, Mekrar began to clap. Arbreu joined in quickly and soon most of the crowd were clapping and cheering.

Arbreu started to glance around to see if Teema had joined in, but Mekrar grabbed his arm. "Don't you dare! If he sees you looking, he'll think you support him. It's time he learned. Anyway, he's not there, he's run away to sulk."

Veld walked over to Ashistar and Borboncha and shook both men by the hand. He was followed by the rest of those who had been kidnapped. Then Loul spoke to both. When she left, Kirym was beside them. She hugged them both, and gestured over to where her friends were sitting.

As they approached, Gynbere glanced at the two former guards, but obviously didn't recognise them. Vellysh did though. He tried to signal to his brother, but Sundas and young Harby stood between them, and blocked the view.

As everyone settled down, Sirasha stood and after Veld

acknowledged him, said, "Veld, have I your permission to pass on some of our history?"

Many of those in the amphitheatre looked perplexed. "Is it relevant to anything happening here now?" asked Vellysh.

Sirasha's grandson jumped to his feet. "Everything my grandsire says is pertinent. In this case, probably the most important information for our families, although it will also have a meaning for those who allow us to share this land."

Sirasha cleared his throat. "Ahem. Before I begin, I beg the indulgence of you leaders. Findlow, may I borrow Sundas, Twig and Blacknight from Wind Runner, Baketer from Imolay, Mekroe from Veld, Paluniis from Garanniis, Dashlan from Bryn, and Walf from Raff."

When the leaders had agreed, those named approached Sirasha and listened to his instructions. Then as one, they ranged themselves around the amphitheatre. Mekroe, with his back to almost everyone, signalled to Armos who had joined the guards on the wall.

Arbreu glanced around the area. For all that Gynbere and his men were with them, he felt this was a peaceful gathering, and yet Veld had put a full contingent of guards on the wall and extra men around the base of the ridge.

Arbreu glanced at Gynbere. "Oh, my goodness. Gynbere has no idea what's going to be disclosed. Why not?"

Kirym looked back at him. "When you pushed the ibith into the channel around the tor, it fell unbroken. I imagine he assumes the inside is equally intact. Perhaps he thinks the information is from after the scrolls were stolen."

As the buzz lessened, Sirasha, surrounded by his sons and grandsons, began to read the scrolls. Arbreu watched Gynbere like a hawk, and if he suspected anything, he showed no sign of it. Even when the details began to be disclosed, he made no reaction. He lounged on a bed of cushions with his eyes shut.

"Why is he not reacting," Arbreu asked quietly.

Kirym glanced over to him. "He's asleep. He may possibly think that if some of the common people are listening to something at the same time he is, it can't be important enough for him to pay attention."

"Should someone waken him?"

"His men are listening. Zeffun is beside him. I'm sure someone will alert him if they feel there's a need. I wonder if he has ever read those scrolls."

"But, why wouldn't he? He held them."

"As the basics of his ancestor's act was evidently passed on verbally, perhaps he didn't see any point in reading it himself, or maybe he didn't feel it mattered anymore."

Some of the detail read out by Sirasha was a repeat of what they heard days before when the scrolls had been first found. Still, everyone listened avidly, to pick up details they'd missed or forgotten. Although the sun was hidden behind clouds, it was getting warm in the amphitheatre. Little wind entered, and the temperature always rose in the afternoon.

Some way into the reading, Zeffun leaned over and whispered in Gynbere's ear, grasping his arm to ensure he roused.

Gynbere looked shocked at whatever Zeffun told him, sat up and frowning, glanced around at the nearest two entrances, the north-eastern and the southern. Both were quite distant and, Arbreu knew, well-guarded.

Arbreu suddenly realised that Kirym had disappeared. He searched the crowd for her. She had collected a basket of juice and water flasks and was handing them out to the guards scattered around the amphitheatre.

The guards on the top of the ridge were well catered for as a matter of routine, water was available there whenever it was needed, but the extra guards inside the amphitheatre did not have the same facilities set up. Arbreu wished he'd thought of that before Kirym had. He'd prefer to keep her a long distance from Gynbere and his men, although that would be difficult. His men were scattered all over the place.

Movement around Gynbere caught Arbreu's eye.

"He's trying to signal his guards," Mekrar murmured in his ear.

"Why?"

"I imagine he feels he may need them. But they're either ignoring him, or they are too tied up in the revelations to notice."

"Ah well, he's given up," Arbreu said. "He's now rearranging his cushions. Maybe he'll go back to sleep and get Zeffun and Vellysh to tell him all about it later."

Kirym was talking to Sundas, having handed him a flask. Just as she turned away, Sundas violently pushed her away with his left hand, and swiped down with his right. Kirym hit the ground, curled in a ball, her high-pitched scream echoed across the amphitheatre.

"What in Faltryn's name—" Before Arbreu could finish, Kirym was on her feet, although she was nursing her right arm and her face contorted with pain. She bent over Sundas, who had dropped to his knees. She held his hand, trying to stem the blood that streamed onto the ground.

Arbreu was one of several people who converged on the two of them, but just before he reached them, he understood Kirym's frantic order.

21

Kirym Speaks

Arbreu! Watch Gynbere! Get armed guards around him. NOW!

There was so much blood, but from the glimpse I got, the third and fourth fingers of Sundas' left hand hung lose, attached by only two small strips of skin. He was on his knees, panting with pain, tears streaming into his beard.

I grabbed my skirt, bunched it up and holding his hand tentatively in my right, pressed the material onto the wound, trying to stem the bleeding as best I could. It was difficult. Using my right hand was extremely painful.

Ubree! I need you!

The crowds parted and Papa was there. "Out of the way," he yelled, pushing people aside. "Let Ubree in."

I was aware of a lot of movement around us, and then Ubree was there.

He leaned his head against Sundas, and slowly Sundas began to relax, his breathing still ragged, but better.

Two claws on Ubree's left front foot dropped forwards and blood welled out, mingling with Sundas'. The rest of Ubree's front right foot turned a strange putrid shade of orange. He sank down to his belly, now panting as Sundas had.

Sundas took a deep sigh of relief, and sat back, staring at his now healed hand. Then he scrambled to his feet and bent over Ubree.

"Come on now, you can do it. You can get—" He looked up at me. "He will heal, won't he?"

As I nodded, the orange in Ubree's foot slowly faded and his normal colour returned. The strands of skin began to connect, the bleeding slowed, and stopped. It took a long time, but eventually his foot was whole again. He flexed it and sat up.

Papa took a deep breath. "Give us some room, here. What happened? Sundas?"

Sundas frowned. "Something flew this way, umm." He frowned. "I thought it would hit Kirym, but..." He shook his head. "I only had a brief glimpse, but it didn't look right. I thought at the time it was one of those really big bees, but it was too big. It moved differently too. Veld, if it missed Kirym, it would have hit Ubree. But I dunno what it was, and it's—well I can't see it."

"Maybe it dug into the ground," said Papa. "It must be under the blood somewhere."

"It's here." I moved my foot, bent down and picked a blood covered disk off the ground. "This Papa. I stepped on it, to ensure it stayed put." I grabbed the flask I'd handed Sundas and poured water over the disk to clean it.

Ubree's head snapped around. "Drop it! Remove your boots. You too, Sundas. Don't stand in the blood."

I pulled my boots off and dropped them on top of the blade. Sundas added his. Ubree stared at me intently. "How do you feel?"

I shrugged. "A bit tired, but that's the excitement of the incident, I think."

Ubree shook his head. "Veld, the boots must be burned, as must anything else that has touched the blood. Kirym, remove your dress."

"Now!" he added as I hesitated. "And Sundas, anything of yours that has blood on it must also be burned. You'll both need to go and wash. Come to me later, there will be a residual effect, and I'll need to deal with that." said Ubree.

I dropped my dress on the boots. I felt strangely cold as I stood there in just my shift and petticoat. I knew blood had gone onto my skin, although there was nothing I could do about that.

"There's some blood on your petticoats, too," said Mekrar.

"Kirym," Wind Runner touched my arm. "There are robes in the wagon. You can wash there too."

Ubree's voice seemed to come from everywhere. "Nothing in that pile can be touched. I will handle them. In the meantime, everyone who sat close to Sundas must be checked in case anything has splashed on them or their clothes.

There was blood on my shift as well, and the bandage was saturated. I didn't know if the blood was mine, or Sundas'. I washed, and re-bandaged my hand with a long strip cut from my petticoat, but there was nothing else I could do. I dressed, thankful that the sleeves of the robe were long enough to pull down over my knuckles. The pile of clothes was larger when I returned. The bandage, wrapped in my petticoats went on the top.

"Ubree, I need to see the weapon," said Papa.

Ubree breathed on the pile, and they seemed to be liquid, a heaving, roiling mass of colour, moving until the disk sat on top.

"Do not touch it," warned Ubree.

The weapon had three curved blades sticking out of a central core. Every edge looked sharp.

Papa stared at it. "Has anyone seen this or something similar before?"

There was a quiet buzz of comments, and then a small voice called out, "I have." Trethia wriggled out of Oak's arms and came over to me. "I saw them in The Rock."

"Who had them?" Papa asked.

"Slaslow and Gynbere."

"She lies!" snarled Gynbere.

"And why would she do that?" asked Papa.

"Always has. Spawn o' that evil black dragon. Always sneaking around, watching. Remembering!" He looked sourly at Trethia. "Always remembering, so she could tell tales. Trying to give the dragon enough information to destroy me."

"Would that be the dragon you blackmailed?" I asked. "The dragon who hasn't been seen since, oh, now when was it you saw him last, Gynbere."

Gynbere's lip curled, but he ignored me. He drew himself to his full height. "Slaslow may have held weapons similar to that, but I never saw them. You can't blame me if someone stole his weapons when he died."

"You threw it," said Trethia, "and he has more of them. He keeps them in his cushions there."

Papa gestured to Mekroe.

"Wait!" said Ubree. "Use thick gloves. Remember though, whatever you use must then be burned."

Mekroe took the first pair offered him, pulled them on and picked up a cushion. He inspected it, dropped it and reached for another. As he dropped it on top of the first, he suddenly grabbed it again and stared at the seam. Then he gingerly pulled out a blade, and flicked it onto the pile beside its twin.

He twisted the cushion around and pulled out a second, a third and fourth, and dropped them and the cushion on the pile to be burned.

He rechecked the first one, and added it to the pile, followed by a third. He plucked a fourth from those around Gynbere, a longer round bolster, checked it and turned to Papa.

"There seems to be at least four blades in every cushion, six or eight in this one. They're cleverly inserted into the seams. If all the cushions have them, I'd say he has a sizable cache at hand."

"That evil little beast must have planted them there," Gynbere snarled. "She's trying to frame me."

"A child?" Papa was incredulous. "Really, Gynbere. That's a little low, even for you."

"Oh, she's not just a child. I said spawn o' that evil lizard and she is. Ask her how long she's been around?"

"You are tiresome, Gynbere. It doesn't matter who placed them in the cushions. You threw one." Papa pointed to the weapon. "Who were you aiming at?"

Gynbere stared arrogantly down his nose. "It didn't matter. Anyone really. I aimed at the girl. If it hadn't been for that great moron pushing her, I'd have had her." He glanced at Sundas. "The dragon sat beyond her, and if I missed her, I'd have him. Almost got him too, and I'm thinking that a direct hit would have done 'im. No way would he be called back after that. No one could do it, and as no one realises how it's done anyway, I've won." He stood up and looked over at the stump, with the dragons nearby. "As much as you wish those dragons to live again, none of you have the knowledge. That huge lump doubly spoiled it in the short-term. He deserved the pain he got for interfering. He'd have died, if it hadn't been for the dragon. But the green will die anyway, and without the rest o' them, I will rise again."

"Ubree came back, the others will follow," interrupted Findlow. "You'll have trouble facing them."

"Huh, they're not allowed to hurt us, or allow us to be hurt."

"Oh, you're not quite right, Gynbere," I said. "They're here to do the leader of The Green Valley's bidding. If they were ordered not to help you in any way, they couldn't."

Gynbere looked shaken. "Veld, it's your job to care for us all. You're foiled, all o' you."

"Oh, no," I said. "The leader's job is to care for everyone. If you are threatening even one, Mama's obligation is to protect them. Therefore," I paused, staring at him and hoping I had it right, "your death may be the best option."

Gynbere went white. "Ah, but only if I have intentions to hurt someone, and I assure you, I no longer do."

"If you were believable, that may be, but you've spent your life lying and destroying," I said.

"My people will object!"

"With all they've all learned about you recently," I said, "they may no longer wish to be your slaves. Especially as they now know they never needed to be in The Rock in the first place. Their decision may be to care for you in the same way you cared for them."

Ubree stood, forestalling any more talk. "Has anyone else found blood splashed on their clothes," he asked. With no answer, he urged everyone back from the pile on the ground.

With sufficient space around them, he snorted a stream of fire onto the contaminated items. The flames roared high, red initially as the material caught, then putrid green, yellow and blue. The fire continued for a long time, much longer than I'd have thought it possible, knowing what clothes were there. As it died, the embers turned to a sickly orange similar to the colour around Ubree's wound. Ubree again snorted flame onto them, and when the flame burned clean, he allowed it to go out.

The poisons love the fire, and it takes a long time for them to become inert, came Ubree's thought.

When the fire finally died, a pile of heat stained disks sat on the burned ground.

Armos arrived at Ubree's side with a large flask of water which he emptied onto them. Steam billowed up from them, hovering above us.

"The steam is harmless," Ubree told everyone.

Dashlan and Tarjin each poured more water over and the steam dissipated.

Papa carefully picked up one of the disks. "You're sure it's safe?"

"Well, not if you cut yourself, for it is a blade. However, it will only be a cut," said Ubree.

Papa brought a piece of parchment from his robe, and slashed it quickly in half.

Gynbere snorted. "Even a blunt knife does that."

"True," said Imolay, "but perhaps this would be a better way to see its threat, Veld." He handed over a piece of thick leather. It was made up of several layers, boiled and glued together while still hot. It had been used as a splint to keep a broken leg from any movement.

Papa raised the blade and slashed downward. He was left holding half of the splint.

"Oh my stars," gasped Mekrar. "That would cut to the bone so easily."

"I wondered how it could take my fingers off, but it could easily have cut my leg in half," said Sundas. He gingerly picked one up. "What will you do with them, Veld?"

Papa frowned and shook his head. "They seem almost too dangerous to have around."

"The healers would find them useful, Papa. They could

excise dead and dying skin quickly and easily. Sometimes that can save a life," I said.

"They would need to be carefully stored," said Mama, "but Kirym is right. They'd be easier to use if they had a handle."

"They belong to your family, Loul, and they did have handles then," said Ubree. "They were a gift from us when we came to your land. How Gynbere got them, well he seems to have been holding a lot of the things gifted to you."

Papa looked shaken. "What? How?"

"Melith, Tamweir, Zandahem, Oakenrock, our robes, the bows and bolts. He held all of those things, and as most of them were left safely locked up in The Green Valley settlement storehouses, Gynbere One or Two must have raided the settlement," I said.

"You can't blame me for things that happened before I was born," screamed Gynbere. "I didn't know where any of those things came from. They were in our possession long before even my grandsire was born. How could I have known?"

"Oh, you knew." The voice was low, but it carried across the amphitheatre. "Those thefts were proudly read to you by your grandsire and your sire. You boasted to your family, as the possession of them showed your supremacy over The Green Valley."

Everyone looked around for the speaker.

Slowly a young man stood and glanced at Gynbere.

"I'm Myrlond Yew. Gynbere is my sire."

"Not any longer, he isn't," snarled Gynbere. "Accusations are easy to make, aren't they? He's a liar. Everything he says is untrue."

Kwarnar stood. "Myrlond speaks honestly. It's the base of your ascendancy over The Green Valley. That a Gynbere could easily walk into any building in The Green Valley, locked or not, and take the items they felt gave them power.

Not of course, the weapons. They were stolen personally from the head man of The Green Valley."

By now, he was speaking over the increasing volume of protests from Gynbere. "I wasn't alive, I can't be blamed. I had no idea how to return them. From all I knew, The Green Valley was deserted."

Sirasha stood. "As a point of interest, may I ask how you knew the land was deserted?"

"I—" Gynbere paused. "The giant told me."

"Why would he," I asked. "Salcan came from here, and he knew it wasn't," I said. "However, you still knew these things belonged to us, so why didn't you return them to Salcan as soon as you met him?"

"Forget what was done by your sire and his ancestors. That is irrelevant," interrupted Mama. "This is about what *you* did. You attacked without provocation. You killed Faltryn and our people. Just now, although everything here was peaceful, you attempted to kill again. For that, you will be locked up until a decision is made for your future."

"Do I understand you have a cage built, Findlow?" asked Papa.

"Yes."

"Then Gynbere goes in there for now. Keep him well guarded, but first, remove all of his possessions including his clothes. Give him one of the night robes to wear. You know how to check for hidden weapons, but be careful with them. Allow cushions and rugs, but none Gynbere has used before, nor any from his family." He turned back to Gynbere. "You are a prisoner. You will get meals; the same as everyone else, a guard will deliver the food. If any of your family object, they are welcome to join you. The restrictions on them would be the same as on you. Let me warn you now. If you use a weapon against anyone from now on, whether you miss with it or not, that weapon will be used against you."

"You have no right to do this," snarled Gynbere.

Mama looked amused. She drew herself up and looked tall and imposing. "We have every right! This is our land, and these are our people. We will protect them and if your death is necessary to guarantee their safety, it will happen."

As a protesting Gynbere was led away, Papa turned to me. "I think there is a lot you have to tell me, Kirym."

"Others will need to hear also, Papa. Perhaps after we've eaten, and those who have heard will have the opportunity to do other things if they wish."

22

Kirym Speaks

I collected a platter of food and took it over to where Morkeen was caring for Amethyst. As was usual, the various groups intermixed, and a lively conversation began. Before I had a chance to more than hand a portion of food to Trethia, Arbreu called me away.

"There's a problem with Teema." His concern showed in his voice.

I glanced around. We were in a quiet place where no one would overhear us. "He wants some time away to think."

"What about?"

"I'm sure he will eventually tell you."

"Can we help him?" he asked.

"He hasn't asked me for help," I said guardedly.

He wasn't finished. "Earlier today I could feel him. Now I can't. I've tried to send him a message, but it's as if I'm running into a cliff. What can I do?"

I looked into his troubled face. "Nothing. Really if he

wants help, he will approach you. Maybe something will take his attention, but right now—" I shook my head.

"You know the way we connect with each other using the tokens?"

I nodded.

"When Mekrar and I joined, I didn't contact you or Teema for two or three days. Then after that, it was easy to contact Mekrar and you, but somehow, I lost Teema. I've never had quite the same ability with him as with you though. Are we limited to the number of people we can include?"

"No, although it is easier for some people than others. Most people continue a close association with parents and siblings, after they join and have their own children."

"So why is Teema gone? The three of us didn't connect in that manner before we came to The Green Valley. What happened to begin it?"

I thought back. "From the time my token darkened after the massacre at Raff's, I could feel Teema's presence. When we met you and we each received a token, the feeling included you and Bokum, although Bokum always to a lesser extent, because his almost immediate connection to Zeprah became so important to him. We did use the messaging back there though. Remember when the lake was ready to burst its bank, and we needed to find Bokum? I think that was the first time for us both in that way. Before then the messages were more involuntary. The first time I needed to talk to you and Teema, you were both happy to answer. We continued from there, and each time it was easier."

"And now?"

"Perhaps Teema doesn't want to listen."

"Aren't you worried about him?"

"Don't yell at me, Arbreu. Of course, I am, but I tried. He's allowed to make that decision, and perhaps he just needs the time away."

"What if he doesn't come back?" he asked.

"That would be his choice."

"Do you know what's actually wrong with him?"

I hesitated. "I think so. But as I said, we can't help him until he wants us to. He may never want our help."

Arbreu's face fell. He shook his head. "With Bokum, Tarl and Peet dying, and then I joined with Mekrar, well he's lost such a lot. I thought Mekrar would just fit in with the rest of us, that nothing would really change. Was that a stupid thought?"

"No, not at all. Mekrar's been with us more and more anyway. Teema's loss was no more than yours."

"Perhaps I shouldn't have joined."

"If he decided to join with someone, would you ask him not to?"

His silence answered that.

"We each carry our own burden. Some do it with less ease than others. Mama is aware of Teema's problems, as are others. He will be watched and cared for, but the three people he won't accept advice from is you, Mekrar and me. He knows where we are, and right now, I have other things to worry about."

He swung around and looked at Trethia. "Is she—"

"Trethia and Amethyst are fine. It's Ubree. He won't live long without his brothers and sisters. Somehow I must find out what can be done to bring them back."

Arbreu fell into step with me as I walked to where Trethia waited. "Why can't he sing to them?"

"I thought it had to be the oldest who did that. Faltryn did sing to them, but it didn't seem to be enough. Then he woke to tell them something more, but he was a baby; He couldn't speak and maybe it wasn't enough. I don't know who woke Ubree. I'm now wondering if there's another dragon around that we don't know of."

We sat down to eat, but I had no appetite.

Mekrar hunkered down beside me. "What's wrong?" She kept her voice low, but I knew from experience that if I didn't give a reasonable answer, she would get louder.

I took a deep breath, a mistake, I almost vomited. The taste of it was raw in the back of my throat. I took a sip from the flask. "Just tired, and I think the shock of someone wanting me dead so badly has just hit home."

"Poor thing," she said, kissing my temple. "It'd be hard for anyone, and you are so young." She squeezed my shoulder, and I heard someone scream.

I lay on the ground, faces hovering over me. Mama's hand was on my forehead, she looked very concerned. "She's far too hot, but I don't know why. Kirym, could any of Sundas' blood have touched your skin?"

"She looked pale all morning, Mama," said Mekrar. "She hasn't eaten. She said it was reaction to all that's happened today, but she's looked unwell since the battle."

Mama made a noise in the back of her throat.

"It's nothing, Mama," I said. "I'm thirsty, and I'd like some peace and quiet for a while." I tried to lever myself up to sitting, pausing as waves of nausea washed over me. I felt sweat break out on my forehead, and hoped Mama wouldn't notice it.

"It's more than that," she said. "I'll get Ubree to help."

I panicked. "No, Mama. It's nothing. Really, nothing. I haven't eaten enough, and I've not slept much."

"You may think me a fool, Kirym, but I've never known a few missed meals and over-tiredness to bring on a high fever, or cause a collapse in this manner. So, what is the matter, and if you try to pass this off, I will have you in the healing area so fast, you won't know what hit you, *and* I will keep you there until I've found out what is going on."

I felt the tears, and tried to brush them away.

Mama leaned me against her shoulder, rocking me, and smoothing my hair.

"She was cut with a knife after the battle, Loul. It's poisoning her."

Mama let go of me and turned to look at Trethia.

I fell back, someone behind me caught my shoulders, and moved up so I could lean on them. Oak's hand gently took my right hand. I leaned my head against his chin. My tears wouldn't stop.

Mama turned back to look at me. "Is that right?"

I nodded.

She shook her head. "Oh dear, let me see."

I gingerly held out my right hand. Mama pushed my sleeve up, and began to unwrap the bandage.

Arbreu was one of those who drew back as the sickening smell of a wound gone bad, hit them.

"Why didn't you come to me or the healers," Mama asked. Her tone alone told me how bad it was. "You of all people. How could you have left it?"

She looked up. "Ubree, can you help her?"

"No!" I pushed myself up. "I killed someone. I don't want to forget, bury it and pretend it didn't happen. It was a life, and—" Tears streamed down my face.

Oak hugged me close, crooning softly.

"Can all of you move away, please?" Mama said. "You'll all find out about this later. You stay Oak, I need you to help her sit."

Mekrar stayed beside Mama; the crowd dispersed. Trethia sat beside me. She had tears in her eyes, and looked scared.

I combed my fingers through her hair. "I'll be all right," I murmured.

Ubree loomed over me. His head seemed to be floating, not attached to any other part of him. It hurt to look up. I closed my eyes. "I'll be better after a sleep." I murmured. I wondered if I had actually spoken out loud, or just thought it.

Kirym, I need to fix your hand, or—

No! I cut through Ubree's message. *I don't want...* I couldn't go on. I felt too tired, too wretched.

"Kirym, open your eyes and look at me."

Despite not wanting to, I did. The sky had dimmed to lavender and grey, the sun was setting. Ubree's face came into focus. A cool breeze wafted across my forehead. He was breathing on me.

"You would not accept that excuse from anyone else. You refused to accept it from Enliah. So why is the level of accountability higher for you? Your weapon may have killed Slaslow, but you did not do it, nor did you intend your weapon to hit him."

I stared up at him, trying to dam the tears that again threatened to spill over. I couldn't think straight.

Ubree touched his token lump to mine. The pain in my hand slowly died and I could straighten my fingers.

Mama removed the last of the bandages, rolled them up and handed them to Mekrar. "Burn them, they shouldn't be used again. She bathed my hand in cool fragrant water. The ghastly smell had disappeared.

"Not all has gone," said Ubree. "You'll have a scar, but you will eventually look at it and understand that some things are better for having happened. You did many good things at the tor. You insisted arrows not be used against Gynbere's marksmen because of the non-fighters around them. You were willing to give up the treasures you value so deeply. You put everyone ahead of yourself in the aftermath of Gynbere's realisation he would not get what he desired. These things are part of your value. Without you, many more lives would have been lost, but yours is important too. There are many things you need to do before your life is over, important things that will make a difference in your world. Don't throw them away on the memory of one man who wanted you dead, and intended to kill almost everyone else."

I still felt wretched.

"You need to sleep, that will help." Ubree's nose touched my forehead again and everything went black.

23

Teema Speaks

"Teema," bellowed Sundas. "Teema!"

I ignored him, but he kept calling. I heard him climb onto one of the wagons, he was searching. I let him. He'd give up soon, especially if I wasn't in the first wagon.

He didn't.

"There you are," he said, as he looked through the entrance. He climbed in and sat opposite me. "I'm worried about you. Come and stay with me. We can sort things out together."

"I don't want your company."

"Then just come and stay—"

"No! Just leave me alone."

"I'll go and get a meal for us."

I shrugged, then shook my head and turned my face to the wall.

"Have a sleep," he said, "and then we'll eat."

As soon as he had gone, I moved to a different wagon. *He won't bother searching again, and even if he does, he won't look in the wagons he's already searched,* I thought.

I woke with a start. Loul stood over me. Someone had thrown a rug over me through the night.

"What do you want?" I knew I sounded belligerent and rude. I didn't care. I stood and tried to walk past her.

She didn't budge.

"Sit down and eat," she said. "Now!"

Stronger men than me, had been unable to say no to Loul. She was used to being obeyed, anyway the smell of the food was too enticing. I sat down and grudgingly accepted the platter of food she held.

"I know you have concerns. Will you share them with me?"

"Why should I? You won't listen."

She breathed deeply. "I have always listened to you in the past."

I didn't say anything, I had trouble putting my words into thoughts.

"Just when you're ready," she said. "Kirym is very sick. Right now, I'm not at all sure if she will live."

"Tell Ubree to cure her. That's his job, isn't it?"

I was sure she was angry, but her voice and face didn't change. She just looked concerned and a little tired.

"Ubree has helped us all. I will ask no more of him. With all he has done, for us and her, there are limits, and now he has reached them."

"He let those mongrels get close to Kirym. She wouldn't have been hurt if it hadn't been for them."

She raised an eyebrow and looked at me. I felt very uncomfortable.

"Teema, if you have concerns *and proof,* I will listen. Veld and all of the other leaders will help."

"None of them care," I snarled.

She just looked at me; I felt like crying.

"Teema, bring me evidence of betrayal and I will do something."

"There's been a war. What other evidence do you need?"

"Gynbere and Slaslow started the war—"

"And Ashistar and Borboncha told them what Kirym carried to ensure they won," I said, interrupting her.

"They didn't win and what Kirym held wasn't a secret. Gynbere guessed what he didn't know, and he got most of it wrong."

I knew I didn't make sense, but I couldn't explain it.

"You're the same as everyone else, determined to dismiss what's obvious." I cast about wildly trying to think of an argument to bring Loul to my way of thinking. Then I realised she was speaking.

"I want you back with the rest of the family, Teema. There are a lot of things to be done. You can choose which dwelling to sleep in, but Zeprah needs help with the children as she travels. She has offered her home to another family, because she doesn't want to face the memories. Nevertheless, she will still need somewhere for Sarel and Trayum, so I'd like you to help her build it."

"There are plenty of people to help her."

"Everyone is overworked. Will you foreswear the promise you made to Bokum?"

And there she had me.

I agreed to do it, but made no effort to hide my resentment towards her. I wondered how she knew about my promise. However, I immediately felt better knowing I had something to do. "I'll help Zeprah, but then I'm leaving The Green Valley."

24

Kirym Speaks

I woke with a start. It was dark, and from where I lay I could see stars, but no moon. Night noises were muted; I couldn't hear the noise of those sleeping nearby.

A light glowed from somewhere behind me. I hadn't heard the rasp of a flint, so assumed the lamp had been hooded.

Mekrar appeared out of the gloom. She helped me to sit and held a flask to my lips. "How are you feeling?"

"Fine." I glanced around. The dwelling was quite small, almost empty, and in near darkness. Two chairs and a bench or table sat on the opposite wall.

"Ubree plans to see you in the morning, unless..."

"Morning is soon enough." I cut her short. "I'm sure he's been doing far too much."

"Are you hungry?"

"That can wait until morning also."

"You need to eat now." Mama walked in, followed by Oak, who carried a large platter. I wondered how they knew I had woken, although probably Mekrar realised I was about to, and sent Oak to get Mama.

Mama sat beside me. "You've a choice, cooked fruit, or some gravy with root vegetables mashed into it."

I reached for the meat juices, and took a mouth full. Moments later, it returned, all over the rug that covered me. Most unexpected, but Oak simply gathered the rug up, and disappeared outside with it.

"Perhaps it was a little rich." Mekrar tucked another rug around me, as Mama spooned a mouthful of fruit into me. "Ubree took the poisons away, but—"

"That can wait until later, Mekrar, when she has more strength."

"She should know, Mama. Withholding the news won't change it nor make it any more palatable. Kirym wouldn't allow anyone else to be shielded from their actions, she shouldn't be either."

"How is Ubree?" I asked.

"He's fine," said Mama, shortly. She sighed. "Very well. The poisons hit him hard, but he came through. The wound was easy for him, but the poisons were something else again. It would have been easier had you allowed him to manage the wound earlier. Even with his help, you still have quite a journey back to full health. You've been asleep a long time."

"How long?"

"Six days."

"What!" I was amazed. "What has happened in the meantime?"

Mama smiled. "Things you could have helped with. The building work is racing ahead, and we have big plans for the next few seasons. For the next few days it all depends on the weather, of course. Ubree says we have another four days before we the next storm hits us. We've been lucky with the weather so far, but it couldn't last, and this one will be bad enough to stop us building. Still everyone is warm and safe, although still overcrowded. It will get better as spring approaches. However, we must get through winter first."

"Temporary dwellings are being built around the settlement for now," said Mekrar. "Relocation for permanent homes will begin in the spring. Those who want total independence are waiting for you, because you know more than anyone where the land is best for each of them, and how to get them there."

Oak returned. "Go and get some sleep, Mekrar." He handed me a water flask.

"I grabbed her hand as she walked past. "You should be caring for Arbreu, not me."

"He's fine," she said. "He's been here a lot, and we've all slept when we've needed to."

"Trethia?"

"She hasn't left you since you collapsed, but she finally fell asleep and Arbreu took her to Morkeen. Others have come and gone, and almost everyone has enquired after you."

I nodded. "Teema?"

Mekrar frowned.

"He's been very busy," cut in Mama. "There are a lot of people without homes. Zeprah offered hers to a family; she felt it was too big for her and the children. Teema has been helping her to build a smaller place. Now, you need sleep. You will not heal unless you obey my instructions, Kirym."

I felt very tired and closed my eyes.

I heard some general movement around me. Someone drew the rug over my shoulders.

"I don't know what Teema is thinking of. He didn't seem interested in Kirym at all." Mekrar sounded very bitter.

"I'm sure it'll all be sorted when Kirym is feeling better," said Oak. "Go and sleep. Come back in the morning."

25

Kirym Speaks

I woke suddenly. I had been thinking of the trip we had taken on Dragon Quest, remembering the rhythmic sound of the water hitting the boat. Even awake, I could hear water, different, but similar enough to bring back happy memories.

It was mid-morning, the sliver of daylight at the entrance showed a grey sky and the bare branches of a tree. There were no trees in the amphitheatre, so we had moved from there. *Did they move me because I've been sick?*

I sat up quickly, feeling lightheaded, and wondered what was happening.

Oak wrapped a shawl around my shoulders, pushed some cushions behind me and eased me back onto them.

"Where are we?" I asked.

"I'll tell you what is happening as you eat," he said. Wind Runner came in carrying a flat platter with an assortment of foods for me to try, and a deep resin-covered platter.

"In case something disagrees with you," she said, sitting it in easy reach.

"I'm feeling much better, but I am thirsty." I reached for the flask.

"We're at the settlement," said Oak. "Ubree told Veld he needed to prepare for the first big storm of winter. Veld wanted some buildings finished to ensure everyone was out of the weather. It's crowded, especially in the dwellings. Everyone else is in the winter hall. We're managing, and it'll be better after today. Four small dwellings will be finished before midday, and a larger hall by tonight or early tomorrow."

"Why am I not at home then?"

"It's too crowded," said Wind Runner, as she sat on the edge of the set beside me. "Along with almost all your family, Loul is hosting Findlow and Lyndym, Cindra's family, Bryn's, Garanniis', a few of the Dwarven leaders and some of their people, along with my immediate family, and quite a few others. Churnyg was there, but he found some oak trees you'd told him about, and he has taken a group to build some hollows. He is now lodging with Armos. All Green Valley families have opened their doors and hearts. Armos utilised the boats for some of us, but you needed peace and quiet, so this dwelling was brought from the amphitheatre."

"How did everyone get here so fast?"

"Ubree brought us here over the nights after you collapsed," said Oak.

"What about the other dragons?" I asked.

"They're well cared for. They came during the first night. Ubree has been amazing."

"The prisoners?"

"When we arrived, there was a stockade and shelter already built for them. Everyone's here. Now eat," Wind Runner said.

The smells were compelling, and I chose some finely ground oats with fruit juice. I was apologising for only managing two mouthfuls when Mama returned.

"That's all right, there'll be plenty waiting for you when you want it," she said, "and you must eat frequently. You won't get well if you don't." She felt my forehead, studied my token and looked into my eyes, searching for residual signs of the poison. "Oak, go, wash and get some food. Wind Runner and I will sit with Kirym until you return."

He obediently left, and she placed a clean robe on the set beside me. "He's a nice young man. He stayed with you for as long as we'd allow him when you collapsed."

She helped me wash, and change. "Kirym, tell me about Salcan. You mentioned him just before Gynbere threw the knife. I asked Mekrar. She just said you'd found him, and would tell me when you woke. I gather Larqeba knows, but he too has kept quiet. So?"

I gave her the major details as briefly as possible and answered her questions.

She was silent for a while. "I should have been more active in organising a search. It seems he wasn't that far away. I thought about him less than I should have. My lack of action could have jeopardised your life."

"Salcan would never have harmed me, Mama. He did the right thing for him. He knew himself; understood his problems. Jalkam explained it to him when she realised what was wrong. He was frightened by his reactions to people, especially large crowds. But in the end, he was happy. He knew those who needed help in The Rock, would get it."

She nodded. "There is such a lot we still don't know about his sort of sickness. Do your healers know anything, Wind Runner?"

She shook her head. "I wonder if Ubree could help there."

"Salcan helped Ubree when he was sick, and I'm sure Ubree would have done all he could in return. But ask him, maybe together you can find some answers." I paused. "Mama, can I sit in the sun for a while?"

She frowned. "Well perhaps after your next meal, but you must promise not to get involved in making any decisions. You will not overtire yourself," and she went on to list the many things I wasn't allowed to do.

I agreed because I knew it was the only way I would see the sun.

I slept again after Mama left me, but when I wakened, Wind Runner was there to ensure I didn't do anything at all except eat, drink and rest. I was bored by the inactivity.

Just before mid-afternoon, Oak arrived with news that Sundas had sorted out a place in the sun for me. I realised how weak I was, when I couldn't walk to the entrance of the dwelling. Oak picked me up and carried me to a nearby set. It was surrounded by wagons and was the most boring place they could have chosen, devoid of any people, or indeed, anything.

"No, Sundas, you don't get away with this. If the wagons are not moved, I will go and find somewhere interesting to sit. And you can answer to Mama."

He chuckled. "Well I didn't think we'd get away with it, but it was worth a try. Do you have a preference?"

"Where I can feel the breeze, see people and talk to a few of them. No one can catch anything from me, and if I get tired, I'll fall asleep."

Once I was comfortable, I took his hand and checked where he had been wounded. There was no scar and he had full movement.

"I slept for most of two days though," he said. "Ubree said it was the residue of the poison. No other side effects. How's yours?"

"As good as yours," I said. I looked around; the trees now red and gold told me how close winter was.

Mekrar, Arbreu, and Trethia were my first visitors, once I was settled. Trethia crawled onto the set beside me and snuggled close.

"Enliah came to see you when you were sick," she said. "She thought it was her fault. Ubree talked to her, and then Splinter talked to her. She's happy now, and so is Splinter. He's helping Bryn and Garanniis build a dwelling for their families, I think he will move in with them when it's finished."

"You shouldn't listen to gossip, Trethia," said Arbreu.

"I didn't listen. I watched."

"She does know these things," I said, and hugged him. "Just wait, you'll see. Now, how are you and Mekrar?"

He shrugged. "We've shared caring for you, and it's been," he paused, "well, different. But not much different from before. We feel right together. Mekrar told me how much you fought for us. Thank you."

"You should get time together alone."

"We do. Not a lot, but we'll get more later, and we have all our lives. There's so much to do here now. Everyone wants Loul to choose an heir. We've been waiting for you to be well enough to attend the meeting. I think it needs to be done before the families separate to live in different areas."

Through the afternoon, many people stopped by to talk to me. Most stayed for a few moments, and went on their way. Sundas watched like a hawk, mainly to ensure I was not fatigued by anyone. It was frustrating.

Morkeen stayed longer, I played with Amethyst for a while. She had grown, although she was still tiny, smaller than most new-borns from the settlement. I asked Morkeen about it, and was assured that although she was small even by their standards, she was growing steadily and doing all the right things for having seen four moons come and go.

Larqeba and Shormel also stayed a little longer when they visited. They were excited about how things were developing. Both had continued with their senior under-guard status, and revelled in the added responsibility.

"We've been doing night duty, Kirym," said Larqeba, excitedly.

"Only around the dragons," said Shormel, "but Veld has real guards around them all the time now."

"You weren't supposed to say that," Larqeba whispered loudly.

Shormel went bright red.

"I'm glad you did. Someone should have told me. Does Papa think they're in danger?"

"I don't know, but as soon as you got sick, Veld ordered they be guarded all the time. And he asked us to help the guards," Larqeba finished proudly.

"I need to see Ubree. Can you ask him to come here?"

They raced off to do my bidding.

Ubree, I know you heard that, but let them tell you. They feel important taking messages to you.

He nodded.

Papa accompanied Ubree, bringing yet another platter of food for me.

After a few generalities, I asked Papa about the extra guards.

"No, no particular reason, except to be doubly sure. Many still support Gynbere, and he's been vocal in his desire to see both you and Ubree die. I know we took his weapons, but there's nothing to say there aren't more out there."

"Delightful person. What will you do about him for the future?"

"I asked Kwarnar to discuss it with the dwarves and try to come up with some ideas. If they agree on a plan that won't endanger others, then we'll make it happen."

"And if they don't agree?"

"Loul will make the decision. She will probably ask you and Ubree for advice."

"Nothing can be done until we solve the mystery of the tor. Gynbere and his people must see it, or there could be unnecessary problems in the future."

"I'll pass that on to Loul. There have already been murmurings about his continued imprisonment without a Judicial Committee meeting. She has no obligation to call the committee, and no one has yet lodged an official complaint. She doesn't want to make fast decision. Too many people are still questioning their own loyalties."

He left and Ubree settled where I could see him, although he said nothing.

"I am sorry," I said. "It was worse than I realised."

He nodded.

"You were right. I let it get too big. And no, I wouldn't have allowed anyone else to get away with it. In fact, I didn't. I asked you to help Enliah, and it was the right thing to do."

"Does your hand still bother you?"

"No, I'd almost forgotten about it."

"And yet you haven't used it, nor have you looked at it."

He was right, I felt myself blushing as I glanced down. My fingers were closed over the edge of the sleeve, hiding the wound. I gingerly opened them. The scar ran from below my forefinger, down until opposite the base of my thumb. Then it curved across the bottom of my palm, and around my wrist to end a hand-span down my arm. It was well healed, white in the centre, and red on the outer edges. I flexed my hand, movement was excellent, although I was aware of the scar.

"Will it fade?'

"The red will disappear. It may be a little sensitive for a while, but you will get used to it quite quickly," said Ubree. "Some of the healers thought your arm should be amputated, you know. It took me three attempts to heal it, I couldn't cope with all the poisons at one time. Rargo's blade was poisoned, and you were also affected by what was on Gynbere's weapon. That was one of the worst poisons I've come across."

"I am truly sorry, Ubree. I've put you to so much trouble. I'll try not to be so stubborn in the future."

He laughed. "I'm sure you have good intentions, but that is what you are, and it would be a shame to have you change too drastically. Now be proud of your scar. You worked hard for it. The boys will be very envious."

"Ubree, I need to go back to the tor. Can you take me?"

"Why?"

"There's something there I missed. I've an idea, and I may be wrong, but I want to check."

"You're not yet strong enough. Once you are, I'll convince Loul to allow it. However, she will not permit you to go alone. Remember, Loul is your mama as well as being your headwoman."

"You'll be with me."

"Oh, I think there will be others too."

I sighed. "I hate to take anyone away from the building work."

He shrugged. "Then wait until the time is right."

"Ubree, what woke you? Is there another dragon we don't know about?"

"I can find no sign of one. My first conscious memory was

flying over the swamp, needing to get to you."

"So, no memory of waking. Just being awake."

He nodded.

I glanced at Trethia. "Was it you?"

"No. But now two dragons have been alive. So, something wakens them."

"Two!" Ubree's head snapped up. "Who?"

My mind was blank for a moment, and then I realised what she meant. "Faltryn. As his body disintegrated, and just for a short time. Then he died again."

"So, it was him."

"What was?"

"I have two sets of memories," he said. "I don't understand where the second set comes from." He paused, shook his head as if to shake off something, and took a deep breath. "Now what makes you think there is something else?"

"Two comments, although maybe I dreamed them. Something like, 'No one realises how it's done'. And then, 'none of you have the knowledge'."

"Gynbere said that just before you collapsed. He's right, I don't know enough."

"But, wait on." I closed my eyes, trying to remember. "He was talking about if he had injured you instead of Sundas. He planned to kill you. Who would have woken you?"

"Normally a reborn doesn't live again until the others sing, so whatever or whoever woke me, must have also woken Faltryn." Ubree glanced at me. "Are you all right, Kirym?"

"Oh, it can't be. Surely there's a..." I tried to think clearly about what happened over the days before the battle, and just after it. "I need to see the other dragons."

I pushed the rug off my legs, pulled my shawl around my shoulders and stood. I felt light-headed, and paused for a moment until everything stopped spinning. I felt extremely weak and tired.

"Ubree, why am I still so weak? Why did I sleep so long?"

"You told me you didn't want me to fix it all. You wanted to accept that your actions resulted in Slaslow's death. So, I ensured you would live, and I've allowed nature to sort out the rest. Have you now changed your mind? I could—"

"No," I interrupted. "Nature is doing very well, thank you. I was just wondering."

I was unsteady on my feet, shockingly weak and horribly slow. I had gone only six steps when Sundas, Oak, Storm, and Mama swooped down on me.

"I said you were to rest!" Mama said. "I can still put you in the healer's area. Try to ignore their rules..."

"Mama," I interrupted, feeling my legs shaking. "I need to see the dragons. It's important."

Oak picked me up, beating Storm and Sundas by moments. "I'll take her, Loul, and make sure she rests there too."

"Storm and I will bring the set," said Sundas.

"No, don't. I can sit on the grass, and lean against the stump."

They ignored me.

Oak settled me onto the relocated set. "You don't have the tokens, shall I get them?"

"You know something, I don't think I need them." I leaned forward. "Iryndal. Please waken. Take your position as dragon leader, guide your brothers and sisters and care for the people of The Green Valley."

I waited, holding my breath.

Nothing happened, and I suddenly felt extremely weary. I closed my eyes, and leaned back on the set. "Stupid to think it was me," I murmured.

Trethia gasped. "Kirym, look!"

I sat up. Iryndal's body seemed to flutter, a movement that went from her nose to her tail. She appeared to expand; was it because she breathed in? Almost as if in a dream, her nose grew a little darker. When the colour reached her eyes, they opened. The darker colour rippled on down her body, waves of it, darker and darker, until the only pale spot was her token mark, which stood out more than ever.

She stood, shook her body, and touched her token bump to my tokens and then connected to Ubree.

Together we repeated the request to Othyn. Again, it took time, but then her body also seemed to quiver, grow and darken. She stood and acknowledged me, Ubree and Iryndal. We turned our attention in quick succession to Egrym, Arymda and Borasyn. All darkened and grew as they woke, and all acknowledged us. Then they all focussed on Ubree, who was, I was sure, telling them all that had happened since he awoke.

I alone turned my attention to Faltryn, calling him to waken also.

Ubree was the first to respond. His head whipped around to look at me. "If he's alive, I'll kill 'im!"

But no dragon appeared. Ubree rolled his eyes, shook his head and relaxed. I studied the dragons, noting the differences from when they were last alive. They were all a little bigger and darker.

Then, "Oh, isn't she sweet."

My head moved as fast as Ubree's. "She?"

We stared at the tiny figure who crept from under a pile of leaves, and immediately fell on its nose. It struggled to its feet.

I glanced at Ubree. He had a strange look on his face, and as what he saw, registered, he seemed to deflate. "Oh, I'd forgotten about that."

"She?"

No one was answering my question; all watched the tiny white dragon as it stumbled over to Ubree and reached up to touch his nose.

"Just stay away from me," Ubree snarled, but Faltryn stared up at him, butted his nose again, and turned to look at the other dragons.

"SHE?"

"Yes, Kirym," said Iryndal. "It's been so long since the eldest died, I had forgotten. I think we all had. With reborns, there must always be a balance. It means a great change when the eldest dies. I believe the dragons on our home planet feared this the most, for some reason."

Faltryn approached each of the dragons in turn, beginning with Iryndal and ending with Borasyn. Iryndal was regal, Egrym was a little dismissive, Othyn was gentle, while Borasyn and Arymda were enthusiastic.

"Wow, how did you get them back?" asked Sundas.

"I have no idea. Their waking as I called them *must* have been a coincidence. Maybe Iryndal can work out what's going on."

Oak hunkered down in front of me and stared. It was a bit disconcerting.

"Kirym, your blue token," he said.

"What about it?"

"It—it's sort of changed again. I don't know, it's different. When I glance at it, it's blue, but when I concentrate, it's—I don't know—darker. The outer colour moves as if it were a blue and green liquid around a blue core.

Iryndal moved fast. Standing behind Oak, she too stared at my token. "You're a dragon caller, Kirym. How did that happen?"

"Because Ubree woke it up when he put himself into the token," said Trethia.

In the stunned silence, Faltryn stumbled over to stand in front me. She stretched her head up to mine, and I leaned down and touched my token to her forehead. Slowly a bump appeared, very blue against her white skin, and began to pulse.

"She's tied to Kirym, too," said Othyn. Her voice showed the awe seen in the faces of the other dragons.

26

Arbreu

The succession meeting to choose the next probable headman, was held on the day of the full moon, two days before the first big storm of winter began. While Loul had originally wanted the building work to continue through the good weather, she was convinced that enough had been done, and one extra day would not finish any more buildings.

The winter hall, finished while Kirym journeyed to and from Faltryn, was deemed the best place for it. Fewer people lived there now, as several other dwellings had been finished. It was temporarily cleared so all of those who wished to, could be part of choosing a successor.

Arbreu expressed surprise at how many attended.

"Each community will keep their own chosen leader, but they'll all be answerable to the leader of The Green Valley," explained Mekrar.

"Wind Runner has already agreed we'll become part of The Green Valley community," Oak said. "Whoever becomes leader will impact on our lives, but Loul said our voice will always be listened to."

"The Tree Dwarves want to see how leaders in The Green Valley are chosen, although I'm sure Churnyg will be leading us," said Borboncha.

"Will you be his successor, Ashistar?" asked Sundas.

"There are too many who, even now, distrust me. And no one quite understands where my duty to Kirym will lead me. So, I doubt it."

"Oh, I don't know," said Baketer. "Churnyg still has many seasons, and things will settle down long before we need to choose someone. I think you are well in there, and the connections with Kirym can only enhance you."

"Why are the prisoners here?" Oak asked.

"They're subject to Green Valley rules, so have a right to hear what is said," Mekrar said, "and to express an opinion. The cage they are in is to protect others, and although it is unusual to have armed guards at such a meeting, Mama and Papa felt it necessary on this occasion.

Veld, Loul, Armos, Zelriff and Old Harby sat at a table at the top of the hall. Veld called for quiet, explained briefly how the process worked and asked for nominations.

Armos' name was given, followed by Mekroe, Young Harby, Gynbere, Cindra, Findlow, Shanyth, Tarl's son, and Kirym.

"Is this position open only to you and your cronies?" called Zeffun Urfit.

"Any who accept The Green Valley as their overlords, and agree to our laws can be nominated," Loul said. "Remember though, even the leader must obey the laws of the land, and changes in law or new laws must be discussed with everyone before they are passed."

"Then I nominate My Lord Gynbere, who has already proven himself a caring, generous and benevolent leader. All his people will vote for him, and I'm sure they will convince everyone else to do the same."

In the silence that followed, and as Grenin noted the name in a book, Sirasha stood and bowed towards Loul. "Is everyone aware that their votes will be made in secret? No one need ever know how they vote."

"Thank you, Sirasha. Now each person named will now either accept, or reject their nomination. More names may be added to the list at any time before the final decision is made," said Veld.

"I accept, Zeffun's nomination," Gynbere called, from his seat in the cage.

Armos declined. "Loul is younger than I am, and will almost definitely outlive me. I will happily support and help train whoever is chosen."

Young Harby declined also. He felt his ability to cope with more responsibility was lacking. Cindra also declined. "Five daughters and Grennin are all of the responsibility I want," she said, although her thickening figure suggested she was about to add to her load before the middle of summer. Findlow, now caring for his family without Natia, also declined. His family had already agreed to accept Loul as their headwoman, with Findlow or Lyndym to be their spokesperson.

The reasons each person gave for declining, they were met with nods of understanding. These answers were expected.

Mekroe stood. "Leading this family, being leader of The Green Valley, was something I never ever dreamed of. Until recently, I was Halse and Tarl's irritatingly irresponsible, younger brother, trouble, the clown, the one most likely to bring disaster to everyone and everything. Now I have joined, married the most beautiful, wonderful woman I could dream of, and I have responsibilities to her and her family. I have already, with Mama and Papa's agreement, aligned myself to Wind Runner and the Faltryners, and pledged to honour the agreements made with the leader of The Green Valley. In that, I will be supporting Starshine when she becomes matriarch of the new settlement of Faltryn, although hopefully it'll be a long way off. That however, disqualifies me from this position. I could not put the best for my new family ahead of The Green Valley, and yet under the promises I made, if I felt the need arose, I would have to. So, I decline, but thank everyone for considering me."

After a momentary shocked pause, Old Harby began to clap, and everyone joined in.

This left Shanyth, Gynbere, and Kirym.

Shanyth was approaching his sixth spring. He and his sister, Tanwyn, sat near their mama, Zhins. Shanyth spent his time hitting his sister's stuffed doll with a small toy cart Tarl had carved for him.

"He's not even aware of what's happening here," Arbreu murmured to Oak. "Other children of the same age are paying attention."

Wind Runner, who sat nearby, leaned over to Arbreu. "He's just lost his papa, and he's still very young. He has plenty of time to mature, and there are many good people to guide him."

"If Zhins allows it," murmured Mekrar. "If he is chosen, she'll sit in his place until he's of age. If Mama dies and Zhins feels he's not ready to take over, it would take a lot to make her step down."

Zhins stood and waited patiently until the crowd had silenced. "Veld, I accept the position of leader for my son. As the eldest of Tarl's children, it is his right to hold this position. I shall be happy to sit in his place to make the necessary decisions as headwoman."

Arbreu had a strange feeling of dread as he listened to her. "It's as if she's pushing Loul aside," he murmured to Mekrar.

Before Mekrar could answer, Young Harby stood and asked to be recognised. Loul and Veld both nodded. "Aren't we still in the nomination portion of this process? There are other choices. We've not heard from Kirym and the nominations have not yet closed. We need to go through the entire consultation."

Before anyone could comment, Zhins turned on Young Harby. "The position belonged to Tarl, and it should rightly go to his son. From eldest son to eldest son. Kirym should only be considered if Tarl had no children."

Zelriff stood and asked for Loul's indulgence. "I think you've misunderstood the way this is done, Zhins. Loul is headwoman, and will be until she dies or feels the need to step down. Veld is her voice and warlord at her agreement only, although it is only recently he has needed to act as warlord. Any of Loul's children could lead us, however, the position is not hereditary, and anyone from The Green Valley family can be nominated. We need the wisest leader. I believe now, all of those nominated should be allowed to speak."

Zhins face hardened. She remained standing.

"Kirym," said Loul. "You also have been nominated. What do you say?"

"No one should consider her at all," Zhins stormed. "She has taken this family to war. It's because of her that Shanyth is without his Papa and she is the reason we buried many other loved ones at the amphitheatre. Kirym pushed Tarl into an attack against his better judgement. No one wants her here."

Kirym's face remained impassive, devoid of emotion. There was silence as she stood.

"I understand and appreciate the honour offered me in being nominated, but I wish to decline."

There was an uproar. Everyone spoke at the same time.

Arbreu was stunned. "Why?"

But Kirym still stood, waiting for the noise to abate. "Had Halse lived, she would lead the family."

"She's dead," snapped Zhins.

"Her sister isn't!" said Kirym. "I'd like to add Mekrar's name to the list. As good as I think Mekroe would have been, I believe Mekrar will be better."

Amid the vocal storm that followed, Arbreu glanced at Zhins. She looked furious.

Mekrar looked stunned.

"What will you...?" Arbreu found he was suddenly talking to Mekrar's legs.

"I accept the nomination," she said.

"So," said Veld, when everyone settled down. "With three people to consider, everyone can comment as they wish, and then a decision will be made."

"Mekrar may be the oldest of your living children, Veld," called Zhins, "but Shanyth is an older child's son. He should have preference."

Gynbere stood. "With this in-family fighting, which is unsettling for everyone, I am the obvious choice. Those who vote for me will be looked on with preference in the days that follow."

"That sounds very like a threat to those who don't vote for you," Zelriff said.

Gynbere ignored her.

The comments, along with many others, were noted. Parchment was placed on the table for the voting, and almost everyone lined up to write their choice.

"What happens now, Arbreu?" Wind Runner asked him, as he returned from making his choice, and sat beside her again.

"Well it's mainly Loul who makes the decision. As in everything she'll look hard at what we all say, but she doesn't have to consider anyone."

"Not even Veld?"

"As Zelriff said, he is simply her spokesman, her voice," said Mekrar. "History tells us she took a long time to make him her voice, because she was joined to him. She could have chosen others to both positions."

Wind Runner frowned. "I should have asked her about it. It seems my assumptions were wrong. Tarl just followed orders from her. He really wasn't needed, was he?"

"He was and he wasn't," said Mekrar. "Tarl had been trained to lead the army, but Papa had trained all of his children and several others, Peet, Bokum, Young Harby, Teema, and Arbreu after he joined us. If Zhins thinks Kirym pressured Tarl, she's mistaken. He did nothing of his own accord. The decision was Mama's. She and Tarl spent a long time talking over the different options, and many of the alternatives were suggested by Kirym. Mama listened to everyone. Mind you, she rarely makes decisions without taking advice. She knows it is far too easy to be swayed by personal desire. Of course, she wanted her people back, Papa especially. However, had it been in everyone's best interest to not approach Gynbere, as headwoman, she would have made that decision, as unpalatable as it would have personally been."

"Why didn't she, as headwoman, lead the army?" asked Wind Runner. "She strikes me as being more than capable."

Mekrar smiled grimly. "She is, but our laws say no, unless there is no other person available. As headwoman, she holds the wisdom of the family, and she understands our mysteries. We protect her, because her wisdom protects us. She'll be hard to follow, and the position may yet go to Kirym."

Arbreu looked as surprised as Wind Runner. "But Kirym declined. Surely it's between you and Shanyth."

"And Gynbere, added Mekrar. "As much as we wouldn't vote for him, we have no idea how many would. Whoever is chosen today, is only doing an apprenticeship, Arbreu. Neither Gynbere, Shanyth nor I may be suitable in the end. Mama can change her mind; any or all of us can approach her with a wish to revisit this. Kirym told me it has happened before, and the provision remains. It's the same for you, Arbreu. If I chose you as my voice and warlord, you may not want the position; you may not be suitable or something may happen to make it impractical. Then I'd choose someone else," said Mekrar.

"Me? Warlord? My goodness, I never thought it would mean that."

Mekrar laughed. "Actually, Voice is more important than warlord. Most of our leaders have known nothing but peace." She brought her finger to her lips as Loul stood.

"Has everyone voted as they wished?" A wave of nodding and murmuring rippled across the group. Zelriff and Old Harby began to sort the pieces of parchment.

"Why four piles?" asked Dashlan.

"Everyone is expressing an opinion, and a different opinion is acceptable. It's part of the process," explained Mekrar. "Obviously Gynbere, Shanyth and myself, but some people may have voiced a concern, or added a condition to their vote, or suggested someone else. If two or three of us receive the same number of votes, the fourth pile will become important. The interim process doesn't end until Loul chooses."

"What if the fourth pile is much bigger than the other three?" asked Dashlan.

Frowning, Mekrar thought for a moment. "I don't believe that's ever happened, although Kirym would know. However, I suspect there would be a great deal more discussion."

"Are you worried about Kirym?" asked Dashlan.

Arbreu glanced over. She sat wrapped in a large shawl, with a rug over her legs, and appeared lost in thought. While her health had improved, she was taking a long time to heal completely, and Loul had insisted she rest. What worried Arbreu most, was that Kirym wasn't arguing against it.

Arbreu was about to go and talk to her, when Mekrar caught his hand. "Don't. She's all right. We'll know if she wants us. Oak is nearby, and the dragons are watching. They won't let anything happen to her."

"Teema should be with her. Where is he, anyway?"

"He's here," Mekrar said. "Even in his present state of mind, he wouldn't miss this."

"I vaguely thought he may be nominated. He's as good as a son to Loul and Veld. Why not?" Arbreu asked.

"He may be mentioned in the fourth pile, but you know, in all of this, I've never even considered him. After Halse died, his name came up then, but perhaps this lapse in behaviour tells us a lot about him."

Sorting the parchments came to an end. Two of the piles held fewer than six sheets of parchment, and one of the others towered over all of them. As Loul stood to announce the winner, Gynbere also stood, accepting handshakes from those sitting close to him.

"The majority have chosen Mekrar." Loul's hand sat on the largest pile in front of her. "I will accept this advice, but please understand, I think this is the right decision."

Gynbere was white, but before anyone could do or say anything, Zhins was on her feet. "That's not fair!" she cried. "Shanyth—"

Before she could say more, Wind Runner moved with a speed that surprised Arbreu, and spoke quietly to her for a few moments. Zhins went quite red, and then sat down. Wind Runner sat with her.

Old Harby stood. "You may join us, Mekrar," and he started to clap. Almost everyone there joined in.

As Mekrar stood, Shanyth walked over to Kirym, and

kicked the set she sat on. "You killed my Papa!" he screamed. The applause died abruptly. "I hate you!"

Kirym stared at him impassively.

Veld rubbed his cheek bone with two fingers, but his face was a mask. Arbreu was amazed at the calm from those at the table, not at all like the inner turmoil he was sure it was felt by everyone there.

"Shanyth," called Loul. There was no response from the child. She called again.

He slowly turned around, but walked only as far as Zhins, who scrambled to her feet and put her arm around his shoulders.

"Shanyth, please come here, now." Loul's voice was quiet, but her tone unmistakable.

Zhins suddenly screamed and bent over clutching her belly.

"Oh, my goodness. Her baby's coming. I wonder how long she's been feeling pains," said Mekrar.

Shanyth looked scared. He stamped his foot on the ground and pointed at Kirym. "It's all her fault," he screamed. "I hate her, I hate her, I haaate her!"

Veld walked over to Shanyth. "This behaviour is most unacceptable. You and I will have a wee chat." He picked Shanyth up, and walked towards the door. Shanyth kicked and screamed for his mama, but Veld never paused. Grennin carried Zhins out, followed by Soojee, Jorlenta, and two other midwives. Loul met them at the entrance. Seba picked a frightened looking Tanwyn up, and took her over to join her children. Tanwyn looked happier when Nysia pulled her into a counting game she was playing with her sisters and friends.

Armos stood and quietened everyone down. "As is usual in the circumstances, the parchment will be destroyed. If anyone wishes to see them, or has any questions about them, now is the time. Other than that, the meeting is over, although we will all gather again when Loul is available."

Arbreu glanced over to see if Gynbere would challenge the votes, but he had turned his back on the crowd, and talking to Vellysh and Zeffun. Neither of them looked happy.

"I'll go see that Kirym's all right," Arbreu murmured, but before he could move, he and Mekrar were surrounded by friends, wanting to congratulate them both.

"It's nothing to do with me," he said, as a beaming Young Harby grasped his forearm and thumped him on the back. "This is Mekrar's moment."

"Oh, you get more training as well," Young Harby said, after he'd hugged Mekrar. "She'll need someone to help with the responsibility, and you're the obvious choice, unless you really don't want to be. Mind you, she could choose me, but somehow I doubt she will."

Finally, the crowd around him thinned and Arbreu moved towards Kirym.

The set was empty. The rug was there, but she'd gone. Panicked, Arbreu searched through the crowd, but many of those still milling around were taller than he was. He stepped onto the set to search over everyone's head, but to no avail. She was nowhere to be seen.

27

Kirym Speaks

The crowd surged around Mekrar and Arbreu and I saw little reason to be jostled and jolted attempting to congratulate them.

The noise was giving me a headache, and when Larqeba and Shormel came to talk, I asked them to get a flask of water, and bring it out to a small shady area overlooking the lake. Then I quietly slipped away.

Half way there, just as I thought I may not make it, Findlow took my arm and helped me the remaining distance.

We sat in the watery sunshine, knowing we would soon be driven inside. The clouds boiled up from the southeast, and although I knew the rain wouldn't hit before next midday, the wind was rising and the air was cooling.

I lay my head on Findlow's shoulder, pleased he didn't speak, although I knew he wanted to. We sat in companionable silence for a short time until Larqeba raced up with a flask, full of chatter about the celebration that was being planned.

I shooed him off to take part, promising I'd watch him and Shormel during the shooting competition later.

"Borasyn told us you were here. Do you want to be alone?" Mekrar asked, as she, Arbreu and Oak sat beside Findlow.

I laughed. "In this family? No, I just wanted some moments to think about a few things."

"Are you all right?" Arbreu asked.

"Why wouldn't I be?"

"Well, ummm!" Arbreu paused dramatically. "Let me see. Zhins! Shanyth! Rejecting the nomination. Why didn't you accept? You should have! You'd have been perfect. I always thought Loul would choose you."

"I'm the youngest. Surely, last in line."

"It's to do with ability, not age. So, what was your real reason?"

I took a deep breath. "I wouldn't necessarily be the best person, Arbreu. I have a lot of other responsibilities, Amethyst, Trethia, the dragons, the tokens, and the weapons."

"But aren't they reasons for you to do it? Those are things that show how suitable you are."

"Mekrar is a better choice. She'll keep the tribes together. She has the time and the desire. If I was chosen, many people would resent it. All those things you site as part of my ability, could cause resentment. Because I am youngest, Zhin's would never accept me. She would agitate and that could split the family. Because I care for Trethia some of the Nythians would have reason to feel unsettled, because I claim Amethyst, some would feel I'd be biased in my treatment of the Valythians. Because I have the dragons, some would fear me. Because I carry the weapons, some would feel I had too much power. The leader needs to pull the tribes together. I would as likely tear them apart."

Findlow nodded. "I knew your reasoning would be sound,

but I didn't think there'd be so many of them. But do you really think they're valid? People are beginning to accept Trethia, and they love the dragons."

"Well, despite that, Mekrar will still do a better job. I'm surprised no one nominated her. Even had Mekroe not rejected his nomination, I think she would have been chosen over him."

"But not over you, surely." said Arbreu.

"That's sweet of you, Arbreu, but let me ask you this. Between Mekrar and me, who would you have voted for?"

"That's unfair, Kirym," interjected Mekrar, before he could answer.

"I know it is, because how could he make that decision here? However, Arbreu, you would have chosen Mekrar, not because you're joined, but because she's the best choice."

Arbreu frowned. "But the choice wouldn't have been between you and Mekrar. She hadn't been nominated. Shanyth had. So, you would have been chosen. If you hadn't declined and nominated Mekrar, it might have been easier."

"Mekrar deserved to be nominated, and I think someone would have before it got to a vote. It should be her position. Even when Tarl led us to save Papa, he was having doubts about his ability and desire to hold the leadership position," I said.

Findlow nodded. "He mentioned it to Loul, suggested she ask you, Kirym. He wanted to step away right then, not lead the armies. Would you have led them, Kirym?"

"No," I said. "Tarl needed to, if only because we were leading many families into the battle. Mekrar will be a better leader than Tarl could have been. She's been trained by the best, Mama, Papa, Zelriff, Armos and Old Harby."

"I never thought Zhins would turn on you in that way," said Findlow. "But isn't Tanwyn older than Shanyth?"

Mekrar sighed. "Only just, and that's another reason there'd have been more discussion. I think Zhins put Shanyth up because he's Tarl's son. He's a reminder to every one of her loss. She's lost the person she relied on. She's hurting and not just the birth pains."

"About the pains. Why didn't she go to the midwives when they started? They'd have helped her."

"The baby isn't due yet, Arbreu," said Mekrar. "She mightn't have realised the birth was imminent. Maybe she just felt uncomfortable and achy."

"Is that the reason she was so aggressive towards Kirym?" asked Oak.

"Zhins has always had a bit of a problem with Kirym," said Mekrar. "She felt Kirym took attention that was due her children."

"I never understood that. There's quite an age difference between them," said Findlow.

"Mama and Papa doted on Tarl's children, but Kirym was their youngest, and she was like a little doll," Mekrar said. "Zhins resentment of Kirym was only part of the issue. She wasn't interested in learning our family history and insisted only she teach the twins. They know a bit about her family, she insisted they would learn about our family later. Her family only had male leaders. Prestige for women came only from their papa, husband and sons. So in her mind, she just lost all status. "

"That's stupid," said Arbreu.

"It's how she feels. The problems may not be over yet. Early babies tend to be too small and sometimes don't survive."

"You kept Amethyst alive, Kirym. She was the tiniest thing I'd ever seen. Tiannii said she was small even for one of theirs, probably born far too early. Could you help Zhins?"

"I doubt she'll accept my help, Arbreu. But I've told

Lantiah and Mama how I cared for Amethyst."

"Can Ubree help?"

Mekrar took his hand. "He heals wounds. I'm not sure if he could do anything in this case. Even if he could, would Zhins will accept his help?"

"Gynbere expected to be chosen," Oak said. "I'm really surprised he didn't challenge the result."

Findlow laughed dryly. "He wouldn't chance the votes being counted in front of everyone. What if the smallest pile was his? He'd never live it down."

"Some of those with him were not looking happy. There may be a few quietly requesting to be let out soon." said Oak.

Trethia sat beside me, as Sundas placed a large platter of food on a small stump in the middle of the circle of people. "We've been watching the men start the competitions, but thought that some food was in order." He helped Trethia to cut a portion for herself. He leaned in close to me as he handed me a portion. "Are you all right?"

"I'm missing something."

"Being headwoman, perhaps?"

I laughed and shook my head. "No. It's something someone said." Before I could enlarge on it, Papa and Wind Runner joined us.

"How's Shanyth?" Mekrar asked.

"We had a chat, he and Tanwyn are now in Seba's care. She and Young Harby will do what is required for a while. Harbs and Zelriff will pop in too when needed. Shanyth'll be all right. He's been learning some intense hatred over the past few days, evidently."

"How much damage has Zhins done to them, Papa?" asked Mekrar.

"Tanwyn is quite sensible for her age. She hadn't been happy with what was being drilled into them. As for

Shanyth, it'll take time, but I suspect it'll be sorted without too many problems. Kirym, now I have you here and you're feeling better, do tell me about the pole Tarl carried during the battle. Loul didn't know all of the details."

"You need to ask Bryn and Dashlan."

"I've asked them, they said the same as Loul."

I laughed. "Perhaps we should all tell you together." I paused. "Iryndal has asked them to join us."

Everyone was impatient until the two men sat down. "The big reveal, is it?" asked Dashlan, grinning broadly.

Papa nodded. "How did you produce a dragon? That was impressive."

"Ownership is nothing if you don't know what you can do with it, Veld," said Bryn. "We used it as a speaking stick. It was only because Larqeba was holding it, that I listened to him long enough to learn about Salcan taking Kirym. Without it, I'd just have thrashed him and tied him to a tree for a few season cycles. After we had passed the lodge on our way to The Rock, Rargo took the pole. You saw that, of course, when he paraded up and down with it. However, it was the head that held the value to us, not the pole. It's been in our family for hundreds of seasons, and yet in the short time Kirym held it, we increased our knowledge so much. That's why she should tell the rest."

I paused for a moment. "All I discovered was that looking through the head showed a shadow. Qwinita and Dashlan then realised the shadow was influenced by several things, the moon in its various configurations, fire, water, and as it turned out, the early sun, although that wasn't realised until they were at the tor. When it was held up to an early morning sun, the shape projected through to the opposite side as the figure of a dragon. When Tarl talked of approaching in the early morning with the sun behind him, it seemed like a good idea to use it, although only because the idea of having it wreathed with smoke could make it appear to be something other than what Rargo purported it to be. Bryn asked Dashlan to replace the pole. That's his story."

"I was at the back of the group bringing the dwarven children to the amphitheatre when the tie on my boot came loose. I was fixing it, and from the corner of my eye, I saw something crawl towards me in the tree above. It was strange, because when I looked there were only branches. Then the wind blew, and it did it again. Gave me a laugh, well a fright too, because it was strange, but I figured then it'd be a great toy. Five stems from a single branch, and the markings on the wood make them appear to writhe when moved slightly. When Pa asked me to replace the pole, I was about to cut a branch from the nearest tree when I remembered it. Great affect, don'tcha think?"

"So, you and Kirym put it together, but who came up with the smoke idea?" asked Bryn. "I didn't expect that."

"Oh, that was totally Kirym," said Dashlan.

I waved the notion away. "No, not me. Those travelling from Faltryn carried fire with them in small baked pots. They stopped using them for the duration of the journey here because the flints were quicker and easier, and the pots were very smoky. Dashlan borrowed one, and carried it under his robe. We attached a dried pig's bladder to the top of it, and a length of dried intestine became a pipe to channel the smoke. Dash held Tarl's shoulder, and the pipe threaded along Tarl's sleeve. Smoke travelled through the tube and was there when needed."

"But how did you ensure it didn't smoke all the time?" asked Papa.

Dashlan laughed. "Again, Kirym's idea. Where the tube met the bladder, she suggested we place a short length of soft leather, long enough to be twisted to hold the smoke. It worked really well 'cause initially it came out as a puff instead of a stream. It took a bit of doing, we sewed it first, but the smoke leaked between the stitches, so we used wood resin. It needed to be pliable after it had dried. Findlow advised us there."

"Wouldn't it have been easier to make the whole thing from leather?" asked Arbreu.

"I thought so," said Dashlan, "but Kirym reckoned the skin would absorb the smoke over the length we needed. She was right too, I tried it over the last few evenings. Wouldn't have worked."

Papa shook his head. "I'm sure it was more difficult than you make out, but it was very effective. What about the noise it made? That was uncanny."

"Ahhhh," said Dashlan. "Another of Findlow's ideas."

"No, not really," Findlow said. "Storm inspired it. I remembered that strange hollow stick he found while travelling back from Faltryn. Starshine allowed me to borrow it. I capped the ends with leather, and added a pile of tiny pebbles. Shaking it created one sound, but Dashlan figured that just allowing the pebbles to run from one end to the other worked better. It sounded like a dragon's roar, but different."

Papa laughed. "Well, ingenious. Going by the comments around me, everyone was intrigued."

"Kirym, you said you were missing something" said Findlow. "What?"

"Well," I said. "Gynbere was at the tor for a reason. There's something there, and we have to find it before he or someone he confides in does."

"The ibith and the stuff in it?" asked Oak.

"He only lost it because he underestimated our reaction when attacked us. What is there that's so important?"

"The weapons," said Mekrar.

"They were offered to him, and he refused them. The

power they present would appeal, but he was too scared to touch them."

Mekrar frowned. "He wanted them at the tor, but whatever he thought they could do, didn't happen."

I shook my head. "He knows something, not everything, but more than I know. There's something I'm just not seeing." I frowned as I tried to think of an answer. "I need to talk to Ashistar, Churnyg, Baketer, and Borboncha?"

Iryndal's voice entered my head. *I'm sending them over, Kirym.*

"How can they help?" Oak asked.

"They may know something. A small something that's vital."

The four men arrived quickly.

"Gynbere knew about the tor, and the amphitheatre. How?"

"To my knowledge, he never left The Rock," said Borboncha.

"Was there ever a time when all of the guards were taken off the wall in The Rock at the same time?" I asked, when they had settled and accepted platters piled high with food.

"It's been happening off and on for about twenty season cycles while I was on the wall, but there were whispers," Baketer said. "It'd happened before with Gynbere's ancestors. Not a lot, but once maybe twice a season cycle."

"Were the guards taken off the tree at that time also?"

Ashistar, nodded. "Why?"

"For how long, each time?

"One night, usually. Occasionally a night and a day for the walls. Never longer," said Ashistar, "except at the time the oak trees were felled. Slaslow said it was because there were evil creatures, aligned to the Oak family out there. He said it was safer to have the Elm soldiers on the wall; they were stronger. When we resumed our duty, the trees were down.

Gynbere said that he was able to protect his people in The Rock, but had been unable to extend that to the trees."

Oak leaned forward. "Did no one ask why creatures aligned to the Oak family, would destroy oak trees?"

"I'm sure many thought it, but it would have been a death sentence to actually ask," Churnyg said.

"But here's a strange thing," said Baketer. "The other times always happened when Gynbere and Slaslow were ill. Both together. The Urfits took over from Slaslow. When we went back onto the wall, there was always an Urfit up there with us. They stayed from dawn to dusk, and they sat opposite where the oak grove was. They stayed thirty to thirty-five or so days, and then we'd have another night off. After that, it'd get back to normal. They never did it any other time."

"Were either Gynbere or Slaslow seen during that time?" I asked.

"No," said Ashistar slowly. "Never. Vellysh made a point of telling us they were avoiding people because their illness was contagious."

"What did the healers say?"

"Nothing, and that was unusual. Normally they'd make a song and dance about how they brought Gynbere back from the brink of death. He'd make a big thing of rewarding them, but not on those occasions."

"Were they sick at other times?"

Ashistar nodded. "But not together, and never for such a long time. I didn't think about it before, but thirty days is a long time to be sick, isn't it? You think it means something."

"Yes, and it's been happening more lately, say in the last eight seasons, hasn't it?"

Baketer nodded. "How would you know that?"

I ignored the question. "How long would it take Gynbere to get to the tor?"

"When we left The Rock, Slaslow told the guard captains that we'd be travelling for about eight days. For the first few days, the people were really pushed hard, but they couldn't keep up, especially as none of them were given food, and no one was prepared. After that, we went slower," said Borboncha. "I overheard a conversation between Slaslow and Thipin back in The Rock. Thipin said, um—" He frowned as he thought back. "He said, 'Five days there and the same back. He'll have time.' Heard no more, they were just walking past."

"And I think seven days'd be right, Kirym," said Papa. "Just going by the information Iryndal has given me, although he must have moved a lot faster than usual. What are you thinking?"

"Did he leave The Rock more after he met Salcan?"

Ashistar smiled slowly and nodded. "And he was gone longer. You know something, don't you."

"Salcan would have told him we were back in The Green Valley again. Suddenly whatever he knew became more important."

"Gunyon and his friend talked about it, a special destination," said Churnyg.

"Gynbere expected to capture Churnyg at the oak grove," said Borboncha. "That failed. The next day Black-Cloak was with us, and then Slaslow told Rookham there was a change of plan. He was ordered to capture this great leader and take them to the seat of power. Slaslow was very specific about the route. We were told to move fast. Very fast. North and then west to the amphitheatre, but we got lost. That threw Rookham. He'd been there several times, so he expected to find it easily."

"Why?" Findlow asked.

"I don't know; I was new to the group. Slaslow moved us around, supposedly so no one can plot against him. Anyway, after we saw you, Kirym, Rookham told us that if we mentioned anything about meeting anyone, we'd be killed. Not that we would've talked, we'd all have been punished had Slaslow found out we'd not killed or captured everyone we met. Then we bumped into another group. They'd been told to get everyone back to the junction where the path turns west."

Papa frowned. "I wonder why."

"While I was waiting for more orders," Borboncha said, "I overheard Slaslow talking to Gynbere. He was in the pavilion, and he said, 'They'll be vulnerable there, and they'll let down their guard.' Then he whispered something about a sacrifice of power couldn't hurt, and it might be what was needed. Does it mean anything?"

"Ahha," said Papa. "Killing Faltryn. The sacrifice."

"But, whatever Gynbere expected to happen at the tor, didn't because Faltryn was killed here, not there," said Oak.

"Faltryn can't have been the sacrifice," I said. "When Gynbere left The Rock, he didn't know we had met the dragons. Anyway, after he killed Faltryn, he still went to the tor, and he still wanted something. So, what do we know?"

"He knew you had the sword and the knife," Baketer said. "Churnyg was alive, but he still planned to go straight to the tor."

A long silence, many frowns.

"He was originally going to the tor," suggested Oak, "and changed his mind,"

"It must have been something Elm told him," Mekrar said.

"Maybe. Gynbere didn't plan to take the sword personally." I paused, as I tried to clarify my thoughts. "At the tor, he itemised the things he wanted. First the weapons, and without jeopardising his life by touching them, he had me put them where he wanted them. Then he asked for the tokens. We know he had prior knowledge of them, because he searched for the statue we saw at Churnyg's door."

"You're right," said Mekrar. "You know, he never asked about those we wore. That's unusual, most people do. So why didn't he?"

I shrugged. "Perhaps he thought they weren't important for what he wanted. But, he got it wrong anyway, because what he did, didn't work. Ashistar, Borboncha, did anything of importance happen during the trip to the tor or once you got there?" I asked.

"Well he spent a lot of time with Black-Cloak and Rargo, especially in the evenings," Borboncha said. "There were raised voices occasionally. Rargo got kicked out at one stage. Spent a few cold nights out in the open. It was rumoured he objected to something said by Black-Cloak, but of course Elm knew more than him."

"The bridge and platform were already built when we got to the tor," said Ashistar. "A group of miners were trying to pry out some of the rocks from the bank beneath the stump. It was hard, some of the workers were injured."

"And that explains something I worried about, Kirym. People disappeared from The Rock. Men mainly, competent rock movers, muscle men, all men who were experienced in moving rocks. They never came back, but the families never spoke of them," Ashistar said. "He sent the men there ahead to do the work."

Borboncha nodded. "Just going by conversations I overheard, a group also left the amphitheatre soon after they arrived. I think they went to the tor."

"How did he get people to go there, when everyone believed they would die if they left The Rock?" Mekrar asked.

"Gynbere told them he alone could protect them, but only in the area of the tor. Of course, that stopped them from running off. A few had tried to escape over the seasons, but their bodies were always seen somewhere nearby at dawn. Slaslow claimed they would have been attempting to return, having realised the truth of what Gynbere had said. He wouldn't allow the bodies to be retrieved. They disappeared though the next night; wild animals, Gynbere said, but none had been heard. I suspect all would have had an arrow in them, and that Slaslow placed the bodies there, and hauled them off.

"So, we know Gynbere had a plan. It showed in who he kidnapped, but who else did he want? Findlow for one," Oak said.

"I think he tried for Bryn," said Armos.

"There were two or three concerted efforts to get you, Kirym," said Oak. "Perhaps he actually wanted the tokens."

"But had he taken me, the sword would have been left here, imbedded in Faltryn's chest."

"He might have thought he could force you to make him the second holder. Then he could take them when he pleased," Oak said.

"But he'd die straight away, because you'd already chosen Ashistar," said Dashlan. "It's a shame he was here when you told everyone. Maybe it would have been easier to let him pick them up."

"Would you really do that, Dash? It's hard to kill a person or allow them to die when they don't have to. The weapons have power, although it is said the power diminishes with each death."

"You're right, but they mightn't have any power left. Maybe that's why the old man didn't die."

"It doesn't work in that manner, Dashlan. I don't know what the power is, but I must act as if the power, whatever it is, is as strong as it's ever been. Anyway, had I invited him to carry them, he would've thought it was a trap. He sees other people in the light of his own thoughts and actions."

"So, what now?"

I shook my head. "I don't know."

"Just thought of something, Kirym," said Ashistar. "When we got to the tor, the guard in charge said the rocks were refusing to leave the mother rock and he hadn't found *it*, whatever it was, anyway. Gynbere went down to check the work, and two rocks fell. It scared him. After that, he sent Slaslow down to check progress, but the rocks clung tight. Slaslow told him to give up. Gynbere went berserk because whatever he wanted to happen, didn't."

"Elm knew about the tokens," I said, "so he may have mentioned them. Rargo may or may not have known. He never saw them, but he may have heard something."

"Enliah probably told him." Arbreu sounded angry.

"They're not a secret, Arbreu," I said. "Many have seen them all here in the amphitheatre. Slaslow probably recognised the yellow for what it was, Gynbere certainly did when Slaslow dropped it. Gynbere still holds it somewhere, I'm sure whoever removed my knife from Slaslow's body would have known to get the token."

"So, we need to find it, but how? Gynbere was searched when he was put in the cage. His clothes were taken and searched," said Findlow.

"Was his hair searched?"

Findlow stiffened. "He wouldn't let us touch it, but he undid every plait, ruffled every curl out. He had a lot of hair, and in retrospect, he could have had the token stuffed in there somewhere." He grimaced. "I'm a fool. I should have checked it, myself."

"Any of them could have held the token for him. It will return to the others when the time is right," I said. "Tokens have a power, and they protect themselves. Now I'd like to talk to the seer who made Gynbere state his wants at the tor."

"Maletta. Strange old woman. Kept to herself, never talked much. When she did, she was always right, although it was rarely seen at the time. She generally appeared to make no sense at all." Ashistar shrugged.

I nodded. "I've not seen her here. Which dwelling did she choose?"

No one knew.

I closed my eyes. *Iryndal, do you know where she is?*

She slept surrounded by the squilute, and spends most of her days near the trees by the stream.

"I'll go get her," said Baketer.

"Thank you, but I think something slightly more formal is needed. Findlow, could you and Sundas invite her to share a meal with us."

When they had left, Papa asked Borboncha and Oak to bring an assortment of food and drink. The circle expanded to give plenty of room for those I expected to join us. I took the opportunity to ask Iryndal to invite, Starshine, Mekroe, Wind Runner and Storm.

"Was Maletta offered a space in a dwelling?" I asked.

"Yes. One to herself if that was what she wanted," said Papa. "She said she'd prefer to meet the trees and animals, she'd keep safer there. I sent food to her. She refused it. Shormel said he saw her collecting berries, roots and stuff, I assumed she was feeding herself. I approached her twice; she walked away. She may not come, Kirym."

"Oh, I think she will," I said.

The others I'd invited arrived; I guessed the dragons had something to do with the speed in which they had turned up.

28

Kirym Speaks

"Well I never expected that, Kirym," Papa said, as Maletta came into sight. "You have more pull than I have."

When Papa and I stood as Maletta approached, everyone else followed our lead.

She was still dressed in what appeared to be a pile of rags, and she had a large lumpy sack, which Sundas carried for her.

She pushed aside the cushions we had placed for her. "Put it there," she said, pointing to a spot beside Papa. When Sundas put her sack down, she sat on it. "You can wait over there," she pointed to a tree some distance away. "I'll call if I need you."

"If you ask nicely, I might assist you," said Sundas, looking grave. "In the meantime, I'll join you in the lovely meal, Kirym and Veld have provided for us." He sat beside her, and cut himself a portion of stuffed bread.

"Hehehe. You chose a right one here, dearie." She patted

Papa on the hand. "The other one's a bit glum, though." She peered at the meal in front of her and sniffed loudly. "Smells passable. I warn you though, I'm hard to poison, and you won't be the first to try. I'll know who added the venom, and they'll feel as if they're sitting on hot coals for the rest of their pathetic lives when I've finished with them." She cackled loudly and stared intently at each person in the group. "I'll remember you all."

She pulled a platter towards her, speared a cube of meat on a long grimy fingernail, and held it up in front of her. Having inspected it from all sides, she held it out to Papa.

With a small smile on his lips, he took it and ate it. She watched him for a short time. "Hehehe, so you thought far enough ahead to take an antidote first." She cackled as she speared another piece of meat and licked the gravy off one side. "Hmmmm, nothing I can't cope with. I'll chance it." She ate it and took another piece, followed by a chunk of bread.

Now everyone was eating, I too took a portion, but didn't manage to eat much.

Maletta leaned back and stared at me. "Lady of The Green Valley. Well that title is even more of a mouthful when I consider the size of you. Wasting away you are. Do none of you here care about her enough to feed her?" She stared balefully around the circle, then sighed deeply. "All right, ask your questions. I don't have all day."

"How did Gynbere know I held the tokens?" I asked.

"Hehehe, why ask what you already know?"

"Elm knew little though, so where did Gynbere get his idea of them?"

She cackled again. "Questions that take you no further in your quest, and are largely irrelevant."

"Why do you answer every question with another question?" asked Mekroe.

She slowly turned to look at him. "Why do you give up leadership, to take up guidance?"

They stared at each other for a moment, and then Maletta turned back to me. "You must act at the right time. Return what has been taken. Put the clues together," she said, and closed her eyes. She didn't speak for a long time. When she finally did, her voice was soft and sweet, the voice of a young woman, not the raspy croak we had heard so far.

"It is as feared, the worst that could be imagined has happened. A new evil is destroying my children. They must flee, flee, and hide in the mists. Destroy what causes desolation. Safety lies in remaining where you are, velour in adventuring through the gate. Meglinor is in danger. You can protect my children; retrieve the stolen figurehead; return it to its place. Help make it as it was; find the lost histories. Recreate the harmony in their land, return the peace we all once had. Find the gatekeeper, but be wary. His loyalties have changed."

Shivers ran up and down my back as she spoke.

Then there was silence for a long time. I felt as if everyone was holding their breath, and only breathed again when I spoke.

"But I don't know. Where are they?" I said.

Maletta's eyes opened. "Some know one thing. Some know another. Some have no wish to tell all they know. You hold a key, but it isn't what you thought. You have time though, but not too much." Her voice returned to normal as she cackled with laughter.

"Hehehehe. No children, poisons don't work on me. I watch and I know." She turned to Papa. "You'll build me a hollow in the cliff behind your dwelling. It won't be an onerous task, it's already been started. Your presence will protect me. You'll send your children to learn at my feet. Send them every season, you may come too." She leaned forward and stared at Findlow. "You too, I'll teach you to laugh. Bring your brother and your son."

Findlow looked mystified. "I thank you for the invitation, and I'll willingly come. But I have no brother, and I have a daughter, but no son."

Maletta screeched with laughter. "'Tis a sad day when you fail to recognise family."

Sundas laughed with her. "I'll visit you, old one. And I'll bring the others as you desire."

She stared at him and nodded slowly. "There's more to you than I thought. I'll welcome you—occasionally!" She looked back at me. "What do you know, child? Tell me!"

"Gynbere demanded the green token. You made him be very precise. Green for the Valley and the people who own the land. Was it more than an acknowledgement that he had no right to The Green Valley?"

She cackled and turned to Papa. "Why did you train her to ask so much? One day she may question the need for you to stay alive?"

Papa laughed. "If you believe that, you are less of a judge of character than I thought you were."

She guffawed loudly. "Protect her while you can. Give her all she asks for. Before long, there will be nothing you can give her."

"Then Gynbere wanted the blue token," said Mekrar. "That was the blue token for the waters, now what was it?" She frowned. "Oh yes, waters directed by the child of The Green Valley. Was that an acknowledgement of Kirym as able to guide the waters from Faltryn, or was he alluding to the old Valythian history? Then again, how would he know of those who lived in the sands?"

Again, there was silence, until. "Ask she who guides the tokens. She who leads the universe."

Arbreu broke the long silence that followed that comment.

"Green and blue tokens. Gynbere was right with those. So why did he then ask for a black token? And why did he name Faltryn."

"Hehehe. Yes. Black for that accursed dragon. Didn't know he'd change, did he? Didn't know anything about the dragons. Only fools pretend to know when they don't. So Kirym of The Green valley. The question on everyone's mind is, where did it come from? One other person knew of it, and even he wonders what's going on."

"We knew Kirym would tell us when she was ready," said Starshine. "The stones decide when to show themselves."

"Hmmmmm. Some of us choose to act, little Faltryn leader, while others let things happen. Think of your future with that in mind. You wish to tell us about the black stone, Kirym?"

"An offering from Faltryn. A gift from one I love. A present from the dragons. A reward to tie us all together."

I'd expected her to laugh again, but instead she stared at me, seemingly almost shocked.

"Just a stone then," murmured Starshine.

Then Maletta laughed. "Nothing is *just anything*, little leader. That's why the universe belongs to the Child of The Green Valley. Miracles have a purpose. What do you think, Lady Kirym?"

"I think things happen, but perhaps the miracle is that they happen *when they do*."

Maletta nodded. "So, the stone is a stone, and it was convenient?"

"Perhaps," I said, "but Gynbere didn't know we held the stones until Elm mentioned them. Elm added no more about them, because he knew nothing. He'd not seen them, but he was a good listener. Gynbere had a little knowledge and assumed he knew it all."

"Hmmmmm! They rightly chose you. You've come further

than I thought." She cackled. "So, you know the next step. Who will you invite?"

"Any who wish to accompany me." I paused. "But especially you, Miarta." I reached out and took her hand. "I'll take you to the caves also. I suspect there is more to them than I found."

"Even with no water entering the canyon, Kirym, it'll be a few seasons before it's dry enough to enter," said Veld.

Maletta's eyes watered as she roared with laughter. "You should spend more time talking to those who know, son of Arjin. Child of The Green Valley, I'll accompany you, to the rock, the cave of dreams and possibly I'll stay until you return the head. Just don't take too long. I'll see you at the tor that isn't. Will the leader of the rock pile demand to come along?"

"He dares not stay away," I said.

She nodded.

"There's something I don't have," I said. "But I don't know what it is."

"You held it, but gave it to someone for safekeeping. They'll return it in due time, and when they do, time will be short." She stood, picked up her sack and walked away.

"You called her by the wrong name, Kirym," said Dashlan.

"No, she didn't," said Oak. "She got it absolutely right."

Dashlan wasn't the only one to look mystified.

Zhins named her baby Tarl. He lived for two days, and as sad as it was, no one, except Zhins, expected him to survive. The surprise was that he drew breath at all. She wanted to bury him in the middle of the settlement, but Mama insisted on a quiet spot on the far side of the gardens where there would be lots of flowers in spring, summer and autumn. After a long argument, Zhins reluctantly agreed, visited him for long periods each day, and, despite objections, began to plan a large monument to sit over his grave.

29

Kirym Speaks

Autumn and winter passed in a flurry of building, interrupted by raging storms. Slowly the numbers of people living in the winter hall diminished, as dwellings were finished.

The guild members moved into various dwellings, and I returned home to Mama and Papa. Mama felt I would rest more there, and it was better for Trethia to be living with a large family and learning to mix with others. She had a solitary life when she lived in The Rock, and even in the small dwelling with me when I returned from the amphitheatre. It took her a long time to happily join in, but I was pleased as spring approached, to see her dive into a group of boys to retrieve a book taken from her.

Papa, Sundas, and Findlow, helped to dig Maletta's hollow, with guidance from Ashistar, who knew about hollows and Blacknight, who had experience with this type of rock. Mama sent up wall hangings, cushions, rugs, along with many other items to make her comfortable, but a few days later, most of these were found sitting on the porch. Mama put them away without comment.

We celebrated with Churnyg during the last full moon of winter, as his people moved from the winter hall to the trees he had chosen. Hollows had formed surprisingly quickly, and the trees thrived under the care of his people. I began to see that these trees would eventually rival those Faltryn had slowed me as he was dying.

Just after the first moon dark of spring, Wind-Runner joined her people in their new settlement half a day to the east, although Mama insisted she retain her own dwelling within the settlement.

I had taken time to rest and build up my strength, and not all of it was forced on me. Through the early part of winter, I was happy to rest for a portion of most days. As midwinter approached, I felt stronger and set out to find and talk to Teema. However, he avoided me, and on the few occasions we were in the same area, he made a point of standing as far from me as he possibly could.

Finally, I made a point of distancing him from my thoughts. I hoped it would give him the space to sort himself out.

Everything changed on the first day of spring. I walked around the corner of a dwelling to find him standing, waiting.

My smile faded when without a word, he removed his blue token, dropped it on the ground, and walked into the one place I couldn't easily enter, the single men's dwelling.

Had it been empty, I would have marched in after him, however, the murmur of voices drifted out. As difficult as it was to walk away, I did so without pausing.

I was relieved when my path took me around the back of the winter hall. With no one in sight, I sank to my knees, closed my eyes and allowed the loss to wash over me. I felt nauseous, and very emotional. My tokens felt strange. Not empty, but now very different to how they had been. As I analysed them, I knew he had gone, completely.

A hand touched my shoulder.

I jumped.

"Are you all right?"

"Mekrar! You startled me." I took a deep breath. "Yes, I'm fine." I stood and looked over to the lake. "I must have underestimated my ability to—"

"If you don't talk to me," she said quietly, "you can explain this weakness to Mama or Sundas. Come on, Quest is back in the water, and Armos has gone for a meal and a rest. We'll have it to ourselves for a quiet talk."

I knew I had no choice.

"Now tell me," she said, once we were sitting in the sun, gazing at the western shore.

I touched my blue token, surprised it was still the same size it had always been.

"Teema cut our token connections," I said.

Mekrar looked shocked.

I took a deep breath and told her what had happened. "I just have to figure out the different balance in my tokens. Before the dragons, it was just the two of us. But it doesn't just affect the blue. My green feels different too."

"Could that be because Bokum died?"

"No, that change happened back at the tor. Arbreu is still there, but Teema has gone."

"Do you want Arbreu to talk—?"

"No," I interrupted. "It won't help. Teema has made up his mind."

"He'll get over it, Kirym, and then everything'll be back to how it was."

I shook my head. "Thing is, I'm not sure it can be. When he initially walked away at the amphitheatre, he was there, but distant. Now he's gone."

Mekrar looked sick. "Mama will deal with it. Someone will find his token and hand it to her. There will be questions."

Arbreu and Mekrar cornered me the following morning. "He's wearing it," Arbreu said, "but he won't talk to me."

"No one mentioned seeing him without it, so he probably retrieved it as soon as you'd disappeared," said Mekrar. "I talked to Mama, she had no answer; said it was your call. If you want to make a formal complaint to the Judicial Committee, you can."

"No," I said.

Arbreu's face fell.

"Arb, it won't make any difference. I can't force his friendship."

"It's more than friendship, and what about when he realises?" Arbreu said. "You know, even my token is different. Before it was us, and you and Teema were equally important. Now I'm only aware of him if I pointedly think about him. You're there as usual, Amethyst is, and Mekrar of course, but the balance has changed."

"I feel the loss less than I thought I would. Maybe it'll be the same for him. Time may change things, but I refuse to mope over it. There's plenty to do, and I'll keep busy."

Early spring was cold and stormy, but the building work continued, and just after the first moon dark of spring, Wind-Runner joined her people in their settlement. It was situated half a day slightly to the east of north, with rolling hills and meadows ahead, and trees to the east and south, to protect them from the winds, and a river nearby. They called it New Faltryn, but soon everyone called it Newff. It was built so a large hall could eventually be added for them to gather in when the weather deteriorated.

We had worried we would miss everyone as they moved away, but we didn't have the chance; there was a lot of visiting between the communities. Mama made the decision that every community would have a guest house once the other building work was done, so we had somewhere to stay when we visited. She also insisted each community retain a dwelling within our settlement. They were frequently used.

When the temperature warmed soon after midspring, I decided to return to the tor. Everyone who wished to, had the opportunity to accompany me, and soon Mama's list had over three hundred names. Others wanted to continue with the building work and setting out spring gardens, and Armos chose to stay as acting headman while Mama and Papa were away.

Gynbere and his fellow prisoners demanded to come along. I knew there would be trouble if I refused, but Mama was not sure. She discussed it with Iryndal, who agreed with me.

The dragons transported us all as far as the amphitheatre. While they could have taken us straight to the tor, I suggested we walk the final distance through the marsh, it would be good for most of them to do the trip during the day, having previously only done it at night, and with the Ubree's assistance.

Mama approached me as I helped Borasyn to unload his packs. "I was told Maletta would be joining us, and yet she has somehow been left behind. Can you return with one of the dragons to get her?"

"She said she'd see us at the tor, Mama. I suspect she's already there."

"And if she isn't?"

"Then I'll go and find her."

"I wish I'd met her. I was busy birthing Zhins baby when you spoke to her. After that, each time I visited her hollow, she was out. I didn't manage time for this one little thing that could make a difference to what lies ahead. Veld thinks she's important to the future."

"Had she needed to talk to you earlier, she'd have found you. Wait until she's ready. She began her trip on the day of the last moon dark in winter."

"Through all those storms." Mama shook her head. "I didn't know she'd left. I should have. There's so much more work to do since the families joined. I miss out on the small things."

"Sundas has been watching, and a few of us have visited her off and on. Sometimes we found her, sometimes we didn't. It depended whether she wanted to see us."

"I heard she visited Gynbere. He was most unhappy about it."

I nodded. "She reminded him about an old prophesy, and laughed when he cursed her. She said, 'You make your own prison,' and walked away."

"Perhaps I shouldn't pry where she is concerned. She's looked after herself for a long time and survived Gynbere." Mama nodded. "But, I sometimes feel I am losing my hold on things."

"You've done all that was needed and more, but you should delegate. Mekrar and Arbreu will thrive on the added responsibility, and there are others too."

"Why were you so sure she'd be the right one, Kirym? I remember you saying something along the lines of that when you first learned to talk, and that was long before

Halse died. I thought you had names mixed up, or maybe was annoyed with Halse and Teema for not taking you on a picnic with them. Now I wonder. What if she had lived?"

"She would have travelled away and started a new settlement. She envied Natia when she left with Findlow. Remember she wanted to go too."

Mama laughed. "That's right. She followed them and refused to speak to Veld for almost a season when he brought her back."

I nodded. "Tarl would have pulled away, he didn't want the responsibility."

Mama thought quietly for a while. "He did say he wasn't happy, although he never said why."

"As much as he loved Zhins, Mama, he knew what she was like. She would laud it over the rest of the family and demand special treatment. He'd be pulled two ways. Wanting to keep her happy, but not wanting the family to be treated as servants."

"I suspect you're right about her, too. And you never ever thought Mekroe would slip into leadership?"

"He's not right for it. He loves the adventure of the new. He'd unsettle everyone, wanting change and innovation. Mekrar will utilise the same ideas, but she'll guide the family. He'd drive them. As advisor to Starshine, Mek is in the perfect place for him. He'll initially be under Storm's guiding hand too. Starshine is so kind, no one will deny her anything she asks and she has an inborn wisdom. She will suggest quietly, and he has the enthusiasm to fire everyone up. Together they're a perfect combination."

"And you? You have everyone else's future tied up. What of yours? Does Teema fit in there somewhere? He is here you know."

"Teema will do what he needs to, but he'll always find it hard to accept that I can make good decisions without him. For me, well I'll take whatever adventures are placed in front of me."

We began our final leg of the journey through the marsh in the morning. The winter rains meant there was more water, but the path was dry, and we were well guided.

The journey was different during the day. The path seemed to be higher and wider, even the wagons we took managed without getting bogged down. Perhaps the narrowness was an illusion of the night journeys.

We arrived at the tor in the late afternoon. Maletta sat on the great stump watching as the wagons we brought with us wove their way around the strange humps that lay on the ground, and settled in the same area they had used in the aftermath of the battle.

"You called that well," said Mama.

Shormel and Larqeba raced towards Maletta, but halted when she waved them away.

"Perhaps it's time you went and made her acquaintance, Mama."

"What if she waves me away too?"

"She won't."

Elsewhere there was a flurry of work as fires were lit for the cooks, a preparation area set up and a few shelters were erected. Iryndal had transported the cage Blacknight had built in the amphitheatre, and Gynbere and his supporters were already locked inside it.

With everything being cared for, I walked over the bridge to the tor, to the centre where Gynbere had tried to erect his pavilion.

Initially I just sat and looked around. I had never taken the time when I was last here, to just look.

"Anything of interest?" asked Oak, as he sat beside me.

I jumped. "I was trying to remember what was said when I was last here, and later in the amphitheatre."

He nodded. "Will Gynbere demand to place the yellow token on the rock?"

"He won't get the chance. The tokens have no connection here at present. They're not needed."

"So, when and how will you get it back?" he asked.

"Tokens do what they wish to do. It isn't going anywhere, and when it's ready to join the others, it will. So, I'll wait." I paused, looking around. "You know, this place is not the work of nature. Did you wonder why Gynbere didn't uncover at least one of those mounds out there? And what made his ancestor destroy the tree?"

"It's an oak tree. Remember he said in that scroll that he was supposed to bend his knee to Churnyg, and wanted to destroy him," said Oak. "Perhaps it's as simple as that."

"That's a huge job just to snub a man who would never know. There's more to it. Why did he focus on this place? What is here that he wants? The tree was cut down many season cycles ago, probably by one of his ancestors. But this Gynbere came back. There's the reference to The Burl of Meglinor. Maybe that's what he was looking for. What is it? Who created it, and why?"

"Did you know he's watching us? He hasn't taken his eyes off you since you crossed the bridge."

"Hmmm, I wonder why?" *Iryndal, can you somehow stop Gynbere and his men from being aware of me for a while?*

"What's going on? They've all just fallen over," said Oak.

I thought they looked tired, came Iryndal's reply.

Oak laughed.

I looked across the top of the tor. "You know, we've been gone since autumn, and yet the grass on the tor hasn't grown at all." I grabbed a handful and pulled. I was surprised at how easily it came away.

The base of the scar was a deep vibrant purple.

"What in Faltryn's name is that?" Oak sounded awed.

"Wait here." I checked under the grass in various places across the tor, before returning to Oak.

"The grass sits on a great slab of purple wood. Dragonheart, I believe. It's the same everywhere I checked." I pulled away another strip of grass, and laid them both aside.

"Wood?" said Oak. "Wow, the work putting pieces together to make something this size."

"I think it's one huge piece. The top is, and possibly the whole tor."

Oaks eyes widened. "A stump? Do you think it's a felled dragonheart tree? Could this be where Churnyg's people lived?"

"No. There is no mention of it in their histories."

"It's chopped down just as the oaks were. And it's shiny. Could Borasyn have done it?"

"No, there's no fallen trunk, and one this size would still be here. The dragons don't seem to be aware of this place unless something specific is mentioned to them. Then they forget again almost immediately. There's something else at work here." I carefully replaced the sods of grass. "Keep quiet about this, I want time to think.

30

Arbreu

They rose with the sun, everyone eager to begin uncovering the mounds.

Kirym and Trethia began as everyone else dawdled over their meal, choosing the hump furthest from the tor. The grass growing over the humps was different to that on the tor. It was made up of the long strands of stringy grass Arbreu had first seen near Salcan's cave.

The long strands initially came away easily, but below the thick green leaves at the top, was a dense mass of hairy stems that wove themselves together. Fine feeding roots sprouted from every joint of the stem and these grew through and around the stems, and eventually set deep roots. Every joint in the feeding root seemed to sprout more green leaves and feeders. The resulting thick mass was difficult to remove, and resisted cutting.

Having hauled as much of the first stems away as she could, Kirym cut them, and grabbed another handful. It was hard work, but before long she had company as the rest of us joined in.

With so many eager to help, Veld organised five teams, each working on different mounds. Soon, it became a game to see who would finish first. Eventually the bottom layer of grass was stripped from the first mound to reveal a stone pillar.

It lay face down, wearing, they assumed by the folds carved into the stone, a cloak. The face was still hidden, as most of the head was covered by a tall collar. Much larger than life, this person was twice Sundas' stature, and the plinth it stood on gave even more height. It almost definitely portrayed someone from The Green Valley. A sword, held in a baldric, was draped across its shoulder.

The pillar had been carved in three uneven sections. The person at the top, a long-ridged plinth and a longer smooth length at the bottom.

"It reminds me of the poles we saw at the stone circles when we were travelling to Faltryn," Arbreu said. "Those had several animals and people standing on top of each other, whereas these appeared to be a person."

"These appear more realistic, although the front view may reveal something different," Wind Runner said.

"It wasn't made to lie flat," said Findlow. "As with the tree, it's been felled. I'm surprised it didn't break when it hit the ground."

Veld nodded. "Standing it could take some time. It's solid stone. It'll be heavy and ungainly. I imagine the holes are around here somewhere."

"I'm onto it," said Findlow, grabbing a spear. He dug it into the ground around the area where the bottom of the pillar lay.

The hole was, as it turned out, easy to find. Although it was well covered with a thick pad of grass, it took little real work for Twig and Blacknight to hack through the grass covering once Findlow located it. However, the hole was not much wider than the base of the pole.

"Let's uncover the rest of them before we decide how to stand them up," said Loul.

They moved on. By evening, six were uncovered.

Everyone was hot and dirty, and one of the deeper pools near the edge of the marsh was put aside for washing. After such hard work, only those on guard remained awake.

The following day, five more were uncovered, and they finished the work on the third day. As the statues all lay on their faces, they were no nearer to identifying them.

31

Kirym Speaks

With the pillars cleared of grass, we faced a problem. All of them had either fallen onto their faces or, more likely, been rolled over once they had been downed. Some were quite distant from their holes, and with two, we weren't sure which hole to stand them in.

"Perhaps the dragons will have some idea," Mekrar said.

"It's not just where they stand, but the direction they look in," I said. "I want that to be right too. There's no indication because the plug that sits in the ground is round, the same shape as the holes."

"Does it really matter?" Arbreu asked. "Just getting them erect would be a great acknowledgment to those who carved them in the first place."

I sighed. "It may matter. Either way, I want to wipe the smirk off Gynbere's face. I wonder if Iryndal remembers."

"No," she said, appearing suddenly beside us. "I've searched my memories, and those of the other dragons. This information hasn't been passed on. Borasyn's memories are still growing, but even he has no idea."

"Faltryn may know. If so would he, no she. Would she be able to tell you?"

Iryndal closed her eyes, suddenly appearing tired. "She's still very young, Kirym. Conversation at with one her age is as with any baby. Interesting noises only. However, I hear nothing at all from her. She can't make me understand. I can't read her memories as we have done in the past. It's one of the mysteries of our rebirth this time. Perhaps we need to leave the statues as they are until she has grown a little. Even then, she may not have seen them before. I think Faltryn slept for well over five hundred season cycles before you found us."

I felt a bit depressed, but then realised what Iryndal had said.

"No," I said. "Faltryn still roamed the land. He was in The Land Between the Gorges on the day Mama and Papa said I could carry the knife. He passed that memory on to me before he died. A great red-leafed oak fell that day, and he saw it. So, he might have seen this. Where is she?"

"Asleep again," said Egrym. "It's all she ever does, useless little—"

"Egrym!" snapped Iryndal. "Behave. She's a baby, and we heard less from you at that age."

Egrym sighed theatrically and rolled his eyes.

"I think I'll ask her," I said. "You never know, she may, well I don't know, but it's time she woke and played for a while."

We sat on the grass by the pillar furthest from the tor and I explained the situation to Faltryn. She stared at the column and turned around to look around the area. As she did so, her tail touched the tip of her nose and she continued around and around trying to catch it.

Phffft, useless, was Egrym's thought. *A waste of space.*

"Stop it, Egrym," snapped Arymda. "We knew at the beginning she was too small to do this. She's allowed to be what she is. You had less ability at her age. If I remember, you needed to be carried everywhere for the first twelve seasons. We'll have to wait until—"

"Perhaps not," interrupted Iryndal. "Look."

Faltryn had stopped circling and was staring southwest of the statue.

"Facing there?" I asked. Faltryn beamed up at me.

"So," said Mekroe, "they all look at the tree stump. That'll make it—owww! She bit me!" He pulled his hand away from Faltryn and inspected his finger.

"Perhaps they don't all face the same way," I said. "We mustn't assume anything. The line of vison might be quite important for each of them. Anyway, this is a beginning."

Ropes were readied and with Storm, Findlow and Sundas in charge, the pillar slowly rose. The end slid into the hole, down, down, down. It hit the bottom with a dull thud, felt more than heard. It had completely disappeared

"Oh!" Papa said. "I didn't expect that."

"Can we assume it wasn't like that originally? Could it be that the holes were deepened later?" asked Dashlan.

"That's a specialised job," said Findlow, "and I don't know of any way it could be done. The holes are too narrow and deep. While you could lower a man into one, he wouldn't have enough room to dig. And how would the soil be removed? Now what do we do about the others?"

I laughed. "The only thing possible. Stand them all up. Then we'll get an idea of how extensive the problem is. After that, I guess I'll start digging."

"Digging?" Mama sounded surprised.

"That's the only way I can think to see what they look like."

"You think they're that important?" she asked quietly.

I nodded. "Have you noticed how strangely amused Gynbere is? Almost choked laughing when the statue disappeared into the ground. He knows something, and I intend to wipe the smirk off his face one way or another."

During the day, we stood another five, and by evening next day all except one was standing and hidden deep in their holes.

We settled by the fire, all voicing different opinions on what had happened, and what we should do next.

"Tell me the problem again, Kirym," said Iryndal. "I've lost the memories of what you've done here in the past few days."

"That's not natural, although it fits in with everything else that's happening around here," I said.

"As the sun sets, I can think clearly, but have no memory of the day. If we talk each evening," she said, after I'd told her, "then we can then think about it overnight, although our thoughts seem to disappear with the dawn. I'll talk to you again before the sun rises."

I carefully described the statues, the tor, the land around it, and what I felt the problems were. Then I left her to her thoughts.

32

Kirym Speaks

It was dark when I woke. Amethyst snuffled in her sleep as she tried to find her thumb, but I didn't think that was what woke me. I tucked her rug around her. Trethia turned and snuggled into Lyndym, who shared the set with us. I felt quite alert, not ready to go back to sleep, so I slipped my cloak over my shoulders and climbed from the wagon.

Something was wrong. I thought it was about midnight, but there were none of the usual sounds and sights I would have expected at that time. Generally, a few of the late cooks would be finishing their final chores, and the last fire would be damped down as the meridian guards took over. The guard's tent, which was in darkness, would have a low light so the head guard could note necessary orders.

In the dark of the night, I was unable to see any guards. This wasn't unusual, Papa discouraged light because it blinded them to movement in the darkness around them. However, tonight the moon should have been shining brightly; we were approaching the full moon. Even the stars were absent. That was unusual, and I was immediately on edge.

I loosened my knife, pulled my hood over my head and began a section search of the camp area.

I had reached the southern sector when I saw a pale shape cross in front of the stump. It was at the far edge of my vision, and unidentifiable.

With my knife in my hand, I sprinted quietly across the open land and into the shadows of the stump. I knew I would not be seen, my cloak was dark blue, but I still needed to be careful, until I knew who it was and what was going on.

He, something in the stance gave me the impression this was male, was very nervous. A dangerous situation.

He backed awkwardly into the shadows of the stump, his knife held inelegantly in his left hand.

Teema fought left-handed, but as soon as I thought of him, I realised he would have held the knife with more confidence.

Then I glimpsed a sword, held backwards along his right arm. Only one person I knew carried a sword that way.

"Twig?" I called softly, as I got close.

He spun around, his knife extended, the sword already angling out, ready to strike. It was obvious he couldn't see me.

"It's Kirym. I'm on your right," I said. "I'll join you."

His sword lowered, but not completely. He was still wary.

I pushed back my hood and moved out of the shadow.

"It is you," he said. "Get over here into the shadows."

Once we were together, he relaxed, stabbed his sword into the ground in front of him, although I noted he kept hold of the knife.

"What's going on? There are no guards. Has there been—?"

"Just wait, I'll find out," I murmured.

Iryndal? What's happening?

Suddenly she was in front of us, only visible because her token bump was much lighter than her body. "Why are you awake?"

"I was going on guard duty," said Twig.

"Did you put everyone to sleep?" I asked.

"It was easier this way. We had work to do. You all should have slept until morning. Your call to duty must be strong for the memory to waken you, Twig."

"What work are you doing?" I asked.

"We talked about it at sunset, Kirym. The changes in the land around here. We're trying to restore it to what it was. We've not finished, and I want it done by dawn. We're not sure what will happen if it's not completed by then."

"Can we see what you've done?" I asked.

"Now's as good a time as any," Iryndal said.

Suddenly the sky lit up, and I remembered Arymda's description of them sending rivers of fire into the sky to entertain the children. It was an extraordinary sight. Once I tore my eyes away from the sky, I could see the changes they had made to the land.

The tor now towered over us, and much of the land around it had been lowered to the same level as that around the stump. Six of the statues were standing tall, the rest still hidden, and a huge cliff stood to the north of us—the land yet to be lowered.

"You're healing the land, Iryndal," I murmured. "Perhaps when it's all restored, there will be answers."

"Amazing," said Twig. "That makes it so much better. How did you get the grass back again?"

"Dragons have many powers," said Iryndal. "I need you both to sleep. It'll make our work easier. It must be finished before dawn. I'm not sure if we will lose memory of this then," said Iryndal, "but if we do, I'll want to talk to you at sunset tomorrow, Kirym."

I woke to sunshine. I lay wrapped in a rug against the stump where I had met Twig during the night. He too was just waking, and now Iryndal had lifted the desire to sleep, everyone was emerging from their dwellings.

We were all in awe at the changes in the land. Most people just stood and stared.

The land around the tor was flat, and on the same level as the base of the stump. The statues all stood as they were meant to, and all now looked in different directions. The area where the tor was, was most arresting. The land curved gently down into a massive bowl. It was centred by a huge, flat-topped, green-tinged, misshapen crag, unlike anything I had ever seen before.

Mama was the first to move. She walked purposefully over to me. "What is it?"

"I suspect it's the Burl of Meglinor."

"Should I have asked a different question?"

"I don't know what that question would be, because I'm still not totally sure what it is. I'm going to find out though."

The top of the burl was even more amazing than I had imagined. The intricate swirls of rich purple dragonheart glowed in the sunshine.

I was surprised at how few people wanted to follow the narrow path to the top. Fewer than one hundred joined me up there.

"I know nothing more about what it is and why it's here, Kirym," said Mama. "It is beautiful, but is it possible it's something as mundane as a viewing platform?"

"I doubt it. Gynbere has no interest in seeing what's up here. I'm thinking he knows it's unimportant at this stage," I said. "He wasn't upset with the change in the land, more annoyed, I thought. I wonder why? There must be something else here."

Mama glanced around. "Where do we start?"

"We've plenty of time. Let's discuss it as we eat. The dragons did more than clear the land overnight."

I washed and dressed in my festival dress, and added the crown I had received with the weapons. Amethyst and Trethia also wore their best clothes, and almost everyone else chose to wear their finery.

Despite wanting to rush to explore, we took our time over the meal; meals the dragons prepared were always special, and needed to be savoured.

We began with the statues. Although Gynbere had no concerns when we began raising them, I had to be sure they had nothing on them of importance. Anyway, we had spent so much time clearing and erecting them, and they had to be here for a reason.

Most were based on the people of The Green Valley, although one was obviously a tree dwarf, and two could have come from Valythia, or possibly one from there; the other from Faltryn. Each, along with looking in a different direction, held one or two items, that seemed exclusive to them, a sheaf of wheat, a platter of tokens, and most interesting, the figure that represented the tree dwarves carried a boat. I wondered what the significance of them was.

Late in the morning, we stopped and rested.

"Did you note that Gynbere showed no interest in the statues?" asked Oak. "He rested and talked to Vellysh and Zeffun. He thinks they're unimportant."

Mama frowned. "Nothing to do with the burl then."

"As much as we haven't picked up every detail, they don't seem to tell us anything about it," I said. "The only other thing here is the stump. That's what Gynbere concentrated on when he came here, and that's where we should look now."

33

Arbreu

At the stump, Kirym brushed away the accumulated debris of the winter.

"Gynbere doesn't look happy," said Oak.

"Good! It means I'm possibly onto something," she said.

"I didn't even think about the stump or the inscription once we left here after the battle," Findlow said.

"Me neither," said Dashlan. "I never realised until now. Did the dragons take the memory, or was it what's been affecting them and their memories?"

"They've been better since they changed the land around. I wonder why," Arbreu said.

"Changing the land to what it was, triggered some of the memories they had," Kirym said. "That's why they did it during darkness. Whatever was distracting them was, if not dormant, at least not as strong at night."

With so many people there, Iryndal passed her view on so all would see what was happening. Kirym wanted no accusations of secrecy or trickery. She specifically mentioned Gynbere and his supporters, wanting them to see it as she saw it.

First Kirym slipped her knife from the sheath on her hip and laid it on the vertical line on the rock. She unhooked her small bow and laid it on the curved line at the top. It fitted perfectly. Then she pulled three bolts from her quiver.

These were not the bolts she usually hunted with, instead they were the three mud-encrusted, filigree-covered cylinders she had found in The Rock, while freeing the last of Churnyg's people just before the whole rock collapsed. She slipped the first bolt into the small round hole.

She's made a mistake, Arbreu thought. The bolt head half sat in the hole, leaning against the edge. It looked wrong. The second bolt also had problems going in very far. Kirym slotted the third bolt in the remaining slot, and suddenly they all slipped down to their fletchings. For a long moment, nothing happened.

Then there was a sound deep in the ground. Arbreu recognised the sound of rock sliding across rock, and understood why Mekrar grabbed his arm and gasped. They had both heard the same sound in the token cave in The Land Between the Gorges during a catastrophic earthquake that ruined their home-land and compelled them to leave and search out the place their ancestors had come from. They heard it more recently when two sections of the outer wall of The Rock fell, allowing The Tree people to escape their imprisonment.

In the moments before Arbreu's panic surfaced, he realised the sound was different. "The ground is still," he said, putting a protective arm around her shoulder. "It's more a vibration than a shake."

"There!" Kirym pointed to the burl. A section of the outer wall had moved, leaving a dark opening. She picked up the baldric containing the sword and shield and, hefting it over her shoulder, walked towards the burl.

"STOP!"

Gynbere stood at the bars of his cage, shaking with anger.

"What about me? You said we'd see what was here."

"Iryndal will ensure you see what we see," said Veld.

"Pah! I wouldn't trust any of them to show me the truth. No dealings my family have had with dragons has ever been what was promised."

"Let him come, Papa. That way he can never claim we held secrets from him," said Kirym. "Any who wish to, can enter, but," she said loudly, as Gynbere and his men retrieved their cloaks from the dwelling, "you do it at your own risk. I know nothing of what's in there, nor what will happen once we cross the threshold."

Gynbere blanched, but filed out of the cage and sauntered towards the burl. "I'm sure the dragons will keep you safe, therefore they will do the same for me."

"Oh, how nice," Oak said. "You do trust them after all."

34

Kirym Speaks

Again, most of those with us stayed outside. Fewer than one hundred, joined us as we again followed the narrow path up the tor to the hole. There was an increase in noise behind me, and I turned to see what it was.

Gynbere was arguing with Twig.

"What's wrong?" I asked.

"He objects to you holding weapons." Twig pointed to the packed baldric I carried over my shoulder.

"What's to say," Gynbere said, "this isn't a trap to kill me?"

"Put him back in the cage. He doesn't have to come in," Papa said shortly, and continued up the narrow track towards Oak and me.

Gynbere's protests rose to a crescendo as he insisted on continuing. After words of warning from Twig, they followed us.

I stepped through the entrance. It was dark inside, and

even allowing time for my eyes to adjust, I could see nothing below me, but I could see the path ahead. It ran north, and angled gently down following the wall around the curve of the burl.

I was aware that Oak, who followed me, was falling behind.

"Are you all right?" I asked.

"I wish I'd brought a lamp. It's so dark in here. The path drops off on one side, but I'm not sure where the edge of it is."

"Just follow the wall. You don't need your knife, there's no danger ahead of us. Would you like me to take Trethia?"

He slipped his knife into its sheath, and with his left hand against the wall, moved faster. "I'll manage her now. How did you know—?"

"About the knife? It's just what you would do. I should have thought about it in advance." I didn't tell him I could clearly see him, Trethia, the knife, the path and wall, although what was below me was still in darkness.

When I was on the opposite side of the wall, Mama and Wind Runner started down the path, followed by Papa and Storm. Others came behind them, but more tentatively, and many carried lamps.

I continued down the long path, and then, suddenly a vast floor stretched out in front of me. As I walked away from the wall, the tokens began to hum and pinpoints within the vast area overhead and around me shone.

The entrance was now above and slightly behind me, the path down had turned on itself three times before reaching the floor. When I reached the centre of the floor, those who had been gingerly feeling their way down, sped up, and soon everyone had joined me.

All around me, I could see the markings of a massive burl. Parts of the walls were as smooth as the top of the tree-stump Borasyn had played with in the amphitheatre. Other areas were rough knotty bumps—the outside of an ancient burl in looks and feel. All of it was the wonderful deep purple of dragonheart.

High above us, the ceiling glowed. Parts of it appeared to move, and for a moment I thought I was seeing clouds, racing across the sky. *Could parts of it be transparent? Perhaps it's just a trick of the eye.*

Most of those who had joined me had close connections with the dragons. The exceptions were Gynbere and his friends, although I knew Gynbere had his own knowledge.

Ubree and Othyn were the only dragons to join us inside the burl. The others opted to remain outside to care for everything there. Othyn sent her view to Iryndal, who passed it on to everyone outside.

Once I'd pulled my eyes away from the ceiling, I wandered around the cave and studied the walls. While I was looking at the west wall, the tokens hum increased in volume. A group of small ledges sat together in front of me. I handed my pocket to Trethia, and she helped me to unwrap the tokens. I placed the blue token in a niche with the green and purple just under it. The next ledge held the rainbow token and I placed the red below that. The bronze sat on the lowest shelf.

Trethia put the wrappings away.

I lay the sword on a longer shelf some distance to the right of the tokens, with the shield alongside it and the knife, scabbard and baldric just below them.

"The tokens aren't balanced, are they?" said Trethia.

"What would you know, you revoltingly, dirty, little troll," sneered Gynbere.

Mama stepped between him and Trethia. "If you wish to remain here, Gynbere, you will keep your comments to yourself. She is welcome. *You* are here under sufferance."

Trethia moved closer to me, hiding in the folds of my dress.

The look Gynbere gave her was pure hatred.

I turned my attention back to the tokens. They glowed softly, and lights from all of them spiralled together and reached out for the pocket.

"Do they not want to be on the shelves?" asked Oak.

"This needs to be with them," said Trethia. She pulled the black stone out of my pocket and handed it to me. I added it to the shelf beside the rainbow token. The stones still weren't balanced, and there were murmurs around me, particularly from those who knew the tokens. For now, though, the stones sang quietly.

There was so much beautiful detail in the walls, I almost missed the single book that sat in a darkened niche low in the west wall. Once I saw it, I realised that many of the longer ledges were designed specifically to hold books. All though, were empty. It was a bonus finding this one. I brushed the dust off the cover.

Ledger Sixteen—Supplemental
The Search

"Mama, I think this is a continuation of the last book our ancestors wrote before we went in search of the dragons. That makes it yours," I said.

"I didn't see it, Kirym, even though I looked at the shelf. Perhaps it's really for you."

"Do as she tells you, leader of The Green Valley." Maletta's voice rang out over the murmurs of the crowd.

Mama glanced up to where Maletta stood at the mid-point of the path above us, took the book and studied the cover.

It was simple, unlike the one I'd found just after the battle of the amphitheatre. As she opened the cover, a scrap of parchment floated to the ground.

I stooped to pick it up.

"Halavash requires your help. Evil came from Athesha. Athesha should come and retrieve it," I read.

I frowned. "Who or what is Halavash, and what is Athesha?"

Behind me someone shouted. I was aware of loud complaints. Someone bumped into me and there were exclamations of protest.

As I leaned down to pick Trethia up, everything went black.

35

Oak Speaks

Darkness. A shrill scream, followed by shouts of protest, a loud bang and a flash of light near the centre of the northern wall took my attention. It was chaotic.

Someone bumped into me, knocking me sideways. It was too dark to see where I was, or what direction I was looking in

"Quiet!"

That's Iryndal. I was confused. *But she stayed outside.*

There was sudden silence and the lights in the northern wall and ceiling glowed. Their light was faint, the air in that part of the cave was thick with smoke. It smelled strange; I couldn't identify what had burned.

White light from the large tokens spiralled up and glowed onto the north wall.

Now the smoke was more obvious, and those nearest the source were moving back towards me. A few had started up the path to the entrance, to be stopped by Othyn.

Sensible for the moment, I thought.

I raced forward to identify the source of the smoke. Ashistar and I arrived at the front of the crowd together. Loul and Veld were already there, Twig and Storm beside them.

"Keep everyone back," Ashistar said.

The thickest smoke now cleared, and I saw what it had hidden.

Gynbere lay against the north wall, eyes closed, his hand around the hilt of the sword. The shield was beside him, still rocking with whatever movement had placed it there.

I mentally visualised the place the weapons had been, and wondered how these two had come so far from their shelf. Gynbere too, because just before everything went dark, he had been just behind Kirym, straining to see what she was reading.

Between the shelf and Gynbere, a few people were still being helped to their feet.

Zeffun pushed past me, took two steps towards Gynbere, but had second thoughts when he saw the weapons. "So, he was right. This was a ploy to try to kill him."

"Had we wanted him dead," Loul said, "we'd have done it long ago. He's given us enough reason too. Now how did the weapons get here?"

"He grabbed them when the lights went out," said Ashistar.

"Why would he have wanted to do that?" Zeffun asked. "Anyway, how would you know? It was dark. Someone pushed them into his hands. He'll tell you when he wakens."

"He's not going to wake up," Ashistar said. "He's dead."

Zeffun's eyes bulged. "What? But he's got to. He said—"

"Only Kirym and Ashistar can hold the weapons and live," interrupted Sirasha Beech.

"He knew that," snapped Zeffun. "So, one of them did it."

"One of whom?" I asked.

"The girl. Her and her traitor friend must have pushed the weapons into his hand."

"How would you know that," Veld paused, "in the dark?"

"Ashistar didn't do it. He was over by the path talking to me," said Storm.

"And it can't have been Kirym," Loul paused and looked around. "Where is she?"

I suddenly had a horrid feeling in the pit of my stomach. In normal circumstances, she would be standing right beside Ashistar.

I pushed back through the crowd towards where I had left her.

Ubree lay across the centre of the cave, south of the path. Kirym must been behind him, I couldn't see her.

I raced down the cave, leapt over Ubree's tail, skidding as I tried to turn at speed.

The tokens glow brightened and began to sing. Their song was mournful, but I already knew there was no good news ahead of me.

Finally, I saw Kirym. She lay on her side against the wall, with Trethia snuggled into her. Kirym had her arm protectively around the wee girl. At any other time, I would have assumed they were sleeping, but I knew they weren't.

Kirym's jaw and Trethia's cheek were both marred by a nasty red wound. Blood from Kirym's wound dripped slowly onto Trethia's temple.

Trethia's blood pooled on the floor under her cheek. The bleeding had stopped. It wasn't a good sign; the two wounds had turned black at the centre; the edges were beginning to turn green.

I glanced back to see what effect the wounds were having on Ubree.

He lay still, his eyes closed, Kirym's left hand against his cheek, her right was clutching Trethia to her. Kirym's wounds hadn't transferred to him as usual. His skin around the area where Kirym touched him, was very dark, and could have been a shadow, but it was growing, visibly.

I don't know how long I sat there watching, waiting and hoping. Hoping they would all open their eyes and smile at me.

A hand gripped my shoulder. I looked up.

"You need to come out now, Oak," said Mekrar. "There's nothing we can do for them. We'll just close off the burl for the night."

I looked around. Everyone else had already left.

"They've gone, Oak. Mama wants us to be together overnight, and we will sort out the details tomorrow."

"Gone? The three of them?"

She nodded. She looked bleak and unhappy, much as I felt.

I leaned forward, took Kirym's hand, kissed it and tucked it back around Trethia. I stood, removed my robe and wrapped it around them both. As I turned to leave, I briefly touched Ubree's head, and with my arm around Mekrar's waist, walked up the path and out into the evening shadows.

I paused as we reached the bottom of the path into the bowl, and glanced up. A massive full moon sat on the eastern horizon. *Kirym would love that.*

Mekrar looked up at me. "Are you all right?"

I shook my head. "I have a headache. My lips sting."

Her eyes widened, a look of horror crossed her face, and everything went black.

The End

If you have enjoyed The Burl of Meglinor, please leave a review on the website of the seller you purchased it from. Good reviews are the life blood of independently-published authors, so please take a few moments to let others know what you thought of the book.

Thank you for reading.

Do look for further adventures as
The Token Bearer series continues.

www.ingramcontent.com/pod-product-compliance
Lightning Source LLC
Chambersburg PA
CBHW051323250626
47155CB00007B/2433